The TURNGLASS

The TURNGLASS

GARETH RUBIN

SIMON &
SCHUSTER

London · New York · Sydney · Toronto · New Delhi

First published in Great Britain by Simon & Schuster UK Ltd, 2023

1 3 5 7 9 10 8 6 4 2

Simon & Schuster UK Ltd
1st Floor
222 Gray's Inn Road
London WC1X 8HB

Simon & Schuster Australia, Sydney
Simon & Schuster India, New Delhi

www.simonandschuster.co.uk
www.simonandschuster.com.au
www.simonandschuster.co.in

A CIP catalogue record for this book
is available from the British Library

Hardback ISBN: 978-1-3985-1449-2
Trade Paperback ISBN: 978-1-3985-1450-8
eBook ISBN: 978-1-3985-1451-5
Audio ISBN: 978-1-3985-2298-5

Typeset in Sabon by M Rules

Printed and Bound in the UK using 100% Renewable
Electricity at CPI Group (UK) Ltd

MIX
Paper | Supporting
responsible forestry
FSC
www.fsc.org   FSC® C171272

For Hannah

Tête-bêche (n)
A book split into two parts printed back-to-back and head-to-foot.
Etymology: French *lit.* 'head-to-foot'.

In the eighteenth century, publishers resorted to printing two books back-to-back and turned upside down. They called these unique works tête-bêche novels. They are strange to read nowadays and the modern bibliophile can find it disconcerting to read one tale and then flip the book over to read another from the opposite direction – only to discover that everything they thought they knew, was an inversion of the truth.

A New History of the Novel, G. Brunswick,
Princeton University Press, 1922

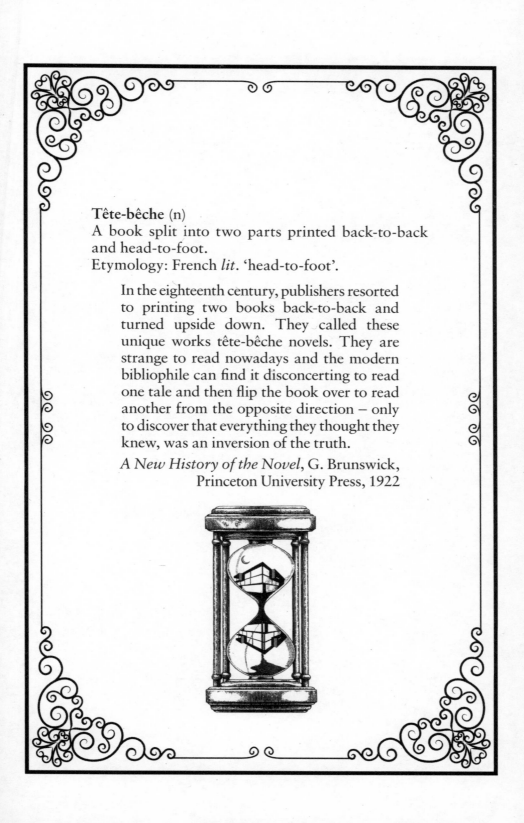

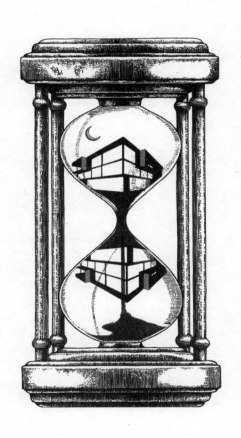

It was the lark, the herald of the morn,
No nightingale: look, love, what envious streaks
Do lace the severing clouds in yonder east:
Night's candles are burnt out, and jocund day
Stands tiptoe on the misty mountain tops.
I must be gone and live, or stay and die.

Romeo, *Romeo and Juliet*, ACT III SCENE V

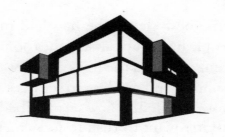

Chapter 1

Los Angeles, 1939

Ken Kourian's eyes, pale green like thirsty grass, bent to the coffee-stained page in front of him. It smelled strongly of coffee too, as if someone hadn't just spilled his drink on it, but had marinated it in the cup for twelve or fourteen hours.

'It's called *The Siege of Downville*.'

'I see, and I—' began Ken.

'You're a soldier just back from the War.'

'Which one?'

'What?'

'Which war? Great War or—'

'Civil. Civil fucking War.'

'Okay. And am I Confederate or—'

'Yankee! You're up for a Yankee. You think . . . look, kid, are you gonna read the lines or am I gonna read them for you?'

This was the best chance he had had in months and there were people lining up outside the room, so he put on a Yankee accent and read the lines. They were something about being injured and needing to see his sweetheart one last time before he died. They seemed badly written to him, but he didn't want to rush to judgement because he had never been in a picture and even his stage credits were only those from college and a couple of years in second-rate shows around Boston.

'Where're you from?' the overweight man behind the desk demanded, staring at him as if he should have a luggage label on his forehead.

'Georgia.'

'Georgia!' He scratched his midriff through straining shirt buttons. 'Then why the hell'd they put you up for a Yankee? Why not one of the slave-keeping sons a'bitches from the South?'

'Beats me,' Ken said. He gazed at the script.

'Beats me too.' The man, the assistant producer, tossed a cigarette butt aside into a bucket of water, where it floated, seeping a brown trail. 'Look, son, it's not your day. Come back another time.'

'I'll be sure to,' Ken replied. And he would. He wasn't one to bow to pessimism, because Ken Kourian was twenty-six and it hadn't yet set in like damp.

As a boy in Georgia, he had seen the distant Blue Ridge mountains and thought of them as separating him from Greek wars and journeys across seas. Then, as he had gotten older, he had come to see them as the hurdle before an unidentified 'more to life'. So he had set out on that journey, as the first in his family to go to college; and now, as a five-year hangover, he was repaying his parents and two banks for the cost, a few bucks at a time.

He picked up his hat, wished the movie well and left through the studio lot, still holding the bad script. Two men with stuck-on moustaches the size of house cats walked past wearing Union uniforms. Ken wasn't sure whether to envy them or pity them for getting into the picture.

Outside the studio, a streetcar was rolling along the road and Ken jumped aboard hoping that it was heading for the beach. Even after months in the city, his understanding of the geography of Los Angeles and Hollywoodland could have been drawn on a playing card. His home town had more elm trees than people and the elms didn't rush around, barging you from the sidewalk, in a hurry to get somewhere to be told to go somewhere else. Sure, he had also been in Boston for eight years – in college and then a little tutoring and a little acting – but his feet still hankered for a path of soft leaves underfoot. In California, wet sand would do as well, however.

'Is this going towards the beach?' he asked the conductor.

'What?'

'The beach.'

'The beach is ten miles in the other direction, pal. You want the beach, get off this car and take one going the other way. Ride it eight stops and then change to another.'

It sounded too complicated. 'Where's this one going?'

'This one? Where do you think it's going? Downtown. Along Sunset. So, you want Downtown or you want the beach?' A woman in a seat was offering a five-dollar bill for a ticket and insisting the conductor take it. 'I can't change that, sister. The fare's only a dime.'

'Well, you should have said that before I got on,' she replied huffily.

'Before you got on? How would I do that? I was in the vehicle, not beside you on the street. Now, do you got change or not?'

'I'll go Downtown,' Ken told him.

'Downtown is ten cents. And I don't got change for a five-spot.'

He paid his money and rode the car.

He had been riding for about ten minutes, watching the passengers get on and off, trying to work out who they were and if they worked in the movies or if they were cobblers or accountants or longshoremen or stockbrokers, when he spotted an endless ridge of trees.

'What's that?' he asked the conductor.

'That? You don't care what that is. You're going Downtown.'

'I'd like to know what it is.'

The conductor groaned. 'That's Elysian Park. Stay away from there.'

'Why?'

'Full'a boogies from Lincoln Heights. Take your billfold, won't give it back even if you ask nice.'

'Oh,' he said. His dad had employed coloured labour alongside white workers on the farm, paying the same rate, but Ken had given up trying to evangelize this system to his high-school class, who stared and then laughed when he put the idea in front of them. At college, a few had nodded knowingly at the idea and said that yeah, it was the future, for sure, but then hired negro butlers at two-thirds the going rate for men with pink skin, leaving Ken wishing he had saved his breath. 'I think I want to go there anyhow.'

'Whatever you say, pal.'

And Ken Kourian, point-jawed, six feet and an inch tall, with healthy farm-boy muscles and a degree in literature from Boston University, jumped off the streetcar and strolled towards the line of elm trees.

The park was cool and lush on a day hot enough to melt automobile tyres. The sensation of grass and fern under his feet soothed him like a drugstore balm. Whatever had ailed them, making the soles bristle in his stiff new patent leather shoes, disappeared, and he could have been barefoot, padding through the undergrowth.

How many trees were there? Ten thousand? A hundred thousand? Ken appreciated the shade, needing to cool down after a frustrating couple of hours. Paramount were casting for a new epic, he had been told at the studio gate. If he put his name down, he might be seen for a small part.

It would be a 'cattle call' casting and that didn't sound good, but it was better than being told to go boil his head.

'Well, I've worked on farms,' he said.

'Then you'll be right at home.'

He hadn't gotten the job. Sure, it was a disappointment, but there would be other chances. They said that the pictures were getting bigger each year. Bigger pictures meant bigger casts. He would stick it out, and in the meantime he had a job writing advertisements for the *Los Angeles Times* and that was enough to pay his modest rent. And his plan was that hanging around the paper's entertainment desk he would hear about the new movies in development, so he could run up to the studio early and ask to be seen. Yeah, maybe it would work.

He walked through the heat of the April afternoon. The birds in the trees were kicking up a hullabaloo before taking off in huge flights in search of food or water or whatever else a bird wants on a hot day in California. He wondered what his own plan for the afternoon was. Keep walking until he stumbled into the town proper or hop back on the streetcar to his boarding house beside a grocery store that he suspected of selling home-distilled hooch from the back door? He had toyed with the idea of calling in there himself some time and seeing what was on the menu.

He just kept walking.

By the time he looked up again, he had walked right through the park to the other side and road noises were rubbing around him like mosquitoes. He thought about turning around and losing himself among the trees again, but he was thirsty and beside the road a diner's neon lights were inviting him.

Ken strolled in to find himself bang in the middle of the late luncheon rush, and the popularity of the place meant there was only a single table left. It was in a corner booth where the fake leather that probably came from a factory a thousand miles from the nearest cow was a deep gold colour. He went over, but as he came close he saw a girl already there. She had been sitting against the wall, out of sight. She looked like she had been trying to keep a low profile.

Ken paused. But she turned two heavy brown eyes up at him expectantly.

'Can I sit here?' he asked.

'Sure.' She said it slowly, like she might change her mind halfway through.

He nodded in thanks and took the seat. She was sipping white coffee and flicking through a magazine about talkies. She was slim, with a pert mouth that looked like it was recoiling from a too-hot drink, and wore a cream turban, a cream blouse and tight cream pants. Ken reached across for the menu in a glass pot at the edge of the table.

'The peach pie is a specialty,' she told him, without waiting for him to ask.

'Does that mean it's good?'

'It just means it's a specialty.'

A waitress appeared at his elbow with her notepad ready. 'I'll have the peach pie,' he told her. 'I hear it's a specialty.'

'Sure it is,' she muttered, writing. 'Anything else?'

'No.'

She pointed at the girl opposite with her stub pencil. 'You covering her check?'

The girl in cream met his gaze. Something in hers said that if he didn't cover it, no one would.

'Okay,' he said.

'I hope it's worth it,' the waitress said, walking away.

Ken and the girl stared at each other for a few seconds. 'Thanks,' she said.

'Don't mention it.'

'But I have to, don't I? I mean, you've just saved me from having to run out on another check. I think this is the last place in Los Angeles I haven't done that.'

'I've only been here eight weeks. I've hardly run out on any.'

Her face lit up. 'Oh, it's the best thing!' she insisted. 'You see, it's redistribution of scarce resources.'

'Failing to pay a lunch check is redistribution of scarce resources?'

'I was told that it was. By a . . .' She silently mouthed the final word: *Communist.*

Ken had met one or two in college. They were very serious young men, intent on growing beards and talking about the Soviet miracle. They hadn't been great company.

'Did he also run out on checks?' he asked.

'No, he had family money.' The conversation lulled because there didn't seem an easy reply, so Ken drew the now-useless *Siege of Downville* script from inside his jacket and placed it on the table. She looked down at it and grinned. 'You're an actor!'

12

'Kinda.' There was a pause and he supposed that she was guessing the truth. 'I just had the audition.'

'Did you get the part?'

'Probably not.'

She sat back, a smug expression crowding out everything else on her face. 'You need to know big people. Know them socially. That's how you get on.'

The subtle 'I've-got-the-inside-track, you-haven't' tone needled him, especially since he was standing her coffee. But during his brief time in LA he had come to understand this was the default position when talking to strangers – a kind of duel for prominence, like two alley cats meeting beside a garbage pail and fighting for its contents.

'Clearly,' he said.

'Do you want to?'

'I . . .'

'Because I can do it. I can.' She leaned forward and rushed on. 'I'm going to a beach party tomorrow. It's at Oliver Tooke's house.' She waited for a reaction. 'The writer?'

Truth be told, the name had rung a distant bell with Ken, but he didn't want to hazard an opinion just yet. 'Okay,' he said, without committing himself.

'At least, I expect he's having a party tomorrow. He does most days. I'll be your ticket in.'

Oliver Tooke. Oliver Tooke. Oh, yes. Yes, now he remembered hearing the name on the radio, a book review programme. But he couldn't recall what the book was about or what opinion the presenter had come up with. 'So you know him?'

13

'I've met him,' she said proudly.

'Often?'

'We've been introduced at a nightclub.'

Friendship was cheap in this city. He looked down at the script. There were breadcrumbs underneath it. 'I'll come,' he said.

'My name's Gloria.'

'I'm Ken.'

Chapter 2

The next morning, he met Gloria outside her apartment. She had a bundle containing a towel and swimsuit in her arms, tied up with ribbon. She was wearing a sea-green kaftan and a blouse and baggy pants of the same hue. Single-colour ensembles were her look.

'So that people always remember you?' Ken suggested, pointing to her get-up.

'You should try it. You need a look for your career.'

Painful as the thought was, he wondered if, at some point in the future, he really would have to have a 'look'. If he could typecast himself – maybe he could use his small-town background and present himself for cornball parts – it would be a foot in the door. He wasn't going to claim his granddaddy was a Cherokee Indian, but if there was a part for a farm boy from Georgia he would happily turn up in cowpoke boots and drawl his vowels long enough to fit whole sentences in the gaps. It might work, so long as they overlooked his college education and love of British literature from the previous century.

'Which way's the party?'

'The beach behind Oliver's house,' she said. It was just 'Oliver' now. 'Jeez, that place sends me! It's up the coast, so we gotta take a cab.'

He clamped his own bundle of towel and swimming shorts under his arm and felt for his wallet. There was a lot of room in it. 'It had better be less than five bucks there and back or we're walking home,' he told her.

'Don't worry about getting back,' Gloria instructed him. 'Someone will give us a ride. They always do.' She waved at a passing taxi and it stopped so sharply the car behind had to swerve into the neighbouring lane. Its driver thumped the horn. 'Point Dume,' Gloria told the cabbie as they jumped in.

'So, what's he like?' Ken asked.

'Oliver?'

'Yeah, Oliver.'

She considered. 'He's a phony,' she said as they pulled into the traffic. 'I don't like him.'

Her calling Oliver a phony was a level of irony. 'Phony how?'

'Oh, he says things but you know he means something else. That kind of phony.'

'Oh, that kind of phony.'

*

16

Forty minutes later, the driver turned off the coastal high-way and took a road so thin it wouldn't even have been ink on a map. It led up to a promontory of land piercing the Pacific Ocean. The headland that was Point Dume rose up like an arching lizard and there was something reptile-like about its surface too: green, scaly and carnivorous. If you stood there staring into the waves that hid more sharp-toothed creatures, civilization must have seemed far behind you.

There was only one specimen of life on the headland: a large three-storey house, built, by its looks, around the turn of the century. It sat on a low cliff, but what really set it apart was that it seemed to be made almost entirely of glass. The exterior walls were glass, the interior walls were glass. The doors were glass framed by a few splinters of wood. You could walk up from the highway and stare right through it, out to the ocean. Only smoked panes on the upper level prevented you looking right through there too. On top of the house was a weather vane, also made of glass, in the shape of an hourglass. It was twisting in a light breeze like it was pointing the way and the way kept changing. The building was an extraordinary sight, but somehow also wrong, Ken thought. There was just something *off* about its character.

'So this is modern architecture,' Ken said.

'What? No, this is Oliver's house,' Gloria replied. There was little he could think of by way of an answer to that. She stared at him for a moment. 'You're not going to say anything stupid and embarrass me, are you? This is *Oliver*

17

Tooke we're talking about. There'll be producers here, directors.'

'I'll try not to.' It was becoming pretty clear that they were not suited. He had, at first, held rough ideas of her becoming his girlfriend, and she was an attractive girl, but they were not of one mind. There was an electric bell button beside the front door, and above it hung a steel name sign for the property: Turnglass House. 'Do we ring this?' Ken asked.

'No, they'll all be on the beach.'

She led him around to the back. The earth became more parched as they rounded the building, coming to a garden with a wide slope that led down to the house's private beach, shaped like a waning moon. Ken was used to open horizons. He had grown up camping before them. But he had never, not even in Boston, lived by the sea. It moved and heaved and boomed, whether anyone was listening or not. He understood why some people could never bring themselves to leave it.

The beach was alive with around thirty young people in bathing costumes: some on deckchairs, others splashing about in the surf. The score to the scene came from a hot jazz quartet.

'Can you see him?' Gloria asked.

'I don't know what he looks like.'

'Oh, no, I guess you don't.' There was a drinks station, where staff in sky-blue uniforms were doling out cocktails and fruit. It sure looked like anyone could come in and claim the booze. She searched the scene. 'Where *is* he?' She stopped a girl walking past wearing a pink two-piece costume. 'Where's Oliver?'

'Oh, honey, I'm so wasted, I don't know where *I* am,' the girl burbled.

Ken took that as an invitation to slink over to the drinks table. 'What's everyone drinking here?' he asked the bartender.

'Everyone's drinking a Tom Collins, sir.'

'Then I'll have a Tom Collins.' The barman handed him the drink. 'Where's our host?' The man pointed to the sea. A hundred yards out, Ken could make out something in the waves. It was a strange sight: a whitewashed structure in the water, built like a lighthouse on a rock poking up through the ocean. It looked a few yards wide and a bit taller. He checked back. Gloria had inserted herself into a group of young things screeching with laughter. He wasn't grabbed by the idea of joining them. But their absentee host, Oliver Tooke, well, he sounded like a man worth meeting. So Ken closed himself inside a wooden changing hut and emerged a minute later in striped bathing shorts.

'Ken!' Gloria called after him, but he pretended not to hear and ran headlong into the surf. There had been enough rivers and creeks around his home town to make him a strong swimmer and he powered through the waves, enjoying the sting of salt in his eyes and mouth, and the chance to use his muscles, which had been wasting away in LA. It was a beautiful day and this was a beautiful chunk of coastline. As he swam, he almost lost himself in his dreams. Right up until the second that the rip tide grabbed him.

The moment he swam into its reach, he felt a funnel

of water dragging him at speed straight out to the open sea. The current was stronger than an ox. But with all the effort he had, he managed to swim parallel to the beach, all the while being sucked towards the empty ocean, and after twenty yards of swimming as hard as he could, he felt the current suddenly return to normal. He trod water as he got his breath back until a mechanical hum made him look up and he saw a red speedboat approaching him. The pilot wore the same uniform as the wait staff. The motor died down as it drifted close to him and he caught on to the short ladder on the side, hauling himself up.

'Rip tide, sir,' the young pilot said. 'Comes on without warning. Very dangerous. Are you going to the writing tower?'

Ken glanced at the miniature lighthouse. 'I guess I am.'

The young man pushed the lever forward and they took off towards the whitewashed structure. As they neared it, Ken saw a man standing in a narrow doorway, leaning against the frame, his hands in the pockets of white slacks. He was tall and slim, with narrow features and slicked-down dark hair. He wasn't going to win any beauty pageants, but somehow you would always remember him.

As the boat closed in, the pilot threw the man a line. There was a tiny jetty, no more than a yard across, and Ken stepped onto it.

Up close, he could see that the building was roughly square, built of cubes of stone and about twelve feet wide and twenty high – a little larger than it had appeared from the shore. Its base was uneven, clambering over big dark rocks, and there was a ring of windows around the top, which made it look even more like a lighthouse squeezed down by time.

'Howdy,' said the man in the white pants. He didn't seem at all surprised by the arrival.

'Hi.' Ken wiped his hair back, pressing some of the brine from it.

'Come on in.'

'Thank you.'

Even though he went in with no expectations, Ken was still surprised when he stepped into the narrow building. No lighthouse, it was a shrunken library, kind of like the one at his college where he had pored over old novels. Dusty spears of light burst down through windows with a fine layer of salt on them, illuminating a thousand volumes clinging to the shelves as if they were afraid of the water.

'This is incredible,' Ken said.

'This?' The man sounded quite surprised himself and gazed around as if the strangeness of the place had only just struck him. 'I suppose it is.' He extended a hand. It had a white signet ring on the pinkie finger. 'My grandfather built it – along with the house – but I made it my own. I'm Oliver Tooke.'

'Ken Kourian,' he said, shaking the hand. It was cool to the touch, as if the man's blood temperature were half a degree lower than everyone else's.

Oliver's brow furrowed a little. 'Kourian, that a Yiddisher name?'

'Armenian.'

'Armenian?' The furrow deepened. '*K'ez dur e galis*

im tuny?' His expression said that he hoped he had the pronunciation correct.

Ken laughed. 'That, sir, is incredible. I've never met anyone who spoke a word of the language before.'

'I know a couple of Armenians,' Oliver said, as if that explained why he could speak it.

'Well, since you ask about the house . . .' Ken turned to face where the glass building sat bird-like on the low cliff. 'It's . . .' he hesitated.

'. . . grotesque?' Oliver suggested. The man was direct, there was no doubting that.

'I wouldn't say that.'

'Wouldn't you?' Oliver leaned against a bookcase. His tone was light, as if this was a subject he had thought much about and had long ago come to the conclusion. 'Wouldn't you say there's just something ugly about it?'

'Ugly?'

'I've always thought so.'

'How so?'

'Oh, just something corrupt about it. Malign.' He said it as if detailing no more than the year it was built. Ken was curious. Accuracy aside – and it wasn't an *in*accurate assessment of the building – it was a strange reaction to a family home. Could a house itself be corrupt? Well, perhaps it could. Oliver changed the subject, jerking his chin towards the doorway. 'Did you come with anyone?'

'Gloria,' Ken informed him.

'Oh, girl who always dresses monochrome?'

'That's her.'

'I've spoken to her a couple of times. Maybe three, I

forget.' But Ken got the feeling that Oliver Tooke knew exactly how many times he had spoken to anyone. He could probably recite each conversation word for word. There was a short pause. 'You want to look through the books?'

He must have read Ken's mind. 'I do. I'm always fascinated by other people's reading habits.'

'Me too.' Oliver sat in a fiery red leather captain's chair that was positioned in front of a walnut secretary cabinet. On the opposite edge of the room there was a chaise longue. Ken toured the room, drifting his forefinger over the collection. The titles spanned a wide range of topics, from surgical techniques to French poetry to cookery. Ken wondered if anything tied them all together, other than what appeared to be a voracious and generalized curiosity on the part of their owner. Maybe it wasn't healthy to be interested in everything at once. 'Why do you think we're fascinated by that?' Oliver asked.

'I guess you learn a lot more about someone from the books they read than where they spend their vacations or which box they tick on a voting paper.'

Oliver looked like he agreed. 'You're from the South, aren't you?'

'Georgia.' Ken felt self-conscious. The South wasn't always so popular with certain types.

'Okay. But college too.'

'Yes.'

'Where?'

'Boston.'

'Not Cambridge?'

'No, Boston.'

'I'm glad, Ken. I've met Harvard men. Some of the most stupid people I've ever met.'

'I've found that too.' There was another pause and Ken glanced back at the books on the walls.

'You think we're heading for war again?' Oliver asked, with intense seriousness. It was another leap of topic. Ken was sure it wasn't a put-on, though; the man's mind really did rush from one subject to the next.

'With Germany? Hitler seems insane, but another war? I don't know.'

'Insane men make the news. Don't overlook him.'

'I won't.'

'Some people would,' Oliver said. It sounded like he had someone in mind. Then another subject. 'You're new to LA, aren't you? You want to be in the movies?'

Well, it was a common question when half the people on the street were hoping for a few lines in the next production from United Artists. 'Just like every other rube you sit next to at the diner.'

'Probably. I guess you need something that stands out.'

'Like always wearing one colour.'

'That kinda thing.'

Ken took a look at the secretary cabinet. His host was working on something. There was a typewriter with a sheet of paper poking out, a sentence suspended halfway through. 'Did I disturb you?' He pointed to the typewriter, which had 'Remington' emblazoned across the top in gothic gilt script, and below that 'Made in Ilion, New York, USA'. But as he glanced at it, he saw that the

24

paper within wasn't a script or a novel, but a letter. It was addressed to some convent.

Oliver reached over and whipped the sheet out, laying it face-down on the desk. 'Sorry, pal, it's private,' he said.

'Of course.' Ken was embarrassed, like he had been caught with his fingers in the cookie jar. 'I should get back, leave you to your work.'

'That's good of you. My boat will take you over if you don't want to swim this time.' He smiled a little, but the atmosphere was cooler.

'Thanks.' They made their way to the little jetty.

'But come back, won't you? I'm throwing a party Monday next week. Night-time.'

That evening, Ken returned to the lodging house that he shared with six other residents and a widowed French landlady who was always perfectly made-up, morning, noon and night, despite being at least sixty years old.

It was lucky that the building was in California, because his room was exposed to the open air at seven or eight points of broken window, damaged wall and penetrated ceiling. It was there that he ate too, with a tin plate and an old scout lock-knife that he cleaned and stored in his trunk after meals.

Coming in tired, he flopped onto his bed with his fingers knitted behind his skull. He had forgotten to say goodbye to Gloria when he left, so he would call on her the following day to apologize – after all, she had invited him to the party. And it had been an arresting afternoon.

After a short nap, his peace was interrupted by the

sounds of violence from the adjoining room. His neighbours, a couple from Montreal who by turns yelled at each other without mercy in French or attempted to kill each other through their pulverizing actions in bed, had started early that night. It took him a while to work out which of their two hobbies they were letting rip. He was glad to hear that it was the angry screaming and decided to leave them to it, going down to the communal room that was used for smoking in the evening. The landlady was there, tidying up. She smiled warmly at Ken.

'Good evening, Mr Kourian.'

'Good evening, Madame Peche.'

'You have been out with a young lady?' Her English was perfect, but her accent heavy, and he suspected she put it on just a little. She had been in LA since the previous century.

'How did you know?'

She breathed in spectacularly, absorbing a scent. *'Fleurs de Paris,'* she said. 'An *inexpensive* perfume.'

He laughed. So a little bit of Gloria had rubbed off on him after all. 'Nothing gets past you, does it, Madame?'

She shrugged a little, like a French woman in a movie. 'Not when we talk about *parfum.'*

He collected an old magazine – there were always a few hanging around, cast off by previous tenants – and was about to return to his room in the hope that the murderous noise would have abated, when he turned back to her. 'Madame, have you ever heard of a man named Oliver Tooke?'

Her eyebrows lifted. 'Of course. Why?'

He sat in a worn-down leather armchair. 'I met him tonight. But I don't know much about him.'

'You met him? The state Governor?'

'The Governor?' Ken was puzzled. If Oliver Tooke was the state Governor, he was damn young for such an office. And on top of his writing career? 'I don't think it can be. The one I'm talking about is twenty-eight or so.'

'Ah!' A light of recognition glowed in her face. 'You mean the son of the Governor. Oh, that tragic boy.' This only confused him more and he waited for an explanation. 'So long ago. Were you even born then? I don't know.'

'When?' he asked, hoping the shutters would be opened on the conversation sooner or later.

She thought for a moment. 'My grandson had just been born, I think. So probably around twenty-five years ago.'

'I'm twenty-six,' he replied.

She sighed. 'Such a pity.' Then she shook away whatever thought was in her head. He wasn't sure he wanted to know what it was. 'Governor Tooke. It was before he was Governor . . . You see the glass in these windows?' He nodded. 'Made by Tooke Glass, I expect. They made just about every window in California at one time. Rich, oh so very rich. But it counted for nothing, didn't it?'

'Why?'

She smiled sadly. 'Because Oliver Tooke had two sons. One had his name, the other was . . .' She pursed her lips in thought. 'Alexandre, I think. He was the younger one, Alexandre. But he was taken.'

'What do you mean "taken"?'

27

She hunted for the word, not one she used often. She pronounced it with unease. 'Abducted. Killed.'

'How?'

She shrugged again. 'I can't remember. So long ago. You met Governor Tooke?' She sounded surprised.

'No,' he said. 'I met the son.'

'Oh, yes.' She tutted at her forgetfulness. 'You met the son. The one who survived.'

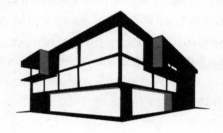

Chapter 3

The next morning Ken was at his desk at eight, sweating over an advert for a soap that claimed to stop men sweating. But the German-sounding client had demanded that words such as 'perspire', 'damp', 'moist' and certainly 'sweat' itself were *verboten*. Ken had to find a way to say something, without using any of the words necessary to convey the meaning. He fixed on the word 'glow' as a code word that might – just – get the message across. The tinkling of a telephone across the room barely registered until his boss, a New York advertising man who had come out west for the sun, hollered over.

'Ken. Phone.'

Ken hauled himself away from the work and lifted the

heavy receiver. He rarely received calls and the heat and frustration with his work had sapped most of his energy. 'Ken Kourian,' he said.

'Ken. *Siege of Downville*. Your screen test was the pits, but someone's giving you another chance. Get here within two hours. Got it?' The words were barked out without any name or introduction.

'Great. Yes. Thank you,' he said, taken aback. There was the thumping sound of a handset being dumped into the cradle. 'I have to go out,' he told the New Yorker.

'Go out? Where?'

'Paramount,' he replied.

'You an advertising man or an actor, Ken?'

'Probably neither,' he replied.

An hour later, he was back in the room where he had had his audition. The assistant producer was watching Ken like you would watch a monkey playing with gasoline and a match. Finally, he spoke. 'You got friends, son?'

'I don't know what you mean.'

'Friends, son. In the business. You must have to be back here.'

'Not that I know of.' He wracked his brains. Unless . . .

'Got a call this morning. Six in the morning. Now, that don't bother me – I'm up at five. Best time of the day. But still – early for a work call. I hear from the producer that some buddy of someone else met some young actor who would be good in one of the small parts.' Ken was about to say something. 'Only it's not such a small part now. Now he's gonna have thirty-something lines. We're getting the rewrite this afternoon. Ring any bells?'

Ken sat back in his seat. This was welcome news: he had a big-shot friend in the industry, something that twenty-four hours earlier had seemed a slim hope.

'I don't even want to know. Well, Wardrobe need to see you. Get down there. You're a Union officer.'

'Union? But I'm from Georgia.'

'That's what I damn well told them.'

He was to play a lieutenant who was the voice of reason next to his bloodthirsty senior officers, which meant that for the next five days Ken spent his lunch breaks in costume fittings and learning his lines. And then when the day came – it was to be an exhausting spin of the earth, because it was also to be the day of Oliver's party – he was ready, waiting in front of his boarding house, only for a runny-nosed messenger boy to turn up and tell him that shooting had been put back for twenty-four hours and he should kick back at home after all.

Knocked out by the nerves and subsequent letdown, he went back to bed. It was a waste of a day booked off from the office but, well, at least he could rest up for the party that evening. Gloria had gotten in touch to tell him they would be going together again and he should pick her up in a taxi. Her voice sounded put out when she asked him why he had abandoned her last time. He made up some need to be back at his lodging by a certain time or the door would have been locked. It sounded hollow because it was.

'Well, this time you're seeing me home,' she said.

'Okay.' He hoped that that meant only as much as its literal meaning.

A stream of cars stopped one by one in front of Oliver's house while jazz soaked the night air. Ken breathed it in, thrilled that this could be his first real movie party, the type written about in the *Los Angeles Times* gossip column: skin against skin, dope and scandal.

Gloria was wearing a short dress decked out with more scarlet feathers than an Amazonian parrot. She dusted down Ken's one good suit as they passed through a black-and-white tiled hallway, past a wide wooden staircase that led upstairs – which, it seemed, was a single double-height storey – into what was described as 'the ballroom'. The spacious chamber was decked with white marble, and at one side a white baby grand piano was in high demand. Whoever was playing knew his way around a keyboard like a surgeon knows his way around a pair of tonsils.

The corner opposite was given over to an indoor sunken pool, where a number of bathing beauties had taken the hint and were submerged in what could have been swimming costumes or just their underclothes. Some didn't appear to be wearing even those.

All around the room, bodies were crowded together: dancing, cooing at each other, bickering. And despite her demand that Ken see her home tonight, in less than five seconds Gloria had spotted some friends and left him at the bar. He really didn't mind.

Looking around, he noted that beside the rows of brightly coloured bottles of whiskey, gin and vermouth, all eager soldiers to the fight, there were small covered silver platters. He lifted the lid from one. It exposed a short line of white powder with a metal straw beside it. He put the lid back. He had been offered cocaine in college and he hadn't wanted it then and didn't want it now. If his fellow guests felt like getting screwy that night, that was their business.

He took a drink – this time everyone was downing martinis with molehills of blackberries stuffed into them – and scanned the place. Outside, he spotted the man he was looking for, drifting down the slope to the beach. Ken pushed through the crowd, but when he reached the garden, Oliver had disappeared.

'Ken! Come here!' It was Gloria. She beckoned him over to where she sat on a linen-covered couch, draped over a man who would have been handsome if it weren't for his cheeks running to jowls and eyes so bloodshot Ken could have seen them at ten paces. 'Ken Kourian, this is Piers Bellen. He's a producer at Warner.' She winked in a manner that she seemed to think was subtle.

'Pleased to . . .'

'I need to powder my nose,' she said, rubbing it in a manner that suggested she wasn't going to the ladies' room to do it. 'But don't let him get away.'

She flitted up, leaving Ken with the man. He was perspiring – or 'glowing' as the *Times* advert would have it – right through a shirt, tie, vest and suit jacket.

'How are you, Mr Bellen?'

'Pissed,' he grumbled.

Ken guessed this was not going to be an easy conversation. 'Any special reason?'

'Fucking Code meeting today.'

'I'm sorry?' He had an idea what the man meant, but he had already decided not to help him out.

Bellen grumbled on. 'Hays Code. It's coming down hard. That man wants to bankrupt us all. What, no sex on the screen? No blaspheming? No rape? What the hell are we going to show? Congress has no idea what we con'ribute to this nation.'

Ken decided he was all in now. 'And what do you contribute?' he asked.

'Dreams. Fucking dreams. Cornball like you should 'ppreciate that.' Well, the insult would have cut deeper if Ken hadn't been sure that Bellen had far less education than him. 'Why the hell else d'you come here? Why didn't you stay down on the farm?'

'I didn't grow up on one.' He had, really, but he also enjoyed lying to people like Bellen.

Bellen wasn't defeated, however. 'Sure. But you know plenty who did. This country? It's a fucking dream. What'd that Jewess write on the Statue of Liberty? "Give me your huddled masses yearning to be free"? You know what yearning means?'

'I know what it m—'

'It means dreaming. They need dreams. We give them dreams. For ten cents. For ten fucking cents, they can dream they're flying to Mexico or eating fifteen courses or screwing Greta Garbo. Hunger? Bills to pay? Not here. None here. They're all 'tside the theatre. That's why they need us. You gotta problem with that?'

'Several,' he said. He wasn't angry, he was just tired by

the conversation, even though it had been raging for less than a minute.

'Then you should—'

'I should nothing.'

'What? You—'

'Look, I've been with you thirty seconds and that's enough for anyone. I'm going to the cocktail counter. I'd ask you what you want, but I don't care.' He heaved himself to his feet and fought his way back into the house.

'You told Bellen where to get off.'

Oliver had appeared with a coupette in his hand. It was swimming with a light brown liquid and ice.

Ken sighed. 'You think it wasn't a smart move. A producer and all that.'

Oliver sipped his drink. 'He's still telling people that?'

So, the man was a fraud as well as a farmyard animal. 'What is he really?'

Oliver put his hand through the crook of Ken's arm and steered him back down to the shoreline. 'A clerk.'

'Who for?'

Oliver hesitated, as if considering whether to reveal something quite secret. 'I forget,' he said.

Well, Ken believed that as much as he believed a seven-dollar bill. But Oliver would tell him if and when he was ready. And there was something Ken wanted to bring up as they looked out on the surf rolling in like white tigers. 'I got a call from Paramount last week.'

'Oh yes?'

'They've given me a part in a film. Someone recommended me.' There was no answer. 'Thanks.'

35

'Don't mention it.'

'I will, though. This is a big thing for me.'

Oliver wandered over to a nearby drinks table and came back having swapped his coupette for a bottle of Crémant and two flute glasses. He twisted away the wire and let the cork blast itself free. Some of the wine fizzed down the neck of the bottle. 'You seem a good guy, Ken. So I did what I could and I hope it leads to bigger things.'

'It might.' He rarely allowed himself to dream. But he liked where the future was pointing.

Oliver hesitated for a moment, then looked out to the ocean and waved. At his signal, the little launch steered away from its course tracing figure-eights in the sea and came to rest a few yards out from the dry sand. 'It's quite the sunset tonight,' Oliver said, gazing out. They waded through the rippling water and jumped into the boat, which spun around and bumped over waves tinted orange by the setting sun. 'Maybe I should write a movie for you to star in,' Oliver yelled over the roar of the engine as they approached the writing tower.

'I think that would be asking a lot.'

'I've never written a movie. There's more money in books. For now.'

'How important is money?'

'I grew up with it, pal. I'm addicted to it. You take it away from me and I'll collapse in on myself.'

This was a surprising thing to say. Sure, money had been tight in Ken's youth – deathly tight in those hungry years they called a Depression – but he had always presumed that those who had money and had always had it looked upon it with carelessness. 'You must have enough, though.'

'No such thing to an addict. That's what addiction means. More drink, more junk. However much you have, you need more.'

'So why not just stay in the family business? Glass, right?'

'Glass, yes. Built this place. Well, I'm probably better for the firm staying away from it. As it is, it keeps rolling out the panes and rolling in the dollars. And so, I have time to write.'

The boat dropped them on the rocky outpost of the Tooke family estate and they entered. Oliver lit an oil lamp overhead that hissed into life, throwing a hot glow over the books. 'I've been working on something new,' he said. 'Something I . . .' He stopped, losing his thought midway through.

'What is it?' Ken prompted him.

Oliver snapped back into the room and went to the secretary cabinet. He took a thin key and unlocked it to reveal a short stack of books. Some were dog-eared modern paperbacks – the type of trash that private school kids would hide from their teachers – others looked quite holy, bound in flaking leather.

He took one from the stack that turned out to be a dime-novel. *He Wanted Her Dead* blazed a lurid cover decked out with a gumshoe pointing his .45 revolver down an alleyway. On the ground was a blond girl with her skirt hiked up her thigh.

'What do you think it's about?' Oliver asked.

'I guess a private dick who . . .' He began to open the

37

book. But Oliver plucked it from his grip, flipped it over and thrust it back into Ken's hand.

'What about now?' Ken looked down, expecting to see a ham-fisted description of the plot and the character of the tough-guy protagonist. Instead, he found another book altogether. *She Needed to Kill* screamed this one. And the gun this time was a little Derringer in the palm of the same blonde, now upright and pointing the pistol at the detective's back. Ken was struck by the book being two, and turned it over to gaze at the first cover again. 'The format is ... gripping, isn't it?' Oliver said. 'One story and then turn it over and it's another, but a sort of mirror image of the first. Maybe the characters look very different from a different point of view.'

'I guess so.'

'It's what I've been working on. In a way. People changing from one viewpoint to another. One year to another.' He stared through the doorway at the black waves lapping on the rocks. 'People do change.' His voice had a thoughtful, faraway quality.

'Oh, not that much.'

'You think?' Oliver paused for a moment, apparently lost in his own thoughts, before continuing. 'When I was very young, I was in a wheelchair – polio, a bad case. I'm told I had to be strapped into it or I'd fall out. I'm fine now, my body adapted and grew.'

'That's good.' Ken had the impression there was more to what Oliver was saying than he was actually saying. He waved the book. 'Did you write this?'

'This one? No, someone else.'

'What do you call them? Books like this?'

'*Tête-bêche* is the term. Head to foot. They're pretty old as an idea – this is how they used to be.' He picked the top volume from the pile and handed it to Ken. The cracking chestnut-coloured leather binding was inlaid with gold letters that were mostly rubbed away but still decipherable. The front was the New Testament with script so tiny that just reading it brought on a headache. Turned over, it was a book of psalms. 'A bit more religious than what they became.'

'That's for sure.' Ken held it next to *He Wanted Her Dead*.

'Gizmo for publishers now. Buy one book, get two! Of course, it doesn't mean that when you think about it – you're getting the same number of pages.' He tidied a few items on his desk that had become disordered.

'I'd like to read this,' Ken told him, flicking through the detective novel.

'Be my guest, pal. In fact, take any of them you like.' He jerked a thumb at the deck of books.

Ken noticed something a little different at the bottom of the pile, a white notebook. He drew it out. The front bore the handwritten name *The Turnglass* – it wouldn't sell so well on the newsstands as *She Needed to Kill*. Ken didn't know all that much about Oliver Tooke's work, but surely detective pulp was a bit of a change of direction? Well, perhaps he wanted to try something new.

He opened the front page. 'Simeon Lee's grey eyes were visible . . .' it began.

But Oliver's hand interrupted and gently closed the book. 'I'm still working on it,' he said. 'I don't quite know

39

how it ends yet.' Ken let him take it back and return it to the bottom of the pile. He locked the cabinet again.

'You know the beginning, though.'

'Sure. But the ending's far more important,' Oliver replied. 'It'll be published soon. You can read it then.'

'How can it be if you don't know the ending?'

'Well, I do and I don't. Anyhow, come the end of June, it's in the shops.'

That was pretty soon if Oliver hadn't finished writing it. Ken guessed the publishing schedules for this kind of pulp novel were short. 'So it's like the others, you flip it over and get another story?'

'It is, but I've only written one of them. The publisher's got someone else to do the other – something they think will fit with mine. One day, though, I'm going to write my own companion piece. The same story but from a different direction. Its reflection.'

'You know, I could read it before it's out,' Ken said, pointing at the secretary cabinet. 'Jemmy the lock, break my way in.'

'You could,' Oliver conceded. 'But you won't.'

'Tell me why.'

Oliver thrust his hands in his pockets. 'Because you're too respectful of right and wrong. And I think that's what I need more of around here. Anyhow, you don't have long to wait.'

'True.' Now that his vision had adjusted to the low light in the room, Ken spotted something unexpected tucked away at the side. It was an easel, with a painting on it covered with a sheet. 'You have a hobby.'

'I find it clears my head.' He sounded almost apologetic. 'To tell you the truth, pal, I find parties pretty exhausting and I like to come out here for a while when they're on. People don't seem to miss me when the bash is in full swing.'

'I can understand that. About parties, I mean. The host has the hardest job of all.'

'I kinda fell into that role.' It was obvious that Oliver wasn't totally happy that he had done so.

Ken could picture him discreetly calling his launch, setting out over the waves and spending a half hour at his canvas or his typewriter – ready to set the party smile back in place and head into the battleground spilling out of his house. 'May I?' he asked as he went to the picture.

'Be my guest.'

Ken lifted the cover and found a medium-sized painting. It was in the early stages, with more pencil lines than paint, ready to guide the artist's brush. But it seemed to be a portrait of a woman in front of the glass house on the cliff.

'Who is she?'

'No one in particular.'

Ken pondered if that could be true. Artists – even amateur artists – never just painted random figures, they always had someone in mind. So he wondered still who she was.

The rest of the party passed in a haze of singing, bathing and people yelling themselves hoarse above the din. Ken took the chance to explore the house a little. Upstairs had five bedrooms, a library and a couple of bathrooms. All had doors made of opaque smoked glass, coloured red, green or blue. Sometime after midnight, Gloria appeared in the ballroom with a silver tray striped with white powder. She insisted Ken try some and he resisted with equal force until she gave up, pouting her lips and calling him a dull son-of-a-bitch and he had better remember he was taking her home tonight or she would make him sorry. And then, half an hour later, she told him that Piers Bellen – 'the producer from Warner that you were so rude to' – was going to see her home, but he had kindly agreed to give Ken a ride even though his rudeness had been totally uncalled for. Ken was so tired by that point that he agreed.

Bellen was already in the driving seat when Ken got into the rear of a tiny white European car. His seat was more suited to a lapdog than a human, and as he eased himself down, Ken saw Bellen's eyes. Even in the glimmers from the house, he could tell the pupils were shrunken, and there were two rough smudges of white under his nostrils. He prayed they would get home – or at least somewhere close – without driving off the road.

'I'm thirsty. And hungry,' Bellen shouted as the ocean road whipped past them.

'Sorry to hear that,' Ken replied with irony that was lost on its subject, but not on Gloria, who glared at him.

'Want a hamburger.' They were passing a billboard advertising meat. 'And Coke.'

'Don't you think you've had enough of that?!' Gloria laughed. But Bellen's face only registered confusion.

'What?'

'I mean, like, white coke. Powder. You know: junk.'

'Oh!' His face cracked into a smile and he guffawed too as he pressed on the accelerator, speeding them even faster and less steadily along the road. But then he suddenly slammed on the brakes.

'Christ!' Ken gasped as he cannoned into the back of Gloria's seat.

'There it is!' Bellen said, pointing and spinning the wheel so that they turned into the parking lot of an all-night grill.

He dragged up the hand brake and ran towards the entrance. Ken and Gloria had no choice but to follow. As Bellen kicked open the chrome door, he turned back to them. His face was curdling as if he had sucked on a lemon. 'Shines,' he called loudly.

'What?' Ken replied.

Bellen pointed to a coloured man and his girl approaching the 'to go' counter.

'Shines. Everywhere.' He made sure the whole room could hear him. For sure the black man could, and gave him a hard look before going back to his conversation with the waitress.

'I said, shines everywhere!' This time, he bawled it.

'Oh, Jesus Christ,' Ken said to himself. He wanted to leave, but they were miles from anywhere and the only transport was Piers Bellen.

And then Bellen changed up a gear. 'We white. You negro. You wait!' He was growling in a fake tribal voice, thrusting a sweaty arm between the couple and the counter.

The coloured man glared at him, then replied, 'We here first. You after.' And he pushed the arm away with the same force. But the man couldn't know what Bellen had been snorting and how it was affecting his brain. Suddenly Bellen's fist – heavy though unpractised, judging by its swinging haymaker – was connecting with dark brown flesh, and a slimmer elbow was thudding into Bellen's solar plexus in return and the waitress was calling the cops and Gloria was screaming her head off and Ken was wishing to God he had found another way home.

Two hours later, Ken sat, drenched in the sweat of night, on a bench in University Avenue police precinct house, three paper cups stained with coffee dregs at his feet. The other couple had been interviewed, processed and bounced. Bellen was at the payphone shouting again.

'Fucking shine hit me, Tooke. A fucking . . . They're uppity now. I swear, they should never have been set free. He fucking smacked me one, you hear?' There was a short silence, as Oliver Tooke presumably got a few words in. 'Isn't it obvious, you numbskull? You come down here and bail me. Fucking police bail.' Another few seconds of calm. And then Bellen lowered his voice to a threatening hiss. 'Because if you don't, then you don't get what I've found out for you. You'll never know what happened.' And, bizarre as it sounded, he put on a high-pitched, wheedling female voice. 'Oh, Ollie, little Ollie. What really happened to me?' He reverted to his previous hiss. 'Only you won't be able to do nothing because you don't know what happened.' And he slammed down the receiver. A rictus grin was affixed to his mouth as he strode over to where Ken and Gloria sat wilting on the bench. 'Tooke'll come. In twenty fucking minutes.'

And the strange thing, to Ken's mind, was that Tooke came. In twenty fucking minutes.

Chapter 4

Ken had a 6am call for some establishing shots for *The Siege of Downville* and had booked another day off from work at the newspaper. That had given him a full two hours' sleep. As the film crew's wristwatches ticked past nine and he sat baking in full costume, waiting to walk past in a group scene, his mind buzzed with questions as to why the hell Oliver would drive from his house in the middle of the night and hand two hundred dollars to the Los Angeles police department to spring a lying boor like Piers Bellen. And whatever the answers, he had a sinking feeling that that lost night might have spelled the end of his friendship with Oliver Tooke.

His mind pounding with the heat, lack of sleep and

the dregs of martinis kicking at the inside of his skull, he dragged himself over to the second assistant director. 'I'm real sorry, but could I go somewhere cool to wait?' he asked.

The young man tried to place him. 'Lieutenant Brooks, right?'

'Yes,' Ken nodded enthusiastically. It was about the first time anyone had recognized him or his part.

'Take your pick. There's the bench over there in the sun, or there's the trailer. It's made outta steel and it's like being in an oven. Take your shitty pick.' And he checked a clipboard with a thick ream of sheets before walking away. Ken went to the bench.

The sun was pummelling down like he had offended it. It scratched at his face and somehow forced its way through the fabric to burn him through his clothes. When he stood up, unable to take it any more, he could feel the skin on his chest crackle. Could the trailer be any worse? He pulled himself over to it, to find twenty extras and a couple of main cast members crowding into its shadow. 'Whatever you do, sport, don't even think of getting in there,' one young man rasped at him. 'You won't come out again.'

Ken squirmed himself between a coloured girl playing a brilliant and dangerous spy for the Union and a one-handed man appearing as a storekeeper. The man had already filmed his only scene, where he got shot in the crossfire between the two armies, but had been told to hang around indefinitely just in case they wanted to bring him back. 'Bring me back? I get killed in the first minute!'

47

he was complaining. 'What kinda doctors they have back then? Witch doctors?'

'That's lunch, everyone!', shouted through a metal cone by a kid who looked like he was excited to be out of his high-school math lesson, were the most popular words of the day. While Ken made his way through a plate of bread and Mexican beans with some unidentifiable meat sausage on the side, he caught sight of the director – an effusive and very short man with a moustache that would have suited nobody on earth – coming out of a trailer, followed a minute later by a red-headed actress who had been cast in a small part. Ken was not one bit surprised when word got round an hour later that the leading lady, who had been found doped out on the floor of her bathroom, was being replaced by the redhead.

'Fun and games, don't ya think?' said one of the older women.

'I guess so.'

'This your first one of these?'

'My first.'

'I've done three in the last month. It's exploitation.'

'It is?'

'I've done Shakespeare. Now this.' She waved her hand to indicate everything. 'Just exploitation.'

They were interrupted by the third assistant director grabbing Ken and marching him over to a scene that was just starting up. 'You're in this one,' he was told.

'Am I? It's not in the script.'

'You're working from the wrong draft. You're on the green. We're on yellow now,' he said, flapping the sheaf of yellow pages in Ken's chest.

'Okay. Do I have lines?'

'Right here.' He pointed some out.

'That's not me,' Ken said, disappointed.

'What?'

'I'm Lieutenant Brooks.'

They both stared at the lines ascribed to another character. 'Ah, shit,' the man grumbled, and he left to find the right actor.

Somehow Ken made it through the day, getting back to his lodging house just after five. By that point, he had walked once up a hill while the cameras pointed in another direction. When he arrived home, he found a note pushed under his door. It was in the olde-worlde hand of his landlady.

'Mr Kourian. Mr Tooke called by. He said that he was sorry for any inconvenience last night and hopes that you are quite well. He would like to invite you to dinner at the Plaza Hotel Friday evening at eight. He has a very nice car.' The last statement was, he was sure, her own thought, rather than Oliver's.

He placed the slip of good-quality writing paper on his bedside table, took off his shoes and jacket and fell asleep in his clothes.

Chapter 5

Over the next few weeks, he saw Oliver a number of times. They would often go to dinner at upmarket restaurants where Oliver would discreetly add the bill to his personal account. In return, Ken would buy them hot dogs from carts at lunchtime. It worked.

'Isn't it tomorrow that your book comes out? The upside-down one?' Ken asked one night. He was yelling because they had ringside seats at a boxing fixture and the crowd was louder than an express train.

Oliver took a while to answer. '*The Turnglass*. Yes.'

The fighter in gold trunks broke out with a vicious upper cut, sending his opponent in black trunks sprawling. The crowd leaped to their feet, baying for blood.

'So you're happy with the ending now?'

'I wouldn't . . .' Oliver trailed off. He was usually so precise with his words. 'Maybe. I guess so.'

'Will you tell me what it's about?'

Oliver hesitated before answering. 'Did I mention, my father's family are from England?'

'No.'

'They are. From a county on the east coast. Essex. That's where the family seat is – our house here is a copy of it, only made out of glass. We used to visit the old place sometimes – it's on a tiny island called Ray. All quite desolate. I've set the book there.'

'Interesting. And what's the story like?'

Oliver was quiet for a while again before he answered. 'It's a sad story.' He didn't often speak emotionally, not like that. He was normally matter-of-fact.

'Will readers buy that?'

The match crowd howled as the black-trunked boxer, charging back from the rope, opened up a wide cut on his opponent's cheek. 'Lots of them,' Oliver told him.

'So who's going to be sad about it?'

'I am.'

At the sound of an urgent brass bell, the fight ended with the gold trunks declared the winner. The victory seemed to put a halt on the conversation and they went out to eat at a place Oliver knew that opened late, then took a walk along Sunset in the cooler air, enveloped by chirping crickets and gasoline fumes. An air of humid desperation was hovering over Los Angeles. Ken felt it, hanging there as the clock ticked to 2am and the drunks and hobos picked through trash heaps.

'Your book'll be out in a few hours,' Ken mentioned, looking at his watch.

'I guess it will.'

'Oliver, I don't know any other authors. But I'm pretty sure most of them are more excited about their new book appearing.'

Oliver stopped and looked back down the street. It was quiet now, no more than a handful of cars winding their way home. 'I'm not sure it's the right thing,' he said.

'Why not?'

'Because of guilt. Because I'm guilty.'

Ken stopped and sat on a concrete bench someone had set beside the road for no reason. 'Guilty of what?'

'Being here,' Oliver replied, remaining standing and gazing down the road.

'Is that really something you can be guilty of? Being alive?'

'Sometimes.'

'That's garbage. So will you tell me what's brought this to your mind right now?'

Oliver seemed to waver. But then he came down on one side. 'Another time.' He made his tone lighter again, as if a part of him, briefly allowed to emerge into the light, had been pushed back inside, and Ken let it drop. Oliver would talk when he was ready.

They walked and spoke about nothing special until

something took their feet along Olympic and they came upon a bookstore with a lit window display. Prominent in it was *The Turnglass*.

'Now let it all come down,' Oliver said, almost to himself.

Chapter 6

It was that weekend, the Saturday morning that the calendar marked as the first day of July, that Ken spoke his first and last words in a talking picture. They were immediately forgettable even to him – something about a senior officer being unhappy with arrangements for billeting the regiment, and a subsequent argument about the time the troops had been marching. But the director accepted the delivery without any sign he had even heard them, and because it was an early-morning scene, Ken was back at his digs by ten o'clock. As he walked from the bus stop, he was surprised to see Oliver waiting outside the house, his arms crossed, leaning on the hood of a big car, a Cadillac Phaeton. Ken's landlady had been right when she had praised it.

'Want to meet my father?' Oliver asked as Ken came near.

Up to that point, Ken had only heard about the man, Oliver Tooke Senior, from his landlady and sometimes read about him in the newspapers. 'Why not?'

A chauffeur opened the door and Ken entered. The car purred out into steady traffic. 'Sorry, pal. I forgot. You probably have no idea who my father is. Dad's state Governor,' Oliver explained. Ken didn't say anything. 'He's back from Sacramento. He usually lives in the Governor's residence there, but he's in town for an event and while he's here W2XAB is interviewing him for the nightly news. Dad wants a show of old family strength at the old family home.'

Ken had barely even thought about the fact that Oliver's glass-walled home wasn't actually his – it was his father's, and all the furniture, the books, the piano, all belonged to Governor Tooke.

'What sort of event?' Ken asked.

'It's a political thing. He's going to run for President next year. He should get the Republican nomination, and he's hosting a little soiree for some of the local organizers.'

'So he's canvassing for votes.'

'Votes? Hell no, nothing so tawdry. Dad's canvassing for money.'

The family were wealthy, but the spend for a presidential primary would probably be beyond even their deep pockets.

On the way, Ken thought of the last party he had attended at the Tooke home. The night hadn't ended well; and if Oliver hadn't been able to place his hands on a couple hundred bucks to post bail for Piers Bellen, it might have turned out worse. As they neared the house, he spoke. 'What does Piers Bellen have on you?'

He thought Oliver would have good reason to send him right back home for prying like that, but his friend didn't even look put out. 'I thought you'd ask that sooner or later.'

'Why?'

'Because you're a perceptive man.'

'And what's the answer?'

Oliver glanced at him but didn't reply.

The cruise-liner-sized car swept into the driveway and they sauntered into the house. Something in the lobby caught Ken's attention: above the fireplace was a painting, and he was sure it hadn't been there before. He recognized it as the one he had seen on the easel in the writing tower, now completed. It was a portrait of a woman aged perhaps thirty, with the house pictured in the background. The subject had chestnut brown hair falling across her shoulders and bright eyes – unnaturally bright, truth be told, because they had been pictured with a sunbeam glaring into them. Her clothes were a little out of fashion, that even Ken could tell.

'Is it anyone in particular?'

'You haven't read my book yet, have you?' Oliver's tone was amused admonishment.

'Not yet – the movie shoot got in the way, but I promise I will.'

'Okay. Let's go up.'

They ascended the stairs and walked the length of the landing, opening the green smoked-glass door to the library. Ken had only had a brief look into the room before. It had dark wood-panelled walls and a slow air to it, as if its summer days were long gone and it was facing a bleak winter.

'Sitting with me today is Mr Oliver Tooke, Governor of California,' barked a bald-headed man holding a microphone in his lap. 'Governor, will you please tell the viewers at home what's on your mind as we approach the presidential primaries?'

On the wall above them hung a family portrait. There was the Governor standing with his hand firmly on the shoulder of his seated wife: a man with bearing and steel-grey hair, a woman with beauty and warm features; and in front of them, their children. But Ken was surprised by two aspects to the picture. The first was that there weren't just the two children Ken's landlady had mentioned, but three: two boys under the age of five and looking like peas in a pod – dark hair framing identical round faces – and a baby held by the mother. One of the boys was in a wheel-chair and Ken remembered that Oliver had said polio had kept him in one as a child.

The other surprise was that the woman in the painting was undoubtedly the subject of the portrait downstairs – the picture that Oliver had claimed was of no one in particular.

'Two words, sir, two words: social corruption,' was the Governor's reply. Ken heard a voice that was almost the same as Oliver's, only aged by time and by heavy smoking that had also turned the Governor's teeth the colour of wheat. 'And I'm sorry to say that a major source of it is the motion picture industry right here in California. Now, I'm a big fan of the talkies myself, but we have a lot of young folk going these days and they're seeing a lot of things they oughtn't.'

'What sort of thing?'

Here we go, Ken thought to himself. Sodom and Gomorrah downtown. Politicians were filling newspaper page after newspaper page with their condemnation.

'Well, they're seeing narcotic use and they're seeing brutal violence and they're copying it. Why wouldn't they when it all looks so sharp on the screen?'

'Countering violent crime is Dad's big thing,' Oliver whispered.

'So I see. It looks genuine.'

'It's personal.'

'How so?'

'I had a brother.' Oliver's face showed a mix of emotions: sadness and something that seemed more like anger. 'I was five, Alex was four. He was abducted.'

'From here?'

'Here? Oh, no. We were at our other house. The one in England. We never saw him again.' He gazed out the window. 'I hate that place.'

It was time to confess. 'Someone told me it had happened, actually.'

'Figures.' Oliver shrugged. 'Someone always tells.' He cleared his throat. 'Anyway, Dad's been heavy on crime ever since.'

A producer put his finger to his lips to tell them to shut up.

The interview ended. 'Have you heard what happened to the President today?' the interviewer asked as they stood.

'I heard he fell out of his wheelchair,' Tooke replied with a smirk. 'Elect a cripple, get a cripple. The American people have only got themselves to blame.'

The interviewer snorted with laughter, then proposed they record a little footage outside in the garden. Tooke agreed and the cameras filmed him walking on the clifftop lawn beside his son, with the sea beyond. 'Your grandfather planted these gardenias,' he was saying. 'He knew that if you have good roots, you have a strong plant. Like strong families. Everything that we are stems from him.' It was baloney for the microphones and cameras. And despite the flowers that surrounded them in regimented rows, Ken couldn't help but remember what Oliver had said when he'd first met him: that there was something corrupt and malign about the house.

Nevertheless, they stopped to admire the gardenias. At the end, the camera crew packed up and the Governor asked Oliver if he was still going around with the sodomites in the movie industry.

'Some of them, Dad. Not all.'

'At least they can't breed.'

'I guess not.'

'I want to lead this nation,' Tooke Senior said, stretching out his back. 'It's vital right now with the situation in Europe – the Democrats would take us into another disaster of a war against Germany. For what? To see a million American boys torn to pieces? And you having faggots for tea doesn't help my chances. People will presume I raised one myself.'

'I'll ask them to stop.'

The Governor nodded. At the end of the lawn, there was a wrought iron octagonal summerhouse with a love seat of the same metal at its centre. Sitting there, impassively watching their approach, was a strikingly beautiful woman with dark hair almost to her waist. She wore a white outfit and a wide-brimmed hat that was keeping the sun off her pale face. Her arm was stretched along the top of the seat. A cigarette was burning in her fingers, and as they neared her, she took a drag, then cast it aside and leaned her cheek on her arm.

'Hello, Coraline,' Oliver said. She looked from him to his friend. 'This is Ken Kourian. Ken, my sister, Coraline.'

He extended a hand and she took it. 'You're a friend of my brother's?' she said. Her voice was soft, as if she was in the habit of only speaking to people within arm's length.

'I like to think so.'

She gazed at him as if he had spoken too quietly to hear. Then she turned to her father. 'How much has Fletcher offered you?' she asked.

'Not enough,' he grumbled.

'You'll have to confront him one day.' And then to her brother: 'I think I'll stay here for a while. I'm tired of Sacramento.' Ken would have been lying if he had then denied the existence of a little civil war inside his chest at the prospect of Coraline Tooke living at the house where he had become a regular visitor. 'Are you in the movies?' Coraline asked Ken.

'Trying.'

'You've got that look about you.'

'What sort of look?'

'Soon-to-be-disappointed.'

A butler intervened and told the Governor that the film crew were leaving and the producer wanted a brief word. He followed the servant back to the house.

'Could you show Ken around the garden?' Oliver asked. 'I need to speak to Carmen for a while.'

'Who's Carmen?' Ken asked, unable to hold his curiosity.

'The maid,' Coraline replied. 'Sure, I'll play house.'

Oliver followed in his father's footsteps, and Ken and Coraline spoke for a few minutes without actually saying anything. The garden, the weather. The things strangers say to each other while waiting for a streetcar. Ken's gaze fell on the house's double-height upper storey. The two rows of windows were arched and large, and he saw Oliver framed in one, speaking earnestly to an old Mexican woman who seemed to be in tears. She ran out of sight and Oliver stood looking just like he had taken a punch in the gut.

'Do you ride, Mr Kourian?' Coraline asked.

'I grew up in Georgia, miss,' he said distractedly. 'If I didn't, I wouldn't get anywhere.'

'Good,' she said. 'I've been looking for a hack. We'll ride today.'

*

An hour later, Ken, Oliver and Coraline entered the gates of a livery stable a few miles up the coast. They wore jodhpur pants, Ken having squeezed into an old pair of Oliver's. 'We've kept our horses here as long as I can remember,' Coraline said.

'She was the most competitive girl rider you ever saw,' Oliver muttered. 'Only thing that ever raised her heartbeat above twenty per minute.'

'And he was slower than the ocean,' she said, leading the way around the back. A stable lad ran to bring her the necessary tack. 'Here we go. This is Bedouin. Don't you think he looks like Oliver?'

The horse was a piebald gelding. 'Sure. It's all in the face.'

'Exactly.'

'Thanks, both of you,' Oliver replied. 'I'll be on Ricky there, and you can have Dad's mount, Stetson. Think you can handle a stallion?'

'He grew up in Georgia – if he couldn't ride, he wouldn't get anywhere,' Coraline told him. Ken detected a sardonic lilt in her voice.

'I guess I'm going to have to prove that, aren't I?'

They saddled up and trotted out. Coraline kicked her heels hard into Bedouin's flank even before they were through the gates, cantering down to the beach. The path was a narrow one with loose rocks and it wouldn't have taken much for the horse to miss a step.

'It's keep up or fall behind, pal,' Oliver shouted as he matched his sister's speed. 'I learned that a long time ago with Coraline.'

'I guess it is!' Ken replied, laughing. It had been a few

years, but the thrill of racing along the track with his new friend and the girl with dark hair streaming behind her like ribbons surged. 'How often do you do this?' he yelled as the path met the damp sand and the horses, getting a whiff of a hunt in their nostrils, took it upon themselves to increase to a full gallop.

'Not often enough. Only when Coraline's death-wish overcomes my sense of self-preservation.' And at that, he smacked his heels into his mount's sides, spurring the horse to leave the ground entirely and fly over a thin creek trickling to the sea.

Ken did the same, feeling the joy of belonging as the three of them abandoned all caution. They were all now bound to live or die as one. And the distance between him, Oliver and Coraline began to close inch by inch. The sun was blazing and the sea was foaming and the horses were snorting and then . . . And then nothing at all as the world spun into confusion and chaos and blackness.

'He's not very good at that, is he?'

The voice was coming through the dark. And as he forced his eyelids up, wincing at the light and the banging pain at the back of his skull, shapes seemed to emerge. The voice belonged to someone looking down at him.

'Are you okay, pal?'

A hand reached for him. Instinctively, he grabbed hold of it. 'I feel like I've fallen off a horse,' he mumbled.

'Yeah, you look like it too.'

'I expect the horses are slower in Georgia,' Coraline remarked.

'We breed them that way. For our own safety.' Breathing in was painful. Breathing out was twice as bad. He tried to work out if he had broken anything except his self-respect.

'How about a little bit of sympathy?' Oliver admonished his sister.

'You give it to him. If you can't stay on a horse, you shouldn't get on one.'

'Give the man a break. His saddle came loose.' Oliver lifted Ken to his feet. 'She's always like this.' Ken focused on his horse, whose saddle was hanging off the side. 'You need me to help you home?'

That would have been more painful than falling off the horse. 'I'll be fine.'

'See, big brother? He'll be fine. Stop your fussing.'

'I don't want him to sue you.'

'Sue me?'

'You encouraged him to race.'

'He's a big boy.'

And even while his head ached, Ken was amused by the tussling between the siblings. This must have been their life – he guessed their father had been a distant one, what with his political career and the business to run. So the kids had probably been raised by nannies and maids, relying on each other more than on their parents. They were quite different in each other's company to how they were with the rest of the world. 'I'll live,' he told them.

'I'll take you to the emergency room,' insisted Oliver.

'I don't need a hospital.'

'Well, you don't need a cabaret show.'

'He should be in one.'

'I don't—'

'We're going.'

Oliver drove them to the Southern California Hospital in Culver City. Coraline arched an eyebrow as her brother helped Ken inside with a hand under his elbow, but said nothing.

'I'm okay. This isn't necessary,' Ken insisted as he gave the attending nurse his details. Only he knew it probably was, but he had no idea how he was going to pay for it.

'Better safe than sorry, pal.'

A doctor came and looked into his eyeballs, took his temperature and blood pressure and seemed, to Ken's wallet, to be running up bills for the sake of it. At the end of it, he was pronounced fit to go, given a pack of aspirin that came out at a buck a pill and went back to reception. 'Where do I pay?' he asked.

The receptionist looked confused. 'You want to pay *again*?' And she looked over to where Oliver stood. Ken understood and thanked her. He didn't thank his friend, because that would only have embarrassed them both. Better to take it as an unspoken part of friendship.

Chapter 7

They got back to the house, Ken easing himself out of the car and trying to keep a lid on the pain in his chest. There was another automobile on the drive and the wisp of a smile spread on Coraline's lips.

'Our grandfather's here,' Oliver explained.

Up the stairs, Ken heard a gravelly English voice spilling from the library. '. . . come across as cold. Be strong, yes, cultivate that image. But don't be a cold fish,' it said.

Coraline was first through the door, then her brother, and Ken brought up the rear. An aged man with a spark in his eye was revealed. He was in a wheelchair and had a blanket over his knees, but there was something about him that said he could have jumped up and shaken out a foxtrot if he had wanted to. The Governor was behind his desk, listening close.

'Hello, my girl,' the old man said as Coraline kissed him on the cheek.

'Ken Kourian, my grandfather, Simeon Tooke.'

'Pleased to meet you, sir,' Ken said, holding out a hand.

'You too, my boy. Why are you limping?'

'Ken had an argument with a horse.'

'It looks like the horse won. Tincture of *Arnica montana*, son.' He clapped Ken on the arm. 'You can get it at any drugstore. It will do for the swelling and the bruises I observe are just budding out under your shirt.'

'Grandfather was a doctor,' Oliver explained.

'I still am,' the old man admonished. 'Now, children, I need to speak to your father for a while. If he wants to be popular, he has to understand people a bit better than he does.'

'We'll be downstairs.'

They left the two men to it. And as Ken lowered himself down the stairs, he heard the old man's voice again. 'Yes, people vote for a man who gets things done. But they *campaign* for a man they want to spend a day with. You need more warmth to come across. And splash out for other people more. They like that. They stay loyal for that.'

'My father listens to Grandfather more than anyone,' Oliver explained. 'For a retired doctor, he sure knows politics.'

'He seems a good man.'

'He is. He's always been generous. When he came over from England he brought his servants with him. He sent their kids to school. Their grandkids, even.' They reached the ground level. 'Will you stay for supper?'

'I can't. I need to go home and put some ice on these wounds.'

'That's fair. Want to stop by tomorrow?'

Ken tried not to glance at Coraline as he replied. 'I'll be sure to.'

Chapter 8

They spent the next day, Sunday, fishing. Oliver gave Ken a hand from the jetty onto his motor launch. 'Careful, pal. After yesterday you must be broken up.'

'Funny. Real funny.'

'Will you be teasing him all the way, dear brother?' Coraline was sunning herself in a tight red one-piece bathing suit. A wide-brimmed straw hat was keeping her face in the shade.

'Just some of it.'

'That's nice to know.' Ken cursed the accident that had made him a figure for friendly ridicule. Well, maybe she would fall into the sea.

'The pain's pretty much gone, thank you for your

concern,' Ken informed them both. 'Where are the rods?'

He found one and an ice box that contained a cocktail shaker full of ready-mixed cosmopolitan.

'Will you fetch me one of those?' Coraline asked. And he couldn't miss that her voice had dropped half an octave and slowed by a mile an hour.

'Fetch it yourself. I'm a cripple, remember.'

Oliver burst out laughing and Ken poured himself a generous measure. And later, when she had drained away the ruby liquid, she placed her highball glass in front of him and he refilled it without a word and handed it back to her; both of them making sure their fingers didn't touch.

It was the kind of day Ken dreamed about: good friends on the open water, a picture in the can ready to be turned into an actual talkie. When he had taken the long railroad out from Boston, he had pictured scenes like this. They might have been in nightclubs or at the races, but the basic elements – excitement, friendship – were just the same. He glanced at Oliver. Despite the brilliant sun, there seemed to be a shadow across his face.

'You okay?' Ken asked.

Oliver looked blankly at him, as if he had just been woken from a dream. 'Oh, sure. Fine, pal.'

'Something on your mind?'

'On my mind.' Oliver looked at the birds above.

'What is it?'

Oliver took his time to answer. 'You ever think about guilt, Ken?'

That was a heavy question. 'Guilt? As a concept? Sometimes. Not often.' It was the same subject that had weighed on Oliver's mind the night of the boxing match.

'No, no, I guess most people don't.' He rubbed his forehead. 'My father and I ... well, I have a lot to say about guilt.'

'You feel guilty about something?'

'Yes.'

'And you want to talk to your father about it.'

'I do.'

'Have you tried?'

'I've started. The book is just the beginning.'

They were distracted by movement behind them. Coraline stood, reached out her arms and dived neatly under the surface of the water. She came up again a few yards away and turned onto her back, floating in the midday sun.

When Ken looked back to Oliver, the shadow was gone and his friend's face held a warm smile. 'I've bought us all tickets to *Mourning Becomes Electra* tomorrow night,' Oliver said.

'I thought that was sold out.'

'I managed to get hold of some seats.'

Ken guessed they were good ones.

They returned home in the late afternoon. The Governor's political get-together was about to begin and fifteen well-fed men dragged themselves out of black sedans arriving one after another into the driveway. A few of them had to be helped out.

The Governor was in the kitchen, reading over some notes before making his entrance. He looked up when his son and daughter and their friend entered. 'I have a meeting in here in two minutes,' he said.

'Who with?' Coraline asked.

'Burrows.'

'What does he want?'

'I'm not interested in what he wants. I have a task for him.'

'On 402?'

'That's right.'

'It's an absurd bill and it's not even popular. I told you to drop—'

'Sometimes, my girl,' he interrupted her, 'you have to do things that are not popular. You understand politics, Coraline, but you don't understand duty.'

'Duty?'

'*Calling.* I tried to instruct you, but it never sunk in. Bill 402 is my duty and I will not be deterred or derailed by anyone. Not even my own family.'

Coraline paused. 'Do you want us to leave?'

He pondered for a second. 'No, stay. Your presence adds to the atmosphere.'

Ken didn't like being part of the Governor's political scheme, whatever it was, and looked for an exit. Before he found one, a man so fat his vest buttons were strained shuffled into the room.

'Governor,' the obese man said, by way of polite greeting.

'Senator.' The Senator peered at the three young people

in the room. 'I have asked my son and daughter and their friend Mr Kourian to wait here and watch what happens,' Tooke said.

Senator Burrows sniffed nonchalantly. He had an accent from another state. Ken thought it might even be his own Georgia. When he spoke long words, he broke them into single syllables. 'You think, sir, that I'm gonna be in-tim-i-da-ted by a few kids?'

'I'm a busy man. I want to get down to business.'

'Business? Well, sure.' He straightened up, lifting his crown by an inch. 'The President does not want—'

Tooke raised the palm of his hand for silence. 'Do you mean President Roosevelt?'

Burrows seemed confused by the question. 'Of course. He does not want—'

'That man with polio? Crippled by polio?' Burrows was taken aback by the description. 'Did you hear that he fell out of his wheelchair? Right out. There he was, kicking his legs about on the soil like a dying bug.'

Tooke waited for a reply. Eventually, the Senator had to give one. 'The President has a medical condition—'

'No, sir, influenza is a medical condition. Gout is a medical condition. Being crippled with polio is an over-whelming reason he should never have been elected.'

Ken recalled Oliver telling him that, as a boy, polio-myelitis had left him wheelchair-bound. Ken glanced at his friend side-on. There was no reaction to be seen.

'What do you mean by that?' Burrows demanded.

'What do I mean? I mean that a man who cannot get to his feet should not try to lead a nation. A nation that has enemies foreign and domestic. He has my sympathy, like any cripple has. But he should have been barred from office.'

'Your personal feelings about the President's state of health will change nothing. He will not agree to fund this kind of hokey science. It is—'

Tooke interrupted him again, this time by speaking right over Burrows's head to a man standing in the doorway. He was kindly-looking, with very thick spectacles and a bushy moustache that almost hid a hare lip. 'Come in, Doctor. Come on in,' the Governor said, beckoning him into the room. 'Senator, this is Dr Arnold Kruger. He comes to us from the American Eugenics Society. Doctor, the Senator and I were just discussing how much money we can find to aid your work.'

'Governor!' Burrows cried angrily. 'The eugenics movement is gaining ground in Europe right now, but I'm damned if I'll let it take root here.'

Tooke stepped forward and snarled. 'Do not raise your voice in my house. This is where my family live and every brick is ours. You raise your voice and I will have you whipped in the street.' Burrows looked furious but bit his tongue. 'That's better. Now, understand this: the President is a sick man in a sick body. He should never have been allowed to get this far. And I will tell you something. I will have your support for 402.'

Burrows could hold himself no longer. 'And why would I do that?'

'Because if you don't, I will rezone and twist about every electoral district in this state to ensure you never set foot in the Capitol again. You'll be lucky to pull together a thousand votes.'

'I'll put you in jail!'

'I'll take the chance. And do you know why?'

Burrows's fat frame began to shake with anger. 'Why?'

'Because this God-given science will transform our land into a nation. The glory of Rome, sir, was no accident. It was breeding. And now we have a scientific way of ensuring that glory.' Burrows stared at the doctor, whose thick eyebrows beetled behind his thick glasses.

Ken and his friends ate out on the sand below the house that evening, grilling the sandbass they had caught earlier over smoking coals. No table, just cloths laid on the soft ground. The Governor and his father had returned to Sacramento, so it was just them in the house.

As he lay back, his fingers knitted underneath his head, Ken felt happier than he had for some time. LA had been a gamble, for sure, and for the most part a lonely one. But in the warm evening, on the sand, with people around him, he could see a future for himself here in this city.

'What's on your mind, Oliver?' Coraline asked as they tipped their final glasses up around eleven.

'My new book mostly.'

'Worried it won't sell well?'

'Maybe I'm just worried.'

'That's not like you.'

Oliver got to his feet. 'I think I'll go to bed,' he said. 'Ken, why don't you stay in the guest room tonight? Jennings will be here at eight, he can run you home.'

'Thanks.'

'And tomorrow, we can talk about what's been on my mind. All three of us, I think. It concerns you too,' he told Coraline.

'What's going on?' Ken asked.

'I want your opinion. Your advice.'

'About?'

Oliver hesitated. 'It's kinda about the book. But it's wider than that.'

'We can talk now if you want.'

Oliver thought it over. 'No, I'll wait until tomorrow. I want to sleep on it anyhow,' he said. He lifted a hand in farewell and went into the house.

Coraline sipped her vodka martini. A single drop of the misty liquid hung on her lip until her tongue flicked it away. Ken watched out of the corner of his eye.

'It's a hot night,' she said as she lay back.

He nodded. 'It is that.' Of course he wanted to pull her to him. But at that moment, he couldn't see the shot. 'It gets hotter in Georgia. A hundred degrees down there.'

There was a long silence before she broke it.

'I'll bet it does.' And at that, she twisted over and onto her feet. Then she was walking away to the house, following her brother. 'Goodnight,' she said.

'Goodnight.' And when she had crossed the threshold, he also stood and sauntered, hands in pockets, towards his room for the night. Maybe he should have gone for it, shot or no shot.

His room was wide and deep, overlooking the bay. He stripped off his shirt and lay, smoking, for a while – he didn't usually, but they had had a few drinks – wondering what had happened to undermine Oliver's mood.

After a while, he heard a mechanical whine on the wind. Peeling back the curtain, he saw Oliver's launch closing in on the writing tower. A silhouetted figure was piloting the pale boat and another stood behind him. What was going on? Presuming it was Oliver at the wheel, he must have taken some care to leave the house quietly.

Ken returned to his bed and for ten or fifteen minutes he thought more about what had happened that day, how Coraline had looked in her swimsuit. But he kept returning to that sight of two figures in the launch.

There was nothing else for it. He had to investigate. As he left his room, though, he was distracted by a creaking at the other end of the corridor. The blue glass door to Coraline's room was ajar.

He waited. No one came, no one spoke. Was the door open as an oversight? Just for the breeze? Something else? Impossible to say. He walked towards it. The gap between it and its frame was no more than an inch, but air was filtering through from an open window.

Of their own accord, his fingers touched the cool glass, ready to push it open. But a sound stopped them, halted in mid-air. It was a sound unexpected and weighted with threat: a sound like a distant explosion. It echoed once, twice around the bay. Ken couldn't tell what had made it, but after the sight of the boat powering towards the writing tower in the middle of the night, he knew something was wrong.

He rushed back to his room and looked out. The tower was black against a purple sky. He ran to Oliver's door and rapped hard. No answer. He wrenched it open.

Inside, the room was perfectly neat and the bed hadn't been slept in. Ken dashed out, through the marble ball-room, down to the beach and stared out at the stone structure, which looked brutal now against the moonlit skyline. Then he stripped to his underwear and charged into the waves.

They were cold and hard, and higher than they had been during the day. He powered through, crawl-stroke, taking short breaths when the swell lifted him and crashed him down again. Yard by yard, he came closer to the rocky outpost of land. All the way, he burned to know what he would find inside that squat stone tower.

Soon his muscles ached with the effort, but he was too far out to turn back. And then he was grabbing the warm rocks with both hands. The launch wasn't there, he noted.

The room was in pitch blackness when he stepped in and he groped for the oil lamp that had hung from the rafter, but found only empty air. He stumbled against something wooden and his foot connected with an object that rang like metal – the lamp. He lit its flame with a box of matches that he discovered by feeling blindly around on the desk. The lamp hissed into life, throwing yellow light on the room, the books, the furniture; and then upon the lifeless body of Oliver Tooke, sitting behind his writing desk, with his back to the wall and his neck torn to shreds by a bullet. Ken felt all the air leave his lungs.

He had seen a dead body once, but it had been his

grandfather laid out in a coffin, wearing his best suit, and his hands clasped neatly, as if he was trying to look nice on a date. Ken, aged ten, had looked on the peaceful corpse with little more than a child's inquisitiveness.

Now he stared at the form of his friend: the life ripped from it, the blood that had moved it spread on books and flung to the wind. There was a small revolver on the desk, next to the hand that had pulled the trigger to tear a man's throat apart.

'Jesus, Oliver. What have you done?' he asked, wanting an answer. He stood there for a time that could have been a minute, could have been an hour; wanting to know why. Just why.

And there was another who would need to know. Coraline, asleep in her blue-doored bedroom. He had little idea how he would break the news to her. All he could do was turn around and prepare for the cold, aching return to shore. Ken cast a last glance at what had once been a man, and stepped to the threshold.

As he did so, something caught his eye: the secretary cabinet in the corner. It held those dime-books with short-skirted women on one cover and dark-coated men on the other. On top of the pile was *The Turnglass*, Oliver's effort at a similar trick-book. The one he had said earlier in the evening he needed to talk to Ken and Coraline about. He never would now.

Ken still hadn't had a chance to pick up a copy, as filming and work had crowded out his daily life. Now he opened it and read again the first line. 'Simeon Lee's grey eyes were visible . . .' He turned it over. As Oliver had said, his story had been paired with another writer's, some run-of-the-mill spook tale titled *The Waterfall*.

Why would Oliver need Ken's advice about the book? And why hadn't he asked for it then and there? There was a chance that it was important; that the novel would give a clue to Oliver's state of mind of late. But that would have to wait: Coraline was in the house and he had to return with the painful news. Without the motor boat, he would have to swim back, and he could hardly carry the book. He would have to leave it here.

He prepared for the exertion. His body remembered the cold and the drag of the current, and tensed like stone before he dived.

It took all his energy reserves to crawl and kick back to the shore, finally pulling himself onto the sand and breathing heavily. At the edge of his vision, a few hundred yards along the bay, he saw what he was sure was the launch, beached. The current might have brought it over.

Or someone had powered it to shore and abandoned it.

He pulled on his pants and hurried through the ball-room and the entrance hall, up the white marble stairs and along to Coraline's room. All the way, he knew that this had become a different house to the one where he had spent happy days.

Her door was open still, wafting in the breeze, as if the room itself was breathing. His hand pushed it open.

'Hello, Ken,' she said softly, as soon as he entered, as if she had been waiting for him. And he saw, in the blue moonlight, Coraline turn over in bed to face him. She was wearing something made of silk decorated with aquamarine stars. He didn't reply but took a step forward. 'No words? No invitation. Just walking in?' Her lips caught a flash of the light. 'Ken?'

'Coraline. I'm sorry.'

'Sorry about what?'

'Something's happened.' He sat on the corner of the bed. He could make out her expression now: quizzical, amused. She waited for him to continue and he searched for the words that would soften the blow he was about to deal her. He hated that it was happening here, now, with the two of them like this. But in the end he could only be direct. 'Oliver has shot himself.'

Even as he said it, he had his doubts that that was the truth; but this wasn't the time.

She flinched as if he had hit her. Then she sat bolt upright. '*What?* What do you mean?'

'He's dead. I'm sorry. I found him in the writing tower.'

She flung back the covers. She breathed deeply twice, down into her core, and pulled on an emerald-coloured satin kimono that hung over the back of a chair. She spoke calmly. 'You've been tricked. He's not dead. It's some sort of a trick.'

A trick. No, no, if only that were true.

'I'm sorry, but I saw him.'

'There's no reason for him to do that!' she hissed. She strode to the drapes and threw them open. The moon – a pale sickle – was dead ahead, dropping milky light onto the stone tower in the sea. She pointed. 'Is he still there?' she asked.

'Yes.' So she had, at least, accepted it.

'I want him back here. I want you to bring him back.'

'I can't.'

'Why not?'

'We need to call the authorities. An ambulance.'

'And what good would that do now?' she demanded icily.

'It's what we need to do.'

She turned to him. Her eyes bore into his. 'Oliver would never do this.'

He could feel the salt on his body, smell the sweat in the air. 'I'll call the police. They need to be notified.'

She watched him leave.

It took twenty minutes for an unmarked police car to arrive at the house. 'Detective Jakes,' a gruff officer said by way of introduction. He was in his fifties, body gone to seed, and sported a moustache that he scratched with his pencil as if colouring in bald spots. 'He's where?' he asked with surprise when the location of the body was explained to him. Ken, now dressed, took him to the beach and pointed. 'Jesus above. How the hell you even get there?'

'The motorboat.' Ken pointed to it.

Jakes swore again. 'All right. Police ambulance is on its way. You know how to run that thing?'

'Sure. But . . .'

'But what?'

Something made Ken look up at the house. The dark figure of Coraline was staring down, with a cigarette glowing red between her fingers. She pulled the drapes across and was gone.

'I'll tell you later.'

'Whatever you say. Let's get going.'

They got going. And soon they were cutting through the waves, then scrambling onto the rocks that had become a tomb for Oliver Tooke's body. Ken let the detective go first. The oil lamp was still burning and the room was as he had left it: threatening and bloody.

Jakes scrutinized the scene, then looked back and raised his eyebrows.

'Yeah, I know,' Ken muttered.

'He do or say anythin' to suggest he was gonna do this?'

'Nothing.'

'Well,' Jakes shrugged. 'Truth is, not many do. With most, it's "He seemed a bit down, but not so bad he was gonna kill himself."' He paused. 'I'm sorry for your loss.'

The phrase was empty. Ken didn't believe Detective Jakes was any bit sorry for his loss. It was form, though, like taking your hat off indoors.

'So what do we do now?'

'Well, there's nothin' suspicious far as I can see. Weapon right there under his hand. Now we just take him back to land. I'm sorry for your loss.'

'Yeah, you said.' He didn't care that he sounded rude.

'We can wait for the ambulance to turn up and come over the same way we did. But be honest with you, it's not gonna be any more dignified than if we just take him back ourselves. Your choice, though.'

Given that choice, it seemed more respectful to take Oliver back themselves instead of watching him carried by strangers who had probably taken five other corpses that week. That day, even; this was LA, after all.

And so they lifted him between them into the small boat and headed back to the headland. But before they did that, as Jakes's back was turned, Ken picked up Oliver Tooke's final story, *The Turnglass*, and slipped it inside his jacket. Little doubts were crawling into his mind like ants, so he wanted to know what the book held – and he wasn't sure the policeman would understand.

Once ashore, they laid the dead man in his bed, with a sheet up to his chin to hide the violence that the bullet had wreaked. As if it mattered now.

Coraline was sitting in an armchair in the corner of her room when he got there. 'Would you like to see Oliver?' he asked.

Without a word, she walked to her brother's bedroom, gazed at the body and returned to her own room.

'Detective,' Ken began, as they went down to the kitchen. It was time to let loose what he had seen earlier.

Jakes was writing something in his notebook. 'Yeah?' He didn't look up.

'I think I saw two people going out there.'

'What d'you mean?' He was still concentrating on his notes.

'In the boat. When I saw the boat going out, I think there were two people in it.'

He paused. 'You think? I mean, you sure?'

Ken closed his eyes and dragged the image out, as plain as day. 'I'm sure. I saw two people.'

Jakes tapped his pencil on his notepad thoughtfully. 'How? You got night-time sun out here?'

'There was enough moonlight.'

Jakes looked like he had chewed something sour and went back to writing. 'Moonlight nothin'.'

Ken tried another tack. 'He bought us all tickets to a play tomorrow night. Is that what a man who's planning on ending his own life would do?'

'I ain't a shrink.'

'But if—'

'Listen.' Jakes closed his notebook. 'You seem to be suggestin' there's foul play here. Well, I hear ya, but there's nothin' at all about this that says so. You said yourself Mr Tooke seemed unhappy yesterday evening, he went out to this crazy outhouse he has on a bunch of rocks – I have no idea how that's legal, by the way – and he uses his own gun.'

'How do you know it's his?'

'What? The rod?'

'Yes.'

'No reason to think it ain't.'

'That's not good enough.'

'And the angle of the bullet.' He demonstrated with his pencil. 'It comes up through the neck an' out the side. If someone else shot it, he woulda had to be sittin' in the victim's lap.'

'You can't be sure of that.'

'Okay, okay.' He put the notebook and pencil into his inside breast pocket. 'Let's say my opinion about this event is based on twenty-five years as a detective. Because in all that time, I have never seen a fake gun planted or a suicide that was anything except what it looked to be: an unhappy man with the means to end things. And I'm sorry. I really am. But we can't help the facts.'

'Can you check it for fingerprints?'

The detective was quiet for a moment. 'Look, Mr Kourian. We can do that. We can try to trace it right back to the manufacturer. We could knock on every door from here to Tijuana askin' people if they've seen anythin'. But I'm gonna level with you: we won't. Because there is absolutely nothin' about this raises any suspicions.'

The doorbell rang and Ken went out to find the police ambulance. The driver apologized for the time it had taken and explained that they had had to stop at every house on the road to ask for directions because he had no idea where in God's name he was. And then the body was taken away, and Jakes drove off and it was just Ken and Coraline alone in Turnglass House. He found her in her room, back in bed in her silk nightdress with aquamarine stars.

'They've all gone,' he said.

'I know.'

'Do you want me to telephone your father?'

'Don't you think it should come from someone he's met more than twice?' Her rejection was offhand, but given the circumstances he couldn't fault her.

'I'll go back to my apartment and leave you in peace,' he said.

He collected his few things – his billfold, his keys – and called for a taxi to take him back to town. As he ducked down into the car, he thought for a moment that the cab had a radio drawling out piano music and he was about to ask the driver to turn it off; but then he realized the music was coming from within the house. Coraline was playing the white baby grand in the ballroom. Something European and melancholy.

Chapter 9

He crawled into his bed around six, and lay there staring at the ceiling, from time to time hearing the couple in the next room argue. They were awake earlier than usual too. It was the heat, no doubt, that had forced them out of their sultry bed.

The detective, Jakes, was convinced it was suicide. Ken hated that because the thought that his only real friend had cut his life short tasted as bitter as brine. But he needed to look at it objectively, so he tried to think of a reason why Oliver might have done it. He had no money worries, for sure; his work was in demand; and if he was in debt, say, he could have tapped his father for cash.

A love affair that ditched? There had been no sign at all

that Oliver had been secretly involved with someone. He hadn't even seemed all that interested in girls – or men, for that matter.

And all that was without the image in Ken's brain of two men going out on that launch. Sure, it was dark, but he had seen what he had seen. So the questions were: who was the second man, and what were they doing out there?

Well, there was one item Ken had lifted from the scene that might help. Oliver had said he had something on his mind, something he needed to talk to Ken and Coraline about, and it was connected to his new book.

The Turnglass turned out to be a hypnotic story about an English doctor investigating the deaths of his relatives during the previous century in the county of Essex – where Oliver had said his family were from. The action took place in a strange house on the coast that could be cut off from the mainland by the tide – and it had the same name as the family's place in California: Turnglass House. So that had to be the Tookes' ancestral home. Yet another connection was that the doctor was named after Oliver's grandfather, Simeon; one of the characters even had Oliver's own name. There was cruelty in the tale, Ken found. Flicking through the pages, a woman's suffering stood out.

I checked the clock in the corner. 'Nearly an hour. She cannot last for much longer. The chill must be into her bones.' I shut the book and removed my spectacles, so I could better concentrate. The sound of her wailing rose again. It had been angry, then plaintive and was now outwardly threatening.

It was odd, but there was even a story within the story, a bleak novelette named *The Gold Field* about a California family living in a house made entirely of glass. That tale's narrator was searching for the truth about his mother's death, but only a few brief fragments of the story appeared. They described a sea voyage across the Atlantic, the unnamed narrator's self-doubt and, finally, retribution for a terrible crime.

Ken began to read from the start, but all the time he was searching for a meaning beneath the meaning. He had gotten about a third of the way through without finding a knot in the yarn when his alarm clock rang like hell. It was eight o'clock and time to get up for work at the newspaper. He was in no mood for it – well, he could barely stand – but given the amount of time he had taken off to appear as a bit-player in the movies, his job was already hanging by a thread. The book went into his bedside table.

So, by nine-thirty – late, but not dangerously late – he was in his wooden seat in the *Times* advertising sales office, his mind spinning. It occurred to him that there were a couple of strange or downright suspicious aspects to Oliver's life that should be looked into if Ken wanted to get to the bottom of what had happened to him: one was the unknown reason Oliver had posted bail for Piers Bellen, and Ken would have to track that barking dog down; the other was the Tookes' first family tragedy. He went to the phone and asked the internal operator to connect him to the library department: the keepers of past editions of the paper and files on every subject that came into the news.

'Library.'

'Hello. This is Ken Kourian. I'd like to see the reports from an abduction case in 1915.' He gave the names of Governor Oliver Tooke and his children.

'Okay. It'll take us a couple of hours. Which desk're you on?'

He knew this could bring down the stop sign. 'I'm on classified.'

'Where?'

'Classified advertisements.'

There was a pause. 'Then what the hell d'you want clippings for?'

He had prepared a story. 'A potential advertiser is publishing a book about old crimes in the state. I said we'd help out. It's a juicy contract.' It was a bad story.

Another pause. 'Okay,' the voice conceded with a clear tone of irritation. 'Couple a' hours.'

'Thanks,' he said. 'And one more thing.'

'What now?'

'Can you see if there's anything about Oliver Tooke, the writer, in the files too?'

'When?'

Ken wasn't certain. 'Any time.'

The voice on the other end of the line didn't sound happy. 'You want me to check every edition ever?'

'How about the last twelve months?'

'Okay, okay.'

Four hours later, a copy boy placed a card box on his desk. It contained editions of the *LA Times* from 1915 detailing the crime; the first was from 2 November.

A police manhunt is underway after the infant son of glass magnate Oliver Tooke was kidnapped from the family's ancestral mansion in England.

The boy, Alexander, four, was wrenched from the arms of his mother, Florence, by two gypsy men. Mrs Tooke was walking in the garden with her elder son, Oliver, five, when they set upon her. The English police speculate that the men may have had accomplices. The family is awaiting a ransom demand or other such communication from the criminals.

The family had been spending the summer at the pile in the county of Essex with Mr Tooke's father, Simeon, who immigrated to California in 1883.

Inspector Marlon Long of the Essex County police department said his men would not rest until the boy was back with his family.

Florence. That name made him sit up. He hadn't known it was her name, and there was a woman in Oliver's story named after her. That had to mean something.

Next, the edition from two days later.

Police in the terrible Alexander Tooke kidnapping case have been rousting gypsy camps around Essex, England, searching for the missing infant. More than fifty men have been brought in for questioning, and although three have been charged with unrelated offences, a police source said the

English coppers are none the wiser regarding the whereabouts of the boy. His father, Oliver Tooke, founder of the glass manufacturing firm, has put up a $10,000 reward for information that leads to the safe recovery of the boy.

It was accompanied by a photograph of a family portrait. Ken had seen the picture before: it was the one hanging in the library at Turnglass House. Here, in rough newsprint, it was captioned: 'Mr Tooke with his wife, Florence, and their children, Oliver junior, five, Alexander, four, and Coraline, one.'

There were other reports in the file, but they were just speculation or updates that said nothing – until a story a year later.

The tragic Tooke family have left England to return to their home on Point Dume, Los Angeles. Ever since the kidnapping of little Alex, four, the family have been holed up in their ancestral home on a small island in the county of Essex, on the eastern coast of Great Britain, with the shutters closed. Oliver Tooke offered greater and greater sums of money for information about the whereabouts of the boy, with the reward now standing at a huge $30,000. But to no avail. Their return indicates that they have now given up hope of seeing the poor little boy alive again.

And there was one final, harsh clipping. A report from 1920 splashed right across the page, headlined: 'Family curse strikes Tookes once more as mother drowns'.

> Florence Tooke, wife of glass magnate Oliver Tooke, has drowned while the family were on vacation in England, visiting their ancestral seat on the island of Ray in the coastal county of Essex. To outsiders, the family seem cursed, having suffered the abduction and presumed murder of their younger son, Alexander, at the same location some five years ago. Mrs Tooke was reported to have been walking across a mud bank when the cruel tide rose and submerged her. Her husband is said by friends to be 'totally distraught' and is doing his best to comfort the couple's remaining children, Oliver junior, ten, and Coraline, six.

The story continued underneath a bleary picture of a slight woman dressed for an evening of dancing, with dark hair loose about her shoulders.

> Mrs Tooke was a society beauty. Born Florence De Waal in New York, she was reputed to be a fine watercolourist in the impressionist style and hosted artistic salons, settling down as a patroness of the arts after her marriage. In recent years, she organized exhibitions of works by artists on the Western Front. Some were controversial, prompting accusations of defeatism and moral turpitude.

At the bottom of the box was the sole recent story about the younger Oliver Tooke. It was from the social pages and an anonymous writer was linking the 'hot young pen-man' to two or three 'sizzling starlets' at some party or other.

> But friends, don't think Olly Tooke's life is a bed of roses. You may remember the Tooke kidnapping case twenty years ago – his brother abducted and never found. His mother dead a few years after that from a broken heart, having pined away for her lost boy. So is Olly hot because he can turn a sharp phrase, or is it his family notoriety and sun-kissed looks? Will his star keep shooting or will he be kicked out of the night sky? Only time will tell. But you know where to come to find out!

Jesus Christ, that was exploitative stuff, Ken thought to himself. *Give the man a break.*

He was drumming his fingers on the desk thoughtfully when his boss returned. 'Hey, George. I'm not feeling well,' he said.

'What's the matter?'

'Something I ate. I need to go home, I think.'

'If you're cutting out early to go to one of your screen tests ...'

'I'm not. I'm sick.'

George jerked his thumb at the way out. 'Okay, just come in early tomorrow if you can to make up.'

'Okay.'

Ken pulled on his jacket just as the telephone trilled and

George picked it up. 'Classifieds.' There was a pause, then George held it out. 'For you.'

Ken took it. 'Hello?'

'Hello, Ken.'

He knew the voice. Very few women called him – one or two secretaries and that was it. This voice was thirty years younger than them. 'Coraline.'

There was a slight hesitation. 'Can you meet me?'

For some reason, he wasn't sure how to answer. Then form took over. She was, after all, a bereaved sister. 'Of course. Where?'

George looked up, his brow furrowing as if he had just heard something he didn't understand but didn't like. Ken pretended he hadn't seen.

'There's a bar on Rodeo Drive called the Yacht Club. Half an hour.'

'I can make that. See you there.'

She hung up and he did the same.

'Feeling better?' George asked sarcastically.

'Her brother died last night,' he replied. He caught sight of the file of cuttings on his desk. He hoped George wouldn't spot it, or it might start to look strange.

'Okay, okay, go. But in future, don't tell me you're sick when you're not. I'm not an ogre. We need to look after each other.'

'Sure.' He went out feeling a little guilty.

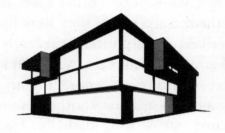

Chapter 10

The bar turned out to be an upmarket place full of movie types. A few want-to-be-actresses sat individually at the bar nursing overpriced drinks and hoping to be spotted.

Coraline wore a tight black dress and pillbox hat with a silk ribbon twisted around it. 'Thank you for coming,' she said formally.

'Not at all.' He felt an urge to make it less formal, but held himself back and signalled to a waiter. 'What's happened this morning?'

'I went to the morgue to formally identify him. My father will arrange the funeral.' She drank from a highball of mint julep.

'Burial?'

The word made her flinch ever so slightly. 'We have a family plot. Oliver wasn't religious – neither am I – so it hardly seems to matter where or how, really.' Was that true? Even those who didn't bother God any more than He bothered them cared where they were laid to rest. She paused. 'He talked about guilt a lot recently.'

'He talked about it to me too. What does it mean?'

'Something on his conscience. I don't know.' She drained her glass and ordered another.

Ken just came out with it, loaded as the words were. 'So, you think he did it himself?'

She fixed him with milky blue eyes and tapped a cigarette out of a packet of Nat Shermans. 'Do you have a reason for thinking otherwise?' Her voice didn't falter.

He had a few splinters here and there that wouldn't have made a safety match. 'A couple of things,' he said. 'He didn't seem depressed; not to me anyway. Did you know he had a gun?'

'No, I didn't.'

It was the sort of thing you would know about your brother. But he stored that thought for now. 'So it might not even be his.'

She drank half the golden-brown julep without flinching. 'Possibly not.'

'And I saw two men go out in that boat.'

She paused lifting her cigarette to her lips. He studied her reaction, trying to pin it down. 'To his writing tower?'

'That's right.'

'Are you certain?'

'I am. But I have to tell you that Detective Jakes isn't convinced. He thinks it was too dark to see.'

'And what's your response to that?'

'That there was a moon and light enough.'

She wrapped her lips around the cigarette and blew a line of smoke to her side. 'That's not exactly conclusive,' she replied.

'No, it isn't.'

'So do I take it on trust that you saw what you think you saw?'

'I guess you have to.' He watched her lift her drink again. 'I pulled the stories that the *Times* ran about your brother Alexander. His abduction.'

With a flash of bitterness, she placed her drink hard down on the zinc table. 'Well, aren't you the little sleuth?' She composed herself again. 'That was a long time ago.'

'Do you—'

'I was a year old. So no, I don't remember a thing.' The air was heavy between them.

'I went to a party at the house a few months back. A man called Piers Bellen gave me a ride home – or he was meant to. He attacked a coloured man at a diner on the way and we ended up in the police station instead. Oliver bailed him out.' She listened without reaction. 'But the really screwy thing is that when Bellen called him, he said Oliver had better come down there and post bail or ... he said something

99

queer as hell about Oliver never knowing what Piers had found out.'

She thoughtfully tapped ash into a glass tray. 'We should speak to him.'

'Agreed.'

First, they would have to find him, though, because Ken had no way to contact Bellen.

But there was someone who did.

'You fucking abandoned me to that pig!' Gloria yelled down the telephone line. Ken and Coraline were in the lobby call booth and it was a wonder the earpiece didn't shatter. He hadn't spoken to Gloria since the neuralgia-inducing night at the police station.

'You wanted to go with him.'

'No, I didn't! I saw him twice. No, three times after that. That's all. I thought he was a big-time producer.'

'So what is he really?'

'What is he? He works for the fucking government,' she sneered. 'State Department, I think. You want to speak to him, call him there.' She hung up.

The State Department. Foreign affairs. Something to do with the family's time in England, maybe. The disappearance of Oliver's brother. Maybe.

After going through information and two DC switchboards, Ken got through to Bellen.

'Ken who?' he huffed. 'Oh, from the party. Did you see what that shine did to me, I—' he spluttered.

'Did you hear about Oliver?' Ken interrupted.

'Tooke? Hear what about that ass?'

'He's dead.'

A pause. 'Wh . . . how?' And did Bellen sound fearful, instead of shocked? Yeah, maybe.

'He died in that stone building he has off the shore; the one he goes to to write. Gunshot.'

'Jesus Chr—' He sounded like he had just seen a man coming towards him with a blackjack in one hand and a noose in the other.

But Ken wasn't in the mood to molly-coddle. 'Tell me, Piers.'

Another pause. And then drawled suspicion. 'Tell you what?'

'Tell me what you had over him.'

Hesitation. 'Nothing.'

'Was it about Alexander?'

'*Alexander?*' He snorted in derision. 'No, it wasn't about *Alexander.*' There was much in the way he said it. But his arrogance was also his undoing, because it told Ken where to go next.

'So it was about someone else. Someone else close to him.' And as he spoke, Ken's hand went, unconsciously, to the book in his jacket pocket and flicked the edges of the pages. There was something in there that he had been thinking about a lot. It was the way one of the characters had been given the name of Oliver's dead mother. And on the phone to Oliver, Bellen had caricatured a frightened woman's voice. 'It was about Florence, wasn't it?' Silence. Guilty silence, for sure. Ken's arrow might have been shot half-blind, but it had gone right through its mark. 'What was it about her that you were holding over him?'

101

His voice became angry. 'You asshole, I—'

'You had something over him about Florence Tooke. And I'm guessing you got it through your work. So you tell me what it was, or I inform your superiors that you've been doing a little freelancing in office hours.'

There was a long hiss on the line. 'He wanted to know about . . . how she died. How exactly.'

He saw Coraline stiffen a little.

'She drowned herself,' Ken said. The newspaper reports had been clear as day.

'But that's just it,' Bellen replied. Ken could feel something coming through the bar, a freight train with failed brakes. 'They held a coroner's inquest. I had a copy of the report sent over. I passed it on to Tooke.'

'What did it say?' Ken prompted him.

'It was the jury . . .' He trailed off.

'What about them?'

'They . . .' He hesitated again, as if the fear of what could come of spilling the facts was rearing in his mind.

'Talk.'

'They . . . returned an open verdict.'

A what? 'What the hell does an open verdict mean?'

'It means they were suspicious. A witness – the house-keeper or something – said Mrs Tooke was pretty happy that day. Took her painting set out to make some art. Didn't seem like she was going to do herself in.' Ken glanced at Coraline; he hoped the words wouldn't be too hard on her. 'So the jury thought it could've been an accident; could've been suicide. Could've been . . . something else. That's what it means.'

Could've been ... something else. It sank in. Coraline's only reaction as she listened was to bow her forehead a little. It was about as emotional as Ken had seen her get, and that wasn't saying much.

'What else do you know?' Ken asked.

'Nothing. Zilch. It took me a long time to get that. And I wanted to—'

Ken hung up. It was obvious that what Bellen had wanted was to milk Oliver for all he could.

For the best part of a minute, Coraline stared across the room at the movie men with girls half their age. Then she spoke. 'Some time ago, Oliver disappeared for a while – a month, I guess.'

'You think he was over in England?'

'When he came back, he was ... distant.'

'There was something he found there.'

'I should say so.'

She put the check on her account and they left the club. Ken followed her to an empty lot where a building would probably go up within a year. For now, it was a scrub of grass and hobos. Ken gave her some space. 'What do you think, Ken?' she asked without looking at him.

'Your father never said anything about doubts over her death?'

'Of course not.'

'Then I think there's a lot we need to know,' he replied. 'And we won't find it by standing here.'

She understood. 'You think we need to go to England?'

'Yeah, I do.'

She reached into her pocket book, took out a fresh Nat

Sherman and lit it with an electric lighter. She blew three long drags into the air before speaking again. 'I haven't been there for a long time.' She paused. 'I hate that house.'

'Tell me about it.'

'What do you want to know?'

'Start at the beginning.'

'My grandfather inherited it from some distant relative. He—'

'Wait, that's true?'

'What do you mean?'

It seemed as crazy as everything else right then. 'In Oliver's book, there's an English doctor named Simeon who inherits his uncle's house.'

'Is there? I haven't read it. Oliver asked me not to for now, but wouldn't tell me why. He said he'd tell me when I could.'

That itself was strange, very strange.

'Tell me about what happened at Turnglass House. The one in England,' Ken said. 'Was there really a body buried in the mud?'

She looked at him curiously. It must have seemed screwed up to her that there was an outsider who knew some of her family secrets. 'Yes, there was. My grandfather told us that when we were old enough to understand.'

'Then it's the story. It's the story in *The Turnglass*. Though Oliver changes your grandfather's surname.'

She laughed sardonically at the revelation. 'Our great family legend. More than a legend, though, it's true, I'm sure. I think my father is a little proud to be descended from that stock – all the great families have a little murder and madness in them, like mediaeval Popes. All starting with my grandfather – after he inherited the house, he lived there for a while before he came here.'

'Was there a woman imprisoned at the house named Florence? In the story, she's sister-in-law to Simeon's uncle.'

'There was a woman, yes. But she didn't have my mother's name. That's Oliver's choice.'

He nodded thoughtfully. What was Oliver saying by naming the woman after their mother? 'I've started the book. I need to finish it. I think you should too.'

'I'll do it on the way to England.'

'All right. There's just one hitch.' A hitch was a polite way of saying he had the spending power of a monk.

She didn't have to be telepathic – his worn shoes spoke for him. 'Don't worry, the family fortune will cover it.'

'I'm . . .'

'Don't mention it.'

Okay. He turned to the practicalities of travel. 'We have two options.'

'Go on.'

'It'll take a week by boat. Two days if we fly.'

The newsreels had been full of the first transatlantic passenger flights, flitting from New York to Newfoundland to refuel, then to Ireland for yet more gas and finally coming in to the port of Southampton on the southern English coast. The flights were in huge sea planes that took off from coastal harbours rather than inland aerodromes.

'Then we fly.'

'If we can get seats.'

'My father is the Governor of California. We'll get seats.'

'Even if it's full?'

'They'll make it less full.'

'I guess they will.' So they were going to England, where her brother had disappeared and her mother drowned. Everything had to be connected to one – or both – of those events. He put his hands in his pockets. This open street with men and women on their ways to grocery shops and streetcar stops wasn't the place for what he was about to ask, but he had little choice. 'What do you remember about your mother's death?'

She stared at the cigarette between her fingers and threw it aside. 'I was in the library, reading. Something about English kings and queens.' Ken could barely think of her as a girl instead of the fashionable young woman in front of him. 'Father came in. He was walking very slowly, I remember that. And he told me straight up that Mother was gone. She had gone out onto the mudflats. We never recovered her body.' Ken gave her a moment to breathe. 'Every year, we went back on the anniversary. Stayed for a week. I stopped when I turned twenty-one, but Father still visits. It's right about now. I always loathed going – as if she would care that we were there.'

It took thirty-six hours to arrange the flights. In the spare day they didn't see each other, but Ken had arrangements to make: he took two weeks' unpaid vacation from the newspaper. And he had to get through the rest of Oliver's story.

It was a ghost story in some ways. No spooks, but the spirits of the past coming back to haunt the guilty living. They, the spirits, were everywhere, even in music.

> She touched her fingers to her heart and began to sing that hymn again. *'Help of the helpless, oh, abide with me.'* And he realized why she sang it over and over: he could just make out the tune itself on the wind. It had to be coming from the bells of the church on Mersea.

Ken followed the characters across their bleak island and through London's winding streets. Through risk and reversal. Friendship and enmity. And when he finally reached the end, he grasped the whole sadness of the story: nobody won. Nobody. No one gained when the buried truth was dug up; or celebrated when the guilty secret was told. Even the characters left standing in the final paragraphs had lost. Reveal the past, it said, and you destroy the present.

That made Ken pause. If Oliver had uncovered secrets and come to wish he hadn't, who was to say that what he found out shouldn't be left to disappear again? But the dog of vengefulness was biting. Look at it hot or cold: Oliver, his friend, was dead and Ken wanted to know who was to pay for it.

The journey began with a regular flight to New York City and then on by railroad to Long Island to pick up the transatlantic airplane at Port Washington.

They had to change trains at Flushing Main Street. The

platform that morning was crowded with day-trippers and men shifting crates of apples and flour to local stores. Some trains were stopping to pick up a hundred or so passengers, but most were expresses passing straight through at full speed.

Ken's mind had jumped about all morning and had now turned to the relationship between Coraline and her father. He couldn't get a handle on it. She advised her dad on drumming up cash from political supporters, but she sure didn't seem warm towards him. But then she didn't seem warm towards anyone, except maybe Oliver. 'Know anyone who's flown across the Atlantic?' he asked just to make conversation.

'Amelia Earhart.'

'You knew her personally?'

'A little.'

Well, that was cute.

They were swamped by other bodies crowding in, desperate to get onto the next train that called at the station. There was another express coming straight through. Luckily, they had been early on the platform so they would at least have seats when one stopped. Coraline checked her wristwatch. 'Two minutes,' she said.

'Good, I . . .' But at that moment, Ken felt something – someone – stamping hard into the back of his knee, collapsing it; and a shoulder barging him forwards, toppling him over. His feet were leaving the concrete platform and his body was rolling in the air. It was a sickening, tumbling fall. But it was the sight of the rails and blackened stones rising up to meet him that made his heart stop.

Even as he fell, he could see the train, no more than twenty yards away, speeding towards him. There was no time to turn over or grab for the platform. He could only put his hands out to shield his face from the impact. Then it came: smacking down on metal and grit, his head cannoning against the bones of his fingers and his stomach thudding onto the steel rail.

The blow stunned him for a second, but he had no time for that. The sight of the charging train bearing down on him shocked his brain into self-preservation and he rolled to his side, right up against the tawny bricks that formed the platform. Someone screamed. The train siren blared. He felt the heat from the wheels rushing towards him and heard the panicked yells of the people on the platform as they watched a man about to die. But the survival instinct is strong, and Ken pressed himself with every ounce of strength he had into the bricks, as if he could turn his flesh to liquid to crawl into the tiny gaps. And he felt something flicker past the back of his head. Something hard and hot.

He knew then that if he had been a hair's breadth further back, a thousand tons of steel would have smashed his skull to pieces.

Then it was right past him, its wheels screeching, brakes jamming the locomotive into the rails like it would tear them apart. And someone, a woman, was still screaming.

'Is he dead?' 'The train hit him!' 'Did you see?' came yells from among the passengers on the platform. 'Someone pull him up!' Ken risked the slightest movement, a twitch of his head that showed him the train stationary just past him. And he collapsed onto his back on the rough ground.

'There's another one in two minutes!'

Okay, okay. He had no time to rest there. He got that.

Ken curled up into a sitting position and carefully stood, which took him face to face with Coraline, whose pale features seemed even paler now, all the blood having drained from them.

He didn't have time for the cries of 'Are you okay?' that were pouring at him. Now that he was alive, he only wanted to know who had knocked him down. 'Call the cops,' he growled, clambering onto the platform. He was more than ready for a fight. He was spoiling for it.

He stared around, his bloody fists tight, searching for a face coloured with guilt. There were young mothers, old men, children. All looked shocked. None ashamed or disappointed that Ken was still alive and ready to kick like a hard-done-by mule. But through the middle, for a split second and no more, he saw a man standing away from the others, in the mouth of the exit. He was completely ordinary in appearance – average height and build, hair the colour of mud. But there was a look on his face that was knife-edge determination. Then the crowd shifted again and he disappeared. 'Get out the way!' Ken shouted, pushing through, shoving out of his path the people who tried to stop him, telling him he was concussed or needed to take time to breathe. He reached the exit at speed and stared up and down the wide new road outside, but there was no one in sight apart from a couple of mothers with babies in strollers.

A policeman ran into the scene, his face redder than a cherry. Someone must have yelled for him.

'You okay, sport?' the officer asked, his heavy breath rattling in a flabby and unfit body.

'I'm alive.' Ken wiped his brow.

'Real dangerous, this place, when all these folks are shoving,' the cop said, taking off his sweaty cap. He should have wrung it out. 'I've told them about it.'

'Someone pushed me. Deliberately,' Ken said in a dangerous voice.

The cop looked taken aback, as if Ken had accused him of being the kingpin behind the attack. 'No, no, not here. Just an accident. People are always pushing and shoving. Don't often go over, but—'

They were interrupted by the driver of the train, who had climbed out of his cab and run across. 'You okay, sir?' he said. He was just a kid. 'I hit the brakes as soon as I saw. Only they—'

'It's not your fault.'

'Just an accident,' the cop said in a reassuring voice.

'That's the last thing it was,' Ken told him. 'Is there anyone here you recognize?' He pointed to the crowd, who were whispering to each other as they watched the discussion.

'Recognize? A few, I guess.' His tone had soured from defensive to evasive. 'This is my beat. I see the same people all the time.' Ken gave it up. Like he said, he was alive, and what was this flatfoot going to tell him anyhow? Only that the folks round here wouldn't hurt a fly if it settled on their nose. And from now on, Ken would be alive and

111

careful. 'You want to come to the station house, make a statement?' asked the cop. It was obvious that he didn't want Ken to do any such thing. It would cause all sorts of paperwork headaches.

Ken shook his head and led Coraline away into the station, where a coffee cart was sitting with no customers, all of them having squeezed onto the platform to see the spectacle. Cheaper than the talkies. Even the girl who attended the cart had left her post to crane her neck, not realizing that the star of the show was right there behind her. Ken poured two drinks and threw a few coins into the box. He had no idea if they would cover the cost, but he wasn't in much of a mood to check the price list.

'You know that was no accident, right?'

'I know,' Coraline replied. 'What do you think we should do?'

'Given the choice, I'm all for staying alive.' He sipped his coffee; it was awful, but he didn't care. The girl who should have been selling it had returned but was keeping a respectful distance just in case falling in front of a train was a communicable disease. 'Any idea who it was?'

'No,' Coraline said.

'Did you see anyone?'

'No. Did you?'

'I just felt someone knock my legs away. But when I got back up, I saw . . .'

'What did you see?'

'Someone. A guy.'

'Did you recognize him?'

'No, but there was something about him, about the way he was looking at me.'

'What does that mean?'

'It was like he planned to do better next time.'

On the harbourside at noon, they stood before a plane the size of a house bobbing in the water.

'That, ma'am,' said an attendant, proud as punch of his charge, 'is a Boeing B-314 Yankee Clipper. Biggest airplane in the world. Ever.'

'It's very impressive,' Coraline said. 'Would you be so kind as to show us to our seats?'

'Glad to, ma'am.'

Coraline thanked him and they were shown into the cabin. It was as luxurious as anything Cunard could sport, with two decks of sink-into-them couches, well-stocked bars and valets in white jackets. The chefs had been hijacked from the best hotels in Washington DC with the promise of a clientele of crowned heads and tips to match them. The nineteen-hour overnight journey would be a vacation in itself.

The plane had seven compartments on the passenger deck, each one holding ten seats, which would be converted into sleeping berths with curtained bunks, all made of polished walnut.

'Quite something, isn't she?' Ken suggested.

'I guess so.'

'Though I wonder how long she'll be flying this route.'

'What do you mean?'

'Your brother and I talked a few times about Germany

and their new Chancellor. Oliver thought war was back on the cards.'

'You thought different?' she replied.

'I did then. Now I'm not so sure. I think Poland's next. I wouldn't be surprised if we're back in. What do you think?'

She thought briefly. 'My father was a lieutenant in the last war. He lost half his men in a single day – and he remembers every one of their names. If he's President, I think we would stay out of whatever happens now.'

Whatever happens? That was a recipe for international disaster if ever Ken had heard one.

'Do you think we should?'

She paused before answering him. 'What I think won't make any difference, Ken.' She called over a barman and persuaded him to bring them a bottle of rye even though he insisted it could only be served by the glass. Ken poured the drinks and Coraline slipped a ten-spot into the barman's pocket. He pretended not to notice. He pretended badly. They stared through the porthole, smoking and watching the stars running alongside the fuselage. 'Who are you, Ken?' She asked it thoughtfully, as if she really did want to know.

'Would you believe a farm boy from Georgia?'

'No, I wouldn't.' She drew a final line of silver smoke from her cigarette.

'It's who I am.'

'It's who you were,' she replied.

'Can't escape our past, Coraline.'

'Watch me.' And she pressed her cigarette stub into a gilded ashtray.

Brandies were being served and a fug of cigar smoke so

thick you could get lost in it for a week hung beneath the ceiling. At the end of the big seaplane was the 'honeymoon suite' – a fully private cabin, currently occupied by some European princeling and his 'friend', according to a whisper from their waiter during dinner. The suite might have seen a lot of people acting like it was their honeymoon, but very few of them wore wedding rings, the waiter added. He hung around until Coraline gave him a ten-spot too. It seemed to be the going rate.

Ken was looking forward to some time to rest, but his mind kept going back to the night he had spent at the Tookes' house, when the door to Coraline's room had been ajar. It had been interrupted by bloody events, but he had felt something powerful that evening and when he had entered her room, before he told her about Oliver, there had been a full four seasons in the way she had looked at him.

They stood beside their curtained miniature cabins now, not yet ready to part. 'This is all better than I had expected,' he said. 'I might just move in.'

'Better than your apartment?'

He laughed. 'In the way that Buckingham Palace is better than a muddy ditch.'

She paused. 'I looked something out for you.'

'What's that?'

An attendant brought her suede shoulder bag from the cloakroom. He didn't get a ten-spot for the trouble and looked disappointed. Coraline took a letter in a faded blue envelope from the side pocket. 'You can read it,' she said.

It was a letter on cream notepaper from her grandfather, Simeon.

Turnglass House, Ray, Essex
6th September, 1915

My dear Oliver, Alexander and Coraline,

I am old now and you have all your lives just beginning. To you, I'm a wrinkly old man, and what do children care for wrinkly old men? Nothing! And that is the way that it should be. You should care for fishing and playing in the trees and learning your school lessons. If only I could be your ages again! Well, that is all behind me now.

I am writing this letter while we are all together because I want you to remember me when I am long gone. Because I will remember you, wherever I am.

There was more about his wishes for them for the future, some advice about getting on with other people and the like. But one part of the letter stood out.

Coraline, one day you will be a fine young lady. But be careful not to be *too* ladylike. Your grandmother wasn't and she was a wonderful woman. So go up in those airplanes that your father raves about. Learn to fly one, even.

Alexander, I know you are going to be a leader of men. A soldier, I think. Maybe the navy for you. But I can see even at this age that you also have a good brain. An artist or writer would suit you well too.

Oliver. Oh, Oliver. I offer you my most profound apologies. You have such spirit and yet that body of

yours lets you down. I have done everything I can
think of, but I am writing this sitting in my usual seat,
watching you in your little glass room in the library,
hoping that I will have some flash of inspiration.

I know I won't.

You probably had no real idea what all those tests
and observations were about, but for these past
few months I have studied you in the wild hope on
your father's part – and mine – that I will come up
with some miracle to cure you of the effects of your
illness. But no, my dear grandson, nothing has shown
any promise. So I sit on the old sopha, watching you
playing with a toy bicycle, turning the wheels around
and around, and knowing that you will never get to
ride upon one. That is a great sadness to me and to
your father, who had such hopes for you, his first son.

'What does he mean, "your little glass room in the
library"?'

'My father had some idea that Simeon could find a cure
for the effects of Oliver's polio. It's not as outlandish as it
sounds – my grandfather's a doctor of infectious diseases
and had some renown for his work on treating cholera. We
were spending a year in England then. So Oliver had to
stay in isolation while my grandfather tried some things.
None of it worked, though he did eventually recover, as
you know.'

Ken checked the date on the letter. It was two months
before the abduction of Alexander. 'In Oliver's book—'

'You want to know about the glass box. In the story.'

So she had been reading it too. That glass chamber held such a central place in *The Turnglass*, it was astonishing to think it might also be true.

'I do.'

'Sure you do. Well, the truth is yes: I think that really happened. At least from what my grandfather told us.'

'Incredible.' Incredible that history had repeated – though this time, it was Simeon sitting on the sofa, watching day and night. 'Why did your parents go back there after your brother was abducted? I would have thought it would hold painful memories.'

'I expect it did. My parents and grandfather left it empty for years, but my father always said it was the ancestral home and ancestry should be revered.' She lifted an eyebrow sardonically in a way that told him ancestry, to her, counted for nothing. 'So they started returning each summer. Until my mother's death.' She looked over the letter again. 'Father lionizes Simeon. He often says, "your grandfather will be proud" – or disappointed, depending on what we've done. Anyway, I wanted you to read this so you know what my grandfather is really like, instead of getting it from Oliver's book.'

'I understand.'

There was a window beside her and the night sky seemed to be pouring through it. Maybe it was the rye or the heat, but he took half a step towards her. The lights above their heads were reflected in her milky blue irises. Her face turned up to his and he felt her breathing, slow and deep, as his hands lifted to her sides, drawing her closer. As he moved his mouth towards hers, her eyes seemed to lose their focus, looking right through him. And her lips turned away. She slowly shook her head, staring out at the night once more.

'Not now,' she said quietly. His hands dropped.

They stared at each other silently for a few seconds, each waiting for the other to move or the waiter to interrupt with a subtle cough or the plane to fall out the damn sky. Anything. There was nothing. She parted the curtains and let them fall back into place behind her.

Chapter 11

They were woken in the mid-morning with thickly steaming coffee and tea. After washing and dressing, they emerged from the plane into the sunlight of an English summer. It was nothing at all compared to a California summer – it would, at best, have counted as spring to a Californian. Also, despite the luxury of the cabin, Ken hadn't rested well and his head was still full of the cigar-smoke fug from the previous evening. So the salty air of the Southampton harbour tingling the back of his throat perked him up, but did little to lift his mood.

As they made their way across the dockside, to be met by some puffed-up dignitary of the town and a senior

120

Pan Am employee, Ken looked around. This was the first sight he had had of Europe outside of newsreels, and it wasn't what he had expected. His image of the Old Country was a mix of mediaeval romance and Dickens novels. Half-forest, half-tumbling tenement. But here was a country gearing up to a twentieth-century war on land and sea: a vast warship was docked, and a swarm of tenders buzzed around it like wasps. In the harbour mouth, a minesweeper was chugging out to sea. Dark blue naval uniforms were all around, dotted with khaki army fatigues.

They look pretty resolved to what's going to happen, he noted. He hoped they could survive without help from the United States this time – if Governor Tooke got his way as President and kept American boys out of a second European theatre of slaughter.

Then they were catching trains and grimy London was passing in a blur. Ken was disappointed he wouldn't get to see this great capital, the source of the literary wine that he had drunk down during his lifetime. But at least there was countryside and genuine little villages with stone churches and maids on bicycles to watch as the train sped past. And finally, they were deposited in the town of Colchester in Essex – an ancient place built by the Romans, a faded sign at the station told them. It wasn't their final destination, but there was something Ken wanted to look into first.

'This is the nearest town, right?' he asked.

'To Ray? Yes, it is.'

'Then this would be where they held the coroner's court.'

'I suppose it would.'

An enquiry at the station ticket office directed them to a brick building no more than two streets away.

The clerk at the front desk replied that yes, anyone had the right to read court transcripts and if the gentleman would like to enter the third windowless room on the right, he would find them labelled by date.

'This one,' Coraline said, opening a wire-fronted wooden cabinet after they had searched for a while. She pulled out a heavy book bound in cheap card. It covered the year of her mother's death.

She laid it on an empty table and they read by the light of a single hanging bulb. British electric bulbs seemed to be far weaker than American versions.

Death of Florence Tooke (Mrs). Inquest the seventh day of July, nineteen hundred and twenty.

Ken and Coraline read of the weather conditions that day – warm and bright – the testimony of a hatmaker who had attended her that morning and said that Florence had seemed happy enough, not at all, in her opinion, in the state of mind of a woman about to kill herself. There was the evidence of Governor Tooke, who said that yes, his wife had been unhappy since the disappearance of their son, but that her mind was quite balanced. But then there was the statement given by Florence's maid, Carmen, who was cleaning the Governor's study when, she said, she saw her mistress drop her easel and wade wildly out across the mudflats into the water, sinking down. Some local residents confirmed that others had died on the same ground. The file finished with the words:

Verdict: Open

And that, Ken knew, meant something suspicious. Something not quite right. He checked the door and quietly tore the pages from their binding, stuffing them inside his knapsack. 'No one else is going to want them,' he said.

'That's true.'

Outside, they took a few minutes in the late afternoon sunshine to think about what they had read.

'It was as Piers said,' Ken said, after a while. He had actually been half-expecting Bellen to have made it up.

'I was hoping it wouldn't be.'

'No, I can understand that.'

Up until that point, Florence's death had been simple. Painful, sure, but explained. And now Coraline was having to come to terms with the idea that both her brother and her mother had died in suspicious circumstances.

She and Ken said nothing more as they took a taxi from Colchester station out through low-lying boggy landscapes. This had been the Vikings' gateway to England, the cabbie informed them. Ken could see why: it was where the sea and land met and married. At times it was solid, at others it was a watery channel. Fields tipped into the freezing North Sea and islets reared up like ghosts.

Finally, the taxi drew up outside a pub. The sight

of it made Ken happy, because, while he might have missed the old London that he had dreamed about, here was an inn that had stood for four centuries and was still handing out weak beer served at room temperature. The sign was warped, but the name of the Peldon Rose was clear. The building was wide and low, with rough whitewashed walls that bowed out here and there with age.

The Peldon Rose had been described in Oliver's story. In it, the hero, the young Dr Simeon Lee, stepped from a coach that had stopped outside the pub on a blustery night towards the end of the nineteenth century, to peer into the murky events at his uncle's home, Turnglass House. Now, in the twentieth century, Ken stepped out of a cab with Simeon's ghost to investigate the death of Oliver at a California copy of that house.

'I'd forgotten this place,' Coraline said. She looked sick as she turned a circle, taking everything in, to end up facing an islet in front of them. That was Ray, the scene of Simeon Lee's investigation, the scene of Coraline's mother's death and Alex's disappearance. A few hundred yards long, it was low and squat like the runt of a litter. Beyond it rose another island, Mersea, where a small town clung onto the rocks.

Ken went to the window of the pub and peered in. He could see low oak beams and an inviting inglenook fireplace. A radio was playing something classical.

'Down from London, are you?' a hoarse voice rattled through the doorway.

Ken checked out his own clothes. They must have

been foreign enough to the locals. 'From a bit further than that!' he called out cheerfully, as he strode in to see a few patrons playing dominoes or sharing a newspaper at the bar.

The voice, it turned out, was attached to the landlord – a man thin as a rake – who was pouring beer from a jug for one of the newspaper-readers. Some of the drink slopped over the rim.

'You sound like it. You Americans?' He didn't sound pleased. The landlord in Oliver's book had been jollier.

'We are that,' Ken responded, in a genial attempt to raise the conversation's spirits. Coraline followed him in and glanced about like she was viewing her own coffin.

'First we've seen here in a while,' the landlord informed him. 'Had a Canadian last month, didn't we, Pete?' Pete, a nervous-looking soul in his forties or fifties with bright red hair, concurred. 'But they're different, aren't they?'

'They like to think so,' Ken confirmed. There was a pause as both parties ran out of road. 'Could we have two of those beers?' He was certain tepid beer in smeared glasses wasn't Coraline's drink of choice, but they couldn't get cute now. The radio continued with its lonely orchestra as they waited for the drinks to be served.

'Come for the oysters?' the barman enquired, seeming to wonder at visitors from so far away.

'We heard they were something special,' he lied.

The drinks were poured and they pushed a few pennies across the bar in return. As they did so, a woman – she looked about fifty and had buttoned up everything that could possibly have buttons – walked up to Pete and placed a single white feather in front of him. 'My boy's in the navy,' she said. 'Going up against the Nazis. You were a coward in the last one and you're a coward now. Same for all you lot. Fine church you have. Just cowards.' She stalked off and Pete, his cheeks reddened to the colour of his hair, quietly put the feather in his trouser pocket and pretended to read his part of the newspaper.

Ken returned to his conversation with the publican. 'Is there somewhere we can put up for a couple of nights?'

'A room? Well, yes, we have some here.' He spoke a little doubtfully. 'Fifteen shillings a night with meals. Ten without. Would that be one or . . .' his eyes undressed Coraline, '. . . two rooms?'

'Two.' Ken moved to block the man's line of vision. Sure, she wasn't actually his girl, but he wanted this guy to back off all the same.

The barman got the message.

After being shown to two rooms with all the comfort of a Trappist monastery and fewer of the amenities, they went downstairs. It was time to get down to business. The evening light was melting onto the roof and there was a smell of moist flowers in the air.

'We'd like to explore a little,' Ken told the publican. 'Those islands opposite. Can we get to them?'

The landlord looked up at the clock, then at a chart pinned to the wall. 'Not now. Tide's too high. The Strood – that's the path to them – it's covered up. Many's drowned trying to get across while the water's over it.' Ken felt Coraline bristle. 'It'll be dark before you can cross, so best to wait 'til tomorrow.'

Ken knew all about the tides over the Strood from *The Turnglass*, how they ebbed and flowed without mercy.

'We would rather go tonight, as soon as it's safe.'

The landlord shrugged his thin, bony shoulders. It was no skin off his nose if the local police would have to fish their bodies out of the mire twenty-four hours later. 'If you must.'

While they waited for the right time, they ate their evening meal. It featured, to Ken's disgust, a rubbery eel suspended in a cold and salty jelly, all presented on rough pureed potato. For form's sake, he forced it down, though it was more like swallowing an insult than food. Coraline didn't bother with form and picked at the potato before pushing the plate away.

'You don't need to tell me,' Ken said.

They kept up the pretence of being holidaymakers who had chosen a queer, out-of-the-way place for a visit by looking through a travel guide to eastern England that Ken had picked up at the railroad station. Eventually, the landlord checked the tide chart and his wristwatch and informed them that it would be safe enough to cross now, but did they have a torch to show them the way? No, Ken replied. The landlord huffed and reached under the counter for a battery-powered flashlight, which he tested and handed them. The ruinous hire of it would be added to their bill.

'Straight down the Strood, then. That takes you onto Ray, then Mersea. Mersea town's on the west side. Won't be much to see at this time, though.' Well, there probably wouldn't be so much more in daylight.

The Strood was a narrow causeway out to the two islets, which were cut off from the mainland by wide creeks. The slippery narrow path was perhaps a hundred yards long from the mainland onto Ray. It ran across Ray for the same distance, and then onto Mersea. At low tide, it was no more than three feet above the lapping waves through the channels, and by the torchlight Ken could see the water rising up to snatch at the road and anyone on it.

As he walked, he knew he was walking literally in the footsteps of Simeon, the hero of *The Turnglass*. That crazy story. From Coraline's information, the tale was all based on the experience of Oliver's grandfather in the 1880s, although it was hard to say how much of the book was history and how much was the product of Oliver's imagination.

Ray itself was a low, flat bully of an island. Its brow jutted over the sea in a bad-tempered challenge. What life it supported was similar: spiky plants grabbing onto the salty soil and a few screeching birds that didn't stay longer than it took to declare the triangular island barren.

Barren apart from a house that stood slate-black against the inky sky.

'That's it,' Coraline said. Ken turned the torch's powerful beam on the building.

Turnglass House, where, in the story, Simeon Lee had disinterred a secret with his bare hands, dragging it out of the mud. And where, in this world, Oliver's brother and mother had both disappeared. The house sat at the southern point of the islet, flanked by mud-flats to the east. It would have been a good place to go quietly insane.

Coraline's voice changed as the beam lit it. She sounded confused. 'What's happened to it?'

It was a good question. A house needs glass in the win-dows, doors in the walls and a roof. This pile of ordered bricks seemed to reach up and up, but on top of its black-ened walls there were only patches of timber and tiles, while its windows were empty.

'A fire,' Ken said. Black scorch marks above the win-dows were just visible in the torchlight.

'I had no idea.' They stared at the ruin. 'So when my father comes, this is what he sees.'

'This is what he sees,' Ken repeated.

Moving off again, wary, as if the fire was somehow waiting out of sight to rush them, they wound along a tramped-down path that was just visible through the tough vegetation. 'If it was empty at the time, that means someone burned it deliberately,' Ken said when they were ten yards from the open doorway. 'Either that or it was struck by lightning, but that's a one in a million chance.'

'Don't write it off. We Tookes have strange luck.' Well, recent events had proved her right on that score.

They reached the entrance, and Ken tugged the bell-pull. Even though his brain told him not to, he expected to hear the same ringing that Simeon had heard. But there was no sound, of course. And anyhow the door that had swung open for Simeon was now just a few chunks of oak held by rusted hinges. It all looked like a beat-up rear-guard after a disastrous battle that everyone wanted to forget.

Inside, the torchlight fell on charred, overturned furniture: a huge porter's chair, a long rosewood table that must once have been very fine, an iron fireplace. The floor was Victorian black-and-white chequer, inlaid with a delicate design of stars but mostly covered by dirt. A musty smell reeked from the house's gizzard.

Coraline went first, treading through scattered soil and splinters. Her feet clipped on the floor. Something in the dark recesses scuttled away. 'So, this is your inheritance,' Ken said.

'Like I said: we Tookes have strange luck.'

Further in was a small sitting room, with a wide hole burned right through the floorboards. 'This must have been where it started,' Ken told her. The wood panelling on the walls had been turned into fuel. There were a few shards of glass inside the room where the windows had exploded with the heat. The iron frames remained. Ken thought again of the story set between these walls. He could see the sick Parson Hawes shuffling through. But what shadows now hid in its corners? Had Oliver found something when he had come to England, something that had led to his death?

'Where are you going?'

Ken had started down a corridor to the rear. He paused underneath a scorched painting hanging skew-whiff on the wall. A hunting scene.

'The kitchen's this way.'

'How do you . . .' She broke off. 'Of course. That damn story.' The torch beam glittered in her eyes.

The kitchen had a huge cast-iron cooking range that could probably have worked as well now as the day it was delivered. 'Stove's bigger than my apartment,' Ken said. There was nothing else there except memories held by the dead. 'Let's go upstairs.' It was time to approach the true heart of the house.

They retraced their steps to the hallway and stared up to the floor above, over which the night clouds hung and a few screeching gulls flitted. A wide wooden staircase led up. Despite the fire, it was mostly intact. They picked their way through a maze of cracks and holes in the timber. A light drizzle began to fall, soaking into the floorboards.

'I had forgotten how insane the proportions of this place are,' Coraline said as they reached the top.

'What do you mean?'

'It's like our house in California. From the outside, it looks like there are three storeys. But there's only actually two. This upper one is just incredibly tall,' Coraline said, her words becoming damp in the air. Ken let the torchlight play up to the top line of bricks and the last vestiges of the roof. 'I wonder why you build a house like that.'

'To get more light in, presumably.' He looked up at the void that was once the roof. 'Well, someone succeeded.'

And then the torch beam fell on something that had fallen from the roof: a man-sized wrought iron bracket that held a huge glass weather vane in the shape of an hourglass. The glass was broken in two. No sands would ever flow from one half to the other.

131

'The house was named after that,' Coraline said. 'I guess the name means nothing now.'

They stepped over wooden joists, along the landing that spanned the upper floor, to a door that still sported some charred green leather. Ken guessed what was on the other side. It was the source of the mystery in Oliver's story, the spring from which all else flowed. He pushed at the door, but it was warped and stiff in its frame. He put his shoulder to it, but it still wouldn't budge. 'I'm going to have to bust it in,' he said. He handed Coraline the flashlight, took a step back and charged at the door with all his weight. It held out for a fraction of a second before giving up and breaking in two. And there he saw it all, just as Oliver's story had described: a thousand or more books lining the tall walls of the library. There was one elemental difference between the novel and the sight itself, though, because in the story, they were fine and revered volumes stretching across the range of human learning; but here they were scorched by fire, covered in lichen and caked in a lifetime of dirt. It wasn't a library, it was a morgue for books. And each one was a John Doe.

Ken looked to the end of the room, wondering just what he might find. The beam followed, as Coraline had the same thought. It fell on a void: a dry, ashen expanse without books, shelves or furniture. No eyes silently glittering. All that was left of that observation chamber was a pile of exploded glass on the floor, malevolently reflecting the room in a hundred broken images. That chamber had once meant something terrible: the imprisonment of sickness and despair. Now those ghosts had been set free.

Ken checked a line of books, running his finger along their spines. He must have been in the natural sciences section, because there were tomes that explained chemical reactions and described frogs in South America. He neatly replaced them among the wreckage. Even he didn't know why he took the trouble when he could have thrown them in any direction and it wouldn't have made a blind bit of difference to the scene.

'What did you think we would find?' Coraline asked.

'Not this. This is a surprise,' he replied. 'It's eerie to be here after reading about it. But the fire? Yeah, that was unexpected.'

It would only ever be a home now for the birds and whatever creatures were skulking in the corners. But the question was whether Oliver had found something else when he had come, something that had started him on a track to his own destruction. From his knapsack, Ken pulled his copy of *The Turnglass*, and read, by torchlight, a passage about the room that stood around them.

He called for Peter Cain. The man came with his hands filthy and a shovel in his grip. 'I been buryin' that dead foal. No use fer lame animals. Wan' ter help me dig him in?' he said insolently. Simeon sent him to bring Watkins immediately, and then went up to the library. Florence was sitting at the small octagonal table, upon which sat the little glass model of the house that held them all, its three human figurines waiting behind the coloured doors of the upper floor like actors ready to play their parts. There was a fire in the grate, and the light of its red flames danced across the yellow silk dress Simeon had picked out for her. She sang a snatch from the hymn once more, '*Help of the helpless, oh, abide with me.*'

Florence. With his story, Oliver had given his mother life beyond the one cut short in the real world. She lived on in the play-scene he had created. It was sad to read.

There was nothing else to see, so they tried the other doors on the landing. Two rooms were bare apart from beds rotted to sticks by the rain. The final door was stiff, but gave way without the need to charge it down, which saved Ken's shoulder another beating.

'This was my father's study when we were here,' Coraline said, peering in like she must have done as a girl. 'I remember standing in the doorway and watching him working. There.' A roll-top secretaire and a high-backed wooden chair dominated the room. The desk had been sheltered by a lonely surviving patch of roof and had been untouched by flames. It was the widow at a funeral that no one else was attending.

An astronomical panorama carved into the desk was as bold as it had ever been, but when Ken looked through the drawers – which turned out to be difficult because the wood had buckled so he had to wrench them out – he found it completely empty.

There was little more to examine – some upturned boxes and a bank of shelves whose entire manifest read: one cracked vase, a small ceramic box and a pile of mouse droppings. Ken sat in the tall chair and sighed. But then his eye fell on something: one of the drawers had refused to push all the way back in. He had thought it was the damaged wood, but it could be something else. He pulled the drawer right out and felt around in the cavity. Yes, there! Right at the back, there was something there. He closed it in his fingers and drew it out.

It was an oval object, two inches long and made of china. Its two halves, which opened like an oyster, were decorated with gilt and delicate curving lines of mother-of-pearl. Someone had paid a good chunk of money for this.

'I know what it is,' Coraline told him the second it appeared in the light.

But Ken wasn't waiting to be informed. He prised the two halves apart and found himself looking at a pair of miniature paintings, done in delicate touches of watercolour that must have taken a tiny sable brush. One was of the house in which they stood, seen from a distance under an evening sky and before the fire that had remodelled it without a deal of care. Its pair, set upside down, was of the house's namesake on a cliff face in California, in broad daylight.

'Tell me,' Ken said.

'My mother painted them sometimes. I have one. This must be Oliver's. I don't know why he put it here.'

No, that was the boulder of a question.

'Maybe so it was with your mother. In a way.' He was far from convinced that was the answer.

'It's possible.'

So, the room had held a secret all right. But it wasn't something that Oliver had discovered; it was something he had left.

Coraline looked out of the room's only window, which faced due south. Ken followed her line of sight down to the muddy shore at the tip of the islet, just visible in the moonlight. 'I want to leave,' she said. 'There's nothing else here.' Nothing but bad memories, she could have added for accuracy.

She walked away, towards the stairs. Ken followed, but something occurred to him and he stopped. He reached into his knapsack and this time pulled out the coroner's inquest minutes that he had torn from their bindings.

'Wait,' he said.

'Why?'

'There *is* something here.' He flicked through the report. 'Yes, here.' He stabbed his forefinger at the page. He read at double speed the words where Governor Tooke had said his wife had been suffering no mental imbalance on the morning of her death, and where the hatmaker who had visited had said Florence Tooke had seemed happy enough. Then to her maid's evidence. 'Look. Carmen's statement to the court.'

'So?'

'Stay here. I'm going out onto the mudflats.'

'What?'

'I'm going to signal to you with the flashlight. Shout when you see the signal.' At that, he rushed out, leaving her in the room lit only by weak moonlight.

With the torch, he picked out his route down the stairs and out the front door. He shone the beam onto his footway. The ground grew soggier, slopping up the sides of his legs. He slowed, knowing exactly what could happen

136

if he stumbled onto the wrong patch, maybe dropped the flashlight, got sucked down . . .

To hell with that. He'd been through too much to go the same way as Florence. He was coming through this, finding what had happened to Oliver and taking it out on whoever had blood on his hands.

And then the ground was more freezing mud than soil. The electric light fell on a brown expanse that could be the shoreline or a dirty sea. Three more steps and his feet sank. One more to be sure. And he was up to his knees in mud. He couldn't risk another. And he turned to the house. He waved the torch left to right, right to left. Then up and down in a holy cross. 'Coraline!' he shouted. The sound echoed, even though there didn't seem to be a single thing for it to bounce off. It was bouncing off desolation. He waved and shouted again.

And then he heard her voice, very distant.

'Yes!'

He waved the cross once more, pulled his numb feet from the mud and stole back to the house. Up through the hall, leaving a filthy trail to the study.

'What did you see?' he asked as soon as he caught sight of her, sitting in the window.

'Nothing.'

Exactly what he expected her to see. 'I thought so. Carmen told the court that she was in here when she saw your mother wade across the mudflats. Quite a trick when the window faces the other direction.' Coraline pursed her lips. 'Tell me about Carmen,' said Ken.

'She's been with us for my whole life.'

Well, that meant she knew more family secrets than a room full of their lawyers and bankers. 'We need to speak to her when we get back. Do you trust her?'

There was a pause. 'Who can you really trust?'

Yeah, that was true.

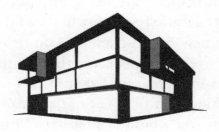

Chapter 12

'I wonder what they do around here for entertainment of an evening,' Ken said as they sat in the corner of the Rose.

'Slaughter a cow, bury themselves alive. Don't ask me.'

Coraline had to be feeling pretty cut up about the lies that were being uncovered. 'Is there anything you want to do to take your mind off things?'

'Like what?'

'Cards? Or I think they play cribbage here.'

'What is that?'

'Something with matchsticks, I think.'

'So neither of us knows how to play it.'

'No. Gin rummy?'

She shrugged in acceptance. Ken borrowed a deck

of cards from the landlord and dealt. They attracted a small crowd of locals, who asked them how to play and then joined in. By the end, they were part of the regular crowd at the inn and everyone treated Ken as a pal and Coraline with respect. He felt guilty about it, but Ken actually enjoyed those few hours in the Old Country with her and their new-found friends. And he could tell that the flickering fire in the grate and their jostling mates had warmed her a little. She smiled at some of the jokes and drank something near to a pint of the pub's gin. It was so watered-down you would need a barrel to get anywhere near drunk, but Ken suspected even the full-strength stuff would have barely touched her.

In the night, he woke with a start. But his dream still flooded his vision: Coraline in the red bathing costume she had worn on Oliver's boat the day they had all been carefree on the ocean. Only this time his fingers weren't handing her a cocktail, they were reaching for the laces that tied her costume at the back. The laces unfurled themselves like snakes and curled around his wrists, binding him.

In the dark of his bedroom, he could feel his chest heaving and his hands stretching out.

'Jesus Christ,' he muttered to himself.

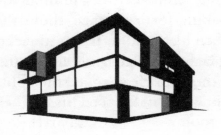

Chapter 13

Ken woke properly before eight. It was too early for breakfast to be served so he took out Oliver's book and began to re-read the story, taking time over it. There was a hell of a lot more to it than lay on the surface, that was for sure. He found himself thinking about how the Simeon character discovered a novel called *The Gold Field* about a Californian travelling to England to find the truth about his mother. It was a reflection of Oliver's own quest; that was a no-brain deduction for anyone who knew his family history. Yeah, Oliver's book was a message to those he had left behind.

Ken read it line by line, checking every word like it

was new in case he missed something, while the sound of the publican sweeping up and shifting chairs around drifted up from the pub below. And when he came to the description of Simeon's first days in the house on Ray, something chimed in his brain. He flicked back and forth looking for a passage about the servants at the house. Then he found it. It was an echo on the page of something he had heard in real life, something he had heard said in the pub. He snapped the book shut, let out a laugh and thumped it down on his bed before hurrying to Coraline's room.

'Come downstairs with me,' he said. 'There's someone we need to meet.'

She checked her wristwatch. 'Is it the mailman?'

'Just come.' They descended to the tap room. The landlord was sharing a dirty story with a barman who was helping him set the place straight, and didn't bother cutting it short when he saw Coraline. 'There was a man here last night,' Ken said, when the tale was over. 'Red hair. His name was Pete.'

'Pete Weir?' the landlord said warily.

'If you say so. He's a Quaker, isn't he? Conscientious objector.'

'How d'you know that?' He sounded even more than before like he wasn't keen on anyone asking questions, let alone Americans who claimed to have come for the oysters, which was about as believable as them claiming to have come for the scenery.

'That woman gave him a white feather, and she was talking about his church being cowards.'

'He's a Quaker, aye,' the barman relented. 'Nothing wrong with that.'

A fine Quaker who frequented pubs, but Ken wasn't going to make a point of it. He rapped on the bar, pleased at the confirmation because this might just send them on a trail that led somewhere, instead of just-about-nowhere like the others they had followed so far. 'We'd like to speak to him.'

'What about?'

'Nothing important.' The landlord's eyebrows were eloquent in their scepticism. 'Where could I find him?'

The man wiped down the grimy wooden counter thoughtfully, deciding whether it was safe to share the information with outsiders who were here for some reason that really wasn't an out-of-the-way vacation. 'His house is down on the Hard. On Mersea.'

'Thanks. How will I know which one?'

'Got a sign outside offering oysters for sale.' Ken thanked him again and the landlord looked at the barman. The other man shrugged, as if the ways of Americans were always hard to understand. Ken was making for the door when the landlord called out, 'He won't be there now.'

'No?'

'Out on his boat, harvesting. Oysters don't just walk out of the sea and into pots.'

'I'm sure. Do you know when he'll be back?'

'Four or five, probably.'

That was frustrating, but there was little to be done. 'Okay. Thank you.'

The barman nodded in reply.

'What's this all about?' Coraline asked, taking Ken aside.

'There's a servant in the book,' he explained. 'Peter Cain. He's a red-haired Quaker who knocks back the drink. Just like Pete Weir. It's quite a coincidence – too much, I think. Maybe Oliver did it consciously, maybe it was unconscious, but he put Pete Weir in *The Turnglass*. We need to find out what he has to say. We'll see when he gets back.'

So they ate their breakfast of mackerel and heavy bread. Then they returned to Turnglass House. It looked better by day, but not by much.

'The fire really did a number on it,' Ken said.

'I wish it had been knocked down.'

It was true that the house was crying out for a bulldozer more than anything else. They explored again, the daylight illuminating more than the flashlight they had had the previous night, but they found nothing more of use and left empty-handed.

Half an hour later, they had padded their way right across Ray and onto its sibling, Mersea. Mersea had a few shrubs and trees, which made it look like a garden paradise compared to scrub-faced Ray. The ground lifted higher above sea level, too, making it large enough to pretend it was a small town. There were a couple of churches, a short street of sad shops and the beach – the Hard, as the locals called it, as if another syllable would have killed them. It was a shingly stretch, deep enough to land fishing boats, with a natural harbour that had been reinforced with a breakwater.

144

A number of fishermen's cottages stood on the seafront, where men were hurrying to and fro with pots and nets. A few of the houses had boards outside offering wares, but only one was advertising oysters: a single-storey weather-boarded building. This was Pete Weir's, but no one was home, as the pub landlord had told them to expect.

What to do to kill time? They weren't spoiled for choice, and so opted for walking about the town, looking into the churches, watching the fishing boats come and go and trying Weir's cottage from time to time without success. 'I grew up by the ocean,' Coraline said, sitting on a concrete bench. 'I found it comforting. Not so much now.'

'I can understand that.'

When late afternoon rolled in, they decided it was time to call on Weir again.

'Are you sure about this?' Coraline asked.

'What do you mean?'

'I mean, you're attaching a lot of importance to a detail in Oliver's book.'

He had been thinking a lot about that book, even while they had sat on the seafront watching the boats unload their catches.

'They call it a *roman à clef*: a novel with a key. The book itself unlocks the truth. And I only just realized something else.'

'Which is?'

'That the "enquiries agent" character – I suppose that's a detective to us – calls himself Cooryan when he wants an alias. I can only guess that's meant to be my surname. I think Oliver left it as a sign to me in case something happened to him. He wanted me to let people know the truth if he couldn't himself.'

She sat for a moment, considering it. 'You think he knew what was coming?' she asked.

'I think he knew it was a possibility. How does that make you feel?'

She stared out to sea. 'Responsible.'

This time, when they approached the little fisherman's cottage, the curtain had been drawn back from the window. Through a cracked pane, Ken could see Pete Weir at a tiny table in a corner, nursing a glass of milk and a plate of pickled fish. It was a single room with a few matchsticks of furniture and an area curtained off to create a sleeping space. Weir was pushing the fish around with his fork, no appetite on show. Ken tapped on the window – afraid it might cave in – and the man jerked up, looking left and right, amazed at the interruption to his routine. Gingerly he beckoned them to enter.

The room smelled powerfully of the sea. 'It's Pete, isn't it?' The man nodded, a little suspicious. He wasn't a man people sought out. 'My name is Ken Kourian. Would it be all right if I asked you something?' Weir grunted something that was probably an agreement. 'Thanks. Tell me, have you lived on Mersea all your life?' He grunted again. 'That's something. Where we come from, people are always moving. It must be fine to have a home and know it's your home.'

'It is, Mister Kourian.' Weir seemed confused by the strange name and pronounced it very carefully. But it appeared that few people chatted to him, and he was settling a bit now, so was keen to keep up some conversation. 'Are you here on honeymoon?' Coraline burst out laughing. Ken stifled a smile. Weir looked bewildered. 'I'm sorry, Mrs Kourian. Have I . . . ?'

'Miss Tooke,' she said.

His face fell. After a moment, his jaw opened and moved as if masticating. 'Miss . . .'

'Tooke. Coraline Tooke. The name means something to you.' Weir looked about the room, seemingly worried that someone had overheard. 'Yes, I can see it does.'

'What does it mean to you?' Ken stepped in. 'Pete?'

The man stretched leathery fingers towards his drink, then thought better of it and withdrew his hand. Ken wondered if there was more in the glass than milk alone. 'I worked for your family,' he mumbled.

'Do you remember me?' Coraline asked. He shrugged, as if that would let him off the hook. 'I think you do.' She paused. 'Do you remember my brother Oliver?' At that, Weir's eyelids lifted, then fell again. 'He's been here, hasn't he?' Another moment of dead air between them. 'What did he say?'

'Pete? Please tell us.'

Silence for an age. Then he broke it. 'Asked me about your ma.'

Ken felt a jolt. There it was, the fork in the road that would take them from 'nowhere' to 'somewhere'.

'What about her?' Coraline demanded. This time, Weir's hardened fingers made it all the way to the glass and he tipped what remained into his mouth. 'Pete?'

'Please. I don't want to be involved.'

Ken met Coraline's glance. He was about to speak when she put her hand in her pocket and drew out her purse. She unclipped it and drew out a five-pound note. She placed it on the table. It was probably a week's earnings for Weir. He sighed.

Five pounds was all it took. It would probably have taken much less. 'Not what he said, is it? It's what I said. What I saw.'

The truth was in sight now.

'And what was that?'

'Shouldn't say.'

'I think you have to now,' Ken told him.

Weir nervously rolled the glass in his fingers. 'It was after they said she drowned.' He briefly looked up to Coraline, then dropped his gaze, ashamed. 'The day after.'

'What was?' Ken demanded.

'I was in the Rose.'

'So?' Ken tried to hurry him to the point.

'A car arrived outside. Big car. Didn't recognize it.'

'Go on.'

And then the punch. 'I saw the mistress's maid, Carmen, carrying some things to it.'

Ken started to comprehend. 'What sort of things?'

'Dresses. The mistress's dresses. Other things. Her vanity set. Not everything she owned. Just the essentials.' And his eyes went to Coraline's for the last time. 'If she'd drowned, where were they going? Tell me that.'

Tell me that. Ken thought of Governor Tooke's continued visits to England and looked to the daughter of a drowned woman who still needed her clothes. A woman whose body had never washed up on the shallow coast-line. A woman whose loyal maid had lied to a coroner's court about witnessing her death.

'She's alive,' Coraline breathed.

And Ken thought of the part that Florence's dresses played in Oliver's novel too, bringing her back to a semblance of life. Perhaps Oliver had thought about his mother's gowns so much that they had made it onto the page.

'I've thought about it a lot,' the leathery man muttered to himself.

'I've thought about it more,' Coraline told him.

'Did you ever tell anyone? Speak to anyone?' Ken asked.

'Never said a word.' He sounded truly remorseful. 'Family business. Didn't seem my place. 'Til your brother came asking.'

Ken probed more, but the man told him nothing else of use. In the end, they went out into the late Mersea afternoon.

'Where is she?' Coraline asked as they walked back.

'I don't know. I think Oliver did. But look. Your father came once a year. He wasn't visiting the place of her death, he was visiting her alive. So we presume it's still in England – London, probably, so he could get there easily. And she's being held there, we also presume.' And once again he thought of the book. He pulled it from his jacket pocket and thumbed the pages. He knew the chapter he needed. It detailed a hunt through London, an incarcera-tion and a secret revealed.

'But it's true. And a few days later, Nathaniel brought me what I was looking for. It was an address in St George's Fields in Southwark.'

St George's Fields. He understood immediately. Yes, he had seen that place himself and had sympathy for any who resided there. 'I can guess the address you mean.'

'I thought you might. Well, Nathaniel asked me if I knew about these places. I told him that I had read about them, but never thought I would be visiting one. "No, miss, not many do."'

'And yet, the very next day, I was in a Hansom heading for it.'

Simeon interrupted. 'The Magdalen Hospital for the Reception of Penitent Prostitutes,' he said. 'You don't forget that name.'

'You don't. So, there I was before this large brick building that looked much like a prison.'

'Ken, are you telling me . . .'

'I don't know. The name is insane, but I don't know if the place is real or if Oliver made it up entirely. It's worth trying.'

'How?'

'Well, they must have a telephone number information system in this country.'

They hurried back to the pub, where the landlord pointed him to a telephone in the corner. It was probably the only one for miles around. Coins fell in the slot and Coraline watched Ken speak into the receiver, wait a few seconds, speak again and then hold for a while before apparently thanking whoever was on the other end and hanging up. 'No listing for that name in London. But it might well have a different name.'

'So?'

'So we can't get there tonight, but tomorrow we go to London and we hunt for it.'

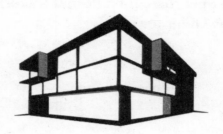

Chapter 14

They were discussing the journey to London over their breakfast mackerel when the landlord casually struck up conversation. 'So, what did you want to speak to Pete about?'

Ken didn't want everyone knowing. 'Nothing in particular,' he said, attempting to dead-end the talk.

'Wasn't about the Tookes, then?'

Ken swallowed his mouthful of fish. There was no point attempting to evade the issue. 'Yes, it was.'

'And you're Miss Tooke, then?' the landlord coolly threw to Coraline. She blinked in agreement, though Ken thought the look on her face right then could have beaten down a marine.

At this, the landlord decided to join them at their table. 'I remember your family well,' he said. 'My dad worked for them a bit here 'n' there. Grandad too, now I think of it.' He stroked his chin with a damp hand. 'Handsome woman, your ma.' He paused. 'Pity, that. All about your brother, wasn't it?'

The man was subtle as a quart of cheap whiskey. 'It might have been,' Ken said. 'We're here to find out what we can.'

'Find out? You're raking all that up?'

'We're raking all that up,' Coraline confirmed.

The landlord went to the bar, where he reached for a couple of plates, a thoughtful expression on his face. 'Know about Charlie White, do you?'

Know about him? Charlie White appeared as a brutal twenty-year-old in *The Turnglass*. The fates of his cousins, John and Annie, were central to the story. It was easy to forget sometimes that the events in the book were based on what had happened to Oliver's grandfather almost sixty years earlier. Were those events connected to what had happened to the family in 1915? At this point, Ken was ready to bet his shirt on it. 'Yes, I do,' Ken said.

'Charlie was *spoken to* about ... what was his name? Alex?'

'Who by?' Ken asked, although he was getting the idea.

'By the constables.'

'Why?'

The publican addressed Coraline. 'He was seen about your house when your brother went missing. No reason to be there. Said he went for a walk. Who goes for a walk

153

on Ray? Reeks, if you ask me.' He settled against the bar. 'But who'm I to say? It was long ago.'

'Is he alive? Does he still live here?'

'Charlie White's going nowhere but Hell,' the landlord muttered in response. 'I'd stay away if I was you.'

'Not a chance.'

The landlord sighed. 'No. Well, he must be nigh-on eighty now. Last I heard of him, he was holed up with Mags Protheroe. He's got a nice little cottage on Mersea.'

If Charlie White's little cottage had ever been 'nice', those days had been lost in time. It was a gap-toothed hovel, at least half the windows were missing and the front door had been kicked in and badly boarded together. More than once, by the look of it.

As they approached the door, a foul cooking smell burst out, closely followed by a woman in her sixties with a dirty linen cap. She glared at the approaching couple.

'Who the twist are you?' she shrieked.

'We're looking for Charlie White.' Ken's accent or tone stopped her dead and she stared at him, then the cottage.

'What for?'

Ken took that to be as good an invitation as they were going to get, and marched up to the door. 'Charlie White?' he called.

A man who had once been huge but now had the skin hanging down on him lurched into the doorway, scowling and spitting by turns. 'Do I know you?' he demanded.

Charlie White was no intellectual giant, but there was animal cunning in his face. It would be better, Ken thought, to be upfront. He said who they were. The cunning look deepened and White's mouth opened to reveal a drunken line of thick teeth.

'How can I be of service?' he sneered.

It was Coraline who answered. 'The police spoke to you about my brother's disappearance. Why?'

'Why not? I was in the "v'cinity", as they put it. Long time ago, girly.'

'Did you see anyone there? Anyone suspicious?'

'Not a stoat.' He crossed his arms. He was enjoying himself.

'What did the police say?'

'Have to ask thems, won't you?'

'They're probably dead by now.'

'Let's hope.'

'You must know something.'

'Know lots've things. Don't mean I'll tell you 'em.'

'Why were you there?'

But White didn't answer that question. Instead, he leaned on the door frame and sneered. 'You know what? I've just thought of something. You never lived here. Never have. So everything you heard about all that, you heard from him.'

'From who?'

He chewed the name like it was cheap tobacco. 'Simeon Tooke.' He watched them beadily as he paused. 'What do you really know about your grandad, then, girly? I mean, *really* know?'

'A lot more than you do.'

He laughed. 'Yeah? Well, then I'm the one to tell you something about him.'

'Go on.'

'He was a swindler.' His face split into the closest thing to a smile that he could muster. 'You know he always wanted that house?' He pointed in the direction of Ray. 'That's what I was told any road. Played there as a boy, set his sights on it as a man. Got it by hook or by crook, they say. By hook *or by crook*. Bumped off his uncle or cousin or what-have-you to get his hands on it, they say. Didn't care who got roughed up along the way, who got made poor.'

Coraline's eyes narrowed. It was a hell of a revelation – if that's what it was. But either way, it was nothing like Oliver's story. 'Who do you mean "got roughed up"?' Ken asked.

'Who?' He chewed the invisible tobacco again. 'Me cousin John. You heard've him?'

Coraline spoke. 'It was my grandfather who found him.'

'Yeah, yeah. Funny that. Him being right there at the right time. Find someone where he found John? Funny that, wasn'it?'

'Are you saying he had something to do with it? He didn't even know your cousin.'

'Didn't he? He said he didn't. How do we know that's true?' White's expression darkened further. 'Now, I've had enough of this. Shog off.' He pulled open his filthy jerkin to show the wooden hilt of a knife tucked inside his belt.

*

They talked it over as they made their way back to the pub. It was all getting as murky as the sea around Ray. Just what had Oliver turned up? What had he been trying to tell people? So many family secrets: Alex, Florence, Oliver, Simeon. But then, they might all be the same secret. That was an idea to pitch and catch.

As they entered the Rose, the landlord beckoned them over. 'Tell me something,' he said. 'You got friends around here?'

'Friends?' asked Ken. 'No.' And already he didn't like the way this conversation was heading.

'Right.' The barman crossed his arms. 'Only someone's been asking.'

'About us?'

'That's right. Sounded like a Yank too. Come in an hour ago, asking if his pals were staying because he's lost the name of the pub they're in. Cock 'n' bull story. Only one pub round here for miles. I told him I've never heard of you. Dunno if he believed me, but he went off again.'

'What did he look like?' Ken had a damn good idea what the guy looked like.

The landlord shrugged. 'Brown hair. Tall as me, I suppose. Ordinary-lookin'.'

'And he asked for us by name?'

'Yeah.'

Ken took Coraline aside. It was bad news. Yeah, it sounded a lot like the man who had pushed him onto the tracks before they caught the airplane.

'What do we do?' she asked.

'Stick with the plan and head straight to London.'

So they took a cab to Colchester and the train on to London, taking a few things with them in case they stayed overnight. It buzzed again and again in Ken's mind that they were retracing the steps of Florence in *The Turnglass*. When they pulled into Liverpool Street Station, he could almost see a venal little postmaster, his palm itching for coins, and a dark-clad parson descending from the train.

They continued in her footsteps, taking a cab to St George's Fields in Southwark – the area still existed, though it had been grossly changed by time and not for the better. There weren't many fields in St George's Fields now, only a pile of dirty streets stalked by buses and underfed children with faces like executioners. Incongruously, something musical was playing in the air and Ken couldn't help humming the holy and hopeful words without even noticing it.

Coraline spotted it, though. 'What are you doing?' she asked.

He realized what he was doing. A tuneful chime of church bells had reminded him of a song and it had taken hold of his brain. 'Nothing. Let's ask around.' The first person they asked – a lad selling fruit from a cart – had never heard of the Magdalen Hospital for the Reception of Penitent Prostitutes. In fact, he sniggered at the name and leered at Coraline, which earned him a few harsh phrases from Ken. A few more passers-by, a housewife counting her change outside a tobacconist's, a drunk leaning against a shop door, a girl dragging a mangy-looking dog, were unhelpful; and as they asked the last one, Ken noticed the music on the air again – the same church clock was striking each quarter hour with a single bar of music.

They took a break in a corner coffee house. Something called 'tea cakes' – which were little more than toasted bread with a few lonely raisins dropped in as decoration – were brought alongside weak coffee. They sipped the drink and chewed the food. They didn't speak, wary that it might bring on bad luck for their quest. And then they were back out on the street, asking questions of people who looked at them as if they were insane. An angry couple, an old woman who didn't know what day it was, a family who apologised for having no clue. A man who burst into laughter and what sounded like Greek, a couple more shaken heads and then, finally, a bow-legged old man who knew something.

'That's it. Was it,' he announced in an accent that it was a wonder anyone could understand. He was pointing at a set of eighteenth-century buildings. 'Not no more now. Now it's 'omes. Been like that fifty year'more.' The workhouse of Oliver's story had been turned into apartments half a century earlier. Coraline's mother could hardly be there. Yet another dead end.

'Did it move?' Coraline asked.

'Move? The 'ospital?'

'Yes.'

The man stroked his chin. 'Now I think of't, it did, yeah, it did. But it changed 's well.'

'How?'

'Become a school. Girls' school. Changed its name, of course.' Well, that could hardly have been a tough debate. 'Moved to Streatham, I fink.'

Coraline swore in exasperation. Her mother couldn't be there either.

Ken was listening to the exchange, but part of his mind

was somewhere else. That part had fixed on the melody in the air. Yes, it was a ringing of bells. He heard the words in his mind to match them. '*Help of the helpless, oh, abide with me ...*' And the words began to crawl out onto his lips. Coraline stared at him. He ignored her and sang more of the tune. Then he lifted his head and listened. The tune was around them. No, it was coming from that road in front. But it wasn't just any song, it was the hymn that Florence sang to herself over and over in Oliver's story as she heard church bells chime it. And it was being chimed now by church bells close by.

'This way!' he shouted, charging into the next road. The tune would end soon. It was the final quarter hour being struck by the church clock. Coraline threw a look at him that said he had lost his mind, but followed him.

Ken ran twenty paces, then stopped sharp, listening hard. The tune was in its last notes. He turned right and ran into a narrow street populated only by an old couple hugging and crying. The melody died as he looked up and down the street. 'Where the hell is it coming from?' he demanded of Coraline as she appeared in the mouth of the street.

'What?'

'The ...' and then his prayers were answered as the same bells chimed the hour itself: twelve strikes. He rode them through a dank passageway into another street. And then, finally, he saw the building. 'There. She's in there.'

At the end of the road, iron gates shut off a small estate. Yellow honeysuckle was climbing out over the walls and an old metal plate on the wall said it was the Convent

Hospital of the Sisters of St Agnes of Jerusalem. The place had an air like it was waiting to wake from a dream.

Through the wrought iron, Ken saw a sprawling building thrown together in a mish-mash of different styles. At least it looked well kempt. He wondered what Coraline was thinking as she saw it all, knowing that her mother was probably inside. Back from the dead, if not actually back to life.

Like Turnglass House on Ray, the gate had an old iron bell-pull, and Ken gave it a sharp tug. It must have sounded somewhere, because a young woman in a simplified version of a nun's habit came quickly to the gate.

'Can I help you?' Her accent couldn't have been more Irish if it had tried. Ken had always thought of the Irish as drunks, rough police or nuns, though what kind of a country could only produce those three professions was a mystery to him.

'We're here to see . . .' he began.

'. . . my mother,' Coraline completed. This was her family story, not his. 'Florence Tooke.'

The young nun looked at her blankly. 'There's no one here by that name,' she said, shaking her head.

Ken saw a flush of something in Coraline's cheek. 'I know she's here. Take me to her or it will be the police you'll be taking to her.'

The nun blinked nervously. 'I promise you, there is no one here with that name. If you want to fetch an officer, you may and—'

'If you make me, I will.'

'It won't make any difference. Upon my word.'

161

Ken put his hand on Coraline's shoulder. There was something in the young woman's expression that made him believe her. The journey they had made through dusty records and over freezing water and muddy tracks, it was all to end here at an iron fence in London. Disappointment was a bitter and rough pill.

'What?' Coraline demanded of him.

'I think she's telling the truth.'

'Then where the hell is she?' All the while, the nun was watching them with confusion visible on her face.

'I don't know. Let's leave. Let's—' He broke off as something clicked in his mind. The nun's precise words: *There's no one here by that name.* And what they implied. 'She's supposed to be dead. Of course they registered her under another name!'

'I'm sorry?' the nun replied, taken aback.

'She's here. Somewhere in your convent, there's a woman aged around fifty who's been here since 1920.'

'We ... We have many patients who have been here that long.' She sounded more nervous now that these people might not just be lunatics.

'But there's something unique about this woman,' he said. 'This woman speaks with an American accent.' The nun's eyes widened and she glanced quickly over her shoulder at the buildings behind. 'I'm right, aren't I?'

The young woman hesitated, then nodded and relented. 'She's your mother?' she asked Coraline.

'Yes, she is. I want to see her.' Coraline was remaining cool, though Ken had the feeling that the young woman behind the gate shouldn't string this out too long.

'I only know her as Jessica. But . . .' She trailed off.

'No buts.' Coraline put her face close to the black iron. 'I'm not going to ask you again.'

Well, threatening a nun took the prize, but there was little else to do.

'I . . . need to speak to the Mother Superior.'

'You need to unlock this gate.'

Ken intervened. 'Go and ask her,' he said, calming the choppy waters. 'I suspect she knows Mrs Tooke's real name. Please tell her that Mrs Tooke's daughter is here. I presume any close family have the right to see their loved ones?'

'Well, y-yes,' the nun stammered. Then she swallowed hard and scurried towards the building.

'I want to kill my father,' Coraline said under her breath. 'How dare he do this?'

'Let's not jump to conclusions,' Ken cautioned. He had a feeling that things might not be as black and white as they seemed. And while passions were running high, it would be better to keep an even head.

She smoked two cigarettes from tip to tip as they waited for a response.

Eventually, the young nun returned, but she wasn't alone. A thick-set woman with a large wimple framing her face was striding towards them.

'Good afternoon,' she said, though her tone said it was a bad one.

'Good afternoon,' Ken replied, before Coraline could unleash the harsher language he guessed was on her mind. 'We're here to see Florence Tooke, or "Jessica", as you call her. This is her daughter, Coraline.'

'And you are?'

'A family friend. Ken Kourian.'

'A lawyer? Doctor?'

'Neither.'

'Then why would I concern myself with you?' She didn't wait for an answer, but spoke to Coraline. 'We will not allow you to speak to any of our patients. For one thing, I have no proof that you are even who you say you are.'

Coraline almost tore her purse apart opening it. She pulled out her crumpled packet of Nat Shermans and tossed it aside to rest in spiky weeds at the foot of the gate, before she found her cheque book. The younger nun bent down and discreetly picked up the cigarette packet. Coraline held out the pad of bank drafts. 'My name's right there,' she said, presenting one.

The elder nun took it from her through the bars and examined it, as if she might be able to detect some signs of forgery, before handing it back with a gesture that said it was unclean. 'You have shown me a banker's book. American. I cannot begin to say if it is yours.'

'What about your passport?' Ken suggested.

'It's in my valise, back at the Rose.'

'Well then,' the nun said. 'If you are who you claim to be, you will be quite able to write to the convent hospital and we will respond in the same way to the registered correspondence address. That is, if the woman you claim is our patient is indeed here.'

'You know damn well she is,' Ken muttered.

'Then you will have no trouble, will you?' she replied with a faint smirk. 'Come away, Sister Julia.' Sister Julia, who was holding on to the gate, followed the older woman. But as she turned to leave, she dropped something from the hand that was grasping the wrought iron. It was the cigarette packet.

'Damn them,' Coraline said under her breath. 'They don't care.'

'No,' Ken replied, distracted by the paper packet.

'My mother could die in there and I would be kept outside.'

His sight was still on the pack of Nat Shermans. 'Hold on, look.'

'At what?'

He stooped and reached through the twisting metal bars to the packet. It was rich green and sported the brand name in gold cursive lettering. But something had been written underneath the logo in pencil: 'East gate. An hour.'

'I think our young friend has a softer conscience than her boss,' he said, showing it to Coraline.

Chapter 15

'Do you remember anything about your mother?' Ken asked as they waited outside a thick door in the east wall.

'I remember her being kind.' Coraline paused. 'Not a specific act, more something around her. I suppose that's being a mother.' She gazed at a pine tree, glowing green in the hot noon light.

'Yes, I guess so.'

They waited until a metal noise alerted them to movement on the other side of the gate. A heavy bolt was being drawn back. The gate eased open and Sister Julia looked out cautiously. When she saw they were alone, she stood back without a word.

They followed her quickly and gratefully through the grounds, keeping to the bushes and trees at the edge, until they came to a rough-looking building connected to the main house by a covered walkway. Deep sounds drifted from it. The nun took a bunch of keys from her habit and let them into a whitewashed passage where the sounds solidified into a brew of humming and chanting.

'It's time for afternoon prayers,' the young woman whispered by way of explanation.

'Who's praying?' Ken asked, although he already knew.

'The patients. They're asking God for mercy.'

Something flared behind Coraline's eyes. 'Where's my mother?' she demanded.

The nun led them around a corner, past doors with heavy locks and numbers screwed to the wood. All were washed with thin white paint. The sister stopped at number five. A whispering from within, fast and low, as if the speaker had something urgent to tell but no time to do it, reached them and the young nun listened for a moment before she pushed in the key.

As she was about to turn it, she paused. 'Please, bear in mind that she's been here a long time. She's different to how you remember her.' The chain of electric lights above them buzzed.

'I was six when I was told she was dead.'

The nun attempted to say something, but the amazement had struck her dumb. She gave up and knocked on the door. 'Jessica,' she said. Then, hesitatingly, 'Florence?' The whispering stopped. The air hung cool despite the heat outside. 'Florence, I've got someone here to see you.

Visitors.' There was another burst of whispering, even faster than before.

The key turned and the door swung open on its own weight. They were looking into a small room like a religious cell. From a single window high up, nearly touching the ceiling, a beam of amber light was filtering in. Dust motes hung as it blazed onto a wall covered with images of the crucified Christ, his side pierced, his head torn by a crown of thorns. The Saviour's face, the colour of ash, spoke of the suffering of the man weighed down by all the sins of the world. And of the pain of the woman who had covered the walls with his image.

That woman was kneeling on the concrete floor, facing a wooden crucifix nailed to the wall below the window. The light made her yellow dress burn like the sun. In her right hand was a rosary, trailing on the floor. All they could see of her was her bent-over back.

'Jess ... Florence?' the sister asked. The whispering began again, slowly now, as her fingers touched the beads in sequence.

'*The fourth sorrowful mystery. The carrying of the cross.*' The sounds bounced around the room. Even the walls didn't want them.

'Florence, we're here.'

'*... full of grace. The Lord is with ...*'

'Mama.' The name fell like a stone into water.

They all waited. The woman kneeling on the floor stiffened. The hand clutching the rosary withdrew towards her chest. 'Who is that?' Her accent was from New York.

'Me, Mama.'

The back unfurled and a woman's head lifted. Her hair had been a deep chestnut colour once, Ken thought, but now it was grey.

'Coraline.' Her voice no longer whispered. It spoke, low and watchful.

'Yes.' She stepped forward.

As she did so, her mother turned her head. The face of Florence Tooke, once delicate and rich with the ease of a wealthy life, had added flesh and lines and age and cares. But for sure it was the same one that had looked out from the newspapers. And the eyes, which were dark, crawled along the walls towards the three people behind her, across the young nun without interest, over Ken and to her youngest child.

'Coraline,' she said again. And it was said with satisfaction, as if she had been waiting a lifetime to mouth the syllables.

The faces of Jesus stared out at them all, faces dead and alive. Florence lifted the rosary, kissed it and hung it around her neck, all the while keeping her gaze on the three intruders into her devotions.

Finally, she turned her body to face them. The light surrounded her with a haze like embers from a wildfire. As she opened her arms, the blaze poured to the ground. 'I prayed to Him you would come,' she said. Coraline stepped forward, unafraid. 'Will you kiss me?'

Coraline could only take her mother's hands. But there was a question that couldn't wait even for the time it took to do that. 'Why are you here?' she asked.

Florence smiled, as if it was the only reply she had expected. 'Yes. Yes, why?'

'Did Father place you here?'

Florence turned back to face the cross on the wall. 'In a sense.' Among the images of Jesus of Nazareth, Ken saw, there was one other picture. It was a copy of a family portrait. He had seen it twice before: once hanging on a wall in the family home and once in grainy newsprint.

'In what sense? Did he force you here?'

The older woman smoothed down her hair. It was perfectly dressed and coiffed, as if she had taken great pains over it. 'Force me?'

Sister Julia interceded. 'I don't think you understand.'

'What do you mean?'

'Your mother's not detained here. She's here voluntarily. All the patients are.'

Florence moved to a bed in the corner of the room and, as she trod, Ken heard a strange noise: a mechanical clanking that he couldn't identify. She sat on the bed, neat and still, as if patience was something she had learned over the years. 'I've thought of you, all the time,' she said, dreamily. 'I asked Alexander about you.'

Her kidnapped son. So she was talking to the dead. That was not a healthy sign.

'You speak to Alexander?' Coraline prompted gently.

Florence turned to gaze at the family portrait on the wall. There they all were: the Governor, her, their three children. But beyond the oils on canvas, two of those figures were dead and one shut away.

'He came to see me.'

'When was that?'

'When?' Her mind became airy. 'Oh, last week. Last year. Time seems to flitter away in this place.'

Yes, not having a wristwatch or a calendar would do that. Ken glanced at the nun, but she didn't have an answer.

Coraline sat on the bed beside her mother. 'Alex died, Mama. More than twenty years ago.'

That revelation would be only one of two cuts, Ken knew. They would keep her other son's death from her for a while; dropping it on her now could have severe consequences. 'Is there a doctor we can speak to about her?' he asked the nun under his breath.

'Not now. He'll be here tomorrow.'

'What are you saying?' Florence asked her daughter.

'Alex died. When he was four.'

Florence sat back on the bed and smiled thinly. 'No, darling. He came to me last month. We spoke. I hadn't seen him for a long time.'

'Mama, he's not here anymore.'

'Why do you say that?' The cheer was fading from her lips.

'I'm sorry, it's the truth.'

'He sat right where you sit now.'

There was a hesitation. 'I don't think so.'

'I know he did.'

'Mama, how did you know it was him?'

'How did I know it was Alexander?'

'Yes.'

'A mother knows her own child,' she replied with quiet confidence.

At this, something occurred to Ken. It could just be that she had known her child, but the wrong one. 'Mrs Tooke,' he said. 'Could it have been Oliver, your other son, who came to see you? Is that possible?'

She gazed up at him. 'Oh, no, no. Not Oliver. It was Alexander. For sure.'

'No, Mama.'

'Is she on any kind of medication?' Ken asked the nun.

Florence relaxed, proud of herself. 'They gave me pills for a while. But I found it hard to think.'

'She stopped taking them,' Sister Julia said. 'We thought it safer not to force them on her.'

'Safer!' Florence laughed. 'For you.'

The news reports Ken had read described a society hostess who liked to paint watercolours. Had she ever been that statue of softness or had she, from the beginning, had a dark flame within her? And her insistence that her dead son had come to visit her could, depending on your point of view, have been an expression of deep-set religious faith or equally deep-set mania.

'The doctors want to help you.'

'No more doctors,' the distracted woman threatened. 'They put me here. They're behind it all. Plotting.' She strode furiously to the opposite corner of the room. The faint clinking sound went with her.

'It's a common delusion,' the nun said as quietly as she could.

'What do you know about it, girl?' Florence snapped, with a filthy look. 'What do any of you know?'

'Your doctor—'

172

Florence interrupted. 'Yes, the doctor. Ask him. He's behind it all. He was in on it with my husband.'

'Which doctor?' Ken asked.

She became angrier. 'That one. With the broken mouth. I told Alexander about him. The injection.'

Ken addressed Sister Julia. 'Do you know who she means?'

She shook her head. 'Are you a little confused, Florence?'

Coraline's mother ignored the question. There was that queer metal noise again as she shifted her weight, like someone was tapping a tin can. 'What's that sound?' Ken asked the nun.

But it was Florence who replied. 'That's my sin,' she whispered. 'A remembrance of my guilt.'

'What?'

In answer, Florence reached down, pinched the material of her dress and began to pull it up, her eyes locked to his.

'Mama.'

'Hush, child.' And the cotton slipped up her flesh, exposing a bare calf, then the pink of her thigh. 'Here, you see my guilt.' The dress rose higher still. The nun let her head drop, as if she knew what was coming and didn't want to admit it. And then the hem lifted over a ring of chain metal studded with sharp barbs. All of them were turned inwards, spiking into angry flesh and piercing the skin to draw pin-pricks of blood. 'I mortify my flesh to atone for what I have done.' She gazed happily upon the item. 'And through my remembrance of sin, I shall sit at the table of the Lord.' Her gaze lifted to the other three in the room, one by one. 'You too shall atone for your sins.'

'What the hell is *that*?' Ken demanded of Sister Julia. He was angry and amazed in equal measures, but the anger won out.

'A cilice. She's right, religiously speaking. But . . .'

'But what?'

'We don't use them for the patients. They're for members of the order.' She touched her own thigh and Ken understood. 'She begged us for one. Eventually, the Mother Superior said that if she wanted to live like a member of our order, there was no shame in that. She got what she wanted.'

Florence touched her rosary to her lips again and began to chant to herself. '*The first sorrowful mystery . . .*' The fire in her withdrew and she turned in on herself.

'Sometimes it's what you want that's going to kill you,' Coraline said, watching her mother. 'So if she's not detained here, she can leave? Right now, if she wants.'

The nun looked like she regretted speaking up. Maybe she should have guessed what would be just about the first thing on a daughter's mind. 'Well, yes, but I'm not sure that's a—'

Coraline was taking no interruptions. 'Mama, would you like to leave here?'

'Please can we speak in the corridor?' the nun asked urgently.

They withdrew, leaving Ken alone with Florence. She smiled at him, and he couldn't miss a hint of something spreading along her lips; a hint of long-forgotten coquetry, like perfume in the air after a party has ended. It wasn't nice to see.

'What's your name?'

'Ken,' he told her. 'Ken Kourian.'

'Are you going to take me away, Ken?' she said, her voice breathy. 'Just you and me?' She stood in the orange beam of afternoon sun. He wondered if this had once been part of her life, her character. The newspapers would never have reported it because the upper classes always closed ranks against that kind of scandal. She came closer. 'Will it be just you and me?' He looked up at the family portrait. She saw where his gaze had fixed. 'That's all gone.'

She came closer again and he raised a hand to press her away from him. 'I don't think that's a good idea,' he said.

'It will be good for both of us.'

'No.'

'And why not?' She pushed out her lower lip in a bad actress's gesture of petulance.

'You're safe here.'

There was a pause, then she spoke again. 'Ken says he's going to take me away. Just me and him.'

He guessed what had happened. Over his shoulder, he saw Coraline and the nun had re-entered the room.

'What did you say to her?' the sister demanded, not bothering to hide the accusation.

'Nothing,' he replied. There was no point trying to explain and it would have seemed in poor taste. Florence sat on the bed but her smile stayed.

'Outside,' Coraline said. She, the nun and Ken withdrew into the corridor to confer. 'I want to take her home,' Coraline declared.

'But it will be a dreadful shock to her,' replied the nun. 'It's hard to say how she will cope.'

'That will be up to us.'

'You need to speak to the Mother Superior.'

Coraline paused for a second. 'I want to know who the doctor is, the one she was speaking about.'

'I have no idea. I'm sorry.'

They heard Florence begin to whisper, fast and low, once more.

'We can try to find him,' Ken said. 'But are you certain you want to take her away? Now?'

'If I wait, and my father discovers we were here, he might prevent it. He might move her somewhere we'll never find her.'

Ken wasn't so sure. He didn't know the right shot and didn't want to do anything that would seem crazy in retrospect. 'We don't know yet why he did this.'

'Whatever the reason,' she said, fixing him with her gaze, 'she's better off not spending her days surrounded by those pictures. If she wasn't out of her mind before she went in, that would be enough to do it. She's coming with us.'

But before he could answer, there was a new voice. It shook the bricks in their mortar. 'That is not your decision to make!' The Mother Superior was coming towards them at speed. There was someone behind her in the narrow corridor, keeping pace.

'Then whose is it?' Coraline demanded.

And the man behind the Mother Superior, a man Ken had met twice on the other side of the Atlantic Ocean, spoke with cold fury as he strode past the nun towards them. 'It is mine,' he snarled. 'You take her out of here and she'll cut her wrists. Or hang herself. Or wade into the sea, and this time she'll succeed.'

'You lied to me for twenty years,' Coraline spat.

Governor Tooke was ten paces away and closing fast. 'I kept you from a truth that would have caused you more pain than you could ever know.' The senior nun, who must have summoned him from somewhere nearby, looked every bit as angry as he did. 'Unlike you, I've had to live with it.' He glared a thousand daggers at Ken. 'My son brought you to my home. Now I find you digging into my family affairs. Get the hell out of here before I have you arrested.'

Ken was about to tell him where to go when Coraline did it for him. 'He's with me, Father. And you have no more jurisdiction here than a farmhand.'

'Please,' begged Sister Julia, trying to get between them. 'Please calm down. This will be upsetting for your mother and for our other patients.'

'That's enough from you!' the Mother Superior growled.

The Governor glanced darkly at his daughter and Ken, then strode into his wife's room and closed the door with a bang. Florence's whispering ceased immediately.

'Hello, my dear,' they heard the Governor say. 'I'm afraid I have some very bad news.' And he told her something too quiet for them to hear, and there was silence before the sound of a woman's voice screaming. Coraline opened the door but her father filled the frame and pushed her away, slamming it shut.

The air in the corridor was stale as they waited, simmering in what they had done. The younger nun took a few steps away, discreetly distancing herself from them. Ken didn't blame her. She had done her best to do the right thing, and now it would rebound on her. The Mother Superior glared at them in succession.

'I want a drink,' Coraline said.

'You and me both.'

For the next few minutes, they heard muffled voices and made out the occasional word: 'Oliver', 'funeral'. And then more silence.

Eventually, the Governor emerged, his face dark as coal. 'Follow me,' he ordered them.

Coraline ignored his instruction and brushed past him into her mother's room. Florence was sitting on the bed, staring up at the carved image of Christ on the cross, beads of wooden blood on his forehead. She didn't seem to realize that her daughter was there at all. The life had ebbed from her, as if the news of Oliver's death had drained away the little she had left.

Coraline sat on the bed too and put her arms around her mother's shoulders. She hadn't done so since she was six, Ken knew. It had to be like hugging a stranger to her. And yet she did it and her cheek found her mother's.

'You want to know why I convinced her to come here,' Governor Tooke said, straightening his tie. They were walking in the grounds of the convent. The scent of the honeysuckle hung heavy on the air. His anger was subsiding into weariness.

'Make it a damn good story, Father,' Coraline cautioned.

'Oh, I have no need to embellish things, girl.' He sat on a felled tree and stretched out his neck. 'You've always thought yourself clever. Well, we shall see. We shall see.' He paused, as if remembering a time that he had long suppressed in his memory. 'When Alexander was abducted, your mother told the police that two gypsy men had taken him from her in the garden at Turnglass and run off to the mainland.'

'I know,' she replied. 'I know it all.'

'So you think.'

'What are you getting at?'

He ignored her question. 'But have you thought about it? What, they just walked up to the house without any of us or the staff seeing them, and waltzed right out again while your mother screamed blue murder?' Coraline's face clouded a little with thought, the change seeming to suggest she understood his drift. 'Oh, yes, I see. You're beginning to think. Not so clever now, are you? And tell me this: why did they do it?' He threw his hands up. 'A thrill kill, they said. Well, they were always talking about those, even back then. Thrill kill.' He shook his head angrily. 'Utter garbage. You get the odd nutjob, for sure, but for the most part they take a hatchet to their own mothers, they don't plan the kidnap of a wealthy man's little boy. And they don't work in pairs. And they don't go all the way out to Ray to do it.' The weariness enveloped him entirely. 'No, I don't believe that pat little explanation dreamed up by cops who had no clue and a bunch of trash newspapermen who wanted to sell more copies

179

of their bilge. Pity, in a way, because it would be easier for everyone if it was some crazy stranger we never had to think about again.' He picked over his own words. 'I've hoped, of course. Hoped that one of those gypsies would get drunk and confess or get picked up for some other crime, then I could tie the rope myself. But I don't think that's going to happen. No, sir.' He took off his jacket in the heat, folded it neatly beside him on the trunk and sat staring at it.

'I presumed it was a kidnapping for money,' Coraline suggested.

'Then where was the ransom demand?' His exasperation burst out like he had been bottling it for twenty-five years. 'We waited weeks for one. If you take someone for money, you ask for it. Even if something had gone wrong and Alexander had died, they would still have sent a demand, a piece of his clothing, and we would have paid up in the hope of getting him back. But there wasn't anything. So what could the motive have possibly been?'

Coraline said nothing for a while. Then she knitted her fingers together and spoke. 'You think Mama had something to do with it,' she said, her voice betraying a fear that hadn't been there before.

'Honestly, I don't know,' he sighed. Ken had to feel sorry for the man, hectoring though he had been until then. 'She had been . . . unstable for some time. And then that happened and the police could find no trace.'

'Whatever made you think you could get away with hiding her like this?'

He lifted his eyes and thought for a moment before

answering. 'Your grandfather taught me that a man does what he knows is right. Even if all other men tell him it's wrong. I've lived by that. All my life.'

Ken looked at the Governor, a man who had had his two sons taken from him. Who could come back from that kind of trauma without scars? Not many.

'She said that Alex visited her,' Coraline said.

'Good God,' Tooke muttered. 'The things she believes. She used to be better – in some ways.'

'What do you mean?'

He took a handkerchief from his top pocket and dabbed his neck. 'When she was taking her medication. She was ... slow in her thoughts. But the ideas weren't outlandish. She's gotten worse. The doctors tell me that's not unusual.'

They sat for a while, listening to the garden birds and gazing towards the block where a number of small barred rooms contained women.

'She wants to go home, Father. It's time. It could help. The scandal's over. If she has round-the-clock supervision, she'll be safe. She might even come back to us.'

'She won't.'

'She might.'

He hesitated. 'How could I even get her home?'

'You haven't broken any law, not back home anyway. And you can make it discreet.'

'She doesn't even have a passport.'

'Then go to the embassy and get one. All the officials will know is that an American woman, the wife of the Governor of California, needs a new passport. They won't do any checking, and even if they do they're not going to rock the boat. You're a powerful man. You can be on an airplane in forty-eight hours. Do it, Father.'

'And then what?'

'Then what? A private nursing home. Somewhere quiet.'

'Nowhere's that discreet.'

'Somewhere must be. And we can cross the next bridge when we come to it. If you don't, I'll do it myself. And that will make a lot more noise.'

Tooke dabbed his neck again. 'All right. All right. I guess it's time.'

'I think your father cares about your mother. And about Oliver too,' Ken said. They were in the lobby of the Savoy Hotel on the Strand. The Governor, who had already taken a suite, had told them to take rooms there while he remained at the convent to arrange his wife's discharge. They could return to Mersea for their baggage when it was all in hand. A commissionaire in green velvet and sparkling war medals had touched his fingers to his top hat as they had entered and Ken had finally got his taste of old-manners London, though he hadn't been in the mood to enjoy it.

'You know what he used to say?' Coraline replied. '"A strong house is built over generations." He told Oliver that he would be the one to follow in Father's footsteps and complete what our grandfather had begun – our family's rise to the very top. That's why Father gave Oliver his name.'

The receptionist was filling out a form for their stay. 'It's not unusual,' Ken replied. 'Many men want their sons to be like them.'

182

'Father wants to be President. If he can't be, he wanted Oliver to be. Now what does he have? The Tookes will die out with him.'

Ken actually felt a slim stroke of sympathy for the Governor, a man who put his family name above everything else. He felt more sympathy for the man's wife, though, whose mind had been broken by her loss. 'It was Oliver who went to see her,' he said. 'She thought he was Alex.'

'I know.'

And that told them something. 'Coraline,' he said, shifting so he could look her in the eye. 'I don't think it's a coincidence that your brother discovers your mother's alive and then dies.'

She licked her lips. 'No.'

There was a long pause. A guest was complaining about the sound of airplanes over London. The concierge was explaining the possibility of war. It was being dismissed as a phony excuse for the noise. 'You ever think about your grandfather and that house on Ray?' Ken said.

'What about them?'

He smoothed his hand over his scalp. 'There's something I can't shake from my head.'

'What do you mean?'

'It's a sense that everything that's happened – to you, your brother, us – is a set of dominoes. The first fell in 1881; the next in 1915; then 1920. Now we're dealing with the last of them.'

'You realize that sounds crazy.'

'Sure it does. But I also think it's true.'

The receptionist arranged for their small bags to be sent up to their rooms and they went to the American Bar to drink martinis. The barman slid them down the zinc bar.

'I'll be square with you,' Ken said, after they had emptied three glasses each in silence. 'I've dreamed of coming to London for most of my life.'

'And what do you think?'

'Well, this isn't what I thought it would be.' He watched a troop of soldiers hurry past the window. Britain was more frantic than he had ever pictured it. It was buzzing with a mix of defiance and fear of the future. The country had been through a bad war twenty years earlier and it wasn't looking forward to another.

'What did you think it would be?'

He stared at the troops and the traffic honking like hopped-up geese. 'Quieter.'

They drank. And hours later, after the electric lights had been turned on, they were sent word that Governor Tooke had returned and required their presence. They drained their glasses and made their way to the elevator. Ken could tell that the alcohol and time to brood had given a bump to the anger Coraline had suppressed at the convent. There was a flinty look in her eyes that turned to hard rock as they rose up the floors.

A hotel page took them to the crown suite, which had been decked out for a king with better taste than most of them actually had. The Governor was talking on the telephone. He was speaking loudly and slowly, and Ken guessed the call was travelling along wires sitting on the Atlantic seabed.

'. . . of course you can. Be my guest.' A pause. 'Oh, nothing to speak of. Only that my secretary had a call from an old friend of his at the *Globe* asking if he knew anything about an automobile accident in Florida.' He paused briefly, and his tone changed, becoming more confidential. 'I don't like that kind of politics, Sam. But if you're going to come up against me . . .' He paused again, this time waiting for a reply, and Ken heard a light creaking through the earpiece, although he couldn't make out the words. 'No, no, of course you aren't. Well, that's fine news. And I'll instruct my secretary to assure his friend that the girl is lying – she had a couple of bruises, no more, it's all exaggerated, not worth the reporter's time. Yes, agreed. November it is. It's been a pleasure speaking to you, Sam, as it always is. And give my regards to Beatrice.' He hung up, stood, thoughtful for a while, then sat in a wing-backed leather chair and waited for Coraline to speak. It was clear that the atmosphere was different to when the three of them had sat in the convent garden and Tooke had seemed apologetic, almost ashamed over what he had done.

It was a while before Coraline spoke. The question was heavy. 'Father, how could you bring yourself to do it?'

He poured bourbon for all three of them.

'I had my family to think of,' he told the bottle.

'She *is* your family.'

'Not all of it. I have ancestors, and one day I expect to have descendants. I have a duty to them too.'

'Duty?' The bourbon remained undrunk.

'Yes, my girl. Duty. You spit out that word like it's dirty. It isn't.'

'Are you going to tell me about being President again?'

He seemed irked but kept his voice level. 'Yes, that will be a duty to our country.'

Coraline slowly drew on a pair of blue kid gloves. It was to give her time to think, Ken could tell. 'Let's just talk about Mother and the arrangements for taking her home.'

Half an hour later, Ken dropped onto his soft bed and ran through all that he knew and didn't know. There was more on the second list. Oliver had been killed, of that he was certain. His death was most likely linked to his mother's incarceration in the asylum where she had taken on a religious bent, obsessed with her own guilt; but why would that push someone to kill Oliver? What if . . .

Something caught his eye.

The handle on his bolted door was moving down and there was the sound of a creaking floorboard outside. He watched the handle move. It could be whoever had been asking questions about them at the Peldon Rose. Or it could be her. The time on the airplane that they had nearly kissed had been playing on the inside of his skull like an orchestra.

The handle changed direction, lifting again, returning to its proper position. He waited. There was a light sound, breathing. And a very slight tapping of feet on the floor.

And then he heard whoever it was try the handle of the next room along: Coraline's.

He jumped up, barefoot, shirtless, and unbolted and flung open the door. No one to be seen, but he hadn't imagined it. He rapped on her door. Nothing. No sound of stirring. He looked down the staircase and tried again, more forcefully.

'Coraline,' he said.

At that he heard movement, the sound of clothes being slipped on or off. The door opened to him on a brass chain. Her eyes appeared above it. He knew they were milky blue, but in that light they were darker than coal.

He was going to explain that someone had tried to enter his room – hers too – and that it could be nothing or something, but then he didn't, he just waited for her to speak.

She didn't. She unhooked the chain and let it fall.

Chapter 16

They stayed in London for two days, then returned to Mersea to collect their bags, before flying back over the Atlantic and then to Sacramento, where they caught a late train to Los Angeles. The lights of lonely small towns flashed past the blind, creating a flicker-book of shapes and shadows. They became less frequent, more remote, until they disappeared completely as the wilderness of the American west took over. Few houses or farms out here. California was a state of cities. The movies were there for the daylight; the actors were there for the fame; Simeon Tooke had arrived half a century ago for the optimism. Everyone was looking to the future in California.

They pulled into Central Station, six days after they left Mersea, as the sun was setting. 'Shall we talk to Carmen now?' Coraline asked.

They knew why she had lied at the inquest about seeing Florence drown, but Ken wanted to know what she had said to Oliver on the day Ken had first met Coraline. Whatever it was had upset them both.

He looked at his wristwatch. 'It's late. We'll talk tomorrow.'

They said goodnight and he took a streetcar back to his lodging house. He managed to spend a night in his own bed for the first time in weeks.

He slept like a log and when he woke he didn't even need a coffee to speed him on his way to the Tooke house.

Coraline was waiting for him in the library, which carried the same lugubrious air as before, as if it was expecting bad news. Carmen was sent for, and entered looking uncomfortable. News of the secrets surfacing within the family must have reached the servants.

'My mother is alive,' Coraline said after a mile-long silence. Carmen bit her lip and stared at her hands. 'Did you know that?' Tears welled in the old woman's eyes and she nodded quickly. 'You've always known.'

'Governor Tooke told me and no one else,' she whispered. 'Sometimes I had to send her things. Clothes or little keepsakes.' She looked up blearily. 'I just wanted to look after her, miss. I've looked after you all.'

Coraline went to the windows that led out to the garden, leaving the maid staring at her back.

189

Ken took up the conversation. 'Oliver found out, didn't he?' She nodded again. 'He said that to you.'

'Yes, sir.'

'Did he say anything else?'

'He asked for old photographs of the family. *All* the family.' She said it with meaning. She didn't want to name Alexander, the missing child. His name was black magic in this house, that was becoming clear.

'And that's it?'

'Yes, sir. Only that and asking about himself when he was young. What I remember about him. Whether he was a happy boy; if he was unhappy in his wheelchair.'

'And what did you say?'

'I only came to the family after Alex's . . .' She shot a nervous glance at Coraline's back. '. . . disappearance. So I didn't know him younger. But no boy's happy in a wheelchair.'

They dismissed her. Ken felt sorry for the woman, who had been forced into a conspiracy she neither understood nor gained from.

He drummed his fingers on a bookcase. 'Your mother said something about a doctor. "He's behind it all. He was in on it with my husband." That's what she said.' He started to ponder. It was following in Simeon's footsteps in *The Turnglass* that had led him to Florence. Oliver had been leaving breadcrumbs through the forest. So where else had Simeon gone? 'A doctor with . . .' He trailed off, as he remembered something. '. . . with a broken mouth,' he continued, more to himself than to Coraline. 'Let me see your copy of Oliver's book.' She went to her room and returned with the novel. Ken searched for a passage: Simeon in the smog-addled Limehouse docks.

> Simeon's vision fell on a man on a bunk. Unlike the others, the man was not smoking his opium, but sipping from a green bottle. He had a hare lip, which was causing the liquid to dribble down his chin.

'Here!' Ken cried out. He read out the lines.

> 'Would you like to try a little, sir?' the man asked. He grinned, to show a maw devoid of teeth. Yet his voice was educated. A university man, by the sound of it. 'The lower-life people in this establishment like to chase the dragon. Me, I prefer to drown it in brandy.'
>
> 'So I see,' Simeon replied. 'But laudanum is just as addictive, you must understand.'
>
> 'Oh, oh, you need not tell me, sir. I am a full fellow of the Royal College of Surgeons.'

'Don't you recall someone who fits that description?' Ken asked.

'Should I?'

'A doctor with a hare lip.' Her face remained blank. 'That doctor your father brought here to bully Senator Burrows just before your brother was killed. He had a hare lip. It's too much to be a coincidence. Oliver included him in the story because he played a part in what happened – and your mother said the doctor behind what had happened to her had a broken mouth; and something about injections too.'

She nodded in agreement. 'His name was Kruger, the one Father brought here.'

'Well, we can see if we can track him down. And I've just realized something else.'

'What's that?'

'All this is coming from the book. But authors write many drafts of their books.'

'So . . .'

'So what if Oliver wrote an earlier version?' He was excited, warming to the idea. 'A draft he cut down to fit into the right number of pages or something. There could be more details to help us.'

'It's possible.'

'Yeah. But first, we'll try to find Dr Kruger.'

A call to the state medical board confirmed that a man with that name did indeed hold a licence to practise, and of course they could supply his surgery address and number. Ken slapped the wall in triumph.

'Dr Kruger's surgery.' It was a pleasant and matronly southern voice hissing through the line.

'I would like an appointment,' Ken informed her.

'Certainly, sir. May I take your name?'

He gave a false one. 'How soon could he see me?'

'I can offer you an appointment tomorrow at two. Is that good?'

'I was hoping to see him before that.'

'I'm sorry, but he's busy until then.'

'I see. Okay, book me in.' He gave her a false address, she made the appointment and he ended the call.

'Do you think anything will come of it?' Coraline asked.

'Maybe, maybe not. Now I want to see if we can find any other versions of the book.'

According to the title page of Coraline's copy, it was Daques Publishing that they had to contact; and their offices were in LA, so Ken and Coraline drove over. It turned out to be a young company not shy about its ambitions, judging by the size of the office. After conversations with the receptionist, and then the head receptionist, in which they explained what they had come for, they were eventually admitted to a conference room with shining silver leather armchairs around a long table and shelves lined with books. On the other side of the table, with a sheaf of papers in front of him that he was scoring with a red pen, a man with a sardonic glint in his spectacles listened to their plea. This was Oliver's editor, they were told, Sid Cohen.

'Mr Kourian, Miss Tooke, I'm in something of a quandary,' said Cohen, sitting back and making a pyramid of his fingers. 'You see, believe it or not, you aren't the first people to come here saying almost exactly the same thing.'

'*What?*' Ken replied. It was a surprise and not a welcome one.

'In fact, I have to tell you, you're aren't even the first people in the last seventy-two hours saying almost exactly the same thing.'

Coraline looked daggers.

'What do you mean, sir?' Ken asked.

'I mean, a guy came here three days ago saying he represented the Tooke family, and politely but firmly requested I hand over any previous drafts of Oliver's latest book.'

'My family has authorized no such individual,' Coraline insisted bitterly. 'Who was he?'

Cohen tapped his pen ruminatively. 'My problem, miss, is that if there is some kind of subterfuge going on, who do I believe? Before the other man came, I got a letter announcing his visit on the headed notepaper of a well-known legal firm. Now, it could have been faked – pretty easily, really, I wasn't on my guard so I didn't exactly check up to see if they really had sent him – but also it could have been real. So here's my quandary: is he the genuine article or are you?'

'Want to see my driver's licence?' she shot back. Ken could tell that after the incident at the convent, she was getting pretty damn tired of having to prove her identity to people who had a very loose connection to her family.

'Yes, I think that would do it.'

Coraline opened the clasp on her clutch bag and drew out her purse. She took out her licence and a photograph and pushed them across the table. Cohen took up the licence, then the photo, peered at them and returned them respectfully. Ken caught sight of a snapshot in which Coraline and her brother were lit by flashbulbs, arm in arm at some party. 'I believe you. But I don't think it's going to help you much. I believed the other guy and gave him the previous drafts Oliver sent in.'

'What did this man look like?' Ken asked.

Cohen shrugged. 'It was a few days ago, so I don't remember all that well. But he looked, well . . . ordinary.'

'Ordinary?'

194

'Yes. But that's what stood out. He was so ordinary it was surreal.'

'Are there any more copies of those drafts?' Ken asked. He knew the man they were talking about.

'Sorry.'

'Do you remember anything from them? Any major changes?'

'I'll be honest with you. I work on ten books at once. I barely remember their titles, let alone changes to the text. So I'm sorry, but I can't help you there.' He sucked thoughtfully on the pen like a cigarette. 'Why do you want to know?'

'Doesn't matter now. Thanks for your time.'

They returned to the car. 'Brick wall,' Ken muttered angrily as he wrenched open the door.

'It seems so.'

'Damn it. Right, screw waiting until tomorrow. I'm pissed. We're going over to Kruger's surgery now.'

'If you say so.'

It was fifteen minutes' drive over to Dr Kruger's consulting rooms in a well-to-do street off Olympic, where it was hard to imagine anyone needing any medical attention unless it was for the effects of too rich a diet. They stopped outside.

'What are you going to say to him?' Coraline asked. She didn't take the trouble to hide her scepticism.

'I'll ask him if he's treated any members of your family.'

'He'll probably tell you where to go.'

'If he does, we haven't lost anything.'

As they spoke, a kindly-looking man wearing spectacles

and carrying a black medical bag emerged from the office. Ken recognized him and began to walk over, but the man raised his hand towards a cab and the car stopped. He jumped in and the taxi drove away.

'Get in,' Coraline said.

They followed the cab through light traffic, keeping their distance. It wasn't hard at that time of day. And when they came to a halt, it was outside an office building that had been completed so recently it probably didn't even have a vermin problem yet. A brass plaque screwed to the wall announced the presence of a medical association: 'American Eugenics Society'. Ken knew of a national body that campaigned to have physically or mentally ill 'defectives' removed from the population. He thought of Florence, how she had been shut away.

Kruger was hurrying up the steps. Ken jumped out and called to him. 'Dr Kruger!' Kruger stopped and looked round. When he came close, Ken saw again the hare lip that Oliver had noted. 'I don't know if you remember, but we met before very briefly.'

'Did we?'

'It was at Governor Tooke's house.'

Kruger's eyebrows lifted in mild interest, a little taken aback by the approach in the street. 'Oh?'

'He has asked me to speak to you about something.'

The eyebrows fell again, his expression narrowing in suspicion. 'Governor Tooke sent you to speak to me?'

'Yes.'

'Why?' He snapped the question; the genial glow had dimmed to nothing.

'About how you treated Mrs Tooke.' The doctor sized him up without speaking. 'My own wife suffers in the same way.'

'Does she?' It was guarded, giving nothing away.

'I might have to put her in an institution.'

'Then do so.' There was a finality to Kruger's tone as he said it. 'I am not the physician you need. So why don't you go back to Governor Tooke – if he did indeed send you – and ask again.' With that, he stomped towards the building entrance. A huge security guard leaning against the doorpost seemed to be taking a keen interest. He had an air about him of wanting to do something destructive with his fists.

'Dr Kruger.'

'I have nothing more to say.'

'Doctor, wait!'

Ken followed him. But the security guard stepped forward and pressed his beefy palm against Ken's chest. 'Back off, chum,' he warned. Ken threw the hand aside and pushed past.

'Kru—' The name was strangled, forced back into Ken's windpipe by a solid arm thrown around his throat from behind. Automatically, his hands grabbed for it, but it held tight and he could feel himself being toppled off his feet. He saw Kruger drop his medical bag in surprise.

Ken could feel the muscular arm was strong, but he wasn't in the mood for heroes. A sharp elbow into the man's gut broke the grasp. He whirled around and launched a fist into the guard's sternum, winding him.

Then it was Greco-Roman wrestling all the way and Ken was motivated as hell.

'You two stop that!' The voice was accustomed to barking orders, and in a second a police officer had come between them. 'What the heck's going on here?'

Kruger came back down from the building entrance. 'That man was harassing me,' he said, pointing a stick-like finger at Ken.

'That so? How?'

'Asking me questions.'

'You know him?'

'Not at all. Keep him away from me.'

Ken could tell he wasn't going to get any answers from the doctor, but at least he could cause him some trouble. 'I just want to know what you did to Florence Tooke.' He rubbed his throat. He was getting tired of sustaining injuries on someone else's behalf. 'That's the wife of Governor Tooke,' he added for the benefit of the policeman. It was always worth throwing in a political connection if you wanted the police to actually take notice of you.

'I've never treated her,' Kruger declared.

'Oh really?' He strung it out like a fishing line. 'Then why did you just tell me you had?'

'I said no such thing.' Kruger was looking rattled. This was not what he had expected this morning.

'Sure you didn't.'

'I've had enough of this. Officer, that man was harassing me. Please get him away from me.'

'You want me to arrest him?'

'Yeah, let's make this official,' Ken said, holding out his wrists for cuffs.

Kruger's mouth opened but he hesitated, deciding if he did want to make this official.

The cop shifted his shoulder blades under his tunic. This was more trouble than he was looking for. He saw the deal and spoke to Ken. 'In that case, I want your name and address, then you're walking away.'

Ken told him, after which the officer marched him up the street with a firm hand on his shoulder, leaving no doubt that he would be better off taking a hike. Coraline raised a pencilled eyebrow at the escort when they got to her.

'That went well,' she said.

Chapter 17

Back at his apartment, nursing a bruised neck, Ken found a telephone message from his boss asking if he was ever going to come back or if they should just sack him now. He screwed it up and threw it aside. No, he wouldn't be going back.

He took a bath, listening to the radio. There was a play on about a man sick of the crime in his neighbourhood. He recruited his friends into a vigilante committee, only for corruption to seep in and the committee to become worse than the criminals they were trying to stop. It was followed by a news programme that reported more military build-up in Europe and a weather warning for the California coastline. A tropical storm was brewing at sea that could make landfall soon. Batten down your hatches, the newscaster said, it could be a bad one.

Ken spent a few hours thinking over what his next move should be. Florence was atoning for a sin that only she knew. But if it was to do with the abduction of Alexander Tooke, it would be best to know more of that crime than he had gleaned from a few newspaper articles.

He went to a phone box and called the Tooke house.

'Hello?' came the soft reply.

'It's me.' He felt determined.

A pause. 'I thought it would be.'

'I want to come over.'

'Come at seven.'

And then there was another voice in the background, a man asking, 'Where to, Miss Tooke?'

'The Yacht Club,' she replied, away from the mouthpiece. The family chauffeur was on duty. 'Ken?' she asked, returning to the conversation.

'Yeah.'

'What do you think happened in 1915? To Alex.'

'It looks like your mother was responsible. And Kruger's mixed up in her being hidden away after that. I guess your father arranged for it to happen in England because there were fewer people around who knew her. No one to intervene. Makes sense, when you think about it.'

It looks.

I guess.

When you think about it.

The only thing around here that was black and white was the floor of the Tookes' lobby.

'At seven,' she repeated. And she put the phone down, her voice replaced by an empty buzz on the line.

So murky, these waters. And it was no stretch to admit that he barely knew Coraline any more than he knew the rest of her family. What she felt, what she was thinking, was only what she wanted him to see.

That evening, as the hour hand on his wristwatch moved to the figure seven and the minute hand clicked onto the twelve, he dismissed a cab and approached the glass-sided house. The lights were off, leaving it to sparkle with reflected glimmers from the sea. It was the wrong house for the Tooke family. It was see-through, allowing everyone to look in, while the people who lived there did their best to hide their lives away.

He pulled the bell and it rang without an answer. She must have been out and running late, but it was a fine night, so he went around to the beach side to sit out on the sand until Coraline returned.

As he sauntered along the shoreline, bathing in the California heat after the European chill, he gazed at the writing tower, standing in the sea like the last debutante at a summer ball. Had anyone been there to lock it up or empty it of all Oliver's books? It would be like picking away at the carrion of a man's life. He glanced back at the house. It had only been a few months since couples had danced and trumpeters blown; now that might well never have happened. And something stood out: the back door wasn't completely shut.

He went closer. 'Coraline?' No answer. He eased

the door open. In the deep copper light, the glass had become a hall of tinted mirrors and the sheen of the sun reflected around the room to make a forest of red discs. Rippling blue sea appeared under each one, surrounding the room so that it was cut off from the land, like the other, older, house. For a moment, he felt an empathy with Oliver, closed in and trapped his whole life by glass.

The waves rolled behind him as he slipped in. But there was something else on top of their sound. Music. Violins – classical – were being played. Vivaldi, he thought. Someone, somewhere in the house, was listening to a record or the radio. He called Coraline's name again, but there was no reply.

He rounded the baby grand piano, went across the room and through to the hallway. He stopped to listen – the violins were stronger now, coming from the upper floor. The white marble staircase glowed faintly and the violins soared to a violent crescendo as he climbed. 'Coraline?' he called once more. The suspicion was growing on him that something was wrong.

His shoes tapped on the marble, a drum-beat below the violins. It was impossible to say where they were coming from. The red doorway led to what had been Oliver's room. It faced the setting sun and the light was bright, picking out the detritus of life: a bed; clothes still hanging in the closet; a set of binoculars on a hook by the window. No one there.

The next room was the green-doored library, there to remind any visitor that this was a venerable family; but a telephone and telex machine were ready in the corner to demonstrate wealth and modernity too.

That left a pair of guest bedrooms and Coraline's own room. The music grew heavier as Ken stalked along the corridor. He came to her door of blue smoked glass and to the source of the strings on the other side. He knocked. No answer. 'Coraline.' Nothing still. But then a new sound: a distant creaking. He took hold of the handle and opened the door a little. A blade of light pierced the gap towards him. 'Are you there?' The creaking again. He pushed the door open and the sea filled his vision: a bank of windows looking out across the ocean, a white leather sofa in front of them. The violins drew above the waves and the groaning wood; but something was breaking the wide expanse of the sea, something hanging from the ceiling. It twisted in the breeze from an open window: a bare foot, a slender form in a cotton dress and atop the shoulders a head hanging forward.

'Coraline!' He charged in, knocking over a side table, so that a collection of perfume bottles broke, spraying little pools of golden liquid across the floor.

The woman's form hung from a rope noose attached to a light fitting. Her back was to him, her head bowed over on a broken neck. He caught hold of her legs in a desperate hope that life might still be there. Below her, a soft leather shoe rested on the floor. But as Ken's hands gripped her calves, one look at the face above him told him a pair of bitter truths.

The first was that the life that had once burned brightly in this body had been snuffed out and could never come back, no matter how many prayers were said, no matter how skilful the doctors who attended. It was gone like the light of a previous day.

The second truth that forced itself upon him, stopping his breath in his chest, was that the woman he held, the woman turning in the breeze, wasn't the unknowable Coraline Tooke.

No. The poor woman he was holding up was her mother, Florence. Tragic, abused, remorseful Florence. She hung by a white industrial cord. It had been meant for rough timber or boats.

He let her go. The metal garter that bit into the flesh of her thigh, to pay penance for old sins, clinked with the movement. It had done her no good. God had not been on her side, had never been on the side of the family who lived in this house. This house that had seen two deaths.

And then a thought struck: *Let there be only two.*

He rushed along the corridor, bursting into both unexplored guest rooms and then the Governor's bedroom, checking them with a single glance, then down into the kitchen. But Coraline wasn't there. No one was. And when he returned to the bedroom and the hanging woman, it was just the two of them in the glass house of Tooke. He went to the radio in the corner and turned it off. The violins faded, leaving only the creaking of the rope.

There was nothing more to be done but to alert the authorities and say that another death had occurred at Turnglass House. He would let them take her down – it seemed more respectful, although he couldn't say why. He went to the telephone in the hallway, all the while concentrating on the words to use: *I've gone to my friend's house. There's a woman here. She's hanged herself.*

But he stopped. Had she? He couldn't know that for certain. Around the Tookes, the more you knew, the less certain you became.

There was no sign that anyone else had been there, though. And when you added in the point that Alex's disappearance sure looked to have been on her hands and conscience, you did come to a conclusion. Sin, guilt, they had chewed her up over the decades to such a pitch that she had seen her dead son come to visit her. Who wouldn't have wanted that to stop?

He lifted the handset of the hallway phone.

'Operator,' announced a tinny voice.

'Police emergency.'

'Hold the line.'

He listened to a series of clicks. How long would it take for the . . .

He froze. There was the sound of footsteps outside, and then a key in the lock. And then Coraline was stepping inside. She was about to speak when he stopped her.

'Coraline,' he began urgently. But he softened. 'I have something to tell you.'

She looked at him with an inscrutable expression, something withheld. There was always so much she was holding back. 'How did you get in?' she asked.

He brushed the question away. 'The back door was open. But listen . . .'

'I closed that.'

'I came in and I found something here.' She waited. 'I found your mother.'

'Mama? She's here?' Coraline began to move into the house. 'Father only brought her over a few days ago. He said he'd keep her somewhere safe.'

He barred her path. 'Coraline, I'm sorry.'

'Sorry about what?'

'I found her dead.'

Coraline took a step back, staring into his face, attempting to find something there. 'What are you talking about?' she demanded.

Guilt, he thought to himself. *I'm talking about guilt.*

He put his hands on her shoulders, as if to steady her. It was the second time he had told her of the death of someone close to her. It was the second time he had been the one to find the body.

'She's hanged herself.'

There was silence for a while. Then a single word that was more cold breath than sound. 'Where?'

'Your bedroom.'

'Is she still there?'

'Yes. I just got here a few minutes ago.' He put his hand on her arm, an attempt at sympathy that brought no more response than if she had been made of glass too.

She placed her purse on a mahogany table beside the door and then, without looking at him, as if she had forgotten his presence entirely, went up to the bedroom. He saw her stop outside the room, looking in. She waited for a while, facing where he knew the body to be turning on the rope, then crossed the threshold out of his sight. He gave her a few moments alone with her mother before he joined her.

It was an ugly scene.

'We need to take her down,' she said flatly.

'Yes.'

He could see the folds in Florence's clothes, her hair in disarray. And as the rope spun, her face slowly turned towards him. It had been lovely once; now it was aged by time and bloated by death. He reached to the cotton of her dress, holding it to keep the body still.

'Well?' Coraline asked. The sound filled the room.

'She's warm,' he said by way of an answer.

'So that means . . .'

'It's a warm day. I don't know how this works, it could make a big difference. But yes.' He knew her meaning and he met her gaze. 'I don't think she's been dead for long.'

Coraline sat on the sofa in the corner of her room, with her elbows on her knees.

'So if we'd come back a few minutes ago, we could have kept her alive.'

'You mustn't think like that.'

'Mustn't I? Who the hell are you to tell me how to think?' It was a rare flash of open anger. 'I want her cut down,' Coraline said.

'I know. But I . . .' He was interrupted by the sound of the bell at the front door. Coraline's head snapped around to stare towards the lobby. 'Who's that?'

'I don't know.'

The bell rang again. Then there was a thudding on the wood and a gruff voice. 'Police. Open up, please.'

As soon as Ken opened the door, he recognized the man. It was Jakes, the detective who had come when Oliver's body had been found.

'Detective,' Ken said, surprised.

'What's happenin'?' Jakes said, straight to the point.

'A woman's killed herself.' He couldn't understand why Jakes was there before he had even alerted the cops, but he would ask that question later.

'Here?' There was only a flicker of surprise. A man who had seen it all, for sure.

Ken led him up. 'Mary and Joseph,' Jakes muttered to himself when he saw the rope and what it held. 'Who is she?'

'My mother,' Coraline replied.

'Your mother?' He looked back up at the body, still now, the warm breeze having fallen away.

'She was in a mental institution in England. My father just brought her back home.'

A light of recognition and understanding seemed to fall on the policeman. No, this wasn't his first suicide. 'You told her about your brother's passin', ma'am?'

'Yes.'

Jakes sighed sadly. 'Figures. Sorry to say, but I've seen that before. No mother should bury her child. Were you the one who called?'

'Called?' she replied.

'Someone called the switchboard a half hour ago. Said I was needed here urgent. Wouldn't say why.' So, someone had called the police before Ken had entered the house.

'Who was it?' Ken asked.

'No idea.' He looked at Coraline. 'Definite wasn't you?'

'I told you, no.'

He stared up at the body above them. 'You think it was her?'

'How would she know your name?' Ken answered.

'Hard to say, but not impossible. I was the detective on your friend's case, after all.' The rope creaked. 'Let's get her down.'

Ken supported her torso as Jakes untied the rope and lowered her to the ground. All the while, Coraline stayed on the sofa, her elbows on her knees. Ken wondered how much of the wall of frost that surrounded her was a real part of her, and how much was thrown on each morning for protection.

'I'll call it in,' Jakes said. As he left the room, he stopped. 'I'm sorry, ma'am. No family should go through this much.' Then he went downstairs and they heard him call back to the station for a police ambulance.

They all waited without speaking, sometimes looking out to sea.

When the ambulance came, the two officers within it entered respectfully into the room, examined the body and slotted together a stretcher.

'Someone has to tell your father,' Ken said.

'I'll call him. I've done it before.'

'Detective!' One of the two officers placing Florence on the stretcher, kneeling at her side, called to Jakes, who was noting something in his pad.

'Hold on, I'm busy.'

'You want to take a look at this.' Ken moved towards the body. 'Please stay away, sir.'

'What is it?' Jakes asked.

'Look at this.' The officer lifted the dead woman's wrists.

Jakes sat on his haunches and pulled back the cotton cuffs. He nodded to his brother officer, who placed the wrists back at the sides of the woman's body.

'Mr Kourian,' he said. 'You found the body of Oliver Tooke, didn't you?'

'You know I did.' He didn't like the cop asking questions they both knew the answer to.

'And you say he was dead when you got to the scene.'

'What of it?'

'Well, now you also say that Mrs Tooke was dead when you got here?'

'That's right.' He could hear a tornado coming towards him.

'Did someone let you in?'

'No, I came in through the back door. It was open.'

'Open, huh? Is that normal?' He looked to Coraline for an answer, but didn't wait for one. 'And Mrs Tooke hanged herself.'

'She . . .'

The tornado hit. 'Then if Mrs Tooke hanged herself, you want to tell us just how she came to have rope burns on her wrists?' He left the words hanging in the air before he lifted Florence's arms, peeled back the material and showed the deep red welts that ran around her flesh. There was blood where they had broken through

211

the skin. His tone fell. 'You want to tell us where that rope is now?'

Ken had known that Florence might not have taken her own life, but he hadn't put that alongside his own presence in the house, his thief-like entry through the rear door and the anonymous call to Jakes. Nothing good was coming from that. 'Someone wants you to think I killed her,' he said.

'Then someone's doin' a damn fine job of it. Anyone know you were comin' here tonight?'

Ken wracked his brain, which was running at full tilt on the back of being accused of a double murder. Other than Coraline herself, he had told no one. 'No. But they could have followed me.'

Jakes stood up and advanced half a pace. 'Followed you? And run in the house, killed her and run right out again without you seein'? That's fast work.'

He was right, of course. But Ken was thinking on his feet. 'Okay, maybe it wasn't me they were after. Maybe they were trying to put Coraline in the frame.' They all looked at her.

'You know anyone who would do that?' Jakes enquired. She shook her head.

'Look, detective,' Ken insisted. 'You don't know that those marks happened while she was dying. They could already have been there. Or who knows, maybe someone did murder her, but it wasn't me!'

Jakes stared into Ken's eyes. 'I get a call sayin' I need to get here pronto. And when I do, I find you lookin' pretty cut up that I'm here, and the lady dead. How d'you think that looks to me?'

'Like a set-up!'

Jakes continued as if he hadn't heard. 'And somethin' else that's been on my mind.'

'What?'

'Table over there. Turned over and everythin's smashed.'

Ken looked at the table of perfume bottles he had knocked over when he entered and saw Florence hanging in the air. 'What of it?'

'It's what we call "sign of struggle". Makes me very suspicious.' His index finger pointed to Ken's chest. 'You're comin' in.'

'I'm not.' Ken was angry, and worried too. He couldn't deny how it looked.

'Then I'm arrestin' you on suspicion.'

'Suspicion of what?'

'You know what.'

The other officers were standing behind Jakes, watchful gazes fixed on Ken. One – he could have been twenty, maybe twenty-five – stepped forward, looking like he wanted to make an impression. He took hold of Ken's arm. Ken shook it off. The cop stepped right in, toe-to-toe, and Ken's blood was hot. 'You'd better step back, officer,' he growled.

'Or what?' He pushed Ken backwards, daring him to fight back.

'I said—'

'Or what?' and he moved to do it again.

But now Ken's blood was on the boil. So when the cop's chest shoved forward, Ken's right fist curved straight up from his hip, punching under the policeman's chin, knocking him to his knees. He sprang up and grabbed Ken around the neck, but before it could get any worse, Jakes had jumped in and wrenched them apart.

'Easy,' the detective warned them both. 'Neither of you do somethin' I gotta make a written report about.'

Ken thought for a second of running for the open door behind him. Two homicides would carry a court-ordered death sentence, no doubt about that. He could dash across the road into the forest and hide. But then what? Live out his life in the undergrowth? No, for now he had to play the game.

'All right. Get on with it,' he muttered. They snapped on a pair of handcuffs and pulled him away. He saw Coraline's face as he was led out. It was like she was seeing him for the first time.

When a paddywagon arrived, he was pushed in to sit on a metal bench screwed to the side. A steel wall separated the driver from the back where he was locked in. 'Watch him close,' Jakes ordered the policeman at the wheel.

'Won't get far with the bracelets on,' the officer replied. The young cop who had wanted the fight jumped in the front.

'Just watch him.' And Jakes went to his own car to lead the way.

With a whine of the engines, they all pulled out onto the road. A panel slid open and the face of the young cop appeared. 'Say, you ever been for a rough ride before?' he asked with a snigger. He didn't wait for a response. 'Hope you like it.' The panel slid back into place and, within a second, Ken felt the van swing right across the road, slamming him shoulder-first against the opposite side of the vehicle. There was nothing to grab hold of to steady himself. Immediately, the action was reversed and the van veered back to its first lane. The floor seemed to fall away from him and he tumbled backwards, the back of his head cracking against the steel bench. He nearly blacked out with the pain. In a second, the van swung again and his cheekbone cracked into a metal cuff, though he barely noticed it as they bounced over a hole in the road, lifting him into the air and then hard down onto the floor again. Without warning, the driver slammed on the brakes, shooting Ken into the dividing wall. He felt something in his nose crumple, and as he slumped down something warm was running down his chin. He heard laughter from the front as the van moved off again.

Laugh it up, boys, he thought to himself. *One day, I'm going to track you down and take you for a ride myself.*

Eventually, the gasoline fumes and angry traffic sounds told him they were in the city. Every one could have been a warning bell and he took them seriously. He was innocent, but he wouldn't be the first blameless man dropped into a prison grave. He sat hunched against the side of the van, his face bust up.

It seemed crazy. Just weeks ago, he had been living his dream: acting in the talkies; boating with good friends. Now his face would still light screens across the nation, but it would be a newsreel as he was strapped to a chair, waiting for the lethal vapour to overwhelm him.

To hell with it. He refused to crawl into self-pity. Someone would be going down for these crimes, but he was damned if it was going to be him.

Chapter 18

At the station house, Jakes stopped to look at Ken's bruised cheeks and glanced at the two cops who had brought him in. He didn't look pleased. Ken had his fingertips inked and rolled on paper to record their prints. Then he was led through the back, into a room that contained nothing but a table and four chairs, all bolted to the ground. Jakes stood over him with his arms folded.

'I want a lawyer,' Ken said.

'Man tells me he wants a lawyer, I think he's done somethin' he needs a lawyer for.'

'Nice try, but I want to see one.'

Jakes leaned his knuckles on the table. 'If you're innocent, you'll want to clear everythin' up sooner rather than later.'

'*I want to see a lawyer.*' He said it slowly enough for the dumbest cop to understand, and Jakes didn't seem dumb at all.

The detective cussed under his breath and left. For an hour, Ken sat or paced around. He had nothing to do but think. Had someone deliberately set him up? The phone call to Jakes sure pointed in that direction. It was possible that a passer-by or neighbour had heard screaming or the like from the house and alerted the police, but they would have left their name.

Eventually, Jakes led a dark man into the room, a fat fellow carrying food stains on his shirt and a canvas bag full of bundled papers. 'Your lawyer,' Jakes said. 'Now, you got two minutes with him before I'm back and we talk.'

As soon as he had closed the door, the man, who introduced himself as Vincenzo Castellina, spoke in a machine-gun fire of words. 'Don't tell me if you did it or not. I don't care. I'm your lawyer. I'll do whatever I can to get you out.'

'I didn't do it,' Ken told him.

'You just broke the first rule. From now on, you do as I say. Got that?'

'Okay.'

'The cops do that?' He pointed to Ken's bust face.

'Sort of. Two cops and a ten-ton paddywagon.'

'Figures. Rough ride. Nothing you can do about it,' Castellina continued, hardly drawing a breath. 'The police told me what they got. It's probably insufficient to press charges. But first we gotta go through an interview. Don't worry, with me here they won't get rough.'

'Do they often?'

'Get rough? Sure. Usually on the hop-heads and queens. The spooks, now they get it the worst. You, you're okay. Wholesome white boy. So—'

He clammed up as Jakes re-entered. 'Had enough time to talk? Good.' He sat down on the other side of the table. 'Why'd you do it, Ken? What'd she do?'

'Having taken legal advice, my client will exercise his right to silence under the Fifth Amendment,' Castellina said authoritatively. 'He has committed no crime.'

'That true, Ken?'

'Having taken legal advice, my client will exercise his right to silence under the Fifth Amendment.'

'Can talk for yourself, can't you?'

'Having taken legal advice, my client will exercise his right to silence under the Fifth Amendment.'

It was obvious this stonewall was the lawyer's favourite tactic and had probably gotten him through a hundred such interviews. And it came out again and again for the next hour. At one point, another officer entered and handed Jakes a note.

'We spoke to Governor Tooke,' Jakes said, after reading it carefully and showing none of the tiredness that was by then hanging off the faces opposite him. 'He says he barely knows you. You been spendin' a lot of time around his family, though.'

'Having taken legal advice, my client will exercise his right to silence under the Fifth Amendment.' Even Castellina's voice was showing signs of strain after uttering the same sixteen words over and over.

Jakes folded the note and placed it in his pocket. 'You and his son. Somethin' between you, was there? You and him? You two have a tiff? What about the mom? You try it on with her? Keep it in the family? She look easy to you?'

At that dreck, Ken broke.

'Look, detective,' he burst out, 'I had nothing to do with the death of Oliver or Florence Tooke.'

'Say nothing,' Castellina ordered him.

Ken ignored him. 'Someone, somewhere, is setting me up for this.'

Castellina threw up his hands and Jakes went for a kill. 'Sure. Why didn't you call emergency when you say you found her? You just sit around takin' a look.'

'I started to, but Coraline came home. Then you turned up.'

'Yeah, you weren't expectin' that, were you? Funny thing, you hardly knowin' this family and suddenly you find two of them dead. Just you there, nobody else,' Jakes said, his voice a low threat.

'Not funny at all.'

'And while we're just shootin' the breeze, you want to tell me what happened with Mr Tooke? The deceased one?'

Ken had been hoping for a chance to float an idea; this wasn't how he had imagined it, but it would do.

'Okay, I will,' he said. 'The fact is, I think that he had something arranged that night, a meeting. If the man had come to the house, Coraline and I would have heard him come in, so Oliver must have met him outside. And he must have trusted this man some of the way, or he wouldn't have taken him out to the writing tower.'

219

'Of course. All part of some plan to kill Mr Tooke, an' the victim played along.'

'No, I don't think that was the plan.'

'Fill me in, why don't you?'

'Because if that was the case, wouldn't the killer do it in a less dramatic way? Knock him out while they're on the water and push him over the side so it looks like an accident. So no, I don't think it was always going to end that way. Some kind of negotiation that went sour would be my guess.'

'Negotiation.' Jakes's tone was one step short of outright mockery.

'Something like that. Then the other man took the boat back and left. The launch was at the beach – I guess it could have drifted there if Oliver hadn't tied it up, but the tide would more likely have taken it some way down the coast.'

'Oh yeah?'

'Yeah.'

'You a sailor?'

'No.'

'Then how the hell can you say what the tides are gonna do?'

'I'm not an idiot. And while we're talking about transport, there's another thing.'

'Sure there is.'

'When I went to the house tonight, I took a cab. The cabbie can tell you that I got there minutes – just minutes – before you did. Not enough time to do anything you suspect me of. Find him.'

'Maybe we will, maybe we won't.'

Their chests were heaving, like they were fighting for real.

Castellina intervened. 'Detective, do you have any evidence linking Mr Kourian to either crime? Actual evidence, not empty conjecture?'

'Empty conjecture, huh?' Jakes paced to the side of the room and folded his arms. 'Right now? No.'

'In that case—'

'But we got enough to hold you while we take a look-see.'

'What does he mean?' Ken asked Castellina.

The lawyer looked put out. 'You're dropping him in the can?' He glanced sideways at the bruise on Ken's cheek.

'Finest hotel in Los Angeles. No charge. And you know what, Ken? When we do find that evidence, you'll be for the gas chamber.'

His words had the confidence of a prediction.

Jakes banged on the door and a custody sergeant took Ken away.

He was led out past the front office, where a bar fight had brought in an army of rowdy drunks, and down through the bowels of the station. The floors smelled of bleach as if they had to be disinfected five times a day. There was no natural light; it was all from a line of caged-in bulbs and even they looked like they had seen better days. From time to time, one of the circling gnats would throw in the towel and land on a bulb to fry.

The sergeant led him through a door, where Ken found himself in a room so bright it hurt his eyes. It took him a second to realize that there were at least a dozen desk lamps all shining straight at him. Hands he didn't register shoved him into a cell, where he dropped onto a wooden bench covered with a stained white sheet that stank of human waste.

He was in the middle cell of three that lay along one side of a larger room, he saw, and a dozen cops were staring at him, stock still like vultures. One, a heavy-set man with bushy side-whiskers, opened his mouth to speak.

'You been places you're not wanted.' The cop looked up and down the bars, as if seeing them for the first time. 'Gotta keep animals in a cage.' Ken's nose rankled at something. There was a bucket beside the bench with the stench of a sewer. 'We'll watch you. All night long.' At that, he ran his nightstick along the bars and left the holding room. His footsteps echoed along the corridor, fading away to nothing, and one by one the other officers went back to their paperwork or reading newspapers or picking their teeth.

The calm before the storm. Where the hell was he going from here?

'Hey, boy,' a voice whispered. The words belonged to an old man with a shock of silver hair and tan skin that suggested he had some Indian in him, who was sitting on an identical stained bench in the cell to his left. 'They really got it in fo' you!' he said, and his mouth cracked open to show a line of black stumps. He fell back against the bars of his cell, laughing hysterically. One of the cops watched and laughed along.

Nobody offered him food or drink and he didn't ask for

any. He lay on the bench, trying not to think what the rag that covered it had been used for. *You been places you're not wanted*. That's what the cop had said. Was he talking about Ken being at the Tooke house that evening, or did it mean that someone didn't like how he had been sniffing around since Oliver's death?

What would Coraline be doing now? Would he be charged? Would his lawyer be able to get him out on bail? There were a ton of questions and not one answer.

Time stretched out. The number of officers thinned to one old man who reeked of garlic when he sauntered around past the bars of the cell, parading his own freedom as the only entertainment he had. Not even a radio would work down where they were, and the old geezer didn't look the type to enjoy a good book. At ten, the lights were switched off. After a couple of hours, Ken's mind gave up on racing between England and doctors and trick-books and men in boats; and sleep grabbed hold of him.

He wasn't sure what it was that woke him. It could have been the breath in his face, it could have been the hands on his wrists and ankles. More likely, it was the arm across his throat, cutting off his air.

His whole body jerked as if he had been hit by lightning. But the weight of men on him held him down, pressing him into the wood of the bench. His eyes were open, but he could only see dark shapes moving over him. He twisted his neck and tried to yell out, to shout an oath or call for help, but something wet and tasting of gasoline was stuffed in his mouth so that his tongue was smothered. And then there was the crunch of impact on the side of his head. And again on his stomach, with knuckles compacted into a fist. He groaned, but it made no noise through the wet rag in his throat. He struggled as hard as he could for what he guessed was his life, managing to drag free one fist that connected with soft tissue above him. Someone yelped like a kicked dog, but Ken's arm was grabbed again and pinned to the bench.

And then something snaked around his neck and tightened. It was rough, scratching into the skin as it bit tighter and tighter. A rope.

'Been places you're not wanted.' The murmur was loud in the still air. He could feel the snake around his neck squeezing. Soon it would squeeze so tight that the blood wouldn't flow. This putrid underground was going to be his coffin. 'But soon it won't matter.'

He could feel the blood in his veins fighting against the rope, a pulse choked off. His brain was getting slower without the oxygen. The dark was getting darker. What could he do? He only had a few breaths left before he would lose consciousness. It was his last chance. Through force of will, he concentrated his mind. He had to change the game. He couldn't speak and couldn't force them off. But he could confuse them. And so, from violently struggling, he went completely limp and held his breath, collapsing into the bench and letting his head roll to the side. There was a pause, then a change came over the men holding him.

'What happened?' he heard a light voice say. 'He have a heart seizure or somethin'?'

The hands on him stayed where they were – the cops

weren't stupid – but they loosened their grip. And then there was cautious movement above him: a patch of pure black moving against slate grey. He heard breathing coming closer. He could smell sweat, and old food on the man's breath. Closer, until he was close enough to listen for Ken's breathing. And with all his strength, Ken jerked his body up and his forehead forward to crack straight into the man's face with the force of a sledgehammer. There was a roar of pain as the cop staggered back. 'Kill this . . . !' he yelled. And then the room was flooded with burning light that caused them all to wince.

'That's enough,' Jakes barked from the doorway, his hand dropping from the switch.

'He just—' bawled the cop, holding his face like a broken egg.

'He just nothin',' Jakes ordered him. And the look the other cop gave him could have killed. 'I said, he just nothin'.'

The other men muttered, spat on the floor and retreated. Ken reached up and tore the rope from his neck. It had been twisted into a noose. He threw it at the feet of the officer he had head-butted – the heavy-set one with thick side-chops.

'Yeah, well,' the cop said. 'Don't matter. Now or 'nother time.' And he swaggered out of the cell, followed by the others. They went to their seats and sat, watching him, as if it was just another day at work.

'You're out,' Jakes told Ken. He jerked his head towards the corridor. 'But you'll be back. We ain't found that cab driver of yours, an' somethin' tells me we won't.' Ken heaved himself to his feet. The strangulation had left him giddy and it was an effort to walk. As he passed Jakes, the detective spoke again. 'Tell me the truth 'bout what you did, or maybe next time I won't be here.' Ken shook his head. There was no point appealing for any understanding.

As he reached the corridor, he heard one of the cops call out, 'You wanna lay charges?' The others laughed.

Cops were corrupt, lazy, often stupid. He knew that. But as he stepped outside, he couldn't get his head around the fact that a squad of them were prepared to kill him too. Any point reporting them? None. All Ken would get out of giving a statement to the higher-ups would be to make sure he rose up their hit list.

No, his best bet would be to finish what he had started. Someone had set the dogs on him. He had to find out who was holding their leash.

Ken might as well have been drained of blood by the time he got back to his lodging house. The cops had decided that the contents of his wallet should go to their retirement fund, so he had had to walk all the way, among the booze-hounds and real criminals who took the Los Angeles night as their playtime. All he wanted was to lie down and sleep. He might not even get undressed. In the hallway, his landlady, perfectly made up and rouged as if it was early evening, instead of the small hours of the morning, stopped him in his tracks. Music came from her apartment and a man's seated legs were just visible through the doorway.

'Mr Kourian. You look ready to drop to the floor,' she said.

'I've had a hard day, Madame Peche.' It was lucky the light was low enough to hide his bruises. They were turning into real peaches and he didn't want to have to explain them.

'You have been working long hours. Or have you perhaps found a little friend?' She had a twinkle in her eye.

Well, let her keep her little fantasy.

'Working too hard.'

'Oh, that is a pity.' She went back to her rooms and he climbed the stairs. Each one seemed steeper than the last. As he was about to fit his room key into the lock, he stopped. He thought he had heard a sound from within. Something shifting about on the creaking floorboards. He listened harder. Nothing now. He tried the handle. It turned, but the door was locked as it should be. Relaxing, he pushed the key in and was about to twist it, but stopped again. This time, the sound was unmistakable: wooden, a sliding sound. He threw the door open and scanned the room. It was neat as he had left it, but the window was open. He rushed over and looked out. At first, he saw nothing except the surrounding buildings and rooftops, lit by streetlamps and house lights. Then he looked straight down. Below his window, the house had a small extension that Madame Peche used to store broken furniture, boxes of winter clothes and the like. And crouching on it, pressing himself into a nook, was the figure of a man, lit by a streetlamp. He wore a light suit and a flat felt cap with a peak that hid his features. But then he chanced a glance upwards, exposing a face extraordinary in its ordinariness – as if he had been specially bred so that no one could describe him to a police artist.

At the sight of Ken, he scrambled to the edge of the building and dropped to the ground, before dashing towards the main road.

For a split second, Ken thought about jumping down from the window and running after him, but from this height he would as likely break an ankle or his neck and he wasn't in the mood to do the guy that kind of favour. He charged down the stairs instead.

'Mr Kourian, what . . .' his flustered landlady voiced as he burst past her. He raced out onto the street, looking in every direction.

There! On the other side of the street, walking quickly but not running, a man in a light grey gabardine suit. No cap, but he had likely thrown that aside. 'Hey!' Ken cried. He sprinted over. The man started sprinting, too, down a long alleyway between high buildings. Ken rushed in his wake, his heart beating faster than a regimental drummer boy.

The alley was full of trash, and a nest of rats squealed as he leaped over them. The man he was chasing had pace, for sure, but instead of running out the other end of the alley, the man ducked through the doorway of a derelict timber building that was more rot than wood.

Ken reached the entry and stopped. The guy could be armed – more people bought guns than bought candy in LA these days – and there was no one else in sight. But the fight had come to his home now, so he wasn't going to back off and hope it all went away.

He trod carefully. It was a big building – it had been some kind of warehouse or factory. Shards of glass splintered under his feet as he entered. All the windows were filthy or broken and the dimmest glow from the street-lamps was filtering in. Some hulking piece of machinery at the side of the room was covered by a sheet and there was an empty doorway at the other end that looked like it led to a stairwell.

Ken stopped and listened. There was something that could have been wind through a broken-down building or the breath of a panting man. He moved in, his tread making only a light tap as he went. There had to be at least one other way out of the building and he wanted to trap his rat. He went towards the doorway at the end, but as he was about to reach it, he stopped. A slight rustling had caught his attention, like the movement of textile. He looked over to the covered machinery. Slowly, he went back to it. It was seven or eight yards square and a couple of yards high. The dirty sheet thrown over it was torn here and there. Ken picked a stone from the floor, one of those that the local boys had used to smash some of the windows. It would do as a weapon.

Was his quarry hiding inside the machine? Ken took hold of the sheet and pulled. It wouldn't come down. As he looked up, something fell towards him, blocking out the ceiling. It fell swiping at him with a heavy metal tool, cracking into his temple, knocking him to the floor, where he sprawled. The pain seared, pinning him to the ground. So when it had abated enough that he could stand to lift his head, it was only to see the figure sprinting away.

He could have staggered to his feet, but he was in no shape to give chase. He lay back on the smashed glass and let the waves of pain wash back over him.

It crossed his mind to report all this to Jakes, but would the detective believe him? Not for a single second.

Back in his room, having drawn the blind and waited a few minutes to make sure no one was waiting to burst in, he reached under his bedframe. He had tied something to the middle slat with thread and now he pulled it out. It was a small, oval, china object, inlaid with delicate mother-of-pearl lines: the holder of miniature pictures painted by Florence that he had found in the house on Ray. He carefully opened the egg-like item to reveal the two images inside: the house in Essex, the house in California, head-to-tail.

The artist had talent. Ken turned it around, so that the two houses flipped. But as it turned, he heard something that he hadn't noticed before: a slight ticking sound, like thin wood tapped by a nail. He spun it again and it happened again. There was something behind one of the pictures.

With the edge of a spoon, he carefully lifted the California picture from its housing. Nothing there. He did the same to the other side. This time, when the picture of the Ray house came away, there was something. It was a tiny model of a horse, carved out of wood, half an inch long. The sort of thing a child might have as part of a nursery menagerie. Wrapped around the horse was a thin slip of paper. Ken unfurled it:

Oliver, my brother. Sleep well.
Alexander

Alexander. He had written this.

And what was unmistakable was that the handwriting was neat and sloping. It wasn't the kind of scrawl that a four-year-old drags across a page. An adult had written this note.

Ken took the little model horse between his forefinger and thumb and held it up to the electric light. The wood was reddish brown and had a faint smell of ripe apples. What was that about a foal in Oliver's book? He grabbed his copy from the trunk. Yes, a foal had been put out of its misery and Simeon shown the carcass.

'Lame fro' birth. Best thin' for 'im,' Cain informed him.

Ken stared at the miniature for a long time. In its shadow was the truth about why Oliver had died. And Ken was beginning to see it.

Chapter 19

The radio was playing in the background as Ken ate breakfast, squawking out band numbers alternated with a warning of severe weather on its way. The tropical storm building a few miles out to sea was expected to hit that night. No one knew how bad it was going to be, but every hour the weather service said that it was getting heavier and nastier. Householders should put up storm shutters on their windows. Children should be kept indoors and adults should leave home only if absolutely necessary. That wouldn't be popular.

He finished his toast and jelly, musing over the fact that he had resigned – well, kinda – from his job. He wouldn't miss it, but he regretted losing access to the newspaper's archive. He wanted to see again the stories he had been given about the family tragedy that had wrapped around the Tookes. No, he *needed* to see those stories.

So after clearing up, he headed over to the office, keeping a look-out for anyone he actually worked with who might question his presence in the building. He was lucky enough to get inside and down the stairs to the library without spotting anyone or being spotted.

'You brought me some cuttings about a kidnapping case back in 1915,' he told a malnourished man with a green dealer's visor.

'You here to complain?' He was at a desk in front of row upon row of bookshelves, each stuffed with large boxes. 'Only we're short-staffed. We can't send everything. You want cuts from the other papers, you need to spell that out and wait.'

Ken perked up at the information. 'You mean there might be more in other papers?'

'Sure. We got the back copies of the *Examiner*, the *Press* and the *Express*.'

'Can you get them for me?'

'What, all of them?'

'Is that possible? Just for 1915. No, make it '16, too.'

'Look, I got other work to do, you know.'

'Okay, I'll do it myself.'

The man in the green visor jerked his thumb towards the shelves. 'Knock yourself out.'

It took Ken a long while just to find the right volumes. The *Press* and *Examiner* had no more details than the *Times* had provided. But the *Express* had really gone to town. It had sent a reporter to talk to everyone and anyone connected to the story, and returned to it whenever it had an excuse. And there was a name, buried deep in one of its articles, that Ken recognized. It was from the 1916 batch, after the family had returned from Europe. There was a photograph of them pushing Oliver in a wheelchair towards an office that he also recognized.

> Some good news at last for the tragic Tooke family. After the shock of his brother's terrible kidnapping, little Oliver Tooke is seen being taken to the surgery of society doctor Arnie Kriger [the reporter had mis-spelled his name, but it was clear who they were writing about]. Kriger is an expert in childhood diseases. One of his staff told the *Express* that the boy's polio had improved remarkably during his time in Europe and he might soon be able to walk, albeit with some difficulty. We at the *Express* pray that he does!

Ken wondered which nurse or receptionist had received a few creased dollar bills in return for that information. He packed up and returned home to work out what that story meant. He left a message for Coraline to call him. They needed to talk.

The storm hit that night.

Sheets of rain shot along the streets, throwing trees against walls, smashing through window panes. Anyone

234

caught on the road – those who had missed the radio messages and the warnings in the newspapers – cowered in shop doorways, looking for a way out. When they tried to shout to each other, they could barely make a sound.

Ken stood in his room. His landlady had run about the house, handing out wooden boards to place inside the windows in case they shattered – it was too late to nail them across the outside. When the power had cut out, Ken had stumbled out onto the landing and found a candle.

He was deciding how best to hold back the flood when a frantic knocking sounded on his door, someone trying the handle, against the bolt. 'Who is it?' he called. He wasn't expecting anyone, so he was on his guard after the last unannounced visitor.

'Coraline,' came the answer.

He slipped back the bolt. The weather had soaked through her clothes and he watched the water trickle down her skin. Her air of sophistication was gone, leaving a natural beauty.

'Come in.'

'No. You have to leave. Now.'

He was alert. He had been through enough to know that the threats around him weren't idle. 'Why?'

'The police. Jakes called me. They have a witness who saw you arrive at the house with my mother. They asked me if I could explain that.'

'It's a lie,' he growled. He pulled her inside and shut them both in. 'I should have seen something like that coming.'

'I know it's a lie. But they told me something else.'

'What?'

'They found a knife, a lock-knife at the house. Kicked under the furniture, they said. It had white fibres in it that look like they're from cutting a rope like the one used to . . . kill her.'

'Okay, well . . .' He was about to say that the knife wasn't his. Then something struck him. He went to the trunk of his possessions and hunted through it.

'What are you looking for?'

He sat back on the bed. Now the break-in of his room made sense.

'I had a knife like that. I use it for meals. It's been taken.' A shadow of scepticism slipped across Coraline's face. 'Save it. I know how it looks. Some cops tried to kill me last night.'

'What?' Even with all the rest that had happened, she sounded amazed.

'Maybe they just wanted to scare me for punching that cop yesterday. I don't know. Anyhow, they held me down in the station and put a noose around my neck. That wasn't a barrel of fun.' He rubbed his throat. 'It could be they're in someone's pocket.'

'Everyone's in someone's pocket.' She paused. 'Will your fingerprints be on the knife?'

'Covered with them.'

'We have to go. Now. I've got Oliver's car.'

He grabbed a raincoat and hurried out with her, doing his best not to make an impression on the other residents, who were standing around with storm lamps and armfuls of boarding. Madame Peche, carrying a heap of bedding that had been soaked through, stopped him on the stairway.

'Mr Kourian. You can't possibly be going out in this,' she told him.

'I have no choice.'

She stared at Coraline with an arched eyebrow. 'I see. Well, the door will be locked when you return this evening. *If* you return this evening.'

'I understand.'

They forced their way out into the torrent. It was coming straight down now, a mass of freezing water pouring from black clouds that had swamped Los Angeles. The power was out everywhere and the only light came from the gas streetlamps and flashes of lightning.

'The electricity's gone,' Coraline shouted.

'Lines must be down. It shorts out the whole city grid when that happens,' he cried back. 'Where's the car?'

She pointed to the other side of the street. The Cadillac stood idle in front of a liquor store. She slipped in the river coursing along the road and he caught her just as she fell.

They closed themselves in the car as a tree branch flew across the road, followed by other debris: a newspaper, some packaging, a billboard that would never convince anyone else to buy Johnson & Johnson's tooth powder.

Coraline started the motor. It must have been warm from the journey she had just made, although the water pouring through it threatened to seize it up.

He reached into his pocket and pulled out the china picture holder. 'You remember this from the house in Essex?'

'Of course. My mother's pictures. God knows why Oliver wanted to leave it in that wreck. God knows why anyone would want to be there at all.'

Ken opened it and lifted out the picture of the house on bleak Ray. The little horse lay nestled behind it. He took it out into the light. 'I think it's something to do with this. I found it last night. At first, I thought it was a horse.'

'It's not?'

'Not quite, it's a foal.' He didn't show her the slip of paper that had been wrapped around the model. The slip that read:

> *Oliver, my brother. Sleep well.*
> *Alexander*

'And the difference is?'

'Oliver's book. There's a foal in it. The foal dies. I had forgotten all about it until I found this. It seems so insignificant when you read the story. So I'm only now realizing what it really means. Oliver was clever. There are a lot of subtle messages in his book. But some are so subtle, only the person they are meant for would understand.'

'Tell me about this one,' Coraline said.

'There's something else we need to know first, but we'll find out tomorrow. And right now, we have to keep out of sight.'

They pulled into the street. The methane streetlights meant they could find their way on the road, but the water, six inches deep on the asphalt, slowed them down. They passed shut-up and shivering diners and stores, but had only gone a few streets when Coraline began checking over her shoulder.

'What is it?' he asked. He already had an idea what it was.

'There's about three cars on the road tonight,' she replied. 'I think the one behind us was parked outside your boarding house.'

He twisted around to see a racing green Desoto Sedan. Someone was screwing with his life, that was for certain. The chances were that it was either a cop or the plain-faced man in the gabardine suit who had previously paid him a visit. 'Are you sure?'

'No.' But Ken kept close watch on the vehicle for two more streets until Coraline took a sharp, last-second turn, spraying a thick wave of dirty water across the sidewalk, and the car made no attempt to follow. Whether it had been thrown off or they were imagining a threat where none existed, he couldn't tell. 'So, we keep running away,' she said.

'Listen. Whoever they are, they're after me, not you. I can get out here. I'll find my own way. You'll be safer.'

She turned the wheel and pressed the pedal. 'I doubt it.'

They drove, buffeted by the wind. Fence posts lifted into the air and cracked down onto the ground. Parked cars shook on their wheels and uncovered windows exploded into fragments. 'We should find somewhere to put in,' he said. 'Take the next right. There are some cheap hotels that way.'

'Wonderful,' she replied.

They hung a right, carried on a few blocks and found a row of flop-houses with names that promised luxury they couldn't even pretend to offer: The King's Hotel, Shangri-La, Excelsior Rooms. All would normally have been lit up, but the electricity grid was out and they looked like cemeteries.

They pulled into one that offered parking, a narrow brick building with an unfinished fire escape. It wasn't even clear if the hotel was yet to open or already closed down, but they took a chance.

Behind the front desk, a man was asleep on a mattress, his wire spectacles still on his nose, all dimly lit by a kerosene lamp. Ken smacked the bell and the night clerk, who smelled strongly of cheap sourmash, roused himself with a groan.

'Buck fifty per night. Hot water extra. Sign here,' he mumbled. 'Got a car?'

'No.' The clerk might take it upon himself to go out and take a look at the number plate.

'Fine. Cash up front.'

Ken handed over the money. The man either didn't notice or didn't care that they had no luggage. He handed them a grimy lamp and they climbed the steep stairs to their room.

It was a ten-feet-square firetrap. The bed was spread with two sheets that between them just about covered it.

'What do you think, Ken?'

Her hair was running with water, delicate beads falling to the floor. And the lamp flame lit her eyes so that he saw the room reflected in them; and he strode across and to hell with it and he pulled her by the shoulders so her mouth turned up to his and he pressed their lips together hard. She was warm and yielding; until she pulled back and away from him, dabbing her mouth with her sleeve.

'I'm sorry,' he said.

'Don't be,' she replied quietly. 'Another time and it would have been—'

'I know. I know what it would have been.'

'I guess I'm just the unlucky type.'

'I guess we both are,' he said, staring out at the dark.

Just as he was drifting off to sleep, Ken heard a new voice coming up from reception.

'Hello, Mick.'

'Hello yourself.' It was the night clerk's voice.

'We had a call come through. Looking for a couple. Twenties. Sound like swells. Could be driving. Anyone arrived in the last few hours?' Ken sat up, alert.

'Last few hours? I been asleep the last few hours.'

'That so?'

'Sure is.'

There was a pause. 'Yeah, well, holler if they turn up.'

'There a reward?'

'Reward? Sure there's a reward. The reward is we don't shut you down.'

The voices fell quiet. Then the stairs creaked. Someone was coming up. Ken jumped to his feet. There were bars across the window, so he would have to make a stand. The footsteps halted outside the room. Ken held his breath, ready for the cop to burst in. But it was the clerk's voice.

'Get the fuck outta here. I ain't seen you.' And the stairs creaked again as he returned to his post.

Ken pulled his jacket on again. They handed back the key, ran to the car and drove it out through the dirty river that used to be Los Angeles. They found a blacked-out, empty lot to park in for a few hours and wait, shivering, on the back seat. The clerk kept their money.

Chapter 20

The wind rolled all through the night, and morning meant no let-up. The solid clouds of the tropical storm – now threatening to turn into a hurricane, according to an excited newscaster on the car radio – meant the whole city was enveloped by a dark grey and lashed by streaming rain. Mid-morning was in twilight and the few cars about were trundling along with headlamps lit so they looked like hellish insects. The road ran with deep, muddy water. Ken parked the car in a spot where he could see their target.

'How long do we wait?' Coraline asked.

'Until he gets here.'

She lit a Nat Sherman. The gusts whipped away the

smoke as soon as it came close to the gap at the top of the car window.

They edged closer to each other, without thinking, to stay warm. It was impossible to see the sun; they could only tell by their wristwatches that it must be above them.

'There he is.' Ken pointed through the windshield, blurred as it was by the rain washing down. She nodded. The tiredness of the night was showing on her face.

Ken got out of the car and waited for the man on the other side of the road to open up his office. Then Ken charged across, into the doorway, barging him inside into a wide corridor and slamming the door after him.

'What are—'

Ken stopped the words with his fist. The doctor squealed in pain and fell back against the wall, holding his hand across his twisted mouth.

'No sound,' Ken warned. Kruger raised a palm in submission. 'I want to know about the Tooke family.'

'What . . . what can I tell you?'

'The mother. What was her mental condition after her son was taken?'

The doctor stammered, unable at first to form words. 'I'm not an expert in diseases of the mind.'

'Hazard a wild fucking guess.' He lifted his fist again.

'All right!' Kruger pleaded. 'She was distraught. Of course. Her son had gone.'

'She was eaten up by guilt, Doctor. And you know why. You know what she did.'

'I don't. *I don't*,' he protested.

Ken seized Kruger's shirt, twisted it in his fist and pinned the man to the wall. 'And the boys. What were they like?'

Kruger seemed relieved to move on to a new subject. 'They . . . Alexander was healthy. Oliver exhibited severe poliomyelitis.'

'What was his prognosis?'

'What does it matter?' the man cried.

'*Answer the question.*'

Kruger threw up his hands in a second submission and gave an impressive performance of a man doing his best to recall facts from twenty-five years earlier. 'Probably a life-long cripple.'

'And what treatment did you recommend?' The man blinked nervously. But this was the crux of it all. This was where it had all gone wrong: for Oliver, for Alexander, for Coraline, for Ken. And he would rather stop Kruger from ever breathing again than let him swallow the truth. 'Tell me now or I'll break your neck in ten different ways.'

A few minutes later, Ken emerged from the building. He went to a telephone booth at the end of the street, where he made a call. Jakes answered and Ken told him a story.

'Oliver's book,' Ken said as he got back into the Cadillac. 'It's all in there if you look.'

'What is?'

'Everything.'

'Where are we going?'

'Back to your house.'

He gunned the engine and pulled out into the river-road.

A wave erupted against the side of the car as the wheels churned the water. The city was drowning, all under the pale amber light from the gas streetlamps.

'There's a car behind us,' she said quietly, her voice almost becoming lost in the rain.

'The same one?'

'Yes.'

He glanced at the wing mirror. He could make out a racing green Desoto. This time, there was enough light to see a man at the wheel. He was wearing a muffler, but Ken knew who it was. 'I thought he was gone,' he muttered. 'Well, we'll see how he drives.'

He stamped down the accelerator and the car jumped forward, skidding as it went.

'He's coming with us,' Coraline said, watching the other car over her shoulder. Ken spun the wheel, hanging around a corner, lifting the Cadillac's offside wheels a few inches from the ground and crashing them down again with a shockwave through the car. The Caddy had a more powerful engine than the Desoto and it quickly put distance between the two. But the conditions meant it couldn't tear away, and the Desoto began to gain. 'What does he want?' she asked.

'Us.'

The green car suddenly roared forward, finding a reserve of acceleration, and its front fender hacked at the Cadillac's rear, screwing the front car on a plane of water before Ken was able to right it again.

'What was that?' Coraline asked.

'He's trying to knock us off the road.'

246

The car behind gained again and thudded into them. Only this time, the two fenders locked into each other, twisting the cars into one hefty machine. Ken pressed and released the accelerator, but the Caddy was trawling a heavy burden. He turned left and right, attempting to shake loose, but it was no good. And now they were coming to a crossroads.

When Ken had been taught to ride, he had learned that when you take a corner, you lean into it and kick your heels into the horse's flank so the beast pushes harder. If you don't, you can be thrown off. It was the same with automobiles. Corners demanded acceleration, and as he reached the junction he put the pedal to the metal. The engine screamed, but the car behind was still holding them back. He hit the gas again, hard enough to put the pedal through the floor. Then, at the last second, he spun the wheel to the right, turning the car on a dime.

There was a bang and a tearing of steel, and the Caddy shot forward. The needle jumped up past fifty, and Ken whirled his head to see the other car spinning away, thrown off by the turning torque and the Cadillac's fury. It was skidding sideways across the wet asphalt, over the broad intersection and straight for the oncoming traffic. Those other vehicles shrieked to halts pointing in crazy directions, but still the Desoto skidded. And then its two left wheels simultaneously hit the opposite kerb, and the car burst upwards, a yard into the air, crashing into a streetlight and breaking it in two like a sapling, before dropping back onto the sidewalk to rest on its side.

Ken lifted his foot from the accelerator and rammed it

down onto the brake. The tyres screeched and smeared the road, stopping about twenty yards down the street. He jumped out, opened the trunk and grabbed a heavy wrench from the repair kit. He ran to the wrecked Desoto with it raised. Twenty, fifteen, ten yards. It took him seconds to sprint it. And as he came close, he saw the driver through the void where the windshield had been. There was blood on his face and for a moment Ken had no idea if he was alive or dead. The broken streetlamp was spewing gas, making the air stink of rotting food.

The man's torso was slumped across the two seats. 'Who are you?!' Ken shouted, ripping away the muffler. The bloody mouth was groggy, attempting to form words, then closing dumbly. 'Tell me!' He lifted his wrench, threatening more pain if the question wasn't answered.

The man's eyes narrowed a little. He reached forwards, towards Ken, shoving at the door. It was already half-open, the bottom of it torn by the crash so that metal ran in twisted spurs. It wouldn't open properly and one of the ribbons of steel scraped against another with a whine. The driver tried again with all his weight, and as the two strips of metal rubbed against each other little sparks flew up, sheltered from the weather by the automobile.

Ken dropped the wrench and stepped back. He could see that the danger wasn't the driver, but what was about to happen. Another burst of sparks and it did. The gas in the air ignited, and Ken hit the ground as the car was engulfed in a fireball five yards across. If the sun had dropped through the sky, it couldn't have burned brighter.

The rush of boiling air was like another gale, and when he lifted his head, he saw a jet of flame from the streetlamp rising ten feet into the dark storm.

He lay his head back down on the road. The man in the car was no threat now. He felt warm blood. A deep gash had opened on his cheek. It was as if, for a few moments, the whole world had collapsed in on itself. All he could do was take rattling breaths.

'Sir, are you okay?'

It was a woman, holding a hat on her head. 'Were you hit by the . . . the . . .' She searched for a word to describe what she had just seen.

'No,' he said quietly, feeling his lungs wheeze. 'I wasn't.'

He wiped his sleeve across his face, smearing ash over it. He dragged himself back to the car. Coraline emerged, shaken up. 'Was he the one who killed Oliver and Mama?'

'Probably.'

'Was he trying to kill us?'

'It doesn't really matter now.'

Chapter 21

The car glided through the iron gates of Turnglass House. The storm at sea could be seen right through the building.

The maid, Carmen, opened the door to them, then folded in on herself, instantly self-conscious, their last talk with her having revealed deeply hidden secrets.

'Where's my father?'

'The library, miss. But he's being interviewed for radio. And . . .'

They ignored the warning and went upstairs. Governor Tooke was sitting in a red velvet wing-backed chair, with a microphone and recording equipment set in front of him. A young presenter had his own microphone.

'. . . KQW speaking to Governor Oliver Tooke, the frontrunner for the Republican presidential nomination. Governor, the storm is raging around us, but America's got a great future ahead of it. Wouldn't you say, sir?'

'Well, Mr Willett, I would say that. And that's because—'

'Father, we need to speak to you.' Coraline stared straight into his eyes without wavering or blinking.

'My dear, I'm speaking to—'

'It's about Oliver. And Alex.'

Tooke looked at her like she was a scorpion.

The radio man spoke. 'Sir, may we—'

'I think my daughter and I need to talk.'

The presenter looked unhappy with the situation, but took his cue and left the room.

Coraline went to the window, took a packet of cigarettes from her purse, lit the last one and stared outside. The Governor looked to Ken.

It was a sad and beat-up road they had travelled. Ken had begun it with a friend, but that friend had had his life stolen from him. And it had all begun with a boy's simple, common misfortune.

He sat in the radio presenter's seat.

'We have a difficult conversation to conduct, Mr Kourian. Is that not so?'

'It is.'

'Well, it's been some time coming, but come it must. Would you like a drink?'

'A drink? No, no, thank you, Governor.'

'It's very early, I know. But I think I might have one.'

He went to a large globe and lifted the top half to reveal glinting bottles. He took a couple out, setting them on the side table, but didn't open any. He was unsure. It must have been unnerving for him to be like that. And he returned to his seat without a glass.

Where to begin?

Ken chose to begin with the story.

'I read the last book Oliver wrote. It's a strange thing. Truly unique.'

'My son was a disapp—'

Ken cut him off. 'Your son was clever, that's what he was. His book took some unravelling.'

'Enlighten me,' Governor Oliver Tooke said, the displeasure returning. He glanced at his daughter. She met his gaze.

'I will. At its heart, it's a story about identity. About being two people at once. Not knowing who you are. And it's about a lame foal put to death in a stable.' Those details should have told him everything. But the truth was so extraordinary, who could have dreamed it? Ken paused and looked out the window. The Essex rain seemed to be running down the glass. Then he could stand waiting no more and asked, 'Why did you do it?'

'Why did I do *what*?' Tooke's jaw was set hard. The smoke rose from Coraline's cigarette and drifted among the books.

The harsh words, the condemnation, seemed to form not in that room, but outside, in the beating rain.

'Mr Tooke, I've been through a lot. I don't care for any more of this today. You had a man end the life of your polio-crippled elder child. And you raised your other son in his place, convincing the world for twenty-five years that he was his elder brother. Why?'

Tooke went back to the table that held the clutch of bottles. He selected a bottle of whiskey and splashed half the straw-coloured contents into two crystal tumblers. He offered one to Ken, who refused it.

'Ah well,' the older man said, returning one of the glasses to the side. 'Time's up.' He dropped into the wing-backed chair and drank a long draught. Enough to get most men drunk in the blink of an eye. 'Why, why, why.' He pointed a scrawny middle finger at Ken. 'Well, you know something? Times are changing, that's why. Once a man would be elected president by his peers – other sharp men who knew what was best for this country. Men who could read and write and think. Men who understood commerce and the law, and what rights a man should have. But now that's changed.' He believed what he was saying, that was clear. He was a man who believed with all his being. 'Now that voting has been extended to every man and woman who can put a cross on a ballot paper, it's whoever looks best on the newsreels and speaks the prettiest on the radio. He's not chosen on brains or ability, sir, he's cast like one of those flickers that you are so desperate to appear in. And that's a dangerous state for a country.'

'Is it?'

'Oh, oh yes, it is.' Tooke nearly laughed. On a run now. 'But I stand for something. I stand for the betterment of this country for the collective good of its people.' His hands knitted together to illustrate society united. 'And a nation is no more than its people; so we have to make the *people themselves* stronger. Finer of mind and body.' Ken pictured Kruger entering the American Eugenics Society headquarters. That building was full of men who thought like Governor Tooke and had been encouraged by events in distant Germany to call openly now for what they believed. 'And I will not be a hypocrite. No, I will not. So I had to practise what I preach.' He took another swig.

'And so?'

'And so.' He lost himself in his thoughts for a moment. 'And so, I had my dear boy taken away, and I let my younger son take his place and his name.' It was the bitterest of vindications. It hung in the air for a while. Ken could hear it echoing. 'Like Abraham, I sacrificed my son. And yes, soon enough Alexander began to believe he was Oliver. He was four years old – you come to believe anything at that age darn quickly. He forgot very soon that we had ever called him anything else.' He swilled his drink around. 'Maybe at the back of his mind, there was always half a memory, I don't know.'

The storm battered at the walls, providing the only sound in the room. Until Coraline spoke. Ken could see the hate in her had turned cold. 'You were always so sure of yourself, Father. Morally. As if it oozed out of your pores.' She went to the drinks table and took the unclaimed glass of whiskey. She drank half without looking at either of them.

'Was it Kruger who took him away?' Ken asked.

'It was the kindest thing for him.'

'And how the hell do you figure that?' It seemed

impossible to Ken that they were sitting here discussing the death of a boy and that Tooke was talking like it had been no more than an unpleasant duty.

'Life as a cripple is no life.' He rolled the glass in his fingers. 'Do you want to try it, having others push you everywhere? Dress you? Take you to the bathroom? Watch your brother run on the athletics field you can't set foot on?'

He seemed, still, to believe every word he uttered.

'What about Mama?'

Tooke glanced at Coraline. 'She didn't want it, of course. Took some hard, hard persuading.'

'It sent her mad.'

'I did my best for her. Put her somewhere they would look after her well. Visited her when I could.' And for the first time, Ken heard the faintest tone of shame. The Governor lifted his glass to his lips, then placed it on the table. But it didn't sit properly and tipped over. He didn't try to right it.

'Christ,' Coraline said under her breath.

'Why the deception?' Ken said.

'What do you mean?'

He felt sick asking it, as if the mechanics of the Governor's actions were what mattered and not the outcome. 'When Kruger took him away, why did you pretend it was your younger boy who had been kidnapped? Why not just say it was the older one with polio who was gone?'

The wind was picking up. Rain was spattering the window, shaking it, threatening to rush right through.

'You tell me, Mr Kourian.'

He had been weighing that question for hours. And there was only one answer that fitted. 'I think it was because your views on eugenics were well-known. If your crippled son had disappeared in strange circumstances, suspicion would have fallen on you. Even if it couldn't be proved, that would have been the end of your political career. But this way . . . this way, you actually gained sympathy.' The Governor made no reply. Ken hated to know that he was right. And that was why his friend, Oliver, had spoken of the guilt he harboured: because his life was a part of his brother's death. 'But everything changed when you saw Oliver's book. You read it and realized that he had found your wife and worked it all out. Didn't you?'

Tooke paused before speaking. 'Actually, you're not quite right there,' he said.

'I'm not?'

'Not quite. For all your cleverness, you're missing a nuance or two.'

'What nuance is that?'

The Governor huffed in scorn. 'My son. My last chance for a man to continue our line and he was no better than the pansies he associated with.' He looked to his side, as if searching for an explanation for how his own child had turned out to be such an embarrassment. 'And then, when he knew what he knew and he summoned up all the courage he had to face me, what did he do? He overshot. Played his hand too high.'

'What the hell are you talking about?'

Tooke looked Ken up and down like he was appraising an animal. 'What I am talking about, Mr Kourian, is that my milksop son was threatening me.'

'How?'

The Governor's pale hand reached for his desk drawer. The wood came out of its housing with a whine. Tooke held a copy of *The Turnglass* up to Ken, before tossing it aside like it was a disease. 'He said this was a taster of what was to come. When I ran for the White House, he was going to go to the police with the full story.' His forefinger jabbed back and forth as anger lifted his voice. 'He thought he would see me in handcuffs. Now! Just as I was about to save this nation from a devastating war against a friendly and admirable country. I could not let that happen.'

The rain washed down the pane. 'So you sent a man to frighten him into keeping quiet, but things got out of hand, maybe he fought back, and he ended up dead.' The Governor reached for the overturned glass, but his fingertips set it rolling over the edge of the table and it fell to the floor, breaking into a hundred pieces. 'Who was it you sent?' Ken asked.

'Does it matter?' The anger had ebbed away.

'Probably not. I think we met him tonight.'

'And?'

'You won't be seeing him again.'

'I see.' Tooke looked at the shattered whiskey glass. 'His family always worked for us. His grandmother was even in Oliver's book. The housekeeper. They always were loyal and I kept them that way.' A thought seemed to come to him. 'Not that it really matters, but what have you done with Kruger?' A sudden burst of wind shook the window; there was a spider's web of cracks in one corner and the rain was seeping through.

'I called a policeman I know,' Ken informed him.

'Are they coming here?'

'Yes.'

The Governor sighed in tiredness, as if he had been awake for months. A clock in the corner passed into a new minute.

Coraline spoke. 'Grandfather would have drowned you if he'd known what you were going to do.'

'Oh yes, miss?' Tooke said bitterly. 'Well, here's something else you just won't credit. You know who is really behind what I did?'

'Tell me.'

'That would be your grandfather himself.'

Ken was struck. 'Simeon?' he said.

'You see, I know what Oliver wrote about our little family intrigue in the last century,' Tooke continued. 'But ask yourself this: where did he hear the story from? All from my dad, of course. And you think that man was telling God's own truth about what really happened? Oh no. I have my doubts about that. You read the story. Do you believe it? The woman running around London like the Lone Ranger, and the old man leaving all his worldly goods to a boy he had barely met? That doesn't strike you as bent out of shape? Oh no. No, miss. My father needed money for his cholera research and a way of getting it fell into his lap. Just a few days of treatment with

258

who-knows-what and the inheritance was his for the taking. And then who is anyone to question his telling of history?'

Ken's mind tumbled. The book, with all its subterfuge, had been a trove of truth for him. But was it really? Maybe there was another layer of lies to dig through.

Tooke was calm as he continued. 'So you see, Mr Kourian, what my father did in that house before me showed me what I had to do there after his example. Because good men do what is right no matter what others would say about it. Like my father, and like Abraham.'

For a while, Ken watched him. There was a light behind the man's eyes that was beginning to flicker and dim. Then Ken spoke. 'Abraham didn't go through with it.'

'Excuse me?'

He met the Governor's gaze. 'He didn't go through with it. The angel of the Lord came down and stopped him. Isaac lived. It was only a test. Of faith.'

There was the muffled sound of an automobile engine. It was pulling up outside.

Tooke's fingers curled into his palms. 'Well, sir, that's fine for the Good Book. But here on earth,' he leaned in to make his point, 'a man's hand is bloodier.'

Ken didn't care about this man's weak, cheap pride. It meant nothing. 'You know, I think I only just understood what the story's about, the way Oliver wrote it,' he said. There was movement somewhere in the house now. The sound echoed off the breaking windows; tread on marble coming closer. 'It's not just about you, or your son, or your father, even. It's really about the past having a will of its own: a will to vindication. To retribution, I guess. The past always wants that.' The leaves of Oliver's book, lying on the cold floor, stirred slightly in the breeze. 'So you can bury it in bricks, or stone, or down in the mud; but when you do that, you only give it time, Governor.'

He watched the web of cracks spread through the glass. *Let it all come down now*, he thought.

THE END

The TURNGLASS

The TURNGLASS

GARETH RUBIN

**SIMON &
SCHUSTER**

London · New York · Sydney · Toronto · New Delhi

First published in Great Britain by Simon & Schuster UK Ltd, 2023

Copyright © Gareth Rubin, 2023

The right of Gareth Rubin to be identified as author
of this work has been asserted in accordance with the
Copyright, Designs and Patents Act, 1988.

1 3 5 7 9 10 8 6 4 2

Simon & Schuster UK Ltd
1st Floor
222 Gray's Inn Road
London WC1X 8HB

Simon & Schuster Australia, Sydney
Simon & Schuster India, New Delhi

www.simonandschuster.co.uk
www.simonandschuster.com.au
www.simonandschuster.co.in

A CIP catalogue record for this book
is available from the British Library

Hardback ISBN: 978-1-3985-1449-2
Trade Paperback ISBN: 978-1-3985-1450-8
eBook ISBN: 978-1-3985-1451-5
Audio ISBN: 978-1-3985-2298-5

Typeset in Sabon by M Rules

Printed and Bound in the UK using 100% Renewable
Electricity at CPI Group (UK) Ltd

MIX
Paper | Supporting
responsible forestry
FSC
www.fsc.org   FSC® C171272

For Phoebe

Tête-bêche (n)
A book split into two parts printed back-to-back and head-to-foot.
Etymology: French *lit*. 'head-to-foot'.

I have recently bought a *tête-bêche*. It is a beguiling thing. Two stories are printed in mutual inversion. One reads the first, then turns the book over and reads the other. These tales are intertwined and parasitic. Beguiling and, I think, a little strange too.

Letter from COUNT HORACE MANN,
20 March 1819

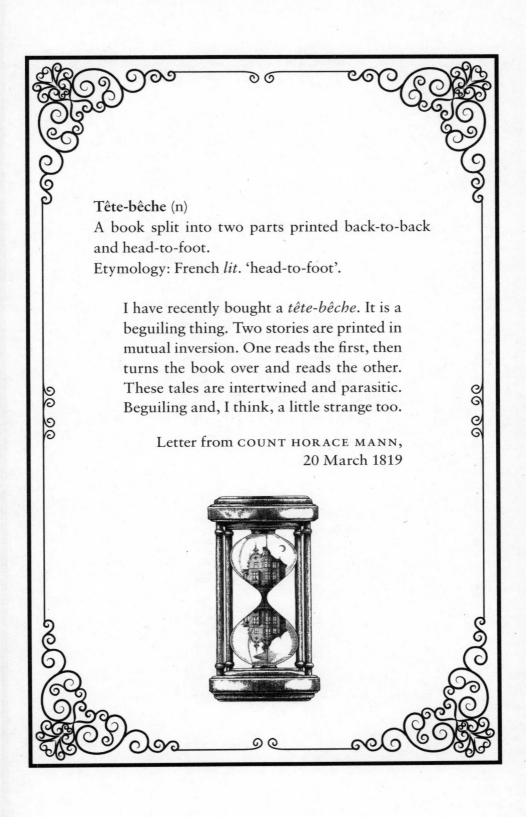

Wilt thou be gone? It is not yet near day:
It was the nightingale, and not the lark,
That pierced the fearful hollow of thine ear;
Nightly she sings on yon pomegranate-tree:
Believe me, love, it was the nightingale.

Juliet, *Romeo and Juliet*, ACT III SCENE V

Chapter 1

London, 1881

Simeon Lee's grey eyes were visible above a kerchief he had tied to keep out the stench of cholera. It was the odour of bodies rotting in doss-houses and mortuaries.

'The King's come knocking,' he muttered.

'Can't we call it something else?' implored his friend Graham, who had a damp scarf bound over his nose and mouth. 'I don't like that name. It implies we owe it something. We don't.'

'And yet it's going to collect.'

'Do you think there will be another epidemic?'

'I hope not.' No, he hoped this was just a local outbreak of the disease.

The two, who had spent years training together for a career healing the sick and reassuring the healthy, walked on through Grub Street, deep in the ancient Roman heart of the city of London. The buildings in the thoroughfare were given over to the print trade – journals and periodicals cataloguing the daily intrigues, pleasures and sadnesses of life. The gutter along the middle of the lane ran with ink.

Simeon cast aside his face covering as they reached their shared lodging. 'We need to find its weak point,' he said. He thought of the disease in animal terms, like a rabid dog. Too small for the eye to see, and yet the bacterium was strong enough to drag waves of men, women and children to their graves. An insidious little murderer. 'Every disease has a weak point.'

Dr Simeon Lee had long, slim features and a long, slim frame that rose lithely up the stairs to their rooms – their garret, in truth – above a print shop whose presses banged without stop around the clock. The place suited him, however, because he could work when most others rested. And it was cheap. Very cheap. After months when his research had stalled due to a lack of money, he needed to save every penny he could.

'It's there, I can feel it's there,' he continued without missing a beat. 'Damn it, we've been able to protect against smallpox for a century. Why not cholera?' He stared out of the grimy tilted window. The sharp darkness of a December smog stared back at him.

'So you have said, once or twice. You're getting a bit

obsessive.' Graham hesitated. 'You know, you're not making yourself too popular at the hospital.'

'You astonish me.' He did not care a cuss what the ancient bewhiskered creatures who ran the King's College Hospital thought of him. Let them work in the tenements and rookeries around St Giles and they might see things differently.

His friend shrugged in dismissal. 'How do you intend to find your miracle cure?'

'How?' He nearly laughed at the question. 'With money. I need money. I need the Macintosh grant.' He undid his tie and dropped onto the fire-damaged settle they had rescued from a pavement in Marylebone. 'Meanwhile, they fall in their houses like it's the Black Death.' He swivelled on the scorched seat, trying to get comfortable. 'A poor man in this street has less chance of making it to the age of thirty than I have of being knighted. Good God, if Robertson and the others would just listen, we could do something about it!' His friend left the air unbroken as Simeon got into his stride, railing against the faculty of the King's College school of medicine who had time and time again demonstrated their utter inability to entertain a single new idea. 'Time and money. That's all it takes to find a cure. Enough time and enough money.'

His anger was born of frustration. Few things could rile him so much as the prospect of his entire body of three years' work growing dusty on his desk. Every month, the grants board of the medical school hummed and hahed over his proposals, and more men, women and children succumbed to the disease.

'Think you'll get it?'

'It's between me and Edwin Grover. Wants it for his stuff on analgesia.'

'He's bright.'

'On paper, yes. In practical terms, he's a cretin. It's all too theoretical. No thought as to how you would actually get a needle in the arm of a seamstress.' He rapped his knuckles on the table in irritation. Grover spent his days in a set of rooms on the upper floor of a rather fine house on Soho Square. He rarely left them. He had no need. No interest, probably.

'What if you don't get it?'

'Then, my friend, I will be out sweeping the street for ha'pennies.' He tugged his forelock.

'Sounds frosty.'

'No doubt it is.'

Graham cleared his throat. 'What about that job in Essex? It would pay.'

Simeon raised his eyebrows in surprise. 'God, I had forgotten all about that.' It had left Simeon's mind almost as soon as he had laid the telegram aside the day before.

'Your uncle, correct?'

'Not quite. My father's cousin.'

'Well, it's a paying job.'

That was true, but it was not an enticing one. 'Ministering to a country parson who has convinced himself he's at death's door even though he's probably fit enough to go ten rounds in the ring with Daniel Mendoza.'

'Simeon, you *need* the cash.'

He brooded. There was absolutely no doubting that point. But he felt like a cheap hireling, treating a man who probably needed no more medical prescription than 'cut down on the port and take a brisk walk from time to time'. And yet the money could restart his progress towards a cure.

'It is an option,' he conceded. 'Though God knows how much I can shake out of him. A country parson isn't exactly rolling in paper.'

'True. Is he at least a pleasant chap?'

Simeon shrugged. 'No doubt one of these quiet old priests who spend all their time reading treatises about Bishop Ussher's calculation that the world is six millennia old.'

'Well, it could be worse. Is it just him in the house?'

'Ah. Well.' Simeon chuckled to himself. 'That is where it does become rather . . . intriguing.'

'How so?'

'It's the family scandal.'

'Scandal? Go on.'

'I don't even know half of it myself – my father wouldn't tell me the details. I believe the parson's brother was killed by his wife in strange circumstances. One of them was mad, I think. I should find out. True, true, a piquant history might be some respite from the boredom of the job. But no, I put my trust in Providence that the Macintosh board will come through first.'

The following afternoon, Simeon sat on a hard, well-polished bench outside a committee room in King's

College. Edwin Grover, primly dressed, sat on an identical bench opposite.

'Still on cholera, are you?' Grover asked.

'Yes. Still on it.'

Grover had no more questions.

An elderly porter creaked out of the committee room. 'Dr Grover? Will you come this way?'

Grover followed him in. The door closed with a bang that echoed up the hall.

It was an hour before he emerged, looking pleased with himself. Simeon swore under his breath at the sight; then it was his turn.

He entered, sat on a wooden chair before a panel of five men and laid out his plans to cure one of the greatest ills of the age.

'Dr Lee. We have been reviewing your application and supporting documents,' one informed him morosely. 'One question kept arising in our minds.'

'What question, sir?'

'What evidence do we have that you will actually get anywhere?'

It was not a friendly question. 'Can you be more specific?'

'Your record seems,' he glanced down at a file, '*inconsequential*. Nothing, we understand, has, in fact, come out of it.'

'I don't believe that—'

'Unlike, say, another candidate's record that shows two papers published in the *Lancet* alone.' Somewhere in the walls, the water pipes banged and hooted with trapped air.

'I have the utmost respect for academic publishing—'

'Whereas all we can see from your work is a series of requests for more funding.'

Simeon gritted his teeth before answering. 'I believe the return will be worth the capital, sir.'

'But what return? And how much capital?'

'I think three hundred pounds would—'

'Three hundred pounds? For a disease now confined to the slums?' There were murmurings of agreement from the rest of the panel. 'It is what those who live in such places are used to. They are born into it. They will live their lives in it.'

'And if you spent as much time in their company as I have, you would know that many of them are better off *not* living in it.'

'Your meaning?' the elderly doctor asked.

'My meaning, sir, is that I can't tell you the number of children younger than five years of age that I have seen who were condemned to nothing more than a short, pain-filled life. At times it has been tempting to cut their lives short then and there rather than watch their inevitable decline.'

'Well, that is between you and God. Here, we are concerned with your application for a grant.'

'Of course. I apologize for becoming distracted. To answer your precise question: we have been unable to identify vaccine-worthy material from human sources. My contention is that non-human animals may possibly produce the material we need. For example, if we expose our closest relatives, gorillas, to the disease, and we extract

their blood, it is possible that consanguination may provide protection against the germ.'

'So now he wants us all swinging from trees,' muttered one of the men.

When Simeon arrived back in his rooms, there was an open bottle of dark wine on the trunk they used as a table. He drained its dregs, glanced at his friend gently snoring in his bed and looked out the window. The street was quiet as the grave.

He noticed then that the bottle had been resting on something: a telegram. The day before, he had sent a cable to his father, asking for details of the murderous events involving his relatives in Essex two years earlier that had set vicious tongues wagging. The reply had been swift. 'Your duties are purely medical. Do them and no more. I understand that nefarious crimes were suspected even before the violence took place. It is no surprise to me. Turnglass House has always had something corrupt and malign about it. Leave it to God and the law.'

Simeon could not help but remark on the fact that his father – not usually a man for flights of poetic fancy – had said it was the house itself that had 'something corrupt and malign' about it, rather than the household. That was curious.

Simeon had never known the distant branch of the family who resided at Turnglass House. He had grown up hundreds of miles to the north, among the stone streets of York, a sole surviving child raised by parents with only a passing interest in him, and sent away for his education at

the age of ten. His father, a solicitor with a dusty practice tending to the needs of dusty aristocrats, accepted medicine as a reasonable profession, although he supposed his mother would probably have preferred if Simeon had set his cap at a more fashionable business in Harley Street. Her subsequent disapproval of a career in researching and combating infectious diseases did nothing to slake her son's thirst for it.

So it's Essex then, he thought to himself.

The island of Ray lies in the salt marshes on the edge of the Essex coast. It is, or is not, an island depending on the tide – resting, as it does, between the open mouths of the Colne and Blackwater estuaries. At high tide it is quite cut off, and the sole house that resides on it feels adrift and isolated. The sea that pours in between the mainland and Ray is topped by a carpet of tangling Sargasso weed, like the fingers of so many drowned men. The weed drifts in its own time through the creeks of the estuary, up to the village of Peldon on the mainland, where the pond outside the Peldon Rose inn has long been a store locker for those supplementing their incomes as oyster fishermen with sales of brandy and tobacco that have been brought from the Continent without paying the ruinous excise duty. The bottom of the pond is wooden and can be lifted to drain away the water, revealing the tar-crusted barrels secreted therein. These barrels supply all the inns of Colchester with wine and all the haberdashers with lace.

Indeed, barely a penny of excise is collected in Essex, even though a quarter of the nation's excisable goods

are imported through that county. And don't imagine that the excise men are unaware of the trade, but since twenty-two of their number were found in a boat one morning some years back with their throats slashed, their friends have been loath to interrupt the local tradesmen.

Beside Ray sits the neighbouring island of Mersea, which is ten times Ray's size and home to fifty-odd homes and a shingle beach known as the Hard. Golden samphire and purple sea lavender decorate both islands, which have a gravel base packed together with clay that attracts wading and floating birds, such as oystercatchers and shelduck.

Yet human visitors to these islands must take care.

At low tide, a narrow causeway from the mainland, the Strood, is revealed by the departing brine. It runs to Ray, across the mile-wide island and then on to Mersea. But anyone who walks it must ensure they have checked the tidal calendar. The danger is not just being marooned on Ray, with its obscure house, but more that anyone caught on the Strood itself as the saltwater rises risks being claimed by the Sargasso weed. Almost every year since the Romans first populated Ray, at least one man or woman has become entwined in that weed. They float there still, making no sound, no complaint, their hands slowly joining.

Simeon could smell sea lavender on the wind as a pony trap set him down outside the Peldon Rose. The driver had laughingly boasted of the local less-than-legal industry

on the way, and Simeon happened to peer into the pond but saw only murky saltwater. The very air tasted of salt, though. It burned a little at the back of his throat, and he tried swallowing two or three times to get rid of it before telling himself he would soon get used to the sensation as part of the landscape.

'Good afternoon, sir,' he heard. The publican, a wiry fellow with huge side-whiskers, was standing in the doorway puffing a long pipe. 'Are ye comin' in?'

'I am, and glad for it,' Simeon replied happily, hefting his travelling bag onto his shoulder and carrying his black leather medical bag in his remaining hand.

'Right then. Ye'll be wantin' somethin' to eat an' a jug-a beer, I shouldn' wonder.'

'That sounds very fine.' He looked over the building. It was a wide, single-storey country inn whitewashed to a dull grey in the winter dun. He was hungry and the prospect of hot food had nourished him for the hour-long ride from Colchester station on his way to see and treat the parson of the parish, Oliver Hawes – Dr Hawes, in fact, that gentleman being a Doctor of Divinity.

'In ye come, then, lad.'

He gladly accepted.

The tap room was populated with seven or eight fellows wearing the clothes of fishermen. Every one was smoking a long, thin white pipe, identical to the landlord's. Simeon wondered if they could somehow tell their own from their friends'. Three women had called in too, forming a trio of Fates in the corner, silently examining him.

'Come on in, lad,' the landlord reiterated. 'Warm

welcome always a' the Rose. Put yer bag down. Tha's it. Jenny! Jenny! Some bread an' twelve – no, sixteen oysters. He looks a hungry one. Sharpish, girl.' He made no attempt to ask if the order met his new patron's needs. Within seconds, Jenny, a girl of about ten years, appeared with bread and a mass of oysters. The landlord handed over a jug of small beer and motioned for Simeon to eat standing at the bar. The whole inn was waiting for him to start eating or announce his business, it seemed. He chose to begin with the food. But if he had been expecting conversation to resume as he ate, he was mistaken. The air remained still, apart from the sound of him, or one other, drinking back ale. Ten minutes later, he had finished his meal.

'Tha'll be four shillings, three pence an' one story,' the landlord informed him.

Simeon chuckled. 'And what story would that be?'

'To tell us all wha' ye're doing here.'

It seemed perfectly friendly, rather than some sort of warning, so Simeon had no compunction regarding a reply. 'I'm a doctor. I'm on my way to look after a relative of mine.'

'Who's tha', then?'

Simeon wondered how they addressed or referred to his almost-uncle. 'Dr Hawes.'

'Parson Hawes!' The landlord's eyebrows shot up and there was a low rumbling in the room. 'Ye're his relative.'

'My father is his cousin.'

'Indeed? Never thought of the parson's family as bein' from anywheres bu' here.'

'I've never actually met him, myself.'

'No, well, if ye're no' from Mersea or Peldon, ye'll no' be doin' so. I heard he was a-sick.' There was a general muttering, but the landlord was clearly the spokesman for them all.

'I'll see him tonight and find out.'

The landlord was concerned. 'Wait 'til the mornin'. Tide's comin' in.'

'Thank you, really,' Simeon replied. 'But I must be going tonight. Dr Hawes is expecting me.'

'Morty, will you take him?' the publican asked one of the knot of men who were making no bones about listening to the conversation.

'I'm the ferryman,' Morty volunteered. He was over sixty and small, but fit as a man who rows in the creeks and seas around Essex must be. 'Ferryman, me.'

'You look a good one.'

'But I'm off home now. Me fire.'

'Is the Strood safe now?' the landlord asked.

'Prob'ly. Won' be running on, bu' he'll get 'cross.'

'Well, that sounds fine to me,' Simeon said. He wanted to get on. 'Will you point me on the way?'

The full population of the inn glanced out the window. There was no rain, but it was past six o'clock and fully winter-dark.

'Ye'll need a lamp,' said the landlord, sounding uncertain that a youngster from the city – probably London – would even know to bring such a thing.

'I have one.'

'Wadin' boots?'

'I didn't know I needed them. I'll cope.' He looked down at his leather ankle boots. Well, they had seen better days anyway.

'See how ye get on, then. Straigh' down tha' way. The road becomes the Strood. Ye can't get the wrong place once ye're on Ray. Turnglass House's the only one on the island.'

He was satisfied. 'It's a strange name. How did the place come by it?'

'Look a' the weather vane as ye come in. Ye'll see.' The publican hesitated a little, as if deciding whether to broach a difficult subject. 'No' a bad old stick, Parson Hawes. A bit funny a' times. Bu' he's been good to his sister-in-law after . . . well, ye know.' He seemed to be probing to see exactly what Simeon did know.

The family scandal. These people most assuredly knew more about it than he did. It would be worth talking, he thought.

'Yes, I know she killed his brother.'

The landlord looked a little relieved to discover that. 'Righ' well. Good an' tha'. Wouldn' wan' it to be a shock t' hear.'

'It isn't.' His father had given him the bald details, but had been vague about precisely how Florence had killed her husband, James, brother to Oliver. 'But I'm in the dark about exactly what happened.'

'In the dark, eh?' He sounded a little sceptical and mulled his response. 'Ask Morty.'

Morty glared at Simeon. 'So, you don' know, then?'

'Not really, no.'

Morty shrugged. 'Well, 's your family. Your business.' Odd to think that the man was right – it was his business, even though he had never met any of the people concerned. Family, he thought, could be a well of strange connections. 'I took the body – yer uncle James or whate'er-ye-calls-'im – away from the house. Terrible state 'e were in.' Simeon felt a curiosity, both professional and human. 'Puffed-up face. Yellow. The bad'd set in.' He paused. '*Infaction* ye calls it, lad.' He pronounced the word carefully.

'What infection? What happened?'

Morty shrugged as if rehearsing a tale everyone knew. 'She gashed his face. Threw a decanter 'gainst it an' the glass smashed. Bad set in. Turned his flesh black here, yellow there.' He pointed to his own cheek and jaw. 'All puffed up like a pig.'

So Florence had cut James's face deeply enough for blood poisoning to kill him. It must have been quite an assault.

'He were a pretty one afore tha',' one of the three Fates called over. 'Prize o' the county.'

'Why did she do it?' Simeon asked. It was a prurient interest, but everyone else knew, so why shouldn't he?

Morty shook his head mournfully. 'Never asked. Bad thin' to happen here. Don' wan' go too low inta it. I jus' put the coffin in the boat, rowed up t' Virley and carried him to St Mary's. He's six feet under now. Go an' ask him any questions ye have.'

'Morty,' the Fate admonished him.

'Well.' He supped some of his drink ruminatively. There

was a pause as they all joined him. 'Ye know where Mrs Florence is now?'

'No.'

Morty glanced at each of his friends in turn. They returned his heavy look. 'Ye will do soon.'

Chapter 2

The words rang in Simeon's ears as he thanked all for their advice and paid his bill. He felt the sting of the salt at the back of his throat again as he stepped outside and set off once more, tramping the single road that would become the Strood. With the inn behind him, he felt quite alone under the night sky and he enjoyed the brief solitude.

The ground became soft, warning of a marsh, and soon the turf beside the path turned to watery mush, lights from the Rose flickering on its black surface. They seemed like signals from lighthouses to him, flitting back and forth. Then he was on the Strood proper. It was just wide enough for a man to pass along and at its end he made out a broad

black mass that bore no flickering reflections: Ray, where his relation awaited him.

Each foot he set down seemed to press lower in the mud. The glittering, glassy water either side of the causeway mocked his laborious progress, and his heels, then his feet and then his ankles sank in. He began to worry that his knees would go in too and that he would be held there until the tide rose above his shoulders. But he chose to trust Morty's assessment that the path was solid enough – just – and to power on. And little by little the way became firmer, until he was on solid land.

Ray, the island that came and went with the tides.

He turned up the flame on his oil lamp and the beam raked the ground for a good distance. He had bought it from a ship's chandler who had assured him it was as strong a light as he would find anywhere, strong enough for ships to find each other a mile away.

It was a bleak place that the light revealed. Deathly so. *Whyever did anyone settle here?* he wondered.

He looked up. A dim prickle of stars was scattered across the sky; but there was a void on the horizon where they were blotted out, where something black and wide loomed up from the waterlogged ground. Turnglass House, the only building on Ray.

A single bright window near its tip was the only sign of habitation.

Coming closer and raking his strong lamp beam over it, Simeon found that the house was three storeys high and wide as a London villa. Beside it stood what looked like a small stable block. A spacious home for a country curate,

although even on the brightest spring day the vista must have been a dreary one.

Turnglass House. He thought of the publican's instruction to look at the weather vane in order to understand the name. Peering up to the roof and angling the ship's lantern as best he could, he saw an unusual vane indeed. It was shaped like an hourglass, with a stream of sand cascading from one bulb to the other; but rather than being constructed of metal, the vane was made entirely from glass, and it glinted in the beam. It had to be lead crystal to withstand the wind and rain with which it was constantly buffeted. As he watched, the vane spun languidly, with a whine. The wind must have been changing.

Reaching the house, Simeon found an old-fashioned bell-pull protruding from the brickwork. He tugged it hard, to be answered by a tolling inside, then footsteps and the drawing back of bolts. *Why lock your door on Ray?* he wondered. *Who would come uninvited?*

'Dr Lee?' A cheery, buxom housekeeper was standing aside and he could feel warmth blasting out from the wide hallway.

'Yes.'

'Won't you come in, sir?' He gladly complied.

The house seemed to have been decorated a hundred years earlier. Busts of long-dead poets lined one wall, and a large oil painting of men on a hunt was set above the staircase. The most striking picture, however, was a portrait over the fireplace that showed a very handsome woman with rich brown hair, standing before a glittering house.

'I'm Tabbers, sir. Eliza Tabbers.'

Simeon set down his carryall. 'Are there any other servants here?'

'Yes. There's Cain – Peter Cain. He's the footman, gardener, what you will. We both live out, sir. On Mersea. I come just after dawn to light the fires and I normally leave around seven. Cain's in from eight until five.'

Yes, it would be hard to attract many to live in at a place such as this – just a mile from the nearest village, and yet remote and cut off at the sea's will.

He handed her his overcoat. She placed it in a press beside a table, upon which a jumble of lamps and rusted iron keys resided. 'Would you please take me to Dr Hawes?'

'Right away.'

She led him up the stairs and along a corridor where every surface was covered in rugs, drapes or wall hangings. It all added to a peculiar atmosphere where the air hung without motion and every tread was thick and noiseless. The upper floor, he found, sported three doors off a long corridor, each padded in coloured leather: green, red, blue. Two more at the end were plain wood.

They stopped at the green one, and the housekeeper tapped: three times softly, then three times hard. She was answered by a painful groan from within. At that sign, she showed Simeon in.

It was an extraordinary sight that met him. A church-at-night darkness was pierced by fingers of light from a partly shuttered oil lamp on an octagonal table in the centre of the room. There were gas lamps on the wall, but

they were unlit. Instead, the cobweb of beams from the brass table showed Simeon that he was in a library – but one quite different from any he had seen in even the few grand houses that had admitted him.

It rose two complete storeys, almost to the roof of the house, with a row of windows on each storey. Ladders around the room gave access to the books that lined every wall from bottom to top. He realized that the staircase he had climbed only came to the first floor of the house, so it must have been built this way with a cliff-like upper level. It would be heaven for bibliophiles, hell for those who loathed the written word.

Within the room were the silhouettes of reading desks and tables with piles of books. Deep seats had been chosen as platforms for consuming the pages. They were arranged in a sort of ring, and in the centre of it all was a sopha, on which a thin, balding man in his forties had fallen back to snoozing, with the octagonal table and its lamp by his side. The far end of the room was in full shadow, though a flickering reflection of the lamp, like the lights on the dark water outside, suggested a wide panel of glass there.

'Dr Hawes,' the housekeeper hemmed.

Slowly, the man's eyes peeled open behind thick square spectacles. 'Hello? Oh,' the older man's voice wobbled. 'Oh, you must be Winston's boy.'

'I am, sir.'

'Oh, I am glad you came. So glad. Come, come.' He had a kindly tone and tried to beckon Simeon to him, but his hand gave up halfway through the motion.

Simeon approached and offered his palm. The patient

gently gripped and shook it. 'Shall I begin by examining you, sir?' Simeon asked, curious as to what he might find by way of disease or hypochondriasis. 'We may speak as I do so.'

'Examine me? Oh, yes, yes. Of course.'

'May I turn on the gaslights?'

'I am sorry, I find their light quite painfully harsh. I prefer the oil lamp.'

'Of course.' The servant withdrew as Simeon opened his medical bag to take out his stethoscope. 'Now, would you please tell me what the problem is?'

'I, oh, I fear I may be dying,' the parson whispered. 'My heart, you know, and I have such sweats and pains. All over. Pains in my joints, in my organs. My head. And my teeth chatter so. But then I have always been cold.'

Simeon thought the house was warm. There was no fire in the grate, so it must have been one of the systems for wafting hot air through vents throughout the building. 'I shall listen to your heart, then I will take a history,' he explained. The patient duly opened his shirt. Confounding Simeon's expectations of an imaginary illness, that muscle was, in fact, anything but healthy. For a few seconds it would gallop, then flutter and then thud deeply. *Not good*, he thought to himself. 'And when did this begin?'

'Oh, now let me think. Yes, it was Thursday. I am usually strong, despite the chills I feel. But as soon as I woke, I felt a pounding in my head. I took to bed, thinking it was merely an unusually bad chill. But today I am far worse – the pains wrack me and I cannot stand or sleep.'

That was five days of sickness. It certainly seemed

worse than a common infection. If they had been in the city, Simeon would have immediately pointed to King Cholera. But out on the sparsely populated coast it was practically unheard of. Malaria? The ground was marshy, but that disease had been eradicated long ago in these parts.

'Have you eaten anything unusual? Perhaps under-cooked meat?'

'No. Indeed, I eat little meat. I find it excites the blood too much.'

'I see. Could your housekeeper have prepared some unusual mushrooms for you, perhaps?'

'None. Simple bread, cheese, occasional fish or mutton, common vegetables. That is all. And Mrs Tabbers and Cain eat the same dishes at the same time – our household is small, there is little point preparing separate meals.'

'Do you take alcohol?'

The parson looked a little sheepish. 'I usually have a drop of brandy as a nightcap, but have not had the stomach for it since I first became ill.' He waved to a small barrel in a corner of the room. A silver ladle lay beside it, ready to scoop out the drink. It seemed that in these parts, where the excise men feared to tread, even the parsons drank from barrels.

'I think it best to stay away from alcohol for now,' Simeon said. 'So no more nightcaps.' A sound – a slight creaking – made his head turn towards the gloomy end of the room.

'If you say so.'

Simeon went through every potential cause of the

curate's illness that he could dredge from his memory of medical school and practice. There seemed nothing apparent. Bad food or drink remained the most likely culprit, however, so he expected he would be there a couple of days while the patient recovered. Then he would return to London, where he would be a few guineas closer to resuming his research. 'I shall give you a restorative and we shall hope that has you up on your feet soon,' he said with confidence.

'If you say so. You are, after all, the qualified one.'

Simeon smiled at the parson's pleasant manners and drew a bottle from his bag. He poured a measure of the restorative into a tumbler. It was drunk, drawing a slight smacking of lips at the bitter taste. 'I shall oversee the preparation of your meals myself. Perhaps there is something your housekeeper has missed.'

'She has been loyal to me for twenty years, or thereabouts,' the older man said. 'It will not have been deliberate.'

Simeon's brow furrowed. 'No, I am sure it won't.' Momentarily, he wondered why such a possibility should have occurred to Dr Hawes.

'London must be a most exciting city for a young man,' the parson said in an off-hand fashion.

Simeon thought he detected the slightest hint of envy in the divine's voice. 'It's certainly invigorating. Sometimes one wishes for a quiet life, though.'

'Ray and Mersea could not be described as invigorating, I fear,' the older man said. 'But I hope you will stay a few days.'

'Until you are better. Of course.' Another creak from the invisible end of the library made him wonder if there was some pet hiding in the shadows and he glanced again that way but could make nothing out.

'And we have not discussed your fee. Would five guineas a day be sufficient?'

'That would be very generous.' Simeon gazed around at the shelves that enclosed them. 'Tell me, how many books do you have here?'

'Books? Oh, three thousand at a guess.'

'That's a good size for a library. I—' He cut himself off as a louder sound from the gloom made him start. 'What is that sound? Do you own a dog?'

'A dog? Good heavens, no.' Parson Hawes peered up at his relation with mystification on his face. 'You do not know? Oh, I would have thought you would have been informed at the Peldon Rose, if not before.' The Rose was clearly the local hub of social intelligence. 'Well, it is best that you take the lamp and look for yourself.' Slightly suspicious of the roundabout way of informing him, Simeon lifted the oil lamp from the table. It threw a yellow glare around no more than two yards of the floor, illuminating stacks of books and a series of rugs – Persian or Turkish. Fine quality. He went towards the dark end of the room. 'But be careful, my boy,' the older man warned. As he moved, Simeon saw the beam glint again on a reflective surface like the black water of the estuary. Glass. The end of the room was indeed one huge glass panel and the light from the lamp seemed to flit about in its sheen. Then another sound, this time a rustling, emanated from it. He

saw his own reflection in the dark pane, like a mirror, coming forward with the lamp in his hand.

As he came closer, the light fell properly on the foot of the glass, rapidly rising up to its full height. And what it revealed seemed strange indeed. The panel was not the end wall of the room, but a transparent partition between the part occupied by Parson Oliver Hawes, with his three thousand volumes, and another smaller section, cut off from the public realm.

'This is rather unusual,' Simeon said.

'It is necessary. Such rage.'

What rage? Simeon wondered, examining the murky pane.

Suddenly, something, a patch of pale colour, appeared behind the glass: a moon-like disc that retreated into the black and disappeared. And something green flashed close to the floor. What had he just seen? Surely it wasn't—? He had an idea, but it seemed insanity itself.

He lifted his lamp to make sure. The beam struggled to penetrate the dark mirror, but he pressed it right to the surface and the light managed to seep through. The scene it lit struck him cold. For sealed behind that glass partition were a writing desk, a table set for dining, a single chair, a chaise longue and shelves lined with books. And motionless on the chaise, wearing a light green dress, sat a woman with dark hair and darker eyes that were silently fixed upon his own.

He watched her, her irises locked to his, her body almost imperceptibly lifting and falling with her breath. Her lips parted, as if about to speak.

30

'You know of my sister-in-law?' Parson Hawes's voice seemed to come from a long way off. The woman's lips closed again, pulling into a wry, sardonic smile. Then she cocked her head to one side, looking around Simeon to glance at the parson. So this was Florence, who had killed James, the parson's brother, by throwing a decanter so ferociously against his cheek that it broke and an infection set in to pollute his blood. 'We are safe, she cannot get out.' That was clear. This was a cell – a glass-fronted cell bedecked with fine furniture, but a cell just the same. 'Simeon, my boy?' Parson Hawes asked.

The smile remained. It stayed with him.

'I had no idea of this.'

She was, perhaps, ten years older than him, and the curve of her chin and cheek marked her as a rare beauty. In country parts, he thought, where men were sure and direct rather than kowtowing to lineage, she would have been aware of it. She might have used it. And it was a beauty he had seen before, for she was undoubtedly the subject of the portrait hanging above the fireplace in the hall.

'Her presence surprises you.'

'Surprises me! It amazes me,' he stated, returning to himself. 'What is she doing there? How can this be right?'

'It was here or the madhouse,' the parson declared with a note of annoyance, as if angered by an insinuation behind the question. 'After she killed James, the judge was ready to put her away. I have done all I can to keep her safe. But if you think she would be better in a straitwaistcoat at Bedlam, please tell me.'

The curate's voice disappeared again as Simeon stared at Florence. She was a striking woman, it was certain. And she was holding his gaze without the slightest concern, as if he was the one imprisoned behind that pane.

'So, she lives in this?'

'She has a bed chamber and washroom behind. You see that doorway.' There was a narrow opening at the rear of her cell. 'So she has privacy if need be. And her food is the same we eat.'

'I see . . .' His mind was racing. No human being should be held like an exhibit at the zoological gardens. And yet she had killed a man, and life in Bedlam would certainly be far, far worse. Simeon had been required as part of his training to enter that terrible asylum: inmates chained to the wall day and night, rocking themselves into madness; others who would scream that they were quite sane, but would have torn at your throat with their teeth given the chance. Very occasionally a patient would be freed, having been cured of their mental affliction, but it was a rarity and only for the mildest patients. No, keep her out of Bedlam if at all possible. Cruel as it seemed, perhaps she really was better off here.

'It has not been easy. It has been a hard balance,' Hawes continued, anger subsiding into something like regret. 'Hard on all of us.' He struggled to wipe his brow with a handkerchief.

Simeon wanted to speak to her, and yet Florence bore no sign of wishing to speak to him. 'How does she get her meals?'

'The hatch at your feet.' Simeon looked down. There

was a rectangular panel in the glass that could be lifted up, large enough to put a tray of food through but little else.

'There must be a way out for her.'

'In order to ensure full security – which is what she needs – there is not. She is quite bricked in. Linen is changed weekly in order to maintain cleanliness, passed through the hatch. Water flows to and from her apartment. Other than that, there is no movement in or out. It has to be thus in order to satisfy the legal authorities.'

Legal authorities be damned, Simeon thought to himself. 'Florence,' he said. And he was sure that her pupils changed at the sound of her name. 'Can you hear me? I am related to you – by marriage. I am Dr Simeon Lee.' He waited for a response, but she remained quite still. The change in her eyes was the only one he would see. 'I am here to treat Dr Hawes for an illness.' And did he then see the slightest alteration in her face? Perhaps the edges of her mouth twitched up a fraction. But the light was low, so he had probably only seen a shift in the lamp's glitter.

'I doubt she will answer you,' Hawes informed him. 'She speaks when she likes, but that is not often.'

Simeon remained fixed on her. 'Will you speak to me, Florence? But a word? A single word.'

'She will not, tonight.'

'How can you know?'

'Because she has had her nightcap too.'

Simeon looked around. 'What do you mean?' He detected something threateningly innocent in those words.

'The doctors who examined her said that she was

suffering from an excess of sugar in the blood. The best way to calm her down was a little laudanum daily and nightly.'

Tincture of laudanum – opium dissolved in brandy – was a common prescription for those of an excited nature. Simeon had indeed seen it used with good effect at calming those whose brains were too hot, but he was not certain that it would have been the ethical course of action in this case. 'She has had a dose tonight?' he asked.

'Her usual amount. The tumbler by her hand.'

For the first time Simeon saw that on a small octagonal table, the twin to the one outside, an empty tumbler lay on its side. And he also saw her look down at it. She was certainly following the conversation. So, her mind was awake even if her body was sluggish. *Of course*, Simeon thought, *that could be the cruellest trick of all to play on her.* Imprisonment behind glass was one thing. Imprisonment in a paralysed body would be a hundred times worse. 'Where do you draw it from?'

The parson indicated a large, lockable secretary cabinet in the corner and produced a key from his pocket. 'The bottle is quite safe, I assure you.'

Simeon tried again to reach her. 'Florence, I'm a doctor. Is there anything I can do to help you?' His hope was not high for a response, but he waited for one nonetheless. It did not come.

'You are a good child, Simeon. Your heart does you credit. But some rivers cannot be crossed.'

He brooded. 'How long has she been in there?'

'Since soon after she killed James. Nearly two years.'

'And she has not been out since?'

'Not for, oh, a little more than a year. For a while she was calmer and it seemed safe, you see. There was a door then, onto the corridor, and I would allow her to sit in here with me of an evening. But then a ... change came over her and I felt it better to have the doorway sealed up.'

Better for you, Simeon thought. *But for her?*

A spark flew up from the lamp so that its reflection rose in the dark mirror. She followed its progress, then returned her gaze to Simeon. He wanted to know the history, how his relations had descended to this strange state of affairs. 'Dr Hawes,' he said.

'Oh, you may as well call me "uncle". I know it is not correct in a strict literal sense, but it will make things easier.'

'Uncle.' He turned to face the parson. 'I know only how she killed your brother. May I know why?'

The divine sat deeper into his sopha, seemingly pressed down by the memory. 'She suspected James of ill behaviour. That is all that I am prepared to say.' The slightest flush of shame appeared on his pale cheeks.

'I understand.' But far from his curiosity being sated by the reply, it was fired.

'I am not convinced that you do,' Hawes admonished him. 'My boy, Ray and Mersea are remote places. More remote than you would understand by looking at a map. Remoteness is bred in spirit.' He shifted his weight. 'Would you be so kind as to pour me a glass of water?' For the first time, Simeon moved away from the woman behind the glass, though he felt her still – perhaps more

35

sharply, even, for not being able to see her. He went to the cabinet where a few bottles stood. The water looked clean enough and he handed a glass of it to the parson. 'Thank you. I was telling you about the spirit of this strange outcrop of humanity. Well, I am forty-two years old. My brother is – was – six years younger. Florence is in between us. Her father is the local squire and magistrate, Mr Watkins. A good gentleman. Due to our ages and the fact that the only other children for miles around were the offspring of fishermen and – well, how should I say?'

'. . . smugglers?' Simeon suggested.

'Let us say, men who are strangers to the excise laws,' Hawes conceded. 'Now, as a man of the cloth, I of course always insist that anything that comes within my house has been properly taxed.' Simeon looked over at the little brandy barrel with the silver ladle ready at its side; he would not have placed money on it being entirely above board. 'And so, we became close. James and Florence were, dare I say it, wilder children than I was.'

'Do tell.' He was still aware that one of the subjects of the conversation was listening intently, albeit in the haze of the poppy.

The parson chuckled at the memories. 'Well, I recall one time I was here happily reading away, Roman history probably, that was my great interest. It still is. They were at Watkins's house on Mersea being tutored in French. The first moment their tutor turned his back, they climbed out the window, ran down to the Hard, cast away their outer clothes and swam through the creeks to the Rose.

They turned up in the middle of the day, soaking wet and wearing only their undergarments. Then they had the gall to hire Morty to row them back again, on the promise of payment from my father.' He laughed gently again. 'Scallywags.'

'They sound it.'

'Oh, but they could be wild. Raging too. When James was, oh, sixteen or thereabouts, they were at the county fair and he was paying all sorts of attention to a farm girl. Florence became quite savage and left the poor girl with a black eye. Well, not very genteel, but they were children. Only children.' A more recent memory seemed to overtake the curate and he stared towards Florence on the darkened side of the room.

'Why does she sit in the dark like that? Does she have no lamp?'

'She has one. Sometimes she lights it. Sometimes she prefers the gloom, I think. It is her choice,' Hawes sighed. 'I am very tired now. I think I shall go to bed, though I doubt I will sleep. I will point you to your room.' He pulled himself up. Simeon tried to help, but he was gently repelled. 'No, I can do this, my boy.' He shuffled towards the door.

Reluctantly, Simeon followed, walking away from the cell that his distant relation occupied. As the light drifted away from it, it returned to shadow; but he felt her watching him still.

'The red door is your chamber. I hope you sleep well,' Hawes said on the landing as he walked painfully away to his own bed.

Simeon bade him goodnight and entered the far bed-room. It was pleasant enough, he found, if a little musty and old-fashioned. *Like the word 'smuggler'*, he thought to himself. He undressed, got into the bed and pulled up the blanket, sorting through all he had heard that evening. He knew he should have been considering what could be causing Parson Hawes's ailment, but he could only think of the woman behind the glass.

Chapter 3

A flock of gulls was cawing when Simeon woke, wheeling noisily about, looking for any pickings on the sea or land. After washing in a basin, he made his way downstairs. As he passed through the entrance hall, he noticed again the portrait above the fireplace and examined it more closely. It was of Florence, he knew now, her head and shoulders under a very bright sky – so bright, it could hardly have been England. No, it had to be somewhere else. She wore a sun-yellow silk dress and had been painted perhaps ten or twelve years earlier – when she had been about Simeon's current age – in front of a most unusual house constructed

almost entirely of glass. The artist had demonstrated great talent because there was something almost disturbingly lifelike about it.

Mrs Tabbers was eating cheese and bread in the kitchen, alongside the manservant, Cain, a hardy-looking man with tufts of bright red hair sprouting here and there from his head, nose and ears. Cain was chewing, mashing the same mouthful for so long that Simeon found it astonishing.

'Good morning.'

'Good morning, sir,' Mrs Tabbers replied.

'Is Dr Hawes awake?'

'He is.' It was a little after eight by the clock nailed to the wall.

'I want to make sure he eats well. I'll take him his breakfast, if that's all right.'

Mrs Tabbers seemed amused by the idea. 'You go and serve him fine, sir. He's in the library. Had to help him there myself.' She stacked a tray with bread and milk.

'It is possible that Dr Hawes has eaten something disagreeable.'

'My cooking is very good, sir,' she returned curtly. 'The parson tells me so often.'

'I'm sure that is true.' Not wishing to offend the woman providing him with sustenance, he took a piece of bread to prove it. 'It is possible, though, that something unseen made its way into his meal. Do you eat the same food as he does?'

'Exactly the same. Both of us. No point making it twice, is there?'

40

'No,' he agreed. 'And the water, milk – all comes from the same source?'

Cain spoke. 'All the same,' he said, in a tone that suggested he thought they were being accused of something and he did not appreciate it.

'Wine?'

'Rare,' Mrs Tabbers told him. 'Christmastide. Communion wine, of course. But that's just a drop and the whole congregation drinks it.'

He was getting nowhere. 'And what about the brandy nightcap he has?'

She shrugged. 'A drop most nights. He finished a barrel a day or two before he fell sick.'

'Which day, precisely, was that?'

'He fell ill on, let me see, Thursday. First of the month.' That concurred with what the parson had said.

'We should test it,' Simeon replied. The timing was interesting. It could conceivably be the source of the priest's sickness, although the continued worsening of his condition suggested it was unlikely. 'I don't know who would want to try it, though.'

'I'll tes' it,' Cain offered.

'What?'

'The brandy. I'll tes' it. Make sure i's safe to drink.'

Mrs Tabbers huffed. 'Fine Quaker you are, drinking. What about that pledge they make you take?' she muttered.

'Quiet, woman,' he snapped. 'Fer medical reasons.'

Simeon interposed. 'You understand it could be a risk.'

'I'll give it ter me dog firs'. Nelson. He likes a drop o'

brandy.' There was no accounting for the risks some people would take for drink. Cain checked the clock. 'Do it 'bout nine. Jus' got ter see ter tha' foal first,' he told Mrs Tabbers.

'What foal?' Simeon asked.

Cain shovelled more food into his mouth and spoke as he chewed. 'Lame 'un. Born few weeks ago ou' of parson's mare. See if i's better now. If no' . . . well.'

'Well what?'

'A drain, isn' it? Costs good money. No good ter the parson nor me. Don' wan' a lame animal.'

'I see.'

'No' a good sign, lame foal.' He chewed his food slowly.

It occurred to Simeon that country folk put great store by the health of their animals, and there was a lot of augury in how the livestock fared. So yes, an ill foal was a curse. 'Are you from Mersea?'

'Born 'n' bred,' he grunted. 'Never been more'n ten mile away.'

That could be useful. 'So you know all the secrets around these parts,' Simeon said jovially. After seeing Florence the previous night, there were certainly some secrets that intrigued him.

Cain put down his cup. 'Ye have somethin' ye wan' ter ask? Ask it.'

The reaction was more aggressive than he had expected; still, there was no point denying his curiosity. 'What happened between Florence and James?'

Cain cut a hunk of bread, buttered it and ate, seemingly stringing out the action to decide on a form of words. 'They say Mr James was involved in thin's.'

'Peter!' Mrs Tabbers warned him.

'Well, i's the truth.'

'What sort of things?' Simeon asked.

'That's enough gossip,' the housekeeper said firmly.

'Mrs Tabbers . . .'

'*No*. Enough gossip.' She poured herself a cup of milk from a jug and set it down as a punctuation point to the conversation.

Simeon thought it best to retire from pressing them for now. He would catch more flies with honey than vinegar and so he left the room, taking the tray of the parson's food to the library.

He entered, keeping his line of vision firmly on his patient, to find Hawes on the same seat as the previous evening, a blanket drawn over him.

'Good morning,' the parson mumbled.

As he set the food down, Simeon could hold back no longer and slowly turned his head to gaze at the other end of the room. She was seated, quietly watching, wearing the same green dress. It might have been the only one she was allowed. She could have been there all night. Did she sleep? Simeon would have been unsurprised to discover that that pleasure, that release, was unknown to her.

But he had to tend to his patient, who was in poorer health than the previous night. His skin was pale, and when Simeon measured his pulse rate, he found it faster and lighter, indicating a worsening of whatever condition ailed him.

'My boy,' the curate said, 'I feel as if an army is marching about in my head. An army.'

Simeon carefully lowered his uncle's wrist. 'I'm sorry to hear that. Have a little breakfast, it will be of benefit.' The parson ate and drank some, before beginning to shiver and collapsing back onto the sopha. 'It's true you're a little worse, sir. But I'm confident you will pull through.' He was lying. The man's signs of life were far weaker than before. It would have been no surprise if he had fainted then and there. 'If you could—'

'Someone is poisoning me!' Hawes suddenly cried, arching his body up, then crashing it back down.

It took the doctor a moment to get over his astonishment. 'Why in Heaven's name would you think that?' he asked.

Hawes panted and recovered a little. 'I am not without enemies.'

Another astonishing claim. The man was a country curate, not a Turkish pasha. 'Enemies? Who?' But despite his scepticism, one identity inevitably suggested itself. Simeon looked to the glass box. She was watching, quite unperturbed. 'Do you mean Florence?'

'Her. Others.'

Simeon's overarching doubt returned at the suggestion of a whole cabal of assassins on the island of Ray. 'And they are capable of poisoning you?'

'More than capable. More than capable,' he insisted. 'You must find out what it is they gave me. There has to be a cure.'

It was not unknown for patients to become delirious during fevers, blaming phantoms for their sickness. Most likely, the priest was suffering a perfectly normal organic

disease or possibly accidental food poisoning. And yet the vehemence of his claim, the history of homicide at Turnglass House and the subsequent strange incarceration of the parson's sister-in-law gave rise to creeping, amorphous doubts in Simeon's mind.

Whatever the cause, it would be best to keep the patient calm. 'I must say, if you have consumed poison, either accidentally or by someone's deliberate action, it is a strange poison that continues to worsen continuously for six or more days after ingestion. I don't know of any that works that way,' he said. 'And the food and drink that you take has all been consumed by your servants. They have not suffered so much as a stomach complaint.' He went over to the new barrel of brandy. 'You have drunk from this, haven't you?'

'It was new the day before the illness took me. I have not drunk from it since then.'

'That makes it very unlikely to be the source of any harmful compound, though Cain's keen to test it anyway.'

'Oh, let him. Why not?'

At that, Hawes, exhausted by the interview, turned over and fell to dozing. Simeon watched over him for a while and, with little else to occupy him, took the time to meander among the bookshelves. They were a strikingly diverse collection – from the religious to natural history to prose fiction. *The Twelve Caesars* here; a collection of Donne's poetry there.

Tap. Tap. Tap. He looked up. The sound of slow, light clinking of glass against glass. It was coming from

Florence's end of the room, where she was rhythmically tapping a tumbler on the partition between them.

'Florence?' he said. 'Do you want something?' She unfurled a finger to point. Simeon followed its line to the priest's octagonal table. On the surface, suggesting recent usage, was a book. He picked it up to find it was a slim novelette. *The Gold Field*, it was named, in appropriately golden lettering. 'You want to read this?' he asked, holding it towards her. 'You want *me* to read it?' Her hand dropped to her side and she returned to her chair.

Simeon turned its dry pages.

I'm going to tell you a story. It isn't a nice story, it isn't really a nasty one. It's just a story. It's a true one, though, and I can put my hand on my heart and swear to that because I was there.

You've probably never heard of me. You might have heard of my father, though. If you're from California, you probably heard his name every time you went to buy whiskey, let alone glass for your windows. I don't think I'm giving away any family secrets when I say the ban on alcoholic drink was a godsend to his bank account. Before Congress decided we all had to take the Pledge, he was a doing-okay man of business. But a cousin in the city of Vancouver – that's in British Columbia, if you don't know – and a natural disposition to make money by any means necessary meant that through the Twenties the barrels came sailing down the Pacific and Dad swapped them for cash. Lots of cash.

The first thing Dad bought was a new suit. The second was a wife. The third was a house made out of glass.

Not all of it, of course. There were timbers and there were metal frames and wood floors. But the walls were almost all glass. That made it hot in the summer, cold in the winter. My father bought it from a man who had built the place and then lost all his money in a stocks scam that Dad said he really should have spotted as a con. The seller thanked my father for taking it off his hands, as if he was doing the fellow a big favour, though the truth was that my father had seen some carrion lying out on the grassland and swooped down to gobble it up.

And now we begin the story, because it has to begin. It begins in February 1939.

Simeon closed the book, keeping his thumb between the leaves, and examined it more closely. Florence had wanted him to read this, so there had to be some significance he could not yet see. The book was no larger than the average cheap novelette, but was handsomely bound in veined crimson leather. Who was the author? He checked the spine. It carried the name 'O. Tooke'. Whoever he was, he was writing about the future and describing it as the past. He opened the pages again.

The snow had come down the day before. We don't see it very often – no more than every few years out on the coast, where our house was built. Back when most of California had no name, not even an Indian

one, somebody called the headland where we live Point Dume, and it suits the name. When I was a kid, the snow would fall on the beach where the sea hit the sand and there would be this crazy up-and-down white layer, like albino skin stretched over a dragon's ribs.

Now, you need to know who was there at the time. The principal characters would include myself, my younger sister, Cordelia, and our grandfather. Then there was my father. My mother had passed away five years earlier in France. I had carried her coffin.

We usually dined late, in the French style, taking supper at nine-thirty. By that time, of course, most of us were on the brink of starvation and the best-fed people in the house were the servants who got to eat three hours before us, their so-called masters.

That evening, I descended the staircase and caught sight of my sister slithering into the dining room wearing a Chinese-style dress that sparkled with gold fibres.

'I can hear your thoughts,' she called over her shoulder as I followed her across the black-and-white tiles.

'What am I thinking?' I returned.

She stopped, waited until I caught up with her, took my arm and whispered in my ear. 'You're thinking that there are just a few more of these dinners to get through before you can get back to Harvard and that nice girl who sends you poetry so bad it should be illegal, but which you keep re-reading because she has a very pretty smile.'

I coughed. Sometimes her insights cut too close to the bone.

It was right then that the butler cleared his throat, his way of getting your attention without actually asking for it.

'Yes?' I said.

'A letter for you, sir.' He handed me one on a zinc platter. It was sealed all around with wax tape and had my name on the front in a handwriting I didn't recognize. It looked like it had been written in a hurry – the ink was smudged and the stamps were stuck on at a crazy angle. There were a number of them, because they were British – this had come all the way from England. And there was something inside the envelope that skidded about when the letter moved.

Not knowing what to expect, I tore it open and pulled out a small card. Its message was short.

'I will tell you what happened to your mother. Charing Cross railway station in London. Beneath the clock. March the seventeenth at ten in the morning.' And left in the envelope was a silver necklace with a small locket. I opened it to find a tiny picture of my mother smiling. I knew it well. She had worn it on the night that her carriage had spun off the highway in a violent storm. No one had known where she had been going that night. Only now someone did. Someone who hadn't signed their name.

So, the story was a quest. A quest for the truth buried in a family history. Not so unlike what Simeon was living right then. Although the words were simple enough and the story was – as yet – unthreatening, still he felt a growing

unease with it. As if it were pulling him somewhere else, to another time, to someone else's world. 'Florence? This book. What does it mean to you?' he asked. 'Why do you want me to read it?' She made no reply in words or actions. He turned to a later page. The landscape became strangely familiar.

> The pub looked shut, but I smacked my fist on the door loud enough and often enough to raise the dead. And finally, the landlord came out looking like he was one of them. So this was where the smugglers met. Some were inside with pistols in their jackets.

Simeon flicked to the end of the story. It came, unusually, halfway through the book and was followed by blank pages.

> So there he was. And there I was. And nothing between us except a hatred that burned like hot coals. I could have put a knife in his ribs and said a prayer of thanks to the Almighty while I did it. For all his declaration of love and piety, he would have done the same to me in the time it took to cuss. The question was: which of us had the plan, and which of us had the gut-ache to put it into practice? In the end, I did.

'Florence, what is this?' he asked.

She looked at the book he held, then rose from her seat and went to her own shelves. She plucked out a thick volume, leafed through it until she found the page she

was looking for and took a pen from her desk. She circled some words on the page, then brought the page to the glass. Ringed in black ink, he read: *Warning. Revelation. Premonition.* The last was circled twice. She returned the book to her shelf and reclined on her chaise longue, watching him.

Chapter 4

Simeon did not want to admit it to himself, but he was, in fact, relieved to close the crimson novelette and place it in the tallest bookcase. He noted as he did so that his hand was actually shaking. Only then did he peer through the glass to Florence. She did not seem disappointed or angry at his failure to read every word. She looked satisfied, as if making *The Gold Field*, and its American vistas and ocean-spanning story, part of Simeon's life was enough for now. More would come of it, of that he was certain.

With his patient asleep, there was little for him to do other than hope that Hawes would rally. True, he could take the parson to the hospital in Colchester, but what good would that do? It would only expose him to the

dirt and germs with which such provincial hospitals were awash. No, he was better off here, where Simeon could monitor his condition.

'Shall we talk, Florence?' he asked. She settled her face deeper into her palm. 'Is there something I can do or get you to make you more comfortable?' She smiled, but it was to herself, he thought. It said that she pitied the man trying to tempt her to speech that would never come. 'Well, if you ever think of anything, I should be delighted to furnish you with it.' He put his hands in his pockets. 'Will you tell me about yourself?' Nothing. And, on the spur of the moment, something more provocative left his lips. 'Will you tell me about James? Will you tell me what you did and why you did it?' He did not know what reaction to expect, only that he wanted to spark one. 'Did you love him or did you hate him?'

And then it came – no screams, no tears. She only drew herself up to her full height, lifting her face to the unseen sky as if bathing in sunlight, and then sighed, with a whole world of words in that one sigh. Then she left for her private space behind the public, where she would be alone. Was the emotion that she had felt regret? Shame? Longing? Anger? It could be all of these or none.

Just as she disappeared from view, Cain entered the room with a plate of bread, some salted beef and a cup of milk on a tray, which he set on the floor before the glass wall. He lifted the hatch and kicked the tray through. The cup turned over, spilling the milk onto the food. He left the room without a look back.

'Cain!' Simeon yelled after him, outraged.

'You must forgive Cain's rough manners.' Hawes had woken and also witnessed his servant's actions. 'He was most attached to my brother.'

'Does that justify this sort of behaviour?'

'One must try to understand the anger of others.'

Well, there was little to be done. But still there was the brandy to test. Simeon took the small barrel downstairs and called for Cain, who attended with a sullen expression until he saw the keg of drink.

'All right, this is your opportunity,' Simeon said, irritably. He wanted to discipline the servant for his earlier behaviour, but it was not his place. 'But try it on your dog first.'

Cain did not need asking twice. He went outside and returned with an ugly-looking hound.

'This's Nelson,' he muttered. He filled a bowl with a mix of the brandy and water. The dog lapped it up – Simeon wondered if the dog really did like booze, as Cain had claimed. They waited twenty minutes and the dog began to stagger about, then fell flat on his face on the kitchen floor, but remained breathing.

'Good stuff,' Cain said. He poured himself a brimming tumbler of the drink.

'You should wait until tomorrow before you try it; watch Nelson for any change.'

Cain shrugged and put the glass to his lips. Men around here were probably weaned on the stuff. Cain sipped it cautiously at first, smacking his lips ruminatively, then poured it down. 'Good stuff,' he confirmed.

Simeon hoped he would not now have two dying

patients and one expired dog to tend to. 'Just wait here a while, I'll watch you.'

'If ye like.'

He calculated what he would do if Cain showed symptoms of poisoning. A purgative would be best. He had a bottle of water filled with mashed mustard seeds that would cause a man to bring up in seconds whatever he had drunk. But they waited thirty speechless minutes and there was no change in Cain's complexion or pulse rate, and Simeon calculated that that was probably it.

The servant thanked Simeon and left, carrying the remains of the barrel and the paralytic canine.

Simeon wandered outside in Cain's wake. It was a foul morning of near-horizontal pricking rain. Over the sea itself, he could see a haar forming – the freezing sea fog that could envelop entire towns, turning them into pits of cold haze.

He strode across the sea lavender, determined not to let the weather defeat him. Turnglass House occupied the sole solid part of Ray, on the western edge of the islet, surrounded by mud and lying a few hundred yards from the Strood. But it was still exposed to the very worst that the North Sea and its Viking ghosts could hurl. As he stared north-eastwards, across neighbouring Mersea, to those countries that had spawned the wild men and their armed longboats, he could well believe there was something malignant in the landscape, ready to leap up and drag a man to his death.

For a second, as he looked that way, something glinted at him from the mud. A sparkle catching the sun's weak

rays just for a flickering moment, then gone again, leaving only the waterlogged ground. He stared where the glimmer had been, but there was nothing now.

The channel that separated Ray from Mersea was in a quandary, surging forward and back, thrusting up towards the Strood, threatening to overwhelm it and then retreating when it found its strength not quite enough at this hour. And someone was making his way along the causeway from Mersea: a boy aged around twelve, carrying a basket on each hip, who was moving quickly, in a practised fashion. Simeon watched him step off the Strood and place one of the baskets on the ground. It held a few packages wrapped in paper and string.

'Are you the butcher's boy?' Simeon called over. The boy nodded a shallow, suspicious nod. 'Don't you bring the meat right to the house?' He jerked his thumb behind him. It was hardly a long way for the lad to venture. The boy shook his head from side to side. 'Why?' The child stood stock still, like a bird watching a cat. 'Tell me.'

The suspicious child hesitated. Then he broke into an evil sort of grin and recited a tuneless schoolyard rhyme. 'Don' run slow. Don' run fas'. Beware the lady in the glass. Whether ye're cat or whether ye're mouse, shun all who live at Turnglass House.' He stayed briefly to savour his courage, then turned tail and ran back to Mersea. Simeon watched him disappear, splashing through the water as it encroached on the path. Mrs Tabbers emerged from the house and collected the basket with a polite nod. This was, it seemed, a normal ritual on the bleak island.

He returned to the house to find Mrs Tabbers preparing

luncheon from the meat the boy had brought. For want of anything to do, Simeon watched her at work until she asked him to stop. He retired, frustrated, to his room, to read a medical journal right into the evening, only emerging to dine or to check on his patient and glance at the glass cell at the end of the room. It remained empty and he wondered why she would not appear.

Simeon woke shivering. At first, his mind was as blank as a cloud and he had no idea where – or who – he was. All he knew was a shooting cramp in his icy limbs. Slowly, shapes evolved through the darkness, picked out by moonlight, and he was able to discern a bed chamber: a taper in a candlestick holder by his bedside and his coat over a chair. He sank back into the pillow, momentarily exhausted by the effort of recollection.

Yet it was not just the cold that had woken him. A rattling from the window told him that it had come unfastened and was clinking in the wind. He rubbed his eyes, feeling a thin layer of ice crystals on them, and forced himself out of the bed. The freezing air woke him fully then, and even after he had secured the window, he was unable to return to sleep so that, as he lay, his senses became attuned to the night and his hearing locked on to a rhythmic wooden creaking like that of a ship at sea. It was too regular to be the weather. It was more like human footsteps.

Immediately, he reached for the candlestick, struck a lucifer match against the mattress and filled the room with an orange glow. An old clock over the mantel showed the

time to be after two in the morning. It was too late for the parson to be abroad, too early for Mrs Tabbers to be lighting the fires. The house was lonely but not remote, so thievery was not out of the question. Simeon took the iron poker from the fireplace.

The sound of powerful waves – inaudible during the daytime, when people and animals were stirring – whished through cracks in the walls as he looked out into the corridor. All was still and dark.

All except for a bar of light under the door to the library.

He listened. There was no footstep-creaking now. Whoever it was had stopped still. Perhaps they had heard his movement and were now waiting for him. Cautiously, Simeon padded to the library. He stopped, straining for any sound from within, but could hear nothing. His heart beating hard, he raised the poker above his head, ready to bring it down hard on the skull of any intruder, and stepped inside.

The room he found was a strange inversion of the one he had first entered. Then it had been bright in the main room and dark in the cell at the end. Now it was the translucent prison that held the light, blazing bright from a lamp, and all the rest was gloomy, with fingerish shadows reaching from the furniture and books.

Florence's tread had made the sound, for she was there, wide awake, in her usual dress. But it was only her back that Simeon saw, bent as she was over her little table, scribbling on a sheet of paper just visible in front of her. Her hand was making long strokes across the page, followed by short back-and-forths, as if she were drawing a picture.

Transfixed by the nocturnal sight, he lowered the poker and watched.

Suddenly, her hand stopped dead in its motion. Her body froze and her back began to slowly unfurl like a serpent's. Her hands smoothed down her dress. One fell on the page, drifted across its surface to the edge and lifted it from the table.

She never turned to see him, but she stooped to the hatch through the wall, pushed the paper through and snuffed out her lamp. Immediately, she was in darkness again and the glass was a mirror in which his reflection, lit by his glowing candle, stared back at him. He heard her dress rustle. 'Wait,' he said, wanting to hear her voice. The rustling stopped. He moved forward. It started again, then faded, and he knew she had gone.

He bent to examine the page she had left. She had, indeed, been drawing. The flickering candle showed a house on the edge of a cliff. Bold, sweeping lines. A clifftop house at the edge of a wide plain. But the landscape was not Ray. It was somewhere far distant. The scene in the portrait above the hall fireplace.

Chapter 5

The following morning, Simeon decided that some fresh air might be of benefit to his patient and Hawes consented to be wheeled outside in a Bath chair, swaddled like a baby. The atmosphere was certainly fresh. 'Take me over there, will you, my boy?' the parson asked, pointing to the edge of the mudflats. Cain and Simeon carried the chair over the uneven ground, setting it down where the priest could look out to sea. Waves came and went, birds above circled and dipped down for skittering fish. Simeon fell to calculating again what could possibly be causing the old man's sickness. He needed his medical texts, but, frustratingly, he had left them in London. A thought hit him: the library was stocked with tracts on a wide range

of subjects – might he be lucky enough to find something useful to his quest there? He could do with Hagg's work on diseases of the gut, or Schandel's on . . .

His thought was interrupted as he noticed, at the edge of his vision, a small clutch of people gathering on the Strood – seven or eight adults and the butcher's boy he had seen the previous day. Even from where he was, fifty yards away, Simeon could see the nasty smile on the boy's face. The child was speaking and Simeon was sure it was the same schoolyard rhyme as before.

The adults were roughly dressed: fishermen or farm workers and their wives. They were eyeing the three men from the house as if watching beasts in a cage.

'What do they want?' Simeon asked.

It was, unusually, Cain who answered. ''Fraid o' us. Think we're goin' ter eat 'em live.' A short grumbling sound from his throat could have been an approximation of laughter.

'It grieves me to say that Cain is right,' Hawes said. 'My flock have not always been the most welcoming and accommodating. Some of them, I say, have been known to be suspicious to the point of, well—' He broke off.

'Of?' Simeon prompted him.

'I could not rule out violence.'

Simeon bit his lip thoughtfully. He had been dismissive of the idea that his uncle was the victim of deliberate poisoning, but was it time to consider the hypothesis more seriously? 'The sickness from which you suffer. Do you think it could be—'

'I am being poisoned. I have told you. Could it be the

61

sinister hand of one of these seemingly harmless folk? I would rule it wholly possible.'

There was, indeed, something in the expressions on the faces of the villagers ranged before them that said maleficent violence was not unknown in these parts.

'Are there any whom you actively suspect? One with a grudge against you?'

Hawes squinted. 'That one on the end.' He pointed an emaciated finger. 'Charlie White. Only twenty years old and yet I have long detected the presence of the Devil in him. Riotous drinking, a use of women for his own purposes. I have warned him from the very pulpit to end his libidinous ways. It fell on deaf ears. I believe he enjoys coming to each service to hear what is in store for him.'

'Is that so?'

'It is. He quite revels in it. He takes pleasure in his sinful rebelliousness. My revulsion at it, he enjoys all the more. But he will not enjoy the endless torment. No, sir, he will not! And he has not the wits to avoid it.'

'The wits?'

'Oh, it takes a mind to escape the fires. He has none. He will burn.'

Simeon made note of the claim. 'Anyone else you suspect?'

Hawes hesitated, cleared a film of mist from his square spectacles and placed them back on his nose. 'There. Mary Fen.' He indicated a squat little woman with hip-length hair. 'The woman has had five daughters in as many years. None of them survived more than a month. Neglect, you say? Yes, perhaps. Or perhaps something

worse. She would not be the first in these parts to give a girl-child a dose of something rather than raise her. And she knows that I am suspicious.' He grunted. 'Those two, they are on trial not just before me, but also before God. But oh, it could be any of them. The Devil is everywhere. He may have taken over one of them or all of them.' The thought seemed to grow in him, anger glowing below his words. 'Yes, yes, one of these overtaken by the Enemy. His hands within theirs, dripping something into me.' His bony finger stabbed towards the onlookers.

Dr Oliver Hawes DD was a country parson, and country parsons tended to have very rigid ideas about the Devil and evil. To men like him, they were not merely abstract concepts but corporeal realities that one could encounter in the nearest rank alleyway. But Simeon kept coming back to his father's cabled words. *'Turnglass house has always had something corrupt and malign about it. Leave it to God and the law.'* He met the gaze of the boy, who was mouthing that schoolyard rhyme over and over.

After luncheon, Simeon set himself to hunting through the library for medical tracts that might be of use. Something on toxicology would be perfect – he might even find a home companion on folk remedies, or a botanical guide that listed poisonous mushrooms and their symptoms, of use. He spent the best part of two hours searching – at first taking books carefully down and replacing them precisely where they had been, then, as frustration grew on him, angrily tossing them aside.

All the while, he watched his uncle struggle to eat. The

parson was drawn up beside the fire, where a small blaze was oozing heat into the room, with a shawl across his knees. His condition had worsened even since the morning. After a long while, Simeon gave up on the collection and threw himself into a wing-backed seat. Florence was in the private rear of her cell. Simeon glanced towards her empty chaise longue. 'Uncle, does Florence draw pictures?'

Hawes's eyebrows rose and he spooned a little milky porridge to his lips. 'Pictures?'

'Landscapes, that sort of thing.'

The elder man dropped his spoon into the pewter bowl. 'She has been known to,' he said with some effort.

'Does she draw them at night?'

'Why would she do it at night?' Hawes paused thoughtfully. 'I afford her ample time during the day for her pastimes. Why at night?'

'I do not know.' Simeon could fathom no more than the curate could.

'Have you . . . seen her?'

He did not wish the clergyman to know he had been stalking the house after midnight. It would seem intrusive. 'No. But I found this in the morning.' He took from his pocket the picture from the previous night and placed it on his uncle's knees. At first, there was nothing. No spark of recognition in the old man's face. And then dark clouds seemed to spread. Hawes's lower lip trembled. He took up the page, peered into it as if there was some great Biblical truth to be found within, crushed it in his fist and cast it into the fire. Simeon was astonished at the reaction to a mere ink drawing. 'Why did you do that?' he asked.

'It is foolishness. For fools. And I want to eat in peace,' Hawes spluttered. 'No more of it.'

Simeon gave no credence to the explanation. There had been hot anger there. 'Uncle, if you want me to investigate what is making you sick, you must allow me to do so. That picture obviously means something to you. Please explain what it is.'

The reaction was instantaneous. The old man thudded his skinny hands onto the armrests and, with some terrible effort, managed to launch himself forward out of the chair, tumbling to his knees. Simeon made to help him back up, but with a flash of fury that bared his teeth like a dog's, the parson knocked Simeon's hand away. Then, like a young infant, he began to scurry across the floor on all four limbs, thrusting the furniture or other obstacles from his path. 'This is my house. My house! I shall command as I please!' he spat. A side table crowded with books was overturned, and then he was at the glass wall, banging on it with his fists.

'Come out! Come out!' he screamed. 'I know you can hear me!'

'Uncle!' Simeon shouted, coming forward to pull the old man away.

'*Come out!*' The fists pounded again on the glass.

And at that, with a swish of her green silk dress, Florence emerged from her sleeping area. She seemed amused and curious at the spectacle of Oliver Hawes on his knees, roaring outside the cell he had built. At the sight of her, the parson stopped his shouting and began to sway. Simeon was reminded of a cobra as it hypnotizes

its prey before striking. But this serpent was spent and he collapsed, dropping his head hard to the floor. He was unconscious.

Astonished, Simeon checked for abrasions and, finding none, rolled the elder man onto his back, gently slapping his cheeks until he began to gurgle. 'You need rest,' he said, lifting the parson into a winged chair. Out of the corner of his eye, he saw Florence placidly smiling, enjoying the show. He was sure she had secrets in her heart as to why her guardian had crawled, livid, across the floor to bang his fists against her gilded cage. He wanted to know what they were. He was beginning to lose patience.

There were also a few last remnants of the drawing that had set the ground ashiver, he saw. At the edge of the grate, some small, charred remains had escaped the flames. He plucked them away. It was the edge of the landscape she had dreamed up. There was nothing more than he had seen before – less, of course – but that imagined scene picked out in black ink took on a greater importance now. For whatever it was, it had had the power to spark violent outrage in Parson Hawes. But how?

As he held it, some of the char coming off on his fingertips, he heard the curate struggle to speak. 'That ... world,' he whispered. 'I told them it wasn't real. They should live under God!'

How were they doing otherwise? Simeon asked himself.

Chapter 6

Over breakfast the next morning, Mrs Tabbers served mutton sausages and black bread.

'I wish to see something of Mersea,' Simeon informed her, tucking into the fare.

'Won' take ye long,' Cain mumbled through overchewed mouthfuls.

'Can I walk the Strood now?'

'Ye can.'

That was to the good. He could still find no organic cause for the parson's condition in the house, but one thought did occur to him: it was possible that the cause lay elsewhere in Oliver Hawes's life. It was just conceivable that the source was in the other building where he spent

most of his hours. Simeon did not want to be away from his patient for too long, but he could spare an hour or two to run over to the church of Sts Peter and Paul on Mersea.

He hoped that when he returned, he would still have a patient to tend to, because when he had risen he had found Hawes moaning on his sopha, with a temperature high enough to boil water. He was worse, far worse, than the previous day. 'My head, it is beating like it will burst,' the priest had mumbled. A line of yellow spittle had hung from his lips until Simeon wiped it away.

So, after finishing his meal, Simeon set out through a drizzle from the clouds. Mersea was the more substantial island by far, he soon found. The village was a mile along the path, nestling on the south coast of the isle. A solid church spire rose up and four or five dozen houses seemed to crowd around its base. They were, for the most part, fishermen's cottages, squat and sturdy – their incumbents no doubt the same.

The church itself was a mediaeval construction in the English Romanesque style. Inside, stone and mortar were uncovered, apart from the occasional regimental colours – troops stationed on the island during the French wars at the beginning of the century, probably. Simeon began to look around, in the faint hope that something would stand out as a possible cause of the parson's sickness.

He checked the nave and the vestry, examined the dry font, the high altar and the locked cabinet that probably held the communion wine. Nothing seemed untoward and he dropped into a pew dejectedly.

'Good morning,' hailed a voice.

It had come from a man entering the nave. Aged around sixty, the man was smartly dressed – far more smartly, indeed, than any of the fishermen would dream of.

'Good morning.' Simeon waited to see if the conversation would be pushed from there.

'I am William Watkins. Magistrate of these parts.' He sat beside Simeon. There was little company to be had in these parts, it appeared, so whatever opportunity presented itself had to be taken. The man had an old-fashioned style of speech that suggested old-fashioned thoughts.

'Simeon Lee. Doctor.'

'Oh, here for Hawes?'

'I am.' He was not the slightest bit surprised that everyone here knew who was well and who was sick.

'Live, will he?'

'We can hope.' He shied away from saying that they could pray – in these remote places, such a saying would probably be taken as an invocation rather than a turn of phrase. His diary was an empty one, but that did not imply that he would rather spend a hunk of it on his knees in the church.

'Hope, yes. Then back to Colchester, is it?'

'London.'

'Oh, London! Gawd. I spent time there as a young blade.' He chuckled to himself. 'I expect you enjoy it too. Yes. Quite the town, London.' He seemed to lose himself in his younger days.

'You're Florence's father.'

'Oh, oh, yes. Florence.' His voice sank. 'How is she? Don't get over there as much as . . . I used to.'

Simeon suspected there was a reason for that. It was not a long trek and there must have been precious little for a Justice of the Peace to busy himself with on Mersea. No, Squire Watkins probably felt rather uncomfortable seeing his daughter in her strange confinement.

'She has appeared quite healthy when I have seen her. Where she is.' Simeon chose not to mention the scorn that bubbled below the daily blanket of laudanum. 'It is not easy for her, you know.'

'No, no. Quite.' Watkins lowered his head and his lips quivered, attempting to form words. Simeon waited. Years with patients had taught him the benefit of waiting for someone who wanted to speak. 'That box,' he said after a while. 'I never wanted it, you know?'

'I'm sure.' Few parents would want their child held like an exhibit. Probably Magistrate Watkins was not a wicked man, only a weak one.

'It was there or the lunatic asylum. The judge said that.'

'Then she is indeed better off where she is.'

'Oh, yes.' He brightened, as if having found a supporter. 'For certain, sir. Would have had her home with me if the judge had allowed it. Wouldn't, though. Worried I would let her loose, I suppose.'

Simeon paused, wondering how accurate it was to state that the arrangement was at the insistence of some unspecified judge. 'Would you have?'

'Would I?' Watkins seemed to be enquiring of himself, not knowing the answer without testing it. 'I cannot honestly say.'

Can't or won't? Simeon thought to himself. 'Dr Hawes

is seriously ill, but the cause is not clear and I am attempting to ascertain it. Have you been unwell yourself? Or anyone you know around here?'

'Unwell? No, not at all. All very healthy.'

Watkins's presence at least offered the prospect of an insight into the strange events that had occurred at Turnglass House over the past couple of years – events that had already left one man dead and one woman imprisoned and might now be connected to the parson's perplexing illness. But it would be better to win a little of the magistrate's trust before probing.

'I would like to see something of the island,' Simeon said. 'To get the feel for it. Where would you suggest I visit?'

'There's not much to it, sir. And I say that as a man who calls this place home.' He was doing his best to buck himself up. 'Oh yes, it's a harsh old place. But come, we can retire to my house for a little ... tea,' he said hesitantly. Simeon suspected it was his medical title that made the magistrate wary of offering harder drink.

'Thank you.'

They walked for ten minutes to the only large house in the vicinity. It was in the modern style, with spires and turrets like a German castle. 'Come on up to the roof,' Watkins said. 'Don't mind the rain. We see far worse.' They climbed through the house, which was more comfortably appointed inside than its outward appearance suggested, up through a trapdoor and onto the roof. Once up there, Watkins happily presented a telescope and invited Simeon to look through it. 'Can see the coast of

Holland if you're lucky. Kent if you're unlucky.' He waited for his little joke to land.

Simeon could see nothing but a violent squall at sea. 'I feel such an outsider here, even though my family – or a branch of them – are firmly rooted here,' he said.

'Ah, yes, it can surely be that way. But we are a welcoming people,' Watkins agreed amiably, if rather inaccurately.

'To tell you the truth, I hadn't even met Dr Hawes before I came here. I know nothing about him, really.'

'Oh, not much to tell. Dependable country parson, sir. No more than that.'

'Everyone has a past, sir,' Simeon countered. 'I think you were quite the young blood once!'

This pleased Watkins such that he began to beam. 'Ha! Indeed, I was, sir. Ah yes, good old days they were.'

'But Dr Hawes must have been a studious sort.'

Watkins hemmed a little. 'Well, yes. Of course, he wasn't always a man of the cloth.'

'No?'

'Oh, no, no. Though I expect he was always destined for it – by temperament, you understand?'

'Oh?' Simeon sounded interested, but not too interested.

'His father, Colonel Hawes – now there was a strict man, an unbending man – wanted his first son for the army. Not the Church.'

'Did he? Then why didn't it turn out that way?'

'Oh, it did. For a short while,' Watkins informed him.

'I don't understand.'

Watkins sat on the crenellation edging the roof. 'The

Colonel was set on purchasing a commission for young Oliver – I told him, I did, I said, "Your boy's not for the battlefield, Henry!", but he wanted a soldier for his first son and that was that. In the end, the best he could do was find a regiment in the Indian army that would take him.'

'Well, that seems fine enough.'

'Oh, you think so, do you?' Watkins replied, warming to the subject. *'Cashiered for cowardice.'*

'No!' And it was a genuine surprise. Watkins looked a little pleased with himself. No matter how much he liked to present himself as the genial country squire, he also enjoyed the gossip of the age.

'As I live and breathe. Rifles regiment, I think – sent into battle in the Duar War. As I understand it – and the details are hard to come by, you understand – he had to be dragged out of the wagon, and within days he had abandoned his post. They had to send a party out to find him. Of course, that also meant he lost his commission and couldn't sell it – came home an indebted coward.'

Well then. The Church did indeed seem a better choice of profession. 'And what about James?' The magistrate stiffened, as if experiencing a sudden bout of nerves. Simeon noted it.

'I . . . I . . .' He peered through the telescope in order to avoid Simeon's gaze.

'Mr Watkins?'

Watkins came shyly away from the spy-glass. 'James was . . . well, he was different to Oliver, of course. Very different. Tearaway, his father thought . . .' He trailed off.

There was something very much on the man's mind that was not being vocalized.

'And what are you not telling me?'

The magistrate shuffled his feet like a schoolboy. 'I . . . I do not wish to speak ill of the dead.'

'Mr Watkins. I should like to know.' The suspicion was growing stronger that his patient's condition really was a product of some of the strange dealings on these islands – and therein lay the road to a cure.

In order to avoid his gaze, Watkins went back to his telescope and bent down to peer through it. 'I can see Holland,' he declared. 'Yes, I am certain that is Holland.' Simeon stepped in front of the lens.

'Mr Watkins. I must know. I could enquire elsewhere. It might cause something of a stink.'

Watkins came away from the telescope. 'James was involved in . . . activity that was not legal.'

Cain had hinted at something of the sort. 'Would you tell me which crimes?'

'I apologize, sir. I have said too much. I must . . . get to work.' He went, nervously, to the trapdoor that had admitted them to the roof. 'Would you come this way?'

'You won't answer the question?' Watkins stared at the trapdoor. 'Then I'll ask another.' He did not wait for a refusal. 'What were the precise circumstances of James's death? And I shall not leave without an answer.'

At this, Watkins seemed to deflate of all air. 'James,' he said, shaking his head.

'Go on.'

'Sir, this is a painful subject!'

'I understand, but more could depend on this than either of us knows right now. Dr Hawes has it in his mind that someone is trying to kill him.'

'*What?* Who?' He sounded genuinely astounded.

'That we don't know.'

'It's not Florence!' Watkins exclaimed. 'I know what you think, but she would not murder a man in cold blood. James's death was an accident.'

'In that case, you will have no objection to telling me about it.'

Watkins was flustered and started a sentence three times before he managed to complete it. 'It . . . it was . . . it was an evening a couple of years ago. Florence and he were heard arguing. Not for the first time. Not at all.' He looked up. 'Well, this argument was about a woman, it seems. Can't tell you who – some strumpet of James's, I expect. Jealous sort, Florence. Passionate. I could never keep her back when her blood was up. Gave up trying before she was even seventeen. She . . .'

'The argument,' Simeon prompted him.

'Yes, yes. Well, they shouted at each other, he denied all, from what I've heard, and then she threw a bottle or something at him. She had been drinking, I think.'

'Did she mean to do it?'

'How could I know?'

'Well, was she proud of her action?'

'Proud? I do not think so, sir. Defiant. Yes, she was defiant.'

Simeon could tell Watkins was keeping something from him. 'Mr Watkins, as a doctor, I would be surprised

75

if such an act alone would have a woman consigned to Bedlam. I believe there is much you are not telling me.'

Watkins let his head hang. He was defeated. 'After James died, Florence began acting quite strangely. She admitted she had killed him, but claimed there was some sort of conspiracy against her. Then she ran away to London, where she utterly shamed herself, and if it were not for a police magistrate taking custody of her, then the Lord alone knows what she might have done. I had to request Hawes take a coach there to collect her and bring her home.'

Well, that was a substantial addition to the story. 'Why did you send Dr Hawes in your place?'

'Why? Because I did not wish to see my own daughter dragged back with an escort of policemen.' He placed his palms over his face. 'And yes, yes, it was shame. I was ashamed that she was mine; that I had not raised her better than that.'

Simeon understood. Shame certainly appeared to be eating the man from within. 'What next? A trial? Hold nothing back now.'

Watkins nodded. 'A trial. At the Assizes. She wasn't fit to attend – she was raving half the time, only laudanum calmed her and then she wasn't up to speaking. The prosecutor said she had to be committed. But I knew the judge, Allardyce. Had a word. He agreed that instead of sending her to the asylum, she could be kept here.'

'In that glass cell,' Simeon said. He was yet to be convinced that her extraordinary incarceration – indeed, any incarceration – was necessary.

'Under supervision, sir! Under supervision! I offered my own home, but even Allardyce couldn't agree to that. "With your father's fond heart, you would not be a reliable warder," he said. But then Hawes offered and Allardyce allowed it. So Hawes had her apartment constructed. It was the best outcome we could gain.'

Simeon had much to say to this, but did not say it. It was time to check on his patient, whom he did not want to leave for more than two hours at a stretch. And so, Watkins led him back down through the house and showed him out. 'Do give my regards to Hawes . . . and to Florence,' he added, with some discomfort.

Chapter 7

Simeon tramped through the village and back along the Strood onto Ray, passing the mudflats that sloped into the channel between the two islands.

As he approached Turnglass House, dreary in the rain, the curious hourglass weather vane slowly turning on its peak, he gazed at those expanses of clayish mud that Cain had warned him to stay away from. Insects ruled over them and rivulets of silty water coursed through them. But he had always had a contrarian streak, and Cain warning him to beware simply resulted in his determination to examine them as closely as he could.

He drew to the edge. They were as foul as Dante's descriptions of the Styx. He could well picture the

ferryman Morty in the role of Phlegyas, transporting souls across the fifth circle of Hell. He was about to move on when something caught his eye. Something metallic was managing to glint in the dismal weather. It was surely the same thing that had reflected the sun's rays the day before but then disappeared from his vision.

Carefully, he picked his course, testing his footing until he found solid earth. Five yards away, it seemed that the prize was lodged on a short, thin stick, caked with mud and washed up from God knows where. Closer still and the metal solidified into a pewter ring. Stretching, his fingers closed on it and pulled it towards him, but the stick was lodged in the mud. Evidently, there was more below the surface because it would not come away. He shifted his position so he could reach it; then he pulled harder. And without a moment's change, without a warning in the mud or the sky, he found he was not grasping a sliver of wood but the freezing, filth-encrusted forefinger of a man's hand.

He fell back and stared at what he had held. Buried in the mud was a part, or the whole, of a man. It was a vile image even for those such as he, who saw the dead and dying by the week. But he drew himself together. A cadaver was a cadaver whether it was on a slab or sub-merged in the ground. And someone, somewhere, was waiting for news of their brother, son or father.

Bracing himself more firmly, guessing the weight of what lay in the mud and quelling any latent human horror at the scene, Simeon set out to reveal the hidden dead. He gripped the palm of the corpse-man, as if they were shaking hands as friends, and heaved.

With a little effort, first the fingers, then the wrist lifted into the light. A dripping, mud-spewing shirt cuff emerged, a metonymic caricature of man's vanity. Yes, it seemed the whole of this poor soul was down there.

Simeon took grip of the cloth and pulled, levering against the soft ground upon which he knelt. And yet with all his strength he could not manage it. Neither, though, could he leave to get help, for he knew that the hand might then be covered up once more, and the body could sink so deep, or be washed away in the channel, that it might never be found again. He had no choice but to get closer.

So he slithered chest-first from the solid ground to the watery mass of mud, feeling it ease over his own body and submerge his splayed legs. He knew he was sinking an inch at a time. If he miscalculated, he could end up interred in the same rough grave as the buried man. Carefully, then, he delved deep into the mud, along the solid flesh of the dead man, until he felt shoulders. The rain was coming down heavily now and his back was soaked with it, but he refused to let his charge disappear once more.

He braced himself. And with all of his strength, he heaved. Inch by inch, it started to move. Closer it came, and deeper he slipped, until they were embracing in the dirt. There would be empty eyes, a throat clogged with mud, but Simeon could only think of hauling this cold body into the light.

He squirmed around until, snake-like, with a yell and the last of his strength, he finally writhed his body and its

dead burden to the solid ground. He collapsed, panting with the effort. With his palm he wiped mud from his own face and spat out brown water. And then he caught sight of the man's face for the first time.

Caked still in mud, it was barely recognizable as human rather than a primordial being. But there it was: a forehead, thick nose and jutting chin. A heavy-set, muscular man who must have once breathed, worked, eaten, laughed and cursed. Simeon stared at what he had dredged from the mud and let the raindrops wash away some of the dirt.

Who are you, my friend? he thought. *Did you drown? Did your heart seize while you were walking? Have you been missed and searched for or has no one noticed your absence?*

The flesh of the body was almost wholly intact. There was some rotting here and there, but little to see. Either the death had been recent, or the clay had perfectly preserved it, as if it had been set in ice. Simeon pulled back the eyelids. The irises were clear and green; the teeth strong but discoloured by tobacco – one of the local fishermen, perhaps.

He considered what to do. He was only a few hundred yards from Turnglass House. At this point, he might as well haul the body there himself. So, with supreme effort, he heaved the man aloft onto his shoulders and slowly made his way on to the house.

When Mrs Tabbers saw what awaited her on the threshold, her mouth drew into a silent scream. 'Calm yourself,'

Simeon instructed her as she staggered back. 'He is quite dead.' He pushed past and headed for the rear parlour, not concerning himself with what he was tramping through the hallway.

There was a table overflowing with religious texts that he swept to the floor and replaced with his burden, mouth up, dirty water dripping to the carpet.

'What in God's name . . .' the housekeeper whispered, having recovered her voice.

'A man, Mrs Tabbers. A dead man.'

'Who is it?' He noticed her surreptitiously cross herself. No doubt the parson would have a thing or two to say about such papistry.

'You will have a far better idea than I have.' He took a vase of flowers, cast the blooms aside and poured the water over the corpse's face, wiping as he went with the doily upon which the vase had been set. Puffed-out cheeks appeared through the remaining clay.

'John White. Tha's who't is.' Cain had entered, drawn by the commotion, and the words were his.

Simeon was opening the man's collar to examine him. He stopped at the name. 'John White?'

'Aye.'

The previous day, when the locals had ranged before them on the Strood like crows, Hawes had pointed out a young man he suspected of many ill deeds, named Charlie White.

'Is he Charlie White's brother?'

'Was Charlie's cousin. No more. Gone now. Look't 'im.' Cain rubbed his jaw.

'So he was from here? Mersea?' he asked.

'Mersea, aye. Dis'peared a year or two back.'

'Well, I think we now know why.'

'Aye.' Cain stepped forward. Mrs Tabbers kept a greater distance. Whether it was respect for the dead or fear of the dead, Simeon could not say. But as a doctor, he felt little of either. To him, cadavers were primarily evidence of medicine's failures.

'Who was he?'

Mrs Tabbers and Cain exchanged a subtle glance.

'Oysterman.'

'I see. And what else?' He waited a moment. Cain returned Simeon's gaze. 'You're hiding something, aren't you, Cain?'

'Hidin' nothin'.'

Simeon fixed him with a look. 'Keep it to yourself for now, but I'll find it out.' He had deep enough suspicion as it was. It seemed the whole population was in on the local criminal trade.

'You do tha'.'

Simeon returned to the body. A dark pool had formed below it on the rug and he set about stripping away the clothing. 'Bring me scissors, cloths and a bucket of warm soapy water,' he instructed Mrs Tabbers. 'And you'll want some sheets to catch it.'

'Shall I wake Dr Hawes?' she asked.

'No, I'll let him know myself later.'

She hurried away to fetch the water. 'Tell me more about this man,' Simeon instructed Cain.

'John? Quie' sort,' he said in a still-sullen tone. He

clearly thought this was not outsiders' business. 'Strong.' If Cain described a man as 'quiet', it must mean he was virtually dumb.

'How did he go missing?'

'Summer the year before las'. Found his boat overturned and run aground on the Hard. Him no' in it. All though' he'd drowned in the sea. Looks now tha' he drowned in the mud.' He squinted through the window. 'Wouldn' be the firs'.'

'Did he have family?'

'His ma died a few months back. He'd a sister, Annie, but she lef'.'

'So Charlie is the closest?'

'S'pose he is.'

Simeon stripped off his upper clothes. They were soaked with rain and mud. Mrs Tabbers returned with the hot water and sheets and he washed and dried himself, then wiped away more mud from the man on the table.

The skin was yellow all over and frayed in places. But as his jerkin was cut away, the flesh of his torso seemed to explode outwards. Mrs Tabbers let out a shrill scream.

Simeon looked down at the ruptures in the flesh. 'Something has been eating him.' Cain mumbled an oath. 'Mr Watkins should be informed.'

'I'll go,' Cain said.

'Thank you.' A thought occurred. 'But don't tell Charlie White. I shall see to that.'

Cain narrowed his eyes. 'If ye like.'

Simeon cleaned up, climbed the stairs and changed into a fresh shirt. It was time to tell the parson.

Entering the library, he found Hawes lying on the sopha, moaning. A glance to the partition at the end of the room showed it to be empty, its inmate out of sight in her apartment behind.

'Uncle,' Simeon said.

The old man's voice was little more than a whisper. 'Oh, Simeon, my boy. I am caught in such shivers.' Simeon placed his hand on the priest's forehead. He was indeed cold to the touch. 'I am not long for this world.'

For once, a patient might be proved right about the gravity of their condition.

Simeon had lost patients before, of course, but always strangers. He hated the idea of allowing his relative's life to slip away, however, because it was his responsibility. 'Don't write yourself off yet, Uncle. You'll be up and delivering sermons to the flock before you know it.'

The older man managed a thin smile. 'I am not so sure,' he wheezed.

'Is there someone you would like me to fetch?'

Hawes lifted his eyes with an effort. 'No one. There is no one. Your father is my closest blood relation. If I die, this house will go to him, and then, in time, to you, you know.' His eyes opened wide. 'What will you do with it?'

Do with it? Among all the other strange thoughts that Turnglass House had engendered over the past few days, the idea of inheriting the place had not been one. What could he do with it? Instantly, he thought of his research, stalled for lack of coin. If he could somehow convince his father to transfer the house to him immediately – his father had, after all, declared a deep aversion towards the

place – he could sell it and restart his work without having to grub around for paid employment or grants. He could devote all his time and effort!

'I'll use it to help discover a cure for cholera, Uncle,' he said. He knew it was a little pompous a statement, but it would give the curate comfort, no doubt, to think of some good coming from his death.

'Oh, that would be a fine use. Yes. But there must be one condition.'

'And what is that?'

'If I die, you must become responsible for her.' Simeon looked sharply to the glass cell at the end of the room. 'It is for her own good. If she is released, she will be immediately caught up and sent to the madhouse.'

Simeon had no desire to become Florence's gaoler. And yet he considered that the parson was correct in his assertion that Bedlam was the other outcome. Well, if it all were to come to pass, he would do his best to treat her fairly. That would probably entail a period of observing her and deciding on the best course of treatment or action. If they were both lucky, her liberty would be achievable. He gave his uncle his word that he would do as asked.

And then the information that Simeon had come up to impart could wait no longer. 'Something has occurred that I must tell you about.'

'Oh?'

'I found the body of a man in the mudflats.'

The parson's head lifted a little in surprise. 'Good Lord, who?'

'I believe his name was John White.'

'John White? Oh, he's a local boy. So that's what happened to him. Poor young man. It happens, you know. Even to those who live here. Poor young man.' He looked to Heaven and whispered a silent prayer. 'Would you like my aid with the arrangements?' he croaked, his consciousness drifting away.

Simeon doubted his uncle would soon be in much of a state to aid with anything. 'I will see to them all. Cain can help.'

White's body would have to be kept at the house until then. He resolved to have Cain remove it to the stable. Mrs Tabbers was unlikely to appreciate having it stretched out on the rear parlour table indefinitely.

With the revelation of the body of John White, Simeon wanted immediately to speak to White's cousin, Charlie, whom the parson had identified as one of Mersea's malefactors. Hawes would likely be out of consciousness for a while, so Simeon took directions to White's home from Cain. After that, he would visit the other person on Mersea that the parson had pointed out as a potential murderer, Mary Fen, who had lost five daughters in infancy. As Hawes had said, she would not have been the first poverty-stricken mother to pour something caustic into her child's drink rather than attempt to feed another mouth. And the baby farms, those places in the stinking cities where women would permanently leave their unwanted children, paying a lump-sum for their upkeep, were notorious for it — the case of Margaret Waters of

Brixton, who had poisoned many infants in her care before being caught and hanged at Surrey County Gaol, was still fresh in the memory.

White lived in a cottage away from the main settlement. It was picturesque in a pastoral style: there was wisteria around the door and the window frames were painted green. And yet Simeon could not put his finger on it, but there was something seedy about the house, as if there were rot in the roots of the wisteria.

White lived here alone, having recently inherited it from a relative, Mrs Tabbers had told him. As soon as White opened the door, Simeon concluded that the well-kept appearance of the cottage was down to the deceased woman and would not last long. White was young and handsome with it. But although each part of his face was fair – the jaw was strong and his complexion clear – still Simeon could not dismiss the impression that, like the house itself, there was something sour about the whole.

'Are you Charlie White?'

'Ye come ter me home. Ye know who I be.' There was a sneer behind each word.

From time to time, in the course of his work, Simeon had had to deal with aggression from some such as White. It did not bother him.

'You are right about that.'

'An' I knows who ye be.'

'I am glad of it. Dr Hawes ...'

'Dr Hawes,' White sniggered contemptuously.

'Yes. He is ill.'

'Then le' him pray.'

'I'm sure he is doing that. He thinks you might know something of his illness.'

'Thinks wha'?' And he laughed a deep, guttural laugh. 'I know nothin' of wha' ails parson.' He leaned in. 'Bu' I know wha' them tha' lives in tha' house desires.' He stopped laughing. 'Wha' they wan's an' wha' they does ter get 'em.'

There seemed to be meaning beneath the verbal confusion. 'Tell me what you mean.'

White hesitated. 'Ask th' woman. Th' mad one's killed parson's brother. If any knows, she knows, now her hubby be dead 'n' done. Ye people say th' Whites don' deserve a taste o' justice. Well, seems maybe we can sup it up anyways.' He made a slurping sound with his lips and started to close the door. Simeon stayed it hard with his hand.

'Your cousin's body has been found.'

'Me cousin?'

'John. He was missing, wasn't he?'

White narrowed his eyes. 'He were. Where'd they fin' him?'

'In the mudflats. He's at Turnglass House.'

White huffed scornfully. 'Where else would he be?' And he shoved Simeon's hand away and slammed the door closed.

Simeon chewed over White's words. For sure, Turnglass House seemed the centre of all these strange events. Simeon's father's claim that there was something malign about the house was becoming truer by the minute. Well, he would think it over as he made his way to his other house call.

Mary Fen lived in a fairly proportioned little house, Simeon found. She blinked in surprise at Simeon's presence on her threshold before giving him admittance – it must have been rare that she had a visitor, let alone one with clean clothes. Her husband, who was some sort of metals artisan, peered over from his work stand, then returned to his labour without a flicker of interest.

Simeon looked around. The place was reasonably well appointed. A few pieces of simple furniture. A rough rug on bare boards. 'Mrs Fen.' She blinked hard. 'I am Dr Lee. Parson Hawes is my patient. I saw you two days ago on the Strood, watching us outside the house.' He waited for a response. There was none but the hard blinking again. 'Why did you do that?'

'Didn' mean anythin' by i', sir. Hones'.'

'So why do it?'

She mumbled her answer. 'Parson don' like us.'

Simeon watched Fen's husband pour a small amount of powdered metal into a wooden dish and mix it with some other compound. He drew out an amalgam on a small glass spoon. 'Why do you think that is?'

'Don' know,' she answered sheepishly.

Simeon could tell this would be a less forthcoming conversation than the previous one, where Charlie White had enjoyed sneering at the clergyman. 'Did you know Dr Hawes is unwell?'

'Had heard somethin'.'

'What had you heard?'

'Jus' he was a-sick.'

'Do you know how he came sick?'

'No, sir.'

'Do you know anything about the household?'

'Not me, sir.'

He changed subject and asked her what she knew of John White. Blinking harder than ever. She knew him, of course, but they were not friends. What of his cousin, Charlie? She had nothing to do with him. And so on and so on.

'Do the people around here talk of what occurs at the parsonage?' Simeon eventually asked.

'They . . . talks.' Her husband began brushing the amalgam over the handles of a box of steel knives on his table. Simeon was distracted by the man's work.

'And what do they say?'

'They says tha' wha'-was-'er-name . . .'

He guessed who she meant. 'Florence.' There was something about the man's actions at the work bench.

'Tha's 'er. Tha' she killed her husban'.' What was he using on the steel?

'That is of public record. What I want to know is . . . Wait!' Simeon stood up and went over. Fen's husband stared up, amazed at the interruption to his work. 'Those knives.' He pointed to the cutlery. 'You're silver-plating them.' Fen blinked hard, just as his wife did. It seemed to be a family trait. Simeon shook his head. He could barely believe that the root of the family's misfortune was so tragically simple. He placed his hand on the artisan's shoulder. 'You have lost a lot of daughters,' he said softly. The man before him sighed deeply. 'You have been . . . suspected of poisoning them, have you not?' He regretted the pricking of the accusation, but there was no way around it.

'Some people—'

'Well, I am sorry. But you *have* been poisoning them.' Simeon lifted one of the untreated steel knives. 'The amalgam you are using.' He tapped the knife on the side of the wooden pot. 'It's silver and mercury, isn't it?'

'Aye.'

'Well, the silver powder is harmless, but the mercury—'

'We made sure the babies never touched it!' Mary insisted.

Simeon softened his voice in sympathy. 'I am sure you did, but mercury is a wild metal. That is why we call it quicksilver. We now know that it can seep into the air and you can breathe it in.' He looked at her. 'I'm sorry to say that you were breathing it in even when pregnant and it would have passed through your blood to your unborn daughters. They would have come out of the womb already poisoned.'

'They were ...' the husband began, but broke off, bewildered.

'I'm sorry, sir. We adults can take that level of poison in the air, but your daughters' chances would have been null,' Simeon said, placing a hand on the man's shoulder and hoping that the knowledge would bring some sort of comfort. The words hung in the air and the couple before him stared at each other, unable to speak. 'If you want to try again for a child, I can advise you how to do it safely.'

Well, the parson's suspicion of Mary Fen seemed unfounded. But Charlie White was surely no stranger to dark intentions.

Back at the house, Simeon found his uncle sitting up, with a letter clutched to his chest and a pen on the floor beside

him. He refused to say what the missive contained. 'I'll fetch you a restorative,' Simeon said, after taking the cleric's pulse rate. He went to his room and poured a glass of tonic, although he was not optimistic about its potential to help. Despite the claims of his tutors, he had always been convinced the drink's effect was more on the mental being than the physical.

When he returned with it a few minutes later, the parson's eyes were closed and he was mumbling to himself.

'Drink this, Uncle,' Simeon said, putting the tumbler to the older man's lips.

Instantly, Hawes was awake. He threw the drink aside, shattering the glass.

'Damn it! Someone is poisoning me!' he cried out. 'I am being killed. It must be her!' His arms writhed in the air and Simeon fought to hold them down – the parson's sudden strength was an amazement after his weakness a few minutes earlier. Simeon could think only of the death throes of a tiger.

'She cannot get anywhere close to you,' Simeon insisted. 'She has been trapped behind that glass wall for more than a year. If anyone is poisoning you, then it is someone else.'

'Then find out who!' the parson snarled. 'Find out! I will not go to my maker in this state.' He whispered something that Simeon could not hear. Then he spoke out loud again. 'If I die, do not let her out. The judge said that she must not be allowed out or she will be taken to the madhouse. Promise me you will not. Not until it has been settled with Watkins and the authorities.'

'Uncle—'

'You must swear.'

'Must I?'

'Yes. Just think what will occur if she is let loose in contravention of the conditions prescribed by the judge.'

Simeon disliked being forced into such a vow, but he relented. His uncle was probably correct that the due process should be followed, otherwise he would probably be cut out of the subsequent decision entirely.

'I do swear it.'

'I am glad. Here. See that this is sent.' He shoved the letter into Simeon's grasp. 'You may read it.'

It was addressed to the bishop.

My lord Bishop,

I beg your most profound indulgence in a private matter. I believe I am the subject of an unholy crime. Someone unknown is doing me to death with the use of a foul poison. Poison, my lord. I make no bones about it. I beg you to send such an inquisitor as will discover the identity of the devil. I know for one that the woman of whom I have guardianship harbours fury towards me, due to my position, although I take on the wardship as a duty to keep her from the madhouse. If not she, then one of my servants or one of the local people who have fomented a secret hatred in their hearts towards me. My nephew, Dr Simeon Lee, knows the identity of those with the greatest reasons to wish me ill.

I remain, my lord, the most humble servant of the Church in your figure.

Oliver Hawes DD

'You want me to dispatch this?' Simeon asked, perturbed.

'Yes. And send for the constable. I want people subject to questions. They must give up their foul secrets or face *peine forte et dure*.'

Torture? It was not the fourteenth century. 'I don't believe there are sufficient grounds for such an action.'

'There must be. It must be sent.'

Mrs Tabbers entered the room. 'I heard something break, sir,' she said uncertainly.

Hawes leaned over the side of his bed and vomited. The servant ran to clean it up with a cloth pulled from a pocket in her apron, while the parson recovered, his eyes blazing.

'I understand, Uncle,' Simeon said. He had severe doubts about the instructions, but it was no time to argue. He tried to understand what lay behind the parson's sense of persecution – it was not uncommon for the brains of the dying to take eccentric turns, even paranoid ones. But if someone nearby really was behind Hawes's illness, it was clear that it could not be Florence. She was where she always was.

And yet Simeon had to admit that poison now seemed a plausible explanation after all. If there was an infection, it was nothing he had seen before and nothing anyone who had been in contact with Parson Hawes exhibited signs of bearing. It could be some sort of internal injury or disease, but there would be no way of knowing without cutting the man apart. 'Mrs Tabbers, would you be so good as to spend the night in the house? I think Dr Hawes needs constant watch.'

'Of course, sir.'

'Tyrone!' the parson barked. 'Fetch Tyrone, he will find who is doing this to me.' He tore his square spectacles from his face and threw them aside as if they burned him.

'Who?' Simeon, bemused, asked the housekeeper. He had never heard the name, but a man does not call on his deathbed for a distant acquaintance.

'Don't know, sir,' she replied, concerned only with cleaning.

Simeon bent down to the parson. 'Who is Tyrone? Is he important? Does he know who is . . . poisoning you?'

'He will find out, I say!'

'Then tell me how to find him.' But the cleric only glared, pulled back and squeezed his eyelids closed. His chest sank, as if all the strength had once more evaporated. It had been an astonishing display.

'Would Mrs Hawes know who this man is?' he asked the housekeeper.

'I don't know, sir.'

Simeon approached the cold wall of Florence's cell and stood before it. His fingers stretched of their own volition towards the reflecting glass.

As if she had been waiting for him, she stepped out from her private apartment and met his gaze. Hers seemed somehow deeper and more forceful than it had been. As if she were returning to herself.

'Do you know what the matter is with Dr Hawes?'

She smiled but said nothing. The previous occasions had taught him to expect such a response. But was it hiding knowledge or ignorance? He could not tell.

He tried another tack. 'Who is Tyrone? Dr Hawes wants him here.'

The woman behind the glass laughed lightly to herself, lifting her mouth and stretching out her throat as she did so. He saw the long, aesthetic line of her throat. Then she turned and passed back into her private room, with the light rustle of moving green silk.

Chapter 8

'Please, sir! Come quick!'

Simeon was shaken into sickly consciousness. The housekeeper's face came into view in the light blue that exists only a little after dawn.

'Mrs—'

'Dr Hawes. I think he's dying!'

Simeon staggered from his bed, not bothering to throw clothes over his nightshirt, and grabbed his medical bag.

The library gas lamps on the wall were lit, but low, affording the room a dim yellow wash. One look at his patient told him the man was on the edge of the precipice between life and death.

'Uncle! Dr Hawes!' he shouted. He slapped the man's

grey, unshaven cheeks. 'Wake up!' He lifted the eyelids, looking for a pupil reaction to the light Mrs Tabbers held aloft. There was none. He tried *sal volatile* beneath the man's nose, blowing air into the man's lungs and shaking his chest hard to get the heart beating.

But it made no odds. Because regardless of the actions prescribed by his textbooks, Simeon knew his patient had expired. The colour was already draining from his lips; there was no pulse in the wrist or neck. No, there would be no more sound, no more fury from the curate.

Upon his weary instruction, Mrs Tabbers departed to fetch Cain from his cottage on Mersea, and Simeon dropped heavily into an armchair. A pang of anger shot through him then and he swept all his instruments from the octagonal table. A jumble of tongue depressors, the useless stethoscope, the heavy bottle of restorative that had never restored, all went tumbling to the floor.

So now there were two dead men at the house. Here, a priest who should have been preaching his Sunday sermon that morning; and outside in the stable, John White, cold as the mud whence he had been dragged. Turnglass House had become a morgue.

'Don't be sad, Simeon.'

The voice echoed around the room. It came from every-where at once. It was low, as if it drifted in the black water and Sargasso weed of the creeks. And every bit as cold. Finally, that voice.

'Florence,' he said, to himself, not to her. He stared at the dark glass. He could see nothing behind it, but she was there, he knew.

And then it surrounded him again. 'He always dreamed of being plucked up to Heaven. And now . . .'

There was a spark in the black as she lit her oil lamp. The glow filled her room, casting her grainy shadow to the floor. He stood and went to her. He could see his reflection twice – once in the glass and once in her irises.

'I thought you would never speak.'

'And then I did.' Her voice had a defiant hint of the local accent below the fine tones of a squire's daughter. It was tugging weeds below the smooth surface.

He glanced at the corpse on the sopha. 'Now that he's dead.'

There was a long pause, heavy air. 'Yes. Now that he's dead, I have found my voice.'

'Do you know what killed him?'

She cocked her head to one side, amused. 'You're the doctor.' She was enjoying the game of evasion.

'Do you have an idea?'

'In here, Simeon?' She waved her hand. 'How could I have any ideas at all in here?'

He wondered if that were true. 'So why are you speaking now?'

She sat and stared into the oil flame. 'I think it's that I want to. I want to hear myself.'

'I want to help you, Florence.'

'You came to help Oliver, Simeon. That didn't turn out so well.' She smirked a little.

'My medical training only goes so far.'

'Oh, I know that. It took two doctors to put me behind this screen.' She leaned forward and tapped the lamp

100

against the glass. 'Such learned men. All that training it took to know that I was best placed here so as not to endanger myself, or them or any other men.'

He wondered where Mrs Tabbers was, how far away Cain lived and how long it would take for them to return.

'They did their best, I'm sure. What people are capable of – that's something we can't learn in a lecture theatre.'

She glanced at the dead priest. 'Oh yes, that's certainly true. People are astonishing at times. The things that I have done, what the others who lived on this godforsaken place have done. I would never have predicted them. No.'

His brow furrowed; there was so much she was holding back. 'What are you talking about? Florence, if you know something, tell me.' She made no reaction. 'Who is Tyrone?' he asked. 'Dr Hawes wanted him here.'

'I'm sure he did.'

'So you know him?'

'You could say that we have met.'

'Can you tell me where to find him? Dr Hawes said he would know who was poisoning him.' The information would be too late for a doctor and medicine, but in time for a judge and the rope.

Florence sat back on her deep blue chaise longue. 'I don't want to meet him again. If you knew what he had done to me, you wouldn't either.'

That gave him pause, but still he had to press on. 'Do you know where he is?'

'Yes.'

'Then for God's sake, tell me where.'

Instead of answering him, she began to sing to herself, a sweet, sad hymn. '*Abide with me; fast falls the eventide. The darkness deepens; Lord, with me abide. When other helpers fail and comforts flee, help of the helpless, oh, abide with me.*'

It did not help him; it seemed a mockery. What would convince her? 'Dr Hawes was good to you. He kept you out of Bedlam.'

'Have you considered that that is where I belong?'

The words were a surprise, but he had no doubt that she meant them. And it went some way to explaining why she had not immediately demanded her liberty after Hawes's death. 'You have no idea what you are saying.'

'How so?'

'I've been in that foul pit. You can't imagine what goes on there.' The game she was playing was beginning to irritate him.

'Enlighten me.'

'Enlighten you?' His emotion widened into anger. 'In the Devil's name, I'll enlighten you. I've seen men take their own lives by drinking the vitriol used to clean the floors. Would you like to know how their screams sounded?' He did not wait for an answer. 'I've seen women give birth and offer their own children up if the men overseeing them would only let them out. My God, I would rather beg on the streets than consign someone there. So no, I will not see you, nor any other human being, degraded to that.'

He strode around the room and ended standing over Hawes's body. Simeon had lost his patient, but that made

him doubly determined to find the cause of the man's death. He thought back to his lectures and recalled one old professor ordering the eager young students to 'consider the environment' when looking for cause. Was there something in the surroundings that he had missed? Hawes had been so certain that he was being poisoned. What if he was, but not by human hand? Toxins could slip so easily into the home – arsenic in the wallpaper, for instance, or mercury in knife handles.

He tore the room apart.

To laughter from the glass box, he upended the chairs, pulled books from the shelves and threw the rugs aside.

'What is it that you are looking for?' she taunted him.

'Whatever killed your brother-in-law.'

'I doubt you'll find it under the Indian rug.'

Half an hour later, he rubbed his aching back. Nothing. Was the house keeping something secret from him? Or was Hawes himself? His eye fell on the locked secretary cabinet.

The parson had shown him the little iron key that he kept in his pocket. Well, he would guard it no longer. Extracted from the dead man's waist, it twisted in the cabinet's lock. The front panel turned down to reveal numerous drawers inside, and within them Simeon found the usual assortment of writing implements, ink, *et cetera*. It was an attractive piece of furniture: decorative brasswork on the cabinet was wrought into images of birds, fruit, weapons; while a horizontal panel supporting the stack of drawers was decorated with a painted relief of a

crowned man asleep below a shining North Star, his name emblazoned below: 'Arthur'. But the cabinet-maker's skill counted for naught as Simeon's hope of a revelation foundered.

He returned to searching the room for anything toxic, all the while watched by the woman behind the glass. He examined again the wallpaper, the leather on the chairs, the rug, but there was nothing out of the very ordinary.

And then his gaze fell on the secretary cabinet again. There was something about that painted panel that itched in his mind. King Arthur slumbering. It was a legend that every schoolboy knew: Arthur was not dead, but sleeping upon Avalon: an island hidden from men's sight.

He got up from the parson's seat and checked the cabinet panel, rapping on it with his knuckles. *Yes*, the sound was hollow! So there was a cavity behind. And a cavity in a secretaire could only mean a hidden compartment.

The thought was not matched to a find, however, as the best part of an hour spent looking for a mechanism to open that panel proved to him that the task was more easily considered than accomplished. He was just about to search in the stable block for a hatchet with which to hack the wood apart when he ran his fingers back over the decorative brasswork. It could hide a button. He pressed and pulled, until by chance he pushed two of the little icons at once.

A click and the panel flipped down.

A voice crawled up his back. 'Well done, Simeon.'

The curate had had a secret indeed, it seemed. For

inside the cavity Simeon found something that struck him with astonishment. It was a smoking implement made up of a long, straight ivory-and-terracotta pipe plugged into a square terracotta bowl. Oh, he had seen pipes like this before and knew what they meant. This one was quite remarkable, however – the ivory was delicately carved with intertwined flowers, making an ugly thing an object of extraordinary delicacy.

'Oh yes, well done, Simeon.'

'Thank you, Florence.' He said it with the same irony that had dripped from her words.

'I think that deserves a reward.'

He looked up from the pipe. 'What do you mean?'

'Something that might, in a sense, go with the item that you have just found.'

'Go on.'

She lay along her chaise longue and pointed at the tallest bookcase. 'That book that you began to read.'

He remembered the strange red novelette with gilded letters, *The Gold Field* written by 'O. Tooke', about a man crossing the Atlantic in 1939 in search of his mother. The novelette that Florence had described, without speaking, only by holding up a page with words upon it circled in ink, as a *premonition*. Simeon had been happy to return its queer time-jumping story to the shelf where she was now pointing.

'What about it?'

'You left it too early.'

'What do you mean?' He took it down and flicked to a point halfway through.

There weren't any sailings for New York for a week. I sat in waterfront bars hoping that a stray ship would turn up out of the blue, offering a quick crossing. I drummed my fingers on the table day in, day out, scanning the horizon and every morning sending to the harbourmaster's office to ask if there had been any stroke of luck. There wasn't, of course. So I had to join the scheduled *Floating City*. It was a huge ship, with cabins for more than a thousand people to skim across the waves on its giant zinc skis.

I had less desire to socialize with my fellow passengers than a murderer desires to socialize with the ghosts of his victims. I kept to my berth as much as I could, venturing out for meals and for an hour's walking up and down the deck so that my muscles wouldn't atrophy. I did this after sunset to minimize the chance I would have to speak to anyone. I needn't have worried – the intense scowl that populated my face scared everyone off. I couldn't wait to get on that airtrain to fly to California and confront the devil.

'No, further in,' Florence insisted.

He went to the end of the story, which finished at the middle of the book and was followed by blank pages.

So there he was. And there I was. And nothing between us except a hatred that burned like hot coals. I could have put a knife in his ribs and said a prayer of thanks to the Almighty while I did it. For all his declaration of love and piety, he would have done the same to me in the

time it took to cuss. The question was: which of us had the plan, and which of us had the gut-ache to put it into practice? In the end, I did.

'It's empty from here.'

'Is it? Turn it over.' She motioned for him to do so.

He flipped the book in his hands. The rear cover was plain red leather. But when he opened it, he found the title page, handwritten in blue ink and fine penmanship, of a very different book.

The Journal of Oliver Hawes DD.

'Why didn't you tell me about this until now?' he demanded angrily. 'It could have been important for investigating his sickness.'

'Perhaps that is why.'

He did not like her insinuation. 'But why on earth did he write it in the back of this book?' he asked.

'Because that is the very best place to hide it.' And he knew she was right. Had she not pointed it out, he would never in a century have stumbled across it.

'His journal,' Simeon muttered to himself.

'He would read it to me at night. To keep me entertained.' She sneered at the words as if they carried a bad odour. 'He had been reading it to me that day you found it. And now that it is time for you to read it, I shall leave you to it.' She retreated into her unseen private apartment.

He leafed through the cleric's words. Most were trivial

records of days passed in prayer or the administration of parochial affairs. But a few stood out.

16 April 1879

I received a monograph today that was most interesting. It came from the Anglican Communion Corresponding Society and described the old practice of 'sin eating'. The custom was once widespread in the eastern parts of England, and survives in pockets. The generalized pattern is that upon the funeral of a person of standing, a penniless man or woman is given money to attend. Small cakes are baked and placed on the body of the deceased and said cakes are then taken up by the sin-eater and consumed. Doing so, they take upon themselves the sins of the dead man and will answer for them upon Judgement Day in the place of the other. Such sin-eaters are thus shunned like lepers by their neighbours, for they carry as much wickedness in their bodies as the Enemy. They have pawned their eternal souls for their living bodies. A poor bargain.

19 April 1879

James worries me greatly. He has been gambling again. He goes to London, stays at some disreputable club — or worse — and fritters away the money that Father left him. He refuses to tell me how much he has lost — I am sure he is losing, rather than winning; after all, who ever beats the gaming table? — but it must be substantial. This afternoon I found him burning a letter in the grate. There was a crest at the top and I suspect it was from the Westminster bank, with whom he holds his account. I shall pray for him.

3 May 1879

I am quite frantic. It is three o'clock in the morning and James
came home half an hour ago. His trousers were wet through even
though it is a dry night and they smelled of the sea. He must have
been wading in the surf. Why does a man wade in the surf at night
around here? There is only one reason.

I confronted him.

'Don't worry about me, big brother,' he said in that infantile tone
he adopts at such times.

'I worry greatly for you. For your mortal body and your
immortal soul,' I replied.

'Ah well. As for the immortal, you have to understand one thing.'
I was terrified, I shall admit. I had a premonition, knowing what
he was going to say. I had hoped he would never actually say the
words, that he would at least keep them to himself. 'Your Heaven,
your G—d. It's all nonsense, man. Don't you see? We live, we die,
that's it. That's the whole deal! Dead as a doornail.'

I always suspected, really, that James was an atheist. But to
hear the words uttered stopped me cold. Of course, the Lord always
knew what was in his heart, so it is no more a sin now than before,
and yet the arrogance of it!

'And what of the mortal, then!' I snapped. 'If you care nothing
for G—d's law, what about the Queen's?'

'What, old Watkins and his revenue men? They couldn't find
their own legs.'

'And what if they do find you?' I insisted. 'What if they catch
you with your wares or whatever you call them?'

'Consignments. We call them consignments if you would know.
Well, if they do happen to trip across us — not that they would,

we're very careful of times and places — but if they do, then I have this.' He opened his jacket and tucked into his belt was a loaded pistol. I demanded then and there that he take it out of the house. 'Why? Afraid I might use it on you?'

'Do not joke about murder,' I warned him. I was angry, and that itself is a deadly sin, but I believe I was quite justified.

Well, he smirked at me and went his way up to his chamber. And I wish I could say that was the last I heard of him that night. But as I sit to write this journal, the sounds I hear from his apartment are too loud to ignore. The creaking, the laughing. The sounds of fornication. I cannot but hear her too.

5 May 1879

I had barely sat down to begin today's entry when James stumbled in half-drunk. I had only a moment to close this book and turn it right-side up, so that it presented the strange futuristic fable. I managed it, but James spied my furtive movement and snatched it from my hands. 'Oho, brother, what have we here?' he chuckled. And to my consternation, he sat and began to read the story. All the while, I worried that he would turn it over and discover my journal — not that there is anything of which I should be ashamed, but a man likes his private thoughts to remain private, and that is why I keep them discreetly here. After all, I know that even if I were to record them in a normal fashion and lock them away, James would get his hands on the key somehow and pry. No, this intelligent method of privacy keeps them far safer than any lock. And the fact that James read the whole of The Gold Field in the space of a three-hour sitting, not once noticing that these thoughts were recorded in the rearmost pages of the book, has proved to me the efficacy of my method. After reading to

the end of the story, he had sobered a little. 'Do you think we will ever be able to fly through the air like that?' he asked, talking about the aerial machines mentioned in the book.

'If G—d wills it,' I told him.

'Oh yes, always "if G—d wills it."' I did not appreciate his mocking tone. 'And what do you think about the story itself – revenge, really, isn't it?'

'"Vengeance is mine, sayeth the Lord,"' I quoted. 'That means it is not for us poor sinners to contemplate.'

'Surely, we have a right to grab recompense from anyone who's hurt us. Just as the hero does here.' He waved the book. As if The Gold Field were as great an authority as Deuteronomy. 'He went through Hell to find the truth about his mother. He deserves his vengeance. It is his for the taking, that's what I understand from this. And isn't the point of reading to make us think about these things?'

'This story is a divertissement. I set store by the message of a more holy book.'

He rolled his eyes in the most infuriating fashion. 'Why on earth do you even bother reading anything except the Bible? Your mind's already made up.'

At that, I asked him to leave. But it did set me thinking: yes, the author of this strange little work certainly seems of the opinion that vengeance is the right of those who have been wronged. I wonder what flex is available in the Bible's words regarding ownership of revenge – for instance: can a man be the instrument of G—d in exacting the due revenge? I do wonder if the author of this red volume – 'O. Tooke' – had a kernel of a grand idea, hidden among his descriptions of hot California landscapes and houses made of glass. I shall have to consider the question more deeply.

111

The earlier events of this morning, those I was going to record, pale in significance such that I shall not trouble myself now to write them.

9 May 1879

I had a pleasant day on diocesan business in Colchester. The bishop required some advice on administrative matters and I was pleased to give it to him. I dined alone and returned around eight o'clock.

10 May 1879

I was in church today, composing a sermon on greed. I hoped to strike James's conscience with it. Even if he is an atheist, and damned for it, he may still have some moral sense. I was writing it, as I prefer to do, in the pulpit, so I can understand how the words will fly out, when I noticed a fellow sitting at the back of the nave. He was not praying, just sitting quietly. I thought nothing of it, until close to an hour later I looked up and he was still there. I wrestled more with the argument of the sermon, and sometime after, when I put the final words down, this man was still in the pew, having been there nearly two hours without moving.

I went down and addressed him. After all, it is unusual enough to see a stranger on Mersea, let alone one who sits in the church for two hours without a word of prayer.

'I am Dr Hawes, parson of this parish.'

'I have heard of you, Parson,' he replied in a rough sort of a voice.

'What have you heard?'

'Oh, very good things. Very good things indeed. You are quite the inspiration.'

'Oh, hardly!' I said. It was flattering, but pride comes before a fall and I have always tried to avoid such pomp.

'No, no!' he insisted. 'I have heard far and wide of your devotion. That's why I came here.'

'May I know your name, sir?'

'My name?'

'Indeed, sir.'

'It is Tyrone.'

'Oh, like the county in Ireland?'

'Just the same.'

'I visited there as a child.'

'Did you?'

'My father was in the government service after he quit the army. He took us there for three years. Overseeing the collection of taxes. I very much enjoyed my time there.'

We talked more, about Mr Tyrone – though I cannot recall what he said – and about my ministry for the Lord. He approved of all I was doing.

'Well, Parson,' he said eventually, 'I must go home.'

'Where is that?'

'Colchester.'

'You came all the way to meet me?' I asked, a little surprised – and, I must admit before our Lord, not unpleased.

'I did.' He stood up and collected his hat. 'And it has been worth the journey.'

12 May 1879

I overheard James and Florence whispering today. I managed to catch the occasional phrase and it struck me that they were discussing The Gold Field. *I thought it most odd, but dismissed the point. I accompanied Mrs Tabbers to the market in Colchester to buy some household wares. They are robbers there, that is for certain. The cost of linen for the bedrooms is quite ruinous now.*

14 May 1879

At James's suggestion, Florence has been painting most curiously. She has been composing images inspired by the very volume within which I surreptitiously write.

One of the canvases has inexplicably appeared above the fireplace in the hall. I nearly fell over when I saw it hanging there in place of the bucolic hunting scene that has hung since our father's time. 'What in the Devil's name has happened?' I exclaimed, forgetting myself. Florence, who turned out to have been watching me enter the house after a brief turn around Ray to take some air, burst into what I can only describe as maniacal laughter. 'I never thought to hear you utter that phrase, brother-in-law. Do you like it?' she enquired, standing atop the stairway. I felt colour rise in my cheeks and could do nothing but stare at it further. It was a painting of her — unquestionably, it was her — but set against a scene that was clearly recognizable from The Gold Field. *For her person was set before a large house almost wholly constructed of glass and perched upon a clifftop. The sun shone hard, as it does in California, where the climate is closer to that of the Indies than our own. And the*

clothes she wore were utterly revealing of her silhouette in a way that none but her maid would normally encounter. I was quite astonished.

'I neither like nor dislike it,' I said, for I did not want to appear churlish. It was something that had meant a deal to her, I supposed, and I wanted to make her happy.

Simeon read those words and thoughtfully closed the journal. He descended the stairs and stared at the painting. The California light was indeed reflecting off glass walls, making the whole imaginary house shine like a lantern. He stood for a while, losing track of the tick of the clock. That landscape seemed somehow more real than the one outside the door. He felt in his muscles that he could step forward through the frame and onto that clifftop, into a search for a lost woman.

When his reverie cleared, he returned to the library and sat down once more with the journal. There were more trivial entries, then another not-so-trivial.

17 May 1879

I could bear it no more this night. Sitting, waiting to see what trouble James was bringing upon our house. I remained in my room until gone midnight without a candle burning so he would think me asleep. Then I heard him come to my door and stop outside. I held my breath. The floorboards creaked away and I heard him going out of the house.

First, I crept up to his chamber, to watch over Florence and ensure she was sleeping well. She was. After a few minutes, I

hurried out of the house myself. James had a lamp so I could follow him easily.

We made it all the way along the Strood, right to the Hard. He went down onto it and waited. I hid behind a tree to keep spy. There was a ship out at anchor and, while I watched James, seven or eight more men came. They came right by me and

And then, without warning, total darkness fell. Simeon could no longer see the book nor his hand that held it in place. The gas lamps on the walls had cut out.

His medical books had once detailed the quirk of nature that means when one human sense is shut off, others can make up for it. And just so, without sight, his hearing became acute. He could hear his own heartbeat – quicker than natural, heavier too, sending more rich blood through his muscles in order to flee or fight.

His heart was not all he could hear, though.

'What's happening, Simeon?' Florence asked calmly through the dark.

'The gas has cut out, that's all.' Of course, that would not be all, he told himself. If it were an actual leak into the house, they would be in grave danger of poisoning or an explosion that could blow the building apart in its entirety. He stood and felt his way to where he thought the doorway was. But he tripped on something wooden, fell and cracked his head on a table. It pounded as he squatted, waiting for the pain to leave him. Then there was a new sound: the library door opening. And footsteps. Someone was coming in.

'Cain?' Simeon called. 'Mrs Tabbers?' Whoever was

in the room, instead of answering, suddenly opened the shutters on a lamp, shining it in Simeon's face and blinding him. 'Is the gas gone?' he asked. But they remained dumb. Instead, the beam swept the room and hit upon the lectern. Simeon, shading his vision, was becoming annoyed by the lack of reply. 'I said, is the gas gone?'

And at that, the light shut off and the room was in perfect darkness again. Whoever was holding the lamp began making their way through the room. Simeon pushed himself unsteadily to his feet.

'Cain, will you say something?'

All he heard in return was a shuffling sound moving around the room. Then the lantern beam blazed again right into him from inches away, making him stumble back as his eyes were seared with pain. He grabbed out at whoever the lamp-bearer was, sure now that they were no friend, but his hands only caught at air. The intruder scurried out of the room, to the stairs.

'I'll find you!' Simeon shouted, scrambling after them. He saw another brief flash of light as whoever he was pursuing found the front door and dashed out. But that left Simeon thrashing about in the pitch black again. Whoever it was, they had obviously turned off the gas and Simeon had no idea where the main tap was. The best he could do was feel his way down the stairs to the hallway, where he knew there was an oil lamp on the table. He found it in the dark, set it aglow and charged outside.

All he saw was the mean, lonely Strood and the gulls overhead. He circled the house and peered into the stable block but found nothing there either.

Back in the hallway, he searched until he found the tap for the gas lamps, turned it back on and lit them. 'Who was it, Simeon?' Florence asked as soon as he set foot inside the library.

'I couldn't tell.' He rubbed the top of his head. He would have a lump there the size of a potato soon.

'Do you know what they wanted?'

Simeon walked over to the sopha. He had a good idea. And the obvious absence of Oliver Hawes's journal confirmed it.

'Yes, I do. I just don't know why. Not yet.' He lowered himself onto the seat. 'Strange little community you have here. Thieves who steal books. Men who shut women in glass. Parsons who die of nothing. I can't think why anyone would live anywhere else.'

'Ray, Mersea – we're different to you people.'

'I'm beginning to come around to that conclusion.' He stood up, winced again at the sheet of pain that wrapped around his skull and headed out of the room.

'Where are you going now?'

'Now? To bed.'

'You're just going to let that man run around?'

'First, we don't know it was a man, and second, yes, I am.'

But as he stood, he noticed something on the floor. The debris of his search had partly hidden it. It was a sheet of notepaper underneath the lectern. He picked it up.

On blue letter paper, headed with the stamp *Metropolitan Police Magistrate, Bow Street, London*, there was a letter to Oliver Hawes. It could only have come

from between the leaves of the parson's journal and fallen out when the book was stolen.

December the fourteenth, 1879

Dear Dr Hawes,

It is now some six months since I entrusted the person of your sister-in-law into the joint care of Mr Watkins and yourself. Since I do not have an address for Mr Watkins, I would be most grateful if you could pass this communication to him. For our records, I would like to know the current state of affairs regarding this woman. Has she stood criminal trial, or has she, as you suggested at the time, been confined to a mental asylum? (And what of the other one she was with, Annie White?)

I thank you for your time in this matter.

Sir Nigel Gant KBE, JP

Annie White? It rang a bell. Cain had said dead John had a sister, Annie, who had left Mersea some time ago. What in Heaven's name was this all about?

'Nigel Gant. Police Magistrate,' he said, facing Florence.

Her lips trembled but she quickly regained her composure. 'I don't know the name.'

Simeon watched her. It was almost like seeing symptoms in a patient: a detached series of colourations and movements. 'I don't believe you.'

She said no more.

*

That night again he woke from a dream. He had dragged John White's corpse from the mud only for its eyes to flick open and its mouth to make sounds that became words. Accusations. Confessions. Condemnations. Whom he was accusing, whom he condemned, Simeon could not tell, for the sounds were in the tongue of Babel: every language and none. Only one utterance made sense, appearing and disappearing through the mire of sounds. *Florence.*

Simeon threw back the covers and pulled himself out of the bed. He had to return to the library.

He padded on bare feet to what had once been the parson's inner sanctum. Like last time he had visited in the night, a light was glowing from that room. And just like last time, she was sitting with her back to him. But this time, she spoke before he did.

'Good evening, Simeon.'

'Good evening, Florence.'

'Neither of us sleeps tonight.' She curled around to face him.

'You have been drawing again,' he said, seeing a page and pencils on the table. She inclined her head to one side. 'What have you drawn?'

'Another house in another time.'

The strange palace of glass perched above an ocean, the one from *The Gold Field*. 'Why do you always draw that place?'

'Why do you have bad dreams?'

He paused. 'I would like to know how you are aware that I do.'

'Why else would you rise in the middle of the night? To

see me when no one else is here? When no one else can disturb us?'

'You are suggesting something, Florence.'

'What should I suggest, Simeon?'

Chapter 9

After breakfast, Simeon wrote to his father, offering to make the arrangements for his uncle's funeral and the disposal of the parson's estate. Watkins, alerted by Cain of the sad news, came to discuss it all.

'One thing to consider,' Simeon said, 'is the situation regarding your daughter.'

'You must not let her out!' Watkins insisted. 'Sir, not yet. Not until the law is clear.'

'The law . . .'

'Aye, sir. If Allardyce gets wind that she is loose, my agreement with him is nullified. She will be bound and taken to the madhouse.'

It was as Simeon had promised the parson, but he had

vaguely hoped Watkins would countermand the promise made. Well, she had been behind the glass for two years; it would only be a matter of weeks, Simeon hoped, before her position could be changed. He was unhappy with the situation, but they could wait that long.

'If you insist. We must also speak about John White,' Simeon told him.

'No doubt we must.'

They went out to the stable where the dead man lay on a pair of crates, awaiting the undertaker's visit. Simeon had performed a fuller examination of the body that morning and the corpse had afterwards been cleaned and wrapped in a winding sheet but had started to smell. 'There's something strange,' he said.

'What do you mean?'

'Well, for a start, John was a local boy. To lose his way and end up drowning in the Ray channel seems a little unlikely.'

'Oh, it happens, sir,' Watkins insisted. 'It happens.'

'I'm sure it does, and for that reason I let it pass as a terrible accident. But then there was something else. Here.' Simeon peeled back the winding sheet and pointed to the dead man's midriff. Watkins looked disturbed by the torn flesh. 'I must insist you look carefully through this tear.'

'My God, must I?'

'I'm afraid so.' He took a pen from a tin in his pocket, pulled apart the edges of a hole in the flesh on top of White's stomach and pointed inside. Watkins, looking unwell, peered where Simeon was pointing. 'His ribs. Look at them. What do you see?'

'Why, his ribs, what else?'

'But what state are they in?'

'In faith, sir, how can I say?'

'You see here and here.' There were a series of sharp little notches cut into the lower edge of two of the bones that he tapped with the nib of the pen. The tip of a third rib was missing entirely, lost somewhere inside the torso or the mud. 'These cuts.'

'Stones in the mud, surely.'

'Not a chance. If he had fallen hard on a rock, that could conceivably break the ribs, but not leave these thin marks. They were made by a knife. A strong blade thrusting in three or four times at least.'

The magistrate stared at him, astonished. 'You are certain?'

'I'm a doctor in the City of London. I see knife wounds each and every week. Mr Watkins, was John White involved in smuggling?' Watkins retreated dumbly and sat heavily on a drinking trough.

Well, that confirmed it. Not only was Watkins's son-in-law involved in contrabanding, but so was the dead man in the stall. The connection was there to be drawn.

'I expect so,' the magistrate mumbled after a pregnant pause. 'They all are.'

'I thank you for your time.' He let Watkins go and took himself to the kitchen, where he found Mrs Tabbers and Cain eating a truckle of sheep's cheese. The marshes around would be sheep and goat land; cows would not thrive there. 'I need to ask you something,' he said. Cain stiffened, as if he could hear a difficult question coming. 'There are smugglers in these parts.'

'Are there now?' Cain replied gruffly.

'Where do they work? When?'

'Nothing to do with us, Doctor,' Mrs Tabbers told him nervously.

'I'm sure that's true. Nevertheless, Mrs Tabbers, I need to know.'

'Then find some'un as knows,' Cain muttered.

He felt irritation building. 'Don't waste my time.' There was a long pause, the air heavy. 'John White was involved, wasn't he?'

Mrs Tabbers busied herself clearing away the cheese and plates. Cain's jaw moved from side to side. 'Say he was. Wha' of it?'

'The man's dead, Cain.'

'Drowned. Happens on the mud.'

'I'll bet it doesn't happen to men who were born on this land. Would you be in danger? I don't think so.'

'Don' get your meanin'.' He stared up defiantly.

'I think you do. And just to make it clearer, White was stabbed. That's what killed him. Not the mud, not the water. A knife.' They looked at the blade in Cain's hand, which he was using to cut the cheese. 'I'm not in the mood for absurd claims that his death was an accident. The man was killed and he was a contrabander. So where do I find them?'

'All righ',' Cain grumbled. 'I'm no Queen's Evidence, so no names. But there migh' be somethin' tonigh'.'

'When?'

He grumbled again. 'Past midnigh' fer the tide. Four bells.' He glared up. 'Tha's two in the mornin' t'ye.'

125

'On the Hard?'

'Where else?'

Two in the morning; well, he had stayed awake longer when working nights at the hospital.

He left them and headed to the library. When he entered, the room's prisoner was staring up at the line of windows that she could not reach. He wondered what thoughts travelled through her. She had little to do but let them loose.

There was something new on her table today, something she must have taken from her private room. It was a small, perfect model of the house, but made entirely from glass, like the one in the book, the one in the painting. Like the real house, the rooms on the upper floor had coloured doors: green, blue, red. And behind each of them stood a human figurine the size of a chessman. The tiny statues were waiting patiently for the game to begin; for the gambit to be played and the king to be captured.

'Do you have someone in London, Simeon?' she asked, apropos of nothing.

'Someone?' He understood her aim, but did not want to acknowledge it yet. He wanted to let her play for now.

'Oh, you know what I mean.' She changed her expression to one he had not seen on her face before. It became coy, like a sixteen-year-old at her first ball. She approached the partition, opened her mouth wide and breathed on the cold glass, her breath turning to mist on the surface. Then she licked her finger and carved a crude heart in the watery film. It lived for a few seconds before melting away.

He chose to be truthful with her. But not open. He did not want her to slip inside him.

'No,' he said.

'Have you ever?'

'Yes.'

'Tell me about it.'

'I choose not to.'

'Are you ashamed?'

'Not at all, but you don't need to know. There's no good in you knowing.'

She smirked. 'So you interrogate me for my past, and yet yours is a mystery.'

'I came to tell you that I was going to observe the Hard tonight. Cain tells me there's contraband coming in.'

'Oh. You are still thinking about John White and his part in our story.'

'I am.'

'Then good luck, my brave one.' She touched her fingers to her heart and began to sing that hymn again. '*Help of the helpless, oh, abide with me.*' And he realized why she sang it over and over: he could just make out the tune itself on the wind. It had to be coming from the bells of the church on Mersea. It was such a mournful hymn, a song of resignation.

'Florence, my uncle Oliver is dead. And regardless of the fact that you cannot have killed him, still you will be blamed. You are a woman said to be so mad that she must be kept in this glass cage. They will condemn you to a lunatic asylum at best, and the rope at worst. Do you not see that?'

127

'I see that,' she conceded.

'And yet you don't help me uncover the truth. In God's name, why?'

Her face clouded in thought. 'Because I choose not to, Simeon. It is my life to lose.'

'And you will lose it! Bedlam or the Tyburn tree: either way, you lose it!'

'Then so be it.'

Nobody in this house knew as much as her about what had happened, of that he was certain. How could he loosen her lips? He set to thinking. He had failed through cajoling or via threats regarding her future. But he might bargain with her. Yes, a deal. He needed something to trade. But what?

Chapter 10

A little after midnight, Simeon buttoned his black coat to the neckline and pulled on navy blue trousers. He did not risk a lantern. Tonight, he had to be unseen, but it was raining and there was no sign of it letting up so his chances were good.

He left the only house on Ray and made his way to the Strood. The tide was rising, threatening to reclaim that thin causeway, the sole route on and off the island. Simeon had been on Ray for a week and it was not nearly enough to understand the patterns of watery encroachment or retreat that cut these islands off.

The ground was marshy as he picked his way along, once or twice sinking up to his knees as he missed the

more solid turf. It took him an hour to walk a distance that would have taken a quarter of that in daylight. But he eventually made it across to Mersea, passing the silhouetted hulk of the church.

All the while, he tried to puzzle out the events of the previous days and the shifting place that Florence held in them. And he kept coming back to that novelette, *The Gold Field*. Why had it become an obsession with her and James? Why did she produce paintings and models of Turnglass House's American twin made of glass?

The rain was whipping across the island now, soaking his clothes. He gave up trying to wipe the rivulets from his face and just let them stream down. It was hard weather but he barely felt it, fixed as he was on a far greater danger.

Criminals came in many forms and he had no idea if these men were cast from the timid or the brutish mould. But with the murdered corpse of John White laid out in the stable, he would make no rash moves. Whoever had done for White could well have been the man – or woman – who had broken into the house, turned off the gas lamps and stolen the parson's journal. If so, that malefactor was desperate and felt no aversion to murder.

The Hard was a strip of shingly beach. At low tide you would be able to walk out for half a mile on the sand and mud, but now the waves were lapping at the shoreline. It was a bleak, hopeless landscape and a couple of timber sea walls extending down into the waves were the only shelter from the wind. He crouched behind one, wrapping his arms around himself for warmth. He only hoped that he would not be there all night for nothing.

By the time an hour had passed, he had lost all feeling in his feet. He remained in his place, though, determined to see the night through. After another hour he had to shake himself to keep the blood flowing.

But finally, close to three o'clock in the morning, he began to see shapes on the low horizon: patches of black moving towards him at speed. And he heard them too: snorting, the distant whisper of horses. But no thumps upon the ground – their hooves must have been muffled with rags. He crouched lower behind the rotting timbers of the sea wall, hoping the horses and their riders would keep to the other side.

Within seconds, they were on the shoreline. Five of them, swinging down from their saddles. One whistled sharply, and from another direction – along the beachline on the same side of the wall as Simeon – came the sound of trotting. Simeon pressed himself to the stony ground and saw a line of five or six ponies, heavy with packs, led by a sixth man. At their rear, two more ponies were pulling a cart.

The rain-sprayed moonlight was not quite enough to pick out the faces of the men, only glimpses here and there, but one seemed to be in charge, and he was the first to speak.

'All righ', lads. Ge' on.' The voice was familiar, though Simeon was unable to place it. They began unstrapping the packs from the ponies and lining them up on the beach. One of the men lit a torch wound with an oil-soaked rag and held it aloft. Simeon presumed a boat was coming in for the goods. He was very soon proved right.

A large dinghy emerged out of the darkness, bearing towards the shore. None of the men made a sound as it approached. The pack ponies were on the beach path, twenty-odd yards behind the men watching the sea. It would probably take a minute to land, Simeon guessed, and his curiosity was pricked. Very carefully, he eased himself up and stalked across the shingle. The men still had their backs to him and he took the chance to open up one of the pony packs. Wool. No doubt bound for France or Holland untaxed. And the return trade would be spirits and tobacco.

He crept back to his hiding place and watched the men's leader, who had his back to the torch. Simeon needed to know who this man was, for he could be the key to the violent death of John White. And then the moment came as the man turned to his fellows and his face was lit full by the flame. Simeon was taken aback to see it was a man he knew. For the face of Morty, the ferryman who had spoken to him at the Peldon Rose when he had first arrived, was revealed, fired red as the Devil's.

So this was the man running the ring that had included John White and James Hawes. He had to know something about their deaths, then. And surprising as it was, it was a welcome revelation, because the man was gruff – and Simeon would still keep his wits about him – but Morty did not seem the type to wield a knife and bury a man in the mud.

He watched as Morty directed the unloading and loading – all done quickly and with barely a sound. Then the boat was on the water once more and the gang were readying their horses.

'See y'all back a' the Rose,' Morty growled. He took charge of the slow pack ponies himself, leading them on foot along the beach path as the others hied away. It was Simeon's chance, and as the others disappeared into the night, he padded after the ringleader. They had gone a few hundred paces when the ferryman left off leading the ponies and went to the shoreline, unbuttoned his trousers and began to relieve himself.

Simeon took the opportunity to quietly approach the train and check the saddle packs. They were now stuffed full of bottles of spirits as he had expected. He took one out and unstoppered it: brandy. He felt guilty as he deliberately dropped it to the shingle ground to smash.

Morty whirled around, his fingers frozen in the act of buttoning up his trousers. 'Wha'?' he spluttered.

'Are you armed?' Simeon asked.

'No.' The man sounded utterly bemused.

'You really shouldn't have told me that.' He took another bottle and tossed it onto the shingle, where it broke in two.

'Stop tha'!' The ferryman started for Simeon, but hesitated. He was on his own, aged in his sixties and not a big man.

'No need to worry, Morty,' Simeon said. 'I'm not the police, not the revenue men.'

'Then who the hell're ye?' The weak moonlight could scarcely penetrate the drizzle, let alone show a man's face well.

'You met me last week. I'm the doctor here to treat the parson.'

'Doctor?'

Simeon approached him, just enough for the moonlight to show them each other's faces. But he kept more than an arm's length away, just in case. 'I'm not interested in evasion of excise. I don't care about what's in those packs.'

'So wha' d'ye wan'?'

'I found something. Buried in the mudflats on Ray.'

'Wha' d'ye mean?'

'I found the body of John White.'

That brought on a change. Morty's head bowed. 'How did he look?' he asked.

No point in lying. 'Not good.'

'Aye, well. Mud'll do tha'.'

And now to play the only good card Simeon had. 'It wasn't the mud that killed him.'

'Wasn' the . . . ?'

'He didn't drown in the mud or in the channel. He was stabbed.'

There was a pause filled by the wind, rain and waves. Morty's voice fell into a growl. 'How d'ye know?'

'I saw the wounds. Someone wanted to kill John and they went about it the right way.'

'Who?'

'I don't know. But I want to. If you help me, we can find the man responsible. Do you have any idea?' Simeon asked.

'Idea? Oh aye, I've an idea, all righ',' he spat. He came close enough now for Simeon to see him grimace at the thought.

'Then who?'

'Am I t'tell ye?' His voice was contemptuous.

'Unless you would rather tell Mr Watkins.'

Morty considered. Then he spoke, the syllables stringing out for a mile. 'James Hawes.'

It was not an allegation that took Simeon wholly by
surprise. For sure, there was bad blood somewhere on this
island. 'Why do you think that?' he asked.

Morty grunted. 'Few days 'fore he wen' missin', John
says tha' James were from a fam'ly o' betrayers.'

'Betrayers? He was selling you out?'

'Don' know exac'ly wha' he mean'. Bu' from tha'
momen', I kep' a watch on James Hawes.'

'And?'

Morty shrugged. 'Never saw nothin' wrong.' *That
might only mean he was a subtle man, as well as an
untrustworthy one*, Simeon thought to himself. 'Then
John dis'pears. So I tells James he isn' wan'ed no more in
the business. Tells him to keep 'way.'

That would not have proved popular with James.
'What exactly did John say?'

Morty hesitated, then seemingly decided the truth was
in his favour. 'We were in the Rose. Storin' a shipmen'
just come in. I says to John tha' James is on his way t'help.
John, he cusses and spi's on the groun'. I asks him wha's
the game. He says Hawes folk ain' the kin' we wan' in
the business. Bu' John won' say no more, no ma'er how I
presses him. Now tha' kinda talk give me heebies. I think
t' myself exac'ly wha' ye're thinkin', Doctor. Tha' James
is blabbin' to Mr Wa'kins. Or worse. Or mebbe he's
plannin' on shootin' us all in the back an' takin' over the

business. Clever man, James. I don' trus' a clever man. Don' trus' 'em.'

A clever man. And a violent one too? But had James Hawes truly betrayed his partners and murdered John White? The supposition was based solely on the word of a dead man. And even if it were true, it only answered for the death of one of the corpses currently in repose at Turnglass House.

Chapter 11

When the undertaker arrived in a hearse the next day, he respectfully placed the bodies of John White and Oliver Hawes in coffins and carried them – and Simeon – away.

'A slight change of plan,' Simeon said, when they were on their way. The other man looked at him blankly. 'Will you please drive us to Colchester Royal Hospital?'

The undertaker protested but eventually agreed to the change in destination, and a few hours later the two bodies were on porcelain slabs, around which shallow gutters ran to drain the blood and other foul fluids that are released when a cadaver is dissected.

Simeon's hand held the scalpel. Behind him was one of the hospital's thick-bearded senior doctors, a Mr Bristol,

who was to supervise the post-mortem examination. Simeon had not objected because it would, in fact, be useful to have a second opinion.

The knife went into the flesh of the first corpse, that of his father's cousin, with ease. It always took Simeon aback just how fragile the human body could be when the right tool was wielded. The hair-thin blade slipped through the dermis and epidermis as easily as if he were cutting into butter.

Death, for Simeon, was a part of life, and one just as fascinating as the stage that came before it. He cut, drew and lifted; but a thorough examination of Parson Hawes's viscera found them to be the normal, complex organs of a man in his forties. No twisted gut, no spots on the kidneys, nothing untoward that would explain his symptoms, let alone his subsequent death. A puckered scar in his shoulder was noted in passing, but it was too historic to be of relevance.

Simeon turned his attention to the contents of the man's stomach. Hawes had been convinced he was the victim of continued poisoning, and while Simeon could hardly check for every compound, there were some that he could rule out. He collected a mass of part-digested vegetables and soupy liquid from within the parson, which he dissolved in a beaker of hydrochloric acid before inserting a strip of copper into the fetid solution, and waited.

'What will it show?' Bristol asked.

'A silver coating means mercury; a dark film would indicate arsenic or possibly antimony – though that would be rather exotic a toxin to find in rural Essex.' He

withdrew the strip and examined it in the light. 'And in fact, it is entirely clear.'

'Is that the result you hoped for?'

'It is *a* result.'

He produced from his bag a small sealed jar of red-brown liquid. 'Brandy that I took from this patient's study,' he explained. 'I don't think there's anything in it, but it's worth checking.' It gave the same negative result.

'There are many other toxins,' Bristol cautioned him.

'Of course. But the patient's pupils were not dilated to suggest atropine. If it were a cyanide compound, he would have been dead in seconds, not days. No strychnine convulsions. Something extracted from plants?' he mused. 'It's possible, but whoever dosed him would have gone to a lot of trouble when they could have just bought arsenic from any chemist and said they had a rat problem. But yes, we should be thorough.'

So, for hours, they tested for a plethora of other toxic compounds, finding nothing untoward. Tired, they agreed that if there were a poison in the man's body, it was an obscure one. 'Well, let's look at the other man,' Simeon suggested.

They turned their attention to John White. Simeon cut him apart in the same way. Folding back the skin and muscle exposed the ribs – a dirty yellow, due to their time in the dirt. He examined the damage to the bones through a magnification lens. 'You see these diagonal cuts into the lower three *costae*,' Simeon said.

'I do,' Bristol confirmed.

'You see how they're deeper at the bottom and peter

away towards the top. The weapon was thrust upwards and forwards. Whoever was holding it was behind this man.'

'Coward.'

'Quite.' He lifted away the skin of the neck. 'Yes, thought so. Look, the neck's been broken at C3.' He pointed to one of the higher bones.

'I see.'

'Our assailant probably grabbed him from behind, reaching around the neck, fracturing it, and stabbed three or four times up into the ribcage with the blade. Must have been quite a substantial one, I would say – the bones look strong enough and he's snapped the end off this one.' They pulled away more flesh to look at the lungs. They had been well preserved in the mud and the left lung had clearly been pierced by the knife that had come through the ribs. 'That's the cause of death there.'

'For sure. How was this man discovered?'

'Submerged in a mudflat. I expect the tides shift the mud banks; if they hadn't uncovered him, he might never have been found at all. This wasn't some drunken brawl that got out of hand – whoever killed him meant to kill him, had the right tool and used it efficiently. We're looking for someone who either planned to kill John that night, or habitually carries a knife and is ready and able to use it.'

'A bad business,' Bristol said, smoothing down his beard.

On the way back to Ray, Simeon considered again. Florence was surely the repository of vital information. How to persuade her to speak? He needed something to

trade. And then the mental picture that he held of her, always in that household twilight, suggested the fee.

As soon as he entered the house, he glanced at her self-portrait that hung above the fireplace, then went quickly up the stairs. There were the three coloured leather-clad doors he had seen on his first approach: to his bedroom, to the parson's and to the library; and the plain doors to the other bedrooms. But there had to be another. He swept along the wall. And here it was, a little, discreet, narrow opening embedded in the elm panelling, a tiny keyhole indicating how to release it.

'Mrs Tabbers!' he yelled excitedly down the stairs. She came up, huffing and puffing.

'Whatever's happened now?'

'This must be the way to the attic, yes?'

'The attic? Yes, sir.'

'I would like to go up.'

'Why?' She sounded not so much suspicious, as bemused.

'A whim of mine.'

She huffed again and drew a bunch of keys from her apron pocket. A slim iron one fitted the lock and turned. She stood back as Simeon rushed in and up a thin winding staircase into the eaves of the roof.

It was full of boxes, dust and bird droppings. Starlings were roosting in one corner and they cawed, startled, at the sight of him.

'Yes, yes,' he replied to them. 'I won't be long.' He started pulling open boxes and lifting trunk lids. They were full of the ephemera of life: broken household items, discarded linen. And then he found one full of bright

colour. He closed the lid and hefted it down the stairs, into the library.

'John White was murdered,' he said as he entered, dragging the case.

'Perhaps,' Florence replied. She was sitting on her chaise longue, waiting for him.

He discounted her evasion. 'Who by?'

She gazed up at the window. 'I wish I could have a window in here. It's not just the light, you see. It's the air. The air I breathe comes to me already tainted, it has passed in and out of your lungs, and the lungs of Mrs Tabbers or Cain. I would like air from the sky, fresh and pure.'

'I can't do anything about that.'

'No.' She sounded sad. 'But one day.' She reached for a pencil that sat beside a sheet of paper on her table. With her fingertip on its lead, she smudged it across the page a few times and admired her work. Satisfied, she went to the small hatch at the bottom of the glass and pushed it through.

Simeon recognized the scene immediately. It was the glass house in California, the one about which Florence and James had developed the strangely keen interest that had angered the parson. Unlike in Florence's self-portrait, the mansion was this time caught in a snowstorm that swirled and smothered. The lines were thin and grey or black, and yet they still had an unidentifiable nature to them that suggested Simeon could reach right through the paper to another world that was peopled with men and women; where a man was searching for the truth about his mother's fate.

The image faded and he returned to the here and now. Florence had powdered her face and her lips were more rubied than the previous day. 'I was thinking about what I found hidden in Oliver's secretaire. That pipe,' he said. He had been struck by the unusual ivory-and-terracotta item. 'It's an opium pipe. I've had to deal with the effects and they're not attractive. It was something that Dr Hawes wanted to keep away from public sight.'

'Oh yes. You would do well to know where that comes from.' She was taunting him with her knowledge.

'Will you enlighten me?'

'Why would I?'

The sheer nihilism of the question struck him hard.

'Because in return for telling me more, I will make you a gift.'

Her eyebrows lifted. 'But I have everything that I need right here. Didn't Oliver tell you?' There was an under-current of malice in her voice.

'I am sure there is more that you want.' He lifted the lid of the trunk. The sheen of sun-yellow silk reflected off the glass of the wall that kept him from her. 'You have lived for a year or more in what you wear now,' he said.

He lifted the yellow dress, the one she wore in the portrait in the hall. It was warm in his hands. Below was another one, peach, and then one in crimson.

The edges of her mouth rose. 'Would you like me to dress for you, Simeon?' She gazed at the gift and sat on her chaise longue. 'Well, my brave one. We shall make a bargain. I shall gain clothing and you shall gain information.' She paused thoughtfully. 'You should return to London.

143

Call at Limehouse. A house on the riverfront with a red lantern. I don't know the actual address, but you can find it, I'm sure.'

He folded the dress and slipped it through the hatch in the glass. She took hold of the sun-blown silk just a second before he let go, and the tips of their fingers touched before she pulled away.

Chapter 12

His breakfast was a rich mutton pie that Mrs Tabbers had taken from the oven with a clatter. She had intended it for luncheon, she said, but since the doctor was going to London for the day, he might as well eat it now. He thanked her profusely.

After mopping up the last of the thick gravy with a hunk of bread, he donned his travelling coat and set out for the capital. He had just stepped out into the fresh air when, without warning, something seemed to shake the very bricks of the house. A rocketing explosion that came from nowhere, before echoing three or four times off the side of the building. Bewildered, his stomach clenched and he whirled around. 'Mrs Tabbers!' he shouted. 'Cain!'

Cain appeared in the stable doorway. In his arm was a double-barrelled shotgun. 'Wha'?' he demanded.

Simeon ran over. 'What was that?'

A sly grin broke over the man's face, exposing five brown teeth and black gaps between them. 'Tha'? Come an' look.' With a certain trepidation, keeping a close watch on the gun, which still had one barrel to discharge, Simeon followed him into the stable. 'There ye go.' There were two narrow straw-carpeted stalls. One – the one where John White had lain – was empty, but in the other the carcass of a young foal lay on the floor, half its head missing. 'Lame fro' birth. Best thin' for 'im,' Cain informed him. 'No use fer lame animals.'

The grin with which he said it made it clear that Cain was taunting the city man.

'Be careful with that gun,' Simeon muttered, leaving the gory scene behind him and stomping towards the Strood.

He made quick time to the Rose, where he hired a trap to take him to Colchester railway station. There he caught the fast train to London, and by the middle of the afternoon he was at Bow Street Magistrates' Court.

'I wish to see the police magistrate, Mr Gant,' he told the porter, who was engaged in sorting mail into low piles.

'His Worship's not sitting today.'

'May I ask when he will next sit?'

The porter consulted a list. 'Monday.'

That was five days away and longer than Simeon was prepared to wait. Gant was the man who had written to Oliver Hawes about Florence and John White's sister,

Annie, suggesting he had placed Florence in Hawes's care following some legal contretemps in London. 'It is a matter of great importance. May I know his address?'

'His address! Lord, do you think we hand out the magistrates' addresses? And have all the desperate beasts from these courts go calling on 'em in the middle of the night? No, sir, I cannot hand over his address any more than I can hand over the keys to the Bank of England.'

It was hardly a surprising reply. Gant would have been in *Who's Who*, with a club listed where Simeon could write to him, but it would likely be no faster than waiting until Monday. Instead, he noticed a signboard affixed to the wall. It pointed to the various courts and offices, and that suggested a different approach.

As the porter turned his attention back to sorting the mail, Simeon surreptitiously followed one of the directions on the signboard, drifting towards a set of stairs leading down into the depths of the building.

Records departments were always below ground, he had found over the years. It could have been something about the temperature being better for preserving paper, but it was more likely that the sort of person who worked in a records department was not the sort to complain about a lack of sunlight. Most of them probably welcomed it.

It was cold as he descended, and damp so that condensation was pooling at the bottom of cream-painted brick walls. He passed a pair of open storerooms containing mops and buckets, a cloakroom for gentlemen and one for ladies, and, at the end of it all, a mottled glass door. 'Files'

had been painted cheaply in white on the door. The lock, he noticed, was a modern spring-lock, the type that made sure the door could not be left unsecured by accident. At waist height, there was a separate handle. It was ajar and he stepped through.

He had had a wild hope that the room might be empty, allowing him free rein, but among a labyrinth of stuffed shelves an immensely fat man was trundling a cart and inserting manila folders bound with white ribbon into their rightful places. He stopped what he was doing and blinked in surprise.

'I was looking for Mr Godfrey,' Simeon told him.

'Who?'

'You're not him?' The man shook his head. 'I'm sorry, who are you?' Out of sight of the fat man, he placed his hand over the lock, gently twisted the knob to draw back the bolt, and pressed the latch into place to hold it there.

'Harrison.'

'Sorry,' Simeon replied, and retreated from the room.

He made his way out of the building and up Long Acre, where he found a post office. He then sent a deliberately garbled telegram to Mr Harrison at Bow Street Magistrates' Court, telling him that there had been an accident at his home and he was needed urgently. He sauntered back to the court, waited half an hour for the telegram boy to scurry in, another minute for the clerk to rush out, and went down to the files room where the latched spring-lock allowed him entry. He stepped in and released the latch so that it locked behind him.

The clerk probably lived in the suburbs – Stockwell or

Clapham, perhaps – which would give Simeon a good hour-and-a-half to rifle the files and discover how and why Florence and Annie White had been entrusted into the care of Parson Hawes by a police magistrate. But if Harrison lived closer, he would not be so lucky with the time. He set to work.

The files were arranged according to the district where the crime had taken place and the date it had occurred. But even presuming a crime *had* taken place – involving Florence, Annie or both – Simeon had little idea where it could have been. His best pointer regarded the date. The letter from Gant had said it was six months since he had put Florence and Annie into the parson's care, and it was presumably shortly before that happened that the crime took place. That meant somewhere around June 1879.

He went through scores of boxes, examining the records from that month. Finally, after forty minutes, with the time ticking away, he found it.

> Florence Emily Hawes. Found fugitive from local mag-istrate, Watkins JP. Suspected in homicide of her lawful husband, one James Hawes, Turnglass House, Ray, Mersea, Essex.

That was interesting. Watkins had declared his daughter fugitive and asked for aid in recovering her. He had told Simeon nothing of this. A weak man, Watkins, a man who would not even stand by his own actions.

> Florence Emily Hawes also known to

The sound of a key being pushed into the lock alerted him. He thrust the lid back on the box, pushed it into place on the shelf and slipped the file inside his coat. The clerk hustled in, evidently out of breath and irritated. His house must have been close by. For now, Simeon was hidden by a wall of shelves, but would not be for long. He had little choice but to brazen it out.

Harrison was pulling off a greatcoat as Simeon stomped towards him.

'Why did you leave your door unlocked?' he demanded angrily. The other man whirled around, astonished by Simeon's presence and at a loss for words. 'As Mr Gant's representative, I will be making a full report of this!' he warned darkly as he made his way out. 'For God's sake, make sure you lock it next time.' He slammed the door behind him and stalked up the corridor.

He heard the man look out. 'Sir?' was called at his back, but he ignored it, climbed the stairs and went quickly out a side exit from the building. He found a narrow passage-way that led out onto Covent Garden market, and wound through the throng to make sure he could not be followed or accosted. After a while he stopped, looked behind him, decided it was safe, and set down in a gaslit coffee house in Floral Street. He opened the file.

'Can I offer you something, sir? Something nice?' A woman was leering over him. She nodded in the direction of the corner. Two young girls were shivering in hired dresses and showing a lack of cleavage due to lack of nourishment.

'Coffee, please,' he replied. 'That's all.'

She shrugged and went to fetch it.

He looked down to where he had left off reading the file. There were just a few more lines.

Florence Emily Hawes also known to have aided and abetted removal of known prostitute from place of asylum decreed by Mr Gant on previous occasion. Prostitute name Annie White.

Strange. Why would Florence be 'abetting the removal' of John White's sister? His mind bubbled with possible explanations, few making sense, but he quelled them to read on.

Florence Emily Hawes and Annie White entrusted into care of Dr Oliver Hawes, clergyman, to be returned to native parish to stand trial.

It was frustrating. The record explained nothing of why Florence had absconded to London and taken Annie White out of an unspecified 'place of asylum decreed by Mr Gant'.

He glanced up at the two streetwalkers in the corner. One was blanched, her eyes half-dead. Probably the clap. He invited her over. She started to walk, but the landlady instantly appeared.

'She don't come free. A crown,' the woman demanded. The girl looked embarrassed.

Simeon slid the coin across the table and the procuress was satisfied, retiring behind a bar stocked with fly-flecked meat pies.

He pulled out a chair for the girl and she sat. 'How are you feeling today?' he asked.

'Well, thank you, sir.' It was surely more formal speech than she would normally have spoken to a client.

'You look unwell.'

'I am quite clean, sir. Certified.'

He was fully aware of the advertisements in newspapers for 'Mrs such-and-such's nunnery' where one of the rooms was occupied by a doctor who would examine the girls before every client visit. He was certain the employ would pay better than his own practice. Such houses were only frequented by gentlemen who paid in paper – indeed, often the very judges and police commissioners who had spent that day shutting down the bordello's lower-class competition.

'I am a doctor.' She visibly stiffened. 'What's wrong?'

'Begging your pardon, sir, but I don't think I'm the right girl for you.'

'No, no, I don't want to be your client. I think you are unwell and I can help.'

She stood and retreated to the corner, where her friend stared at him aggressively. The landlady came over.

'What's this?' she demanded.

'I told her I'm a doctor and I think she's unwell.'

'Doctor?'

'Yes.'

Her expression tightened. 'Then you're not welcome.'

First, he was surprised; then he was curious. 'Why?' he asked.

'Some bad sorts are doctors.'

'I know, I've met some. But what are you referring to?'

She glared at him for a few moments. 'Some cut up girls,' she said.

'What on earth do you mean?'

She hefted herself up. 'Just down the road. They say he was a doctor anyway. Handy with a knife. Enjoyed himself, they say.' She sniffed, then dropped his coin in front of him.

'Tell her to present herself at the Royal Free Hospital. They'll treat her,' he said. He knew the men there. They would see her as well as they could without payment.

She glared at him again.

He took up the file and left. Out on the street, he glanced along the road where the woman had indicated some girls had been 'cut up'. They were right beside the flower market. Such beauty and such ugliness within a spit of each other.

It was too early to head to the location Florence had told him could provide an insight into some of the secrets held at Turnglass House, and so he had to kill some time. He set out on foot through the market. There were stalls selling every flower and every spice that could be obtained throughout the Empire, the latter stacked in baskets piled with golden, dun-coloured or bright green dust. It was, he realized, probably the first time he had been to Covent Garden and really looked through the market. From there, he wandered along Floral Street. There were more girls on that street, some beckoning him, but he kept his mind on the wares in the shop windows.

His feet naturally turned towards King's College

Hospital to the east. He walked along the Strand, past his home in Grub Street, under the shadow of St Paul's dour dome, stopping to buy a fizzing soda in Paternoster Square that he drank leaning against some iron railings. He peered up at a window wherein he was sure his rival for medical research funding, Edwin Grover, was hard at work over his tables and calculations. Grover's work was not entirely without merit, no, but it had no real application. Simeon discarded the dregs of his drink and went on to the hospital.

After twenty minutes wandering through its wards, he found his lodging-mate, Graham, among the beds for those who had broken limbs. He was examining a man's leg. The man, a vintner to guess by his florid face, was wincing in pain, although Graham was paying little attention.

'Simeon, old man!' Graham proclaimed, dropping the limb to the stiff sheet. Its owner showed intense relief. 'Back so soon?'

'Just for the day. There's something I need to find out.'

'Ah, more research.'

'Indeed.'

'So, what's the scenario in Essex?'

Simeon outlined the strange situation. His friend seemed, by turns, astonished and aghast. 'My God,' he said. 'I thought it was just some ill parson.' The man on the bed had let his mouth fall open in amazement.

'Oh, I wish it were that. But I fear there's much worse behind it.'

'Well, be careful. It seems you're poking about in some dangerous corners.'

Simeon agreed and they chatted for a while, until it was late enough to resume his journey.

It was a grim evening in London as he stepped out of the hospital. The smoke from ten thousand home fires had mixed grittily with the sheet fog rolling up the Thames. The blend had a vile green hue – like pea soup, the locals joked as they spat out thick sputum. Aristocratic ghosts were stumbling through the smog in their toppers and tie studs while youthful street sweepers cleared a barely visible path through the horse dung for them.

Hailing a cab, Simeon told the driver to take him to Limehouse.

'You sure, sir?' the cabbie asked. 'Rough 'round there. Gentleman like you.'

'Thank you. I know what I'm doing.'

'If you say so.'

The driver whipped up the horses and they clipped through the smoky mist. Simeon reached into the pocket of his travelling cloak and drew out the flower-carved pipe that he had found in the secretary cabinet at the house. In preparation for the task ahead, he broke it in two.

Chapter 13

Within the Hansom, Simeon covered his face with a muffler, hoping to breathe in less of the smog stink. There was no point looking out the window, he could hardly see to the other side of the cab. On the way, he thought about the teachings of the new psychologists and how some believed that in each of us our base desires fight against our conscious morality. He had never believed in wickedness in the way that religious men, such as his uncle, believed in it. He thought actions were right or wrong, for sure – who did not think that? – but not that they laid an indelible stain on one's character.

'I'll set you down here, sir,' the driver called down.

'I have no idea where we are,' he replied.

'Well, that makes for two of us. Only I daren't go further 'cause we're as like to end up in the river. Can't see me own hand in front of me face.'

Simeon relented, unbolted the door and jumped out. The beams from the carriage lamps stared into the smog, turning it yellow, but penetrating no further than the doctor could reach. It was strange to end up in London's docklands. He had been called there a few times – it was outside his normal patch, but occasionally he had heard of a particular case that could have helped his research. This time he was going not as a doctor but in the guise of a client of the worst kind of house.

Somewhere close, he heard two people – women – arguing. 'Give it back, bitch. Give it.'

'It's mine! He gave it me!'

'Give it, or I'll do you!'

Simeon turned his head away from the sound.

'You sure you want leaving here, sir?' the cabbie called one last time.

'I'm sure.'

'Your funeral.'

He hoped that the phrase would be just a form of words, rather than literal truth. In Limehouse, it could easily be the latter. He handed up some money and the driver tapped his whip to his hat.

Simeon's feet swished through running water. Something scuttled over his boot and squealed as he kicked it away. So many creatures around him. All as sinful as they were unseen. Well, he was going to a place where fresh sins blotted out the old.

Men throughout London had succumbed to the poppy pipe. Of course, most opium was now grown in the British Empire, in India, and shipped to China for consumption, much against the wishes of the Chinese Emperor, yet it was the Chinese who ran the houses in London.

And even though it was a decade since the Pharmacy Act had stopped everyone from barbers to ironmongers selling opium, the fancy of the age would not let it pass into history – there were a dozen poppy houses in this street and the next. Calling in, three or four politely told him they did not sell pipes, however; a few more said they did, but none quite like this one; and one owner took exception to any questions at all and bade Simeon leave without delay.

After the last rejection, he felt his way along the damp cobbles, from time to time catching sight of hulking shades through the river-bound fog. Huge screw steamers bound for Canton or California. California – that place that had occupied the thoughts of the inmates of Turnglass House. He had, in actual fact, thought sometimes of going to that state himself. The gold rush of thirty years earlier had made some men very rich and all men avaricious, but what it represented to Simeon was opportunity without the stifling constraint of the medical establishment or men's petty minds. And opportunity was what he wanted above all. Just the chance to make his mark.

And then he found the place for which he was searching. It looked to have once been a seaman's mission. Its red roof pitched over a squat building of misshapen

yellow bricks with two rows of small windows, while a wide entrance was flanked by two black sailors who nodded to him as if passing an acquaintance in the street. And above them was a red lantern, just as Florence had said.

Even before he had requested admission, a tiny Malay man hurried him in, overjoyed to have a customer, it seemed, and pushed him through an inner door into a big open hall. He found the walls were lined with bunk beds crowded with gaunt faces; while a thick blue haze drifted from mouths and spurted from pipes bubbling over little lamps.

Most of the faces were men whose wan features suggested that they were past the middle of life, but Simeon knew well how the poppy aged a man, so that you should take ten years from an opium-smoker's looks to reckon his real tally. Neither poverty nor war nor disease could wear someone down like the pipe could. They became bestial faces then, turned into chattering monkeys, all humanity sucked away.

'Noooo ... I'll ... I'll ... pay. I have ...' one of the few woman burbled as she was hauled from her bed. Her gaze fixed on Simeon as he walked. 'Sir, will you lend me ... Lend me a ...' She fell to her knees before him.

He bent down and took her pulse. 'Calm yourself,' he said. Her heartbeat was slow but regular. He took two coins from his pocket and handed them to the Malay. 'One for you, one for a cab to take her to the nearest doss-house.'

The Malay bowed and took the coins, propelling the

woman towards the street. Simeon would have to start looking after his purse more closely; the trip was becoming expensive.

There was precious little heat in the vast room, but what warmth there was came from a sparse fireplace at the end, around which a dozen bodies were dozing or lying unconscious. One or two were warming their bones before returning to the world outside, having exhausted their persons and their pockets. One staggered away, muttering to himself, 'Who am I now? Who am I now?' He fell onto an empty bunk and snatched at the pipe there, putting it to his lips and sucking hard, wholly unaware that it was cold and empty. A man wearing only trousers came along, grabbed the other man's ankles and wrenched him out. 'My pipe,' he growled in an accent Simeon could not begin to place.

Simeon's vision fell on a man on a bunk. Unlike the others, the man was not smoking his opium, but sipping from a green bottle. He had a hare lip, which was causing the liquid to dribble down his chin.

'Would you like to try a little, sir?' the man asked. He grinned, to show a maw devoid of teeth. Yet his voice was educated. A university man, by the sound of it. 'The lower-life people in this establishment like to chase the dragon. Me, I prefer to drown it in brandy.'

'So I see,' Simeon replied. 'But laudanum is just as addictive, you must understand.'

'Oh, oh, you need not tell me, sir. I am a full fellow of the Royal College of Surgeons.'

Simeon sighed. He had seen other brother medics

succumb to their own drugs. There was something especially tragic about a man who predicted his own rotten
fate and still fell into it. 'Then I advise you to take a care:
look to your training and consider the dangers of opium,
as well as the pleasures.'

'But I do take a care,' the man insisted, more wildly.

'And how may that be?'

The fallen surgeon was more addled than he had first
appeared, Simeon realized. 'How? Just so!' He took a
long spoon from within his grimy shirt, inserted it into
the bottle and stirred the drink vigorously. 'You must
stir it well. Otherwise, the opium falls to the bottom and
the dose grows as you eke through the bottle. You must.'
He took another swig and offered it to Simeon. 'Try for
yourself, sir.'

'I thank you, but no.' His thoughts were depressed for
a moment. This man should have been curing the near-
dead souls who surrounded him, not joining them. If
he could be drawn out of this hell-mouth, he might still
shake off the addiction and return to his former profession – although there would be horrendous shaking and
sweating consequences for his body as the opium left its
conquered land. 'Is there anyone you would like me to
contact on your behalf? Family or friends? Maybe some
of your old colleagues could help.'

'Help? Help how?' The man seemed alarmed. 'I am
more than happy, I assure you, sir. I am delirious! I wish
to stay! I wish to stay!' He grabbed Simeon's shirt and had
to have his fingers gently eased away.

'You can stay if you like, sir.'

'I do! I must!'

There was no point arguing with the already dead, Simeon wearily told himself.

'You are not like most of my customers.' The voice was young and female. The accent Chinese. He turned to face her and beheld a young woman in the habit of a nun.

'You are not like most of the women in Limehouse,' he replied.

'Do you mean this?' She plucked at her wimple. 'I was brought up by the Holy Sisters of Penance in Canton, sir. My heart will always be with them. A pipe I can fetch you.'

'I have a pipe, but it's broken and I would like it replaced.' He drew it from his pocket and showed it.

She took the pipe and examined closely its two severed halves. 'Ivory and terracotta is unusual. Most men like the porcelain.' Her eyes invited his. 'The smoke is warmer. That is why.'

'Is this pipe yours?'

Her voice was like honey as she replied. 'I made this pipe myself. It was mine. Now it is yours.'

'You recognize it?' She delicately traced her finger along the pipe, along the stem of the carved flowers, and winced when her finger came to the break in the ivory. She nodded. 'Then this must be the place my brother came,' he said.

'It must be.'

'Maybe you remember him?'

'Maybe I remember many men.'

'He is different. A parson. Oliver Hawes.'

She paused, rolling the name on her tongue. 'I do not know him. But I know the pipe. This pipe was bought by a man by another name.'

'Who?' She stood quite still before leading the way into a room at the rear. It was full of the style of her homeland. Pink silks wafted over stools and tiny porcelain figures of animals were arranged on a mantelpiece. It was infused with the scent of jasmine. 'Who?' Simeon asked again. He placed a bright guinea coin on the table. Yes, he would have to watch his purse very closely.

The woman opened a green jade box containing a neat row of cigarettes. On each, there was a long brown stain up the middle of the paper that said they contained more than tobacco.

'Thank you, but no.'

She lifted one and lit it, allowing the smoke to stretch up to the ceiling, before opening another box. It proved to be filled with drawing materials, and she extracted a pot of purple ink that sat beside three pens arranged impossibly neatly in order of thickness of nib. She selected the smallest, dipped it in the ink and curled it across a leaf of paper. Simeon waited. The nib was dipped again, and another curving line appeared. Again and again ink was added, until a face emerged. It was a European face with round eyes and a strong nose, although the life of its artist animated it such that the man wore the clothing of an oriental emperor. And yet the face was familiar.

'This man is the one you are looking for,' she said.

'What is his name?'

'His name is Mr Tyrone.'

Simeon once more heard his uncle crying out, in his death throes, for Tyrone.

'What do you know of him?'

'Know of him? We do not ask many questions of our patrons,' she told him.

'I'm sure. But there will be something.'

She held out her palm, dimly pink in the yellow from the oil flames and the orange from the fire. He placed his last bright crown within it and it closed on the metal.

'Many of our customers have something they are missing,' she said. 'Mr Tyrone struck me as a man missing everything. Do you understand my meaning?'

'I believe I do.'

'I often feel sorry for my customers. But I do not think anything could make me feel sorry for Mr Tyrone. You cannot feel sorry for a man who is hollow.'

A hollow man. Simeon had treated patients like that. Men at the end of hard, scrabbling lives who seemed to have died long ago and only their bodies were moving and breathing and eating. This man, Tyrone, who was at the heart of all that had befallen Florence and the Hawes family, was of their number.

'I should like to meet him.'

'He is a man who can cause trouble. Why would I help you find him?'

'Because you don't want him coming back here.'

She paused, then, from nowhere, she produced a small bell and shook it. A part of the pink-papered wall slid away – a doorway deliberately obscured

from the uninitiated – and a dark, heavy-set man approached. The patroness addressed him while still gazing on Simeon.

'When did you last see Mr Tyrone?' she asked.

'Tyrone?' The man's accent was as Irish as the name he growled. 'That bastard still owes for services. Haven't seen him for a year or more.'

'And what services did you render him?' Simeon enquired.

The woman nodded to her assistant, telling him to speak.

'Sent a man to help him recover some property of his, down St George's Fields. Seemed easy enough from what he said. Turned out to be a rum bash – not what he said it was. You see him? You tell him that Frank at the Red Lantern hasn't forgotten him.'

'I think that will be all we can help you with,' his mistress said.

Outside the building, Simeon began walking in search of a cab. Through his thoughts fell Tyrone, the poppy pipe, John White's corpse laid out, *The Gold Field* and Florence imprisoned behind glass. They all tumbled like grains of sand through Turnglass House's hourglass weather vane.

He passed along the edge of the dock. In the water, he caught sight of a house behind him. The reflection rippled. And as he watched it move, disintegrate and reassemble by the second, a thought struck him like an arrow. It was a searing realization, a sudden comprehension about the killing of Dr Oliver Hawes. He, Simeon,

had been looking at the death from the wrong angle – reflected, indeed, in the dark mirror that bound one end of the man's book-filled domain. Simeon knew now how the parson had died.

Chapter 14

He returned at speed to Ray with his mind a riotous theatre. Actors seemed to be running onto the stage, shouting out a confusion of lines, dying, stabbed by wooden knives, and returning in different guises.

When he reached the house, Mrs Tabbers came to him in the parlour and offered him a fish stew. He set aside the question, instead posing one of his own. 'How long would the parson eke out one of his barrels of brandy?'

'A whole barrel? Oh, he wasn't a big drinker, sir. Could be a year with ease.'

'I thought so,' he replied. 'I would probably do the same. No fish stew, thank you.'

She gave him a bemused look and took her leave. He

stared out the window over the wild landscape of Ray, illuminated by the house's gaslight. His mind was settling, and yet the truth he now knew was as bleak as the scene outside.

And is this what brought it all into being? he asked himself. *Men and women on a blasted turf. Wouldn't it drive anyone to a blasted mind?*

He called for Peter Cain. The man came with his hands filthy and a shovel in his grip. 'I been buryin' that dead foal. No use fer lame animals. Wan' ter help me dig him in?' he said insolently. Simeon sent him to bring Watkins immediately, and then went up to the library. Florence was sitting at the small octagonal table, upon which sat the little glass model of the house that held them all, its three human figurines waiting behind the coloured doors of the upper floor like actors ready to play their parts. There was a fire in the grate, and the light of its red flames danced across the yellow silk dress Simeon had picked out for her. She sang a snatch from the hymn once more, '*Help of the helpless, oh, abide with me.*'

Simeon felt the urge to pull an atlas from one of the bookshelves, opening it at a map of the Americas. He placed the tip of his index finger on California and tapped it on a headland that bore no label, but that he knew would one day be named Point Dume.

'Don't go, Simeon,' she said softly.

'Why not?'

'It won't end well. Tragedy for you and your family.' She ran her palms over the glass model she had made.

'And how do you know that it will end badly?'

'Oh, Simeon, we both do. It's all in *The Gold Field*. It won't take much: a spark of ambition here, a flicker of wrath there. The sins rack up until the whole house burns. It's the dust in the air; it makes the blood foul.'

When Watkins finally arrived, around ten o'clock, Simeon offered him a drink, which he accepted.

'And now, Mr Watkins, may I have the book?'

'What book?' The magistrate stared at his feet.

Florence lifted the three figurines from the miniature of Turnglass House, setting them down, one by one, in front of it.

'You know quite well what book. Oliver Hawes's journal.'

'I have no idea—'

'Please don't waste my time, sir. I know you took it. And I know why.'

Watkins seemed ashamed still, but summoned a little strength. 'Do you, sir? Then please explain how you came to that conclusion.'

'I will.' He paused to gather his thoughts. 'I have been unable to understand how Oliver Hawes came to die.' Florence knocked one of the figurines over. It rolled a little on the table top. 'It could have been an infection, but if so which one? None that I recognized. And nobody else appeared to have it. You're all hardy souls here. And there was no sign of serious internal disease when I performed an autopsy. No, I eventually came around to Dr Hawes's own hypothesis: that he was poisoned last month.' He ignored Watkins's apparent shock. 'But again, the question of how had me utterly stumped. He ate the same food

169

as Cain and Mrs Tabbers and neither of them displayed any symptoms. It could have been one of them, of course, but quite why they would want to make themselves destitute by murdering their employer would be hard to fathom. And even if they did, there would be easier methods – they could have smothered him in his sleep and no one would have been any the wiser.'

Watkins looked like he wanted to raise an objection but could not think of one. Simeon continued. 'There was only one source of food or drink that Dr Hawes alone consumed: his nightly nip of brandy. The barrel was new the day before the onset of his sickness, but he became increasingly ill for more than a week after he stopped drinking it at my direction; and in addition, we tested the barrel on Cain's poor dog – apart from getting the poor mutt blootered, it had no effect. I also tested it myself later at Colchester Royal and it was quite harmless. No, the barrel had not been poisoned. Indeed, nobody poisoned Oliver Hawes last month.'

'Then what are you getting at?' Watkins demanded, at last rousing himself.

'It is simple, sir.'

'Then tell me!'

'Somebody poisoned him a year ago.' He felt little elation. He was angry that it had all come to this.

'A year ago? Impossible. Who?'

'Your daughter, Mr Watkins.' It was a relief to say the words and to look at her as he spoke them.

'Florence,' Watkins gasped. The game was up, it seemed.

She swept all the glass figures to the floor, leaving only the transparent house.

'Yes. Florence.' His eyes remained locked on her. 'She poisoned Oliver Hawes more than a year ago, the last time she was let out of her glass prison cell.'

Watkins collapsed back into his chair. 'But how could . . .' He trailed off.

Slowly, to the beat of a funeral step, she lifted her hands and brought the palms together. *Clap. Clap. Clap.* 'Bravo, Simeon. You are a sharp little knife.' Her voice sounded like one. 'I wonder what else you have learned or guessed.'

He gazed at her. 'Since you ask, I have a strong suspicion regarding the death of John White and how the inmates of this house were involved in it. How James was entwined in it. And then there is John's sister, Annie, whom you sought out in London. Where is she now? That's a question we need answered.'

Watkins burst out again, 'You think something untoward happened to her too?'

Simeon did not turn away from the woman behind the glass. 'Yes, I do. Don't you, Florence?' But he did not elaborate. Watkins would always be three steps behind his daughter. 'What happened after you found her?' She beamed at him. 'It's all in Hawes's journal, isn't it?' He addressed Watkins. 'And that's why you stole it. To protect your daughter. Something you had failed to do previously. Because its contents would have led me to the conclusion that Florence is guilty of murder.' Watkins let out a small moan and drank down his glass. His daughter laughed lightly. But Simeon's mind was fixed still on the

book and nothing else. 'I presume she told you of its contents after Oliver's death.' The magistrate made no demur this time. 'Then for God's sake, let's end this charade. Give me the journal!'

'I . . .'

'I say we give it to him, Father,' she said, her voice less muffled by the glass than of late. 'What do you care now? What do I care?' She waved her hand without concern.

'Send Cain to your house for it,' Simeon ordered him.

'There is no need,' Watkins mumbled. 'It never left the room.'

'*What?*' Simeon was outraged. It was still here! All that time spent pondering over its location.

Watkins wiped sweat from his brow. 'I was afraid you would catch me when I ran. So I hid it here safely, in the dark. That way, you wouldn't get your hands on it.'

Simeon took a moment to consider the information. The man had hidden it in the room, but where could he have placed it such that Simeon could not have come across it by chance? Oh, one place only. Simeon turned to the glass.

'Give me the book, Florence,' he said. 'I want to read of the second life of Oliver Hawes.'

She placed her hand on the miniature glass house on the table, tipping it onto its side. 'Do you think we are masters of our own fates, Simeon? Oh, I see that you do. Well, you are wrong. We are but the playthings of others.' Her voice was low, tangled up in the Sargasso weed once more. 'A second life, you call it.'

'Yes. That's what it was, wasn't it?'

'Perhaps.'

She went to the shelves that lined the rear wall of her cell, reached up to run her finger along the highest shelf and stopped it on a slim red volume with gold lettering on the spine. She could have taken it through to her private apartment, where it would have been wholly out of sight, but she had evidently enjoyed the fact that Simeon had seen it hour in, hour out, and yet never *seen* it. She pulled it down and stepped to the small hatch through which her meals were supplied – no doubt that was how Watkins had got it to her – and her pale hand pushed it through. For the second time, their fingertips touched and held for a moment, before she slowly drew back into her own world.

'Why did you keep it from me? You wanted me to read it before.'

'It was Father's doing. He came to me and begged me to keep the full facts from you. It was more to save his own reputation than my neck, but I relented.' Watkins seemed to fold even more into himself.

Simeon let that go. He was desperate to know the contents of the journal, those that he had not yet read. He turned the book over and opened the back cover to once more reveal the secret journal of Oliver Hawes. He continued whence he had left off.

19 May 1879

That good man Tyrone found me this evening. I was at the Bricklayer's Arms in Colchester, having been to speak to the Dean about financial matters. I was eating some leek soup and reading a

treatise on poverty in the Church. 'Hello,' I said, looking up. There were many other people in the saloon and I was sure most of them should have been in the public bar.

'I've been looking for you,' he said to me.

'Oh, why is that?'

He sat down. 'I'm famished,' he declared. And he took the spoon right out of my hand and drank some of my soup. 'I have been busy, that is why.'

'Busy doing what?' I was annoyed that he had taken the spoon from me, but I let it pass because I had an inkling that he had something important to say.

'Checking. Looking into things. And I'll tell you something, my friend, I believe we are missing – well, you are missing – a trick to play.'

'To what do you refer?'

'Something tells me that you are not a free man.'

'Not free? Absurd,' I replied. I must admit I was a little irritated by his insolent tone. 'Look at my wrists, do you see chains upon them? Observe the door – is it locked? Can I stand and walk right through it and mount my horse to ride home?'

'No, no chains on your wrists.' Here he leaned in and I could smell something cadaverous on his breath. 'And yet . . .' He sat back on the rough bench. I supposed he would say more. But he waited. And I realized right away that he had, indeed, hit upon a problem that had confounded my brain for too many years. A question about the freedom of will granted to us by our Heavenly Father.

'And yet?' I prompted him.

'And yet you cannot. Because it is against all that the Scripture tells us.' And there it was indeed.

'Do tell.' I pushed the bowl away. It no longer interested me.

'You wish for what I have.'

'You do not strike me as a rich man.'

'Confound my cash money!' he snarled. 'You want what I truly have: the freedom to grab and blow hard. The freedom to make merry as I will.'

He was becoming quite animated on the subject. 'And what makes you believe I would countenance any such addition to my life?'

'I've seen you read the Scriptures day in, day out.'

'I have not seen you,' I said, slightly surprised by the assertion.

'I sat at the back of the church.'

'I see.' I was unsure whether to believe him.

'And each time, I caught something in your eye or the turn of your mouth. For each one of those deadly sins or commandments, there was . . .'

'Was what?'

He avoided the question infuriatingly. 'I've sailed around the world. You have the look of the sailor as he nears a new land – a desperation to leap ashore and savour what he can.'

I took a sip of my small beer and gazed at him over its rim. 'Indeed?' And I relaxed. 'Oh, but you are making a mock of me, a poor country parson.'

'Poor! Hah! We can be agreed that you are certainly none of that. A country parson, yes, but poor, oh no. I cannot allow that.'

Yes. This one had depth. I stood and left the saloon bar. I knew that he would follow.

'Your speech I find interesting. Not that I will act upon it, but for now I am curious as to the endpoint of your argument.'

'You'll see that soon enough,' he said somewhat cryptically. 'There's something I've wanted to show you for some time. The time's come.'

175

'I am a busy man. I cannot run on fools' errands.'

'True, true,' he conceded. 'But this you will benefit by.'

I realized that we had walked to a wealthy part of the town I had only entered once or twice at the invitation of the Dean or other such luminaries. I was wearing my travelling coat and wrapped it tighter to keep warm. I have always been a martyr to the diseases of other people.

Tyrone was in front of me and he went up to a house that had lights on. He knocked and it was opened by a butler in full livery.

'Yes?' this man enquired.

'I've heard of this house,' Tyrone told him. I thought it strange behaviour and was ready to apologize for my companion's gruffness.

'Have you now? What have you heard?'

'Oh, stand aside, man,' Tyrone ordered him. I was somewhat taken aback. I had thought this to be the house of a friend of his. Even men such as him — I had it in my mind that his morality was open to question, despite his regular attendance at Holy Communion — have friends.

'I will stand aside only when you tell me who sent you,' the butler insisted.

'Sent me? Sent me, you say? This gentleman sent me.' It took a moment for me to realize what he was getting at: he had put his hand in his pocket book and pulled out a whole guinea. Such wealth some men have to give away! The wind was very strong then and it muffled a bit what Tyrone said, but whatever the precise words were, the man stood back and we were across the threshold.

What a surprising sight it was inside. It looked as if a prince was in residence. All around were plush leather armchairs — far better than those in my library — and love seats and potted plants.

And a wide marble staircase leading up. 'Well, don't just stand there with your mouth agape like the Colne estuary,' Tyrone said to me. And he laughed. 'Come in. We'll taste the delights.'

There was drink to be had, I could see that, because there were bottles and glasses on tables, but to what else he was referring I could not tell.

He went to one of the tables and took up a decanter of what seemed to be sherry.

'No excise paid on this, I'll say,' he muttered.

'I am sure you are correct there.'

And then something made me look up, up the staircase: steps on the marble. Three young women were tripping lightly, led by an older dame. They were dressed for an evening at the opera or such and they were all quite beautiful and beautified. Poets would have had them looking like birds.

'Good evening, gentlemen,' the older one said. She wore attractive stones around her neck and her dress positively floated as she walked.

Tyrone sat on a settle and motioned to me to do the same. I felt a little unsure, but did as he instructed me. 'Good evening, madam,' he said. 'I would have some entertainment.'

'That we can offer.' She looked at me and my clerical garb. It upset her not a bit. I think it might even have tickled her. She waved her hand towards the younger ladies. 'Isabella, Clarice and Amelia are new to this, and yet I know they will provide pleasure.'

'New to this?' Tyrone burst out. 'Ha! That's a good one. I had the yellow-haired one last month and she was fine for the use. I'll have her again, I think.' And then he stood up and made towards the young lady at the back.

'And for you, sir?' She addressed me without my divine title, defrocking me.

Before I could speak, Tyrone spoke for me. 'I go in his place,' he informed her. She looked to me and her delicate brow arched. I made no reply and she took that as consent.

'As you will, sirs. Go with the gentleman, Isabella.'

She began to ascend the stairs and Tyrone followed. 'Wait,' he said. 'I don't like the name Isabella.'

'You do not, sir?' the procuress enquired.

'No. I want it changed.'

'What would you like it to be?'

Tyrone said nothing, but looked to me.

'Florence,' I said.

'Florence, sir?' the girl asked. She had a light voice, from the north of our country.

'Yes,' I said. 'You are to be Florence.'

Chapter 15

Simeon paused reading and looked up. How strange it was. Florence seemingly read his mind.

'A hidden journal, a hidden man,' she said.

'He was.' He read on.

25 May 1879

Parish business took me to Colchester again and I ate at the Bricklayer's Arms. When I arrived, Tyrone was there, the only one at the inn.

'Dr Hawes,' he greeted me cheerily. Indeed, he was cheerier and more vivacious than usual. And I guessed why. One of our village girls, Annie White, the daughter of an oyster fisher, was pouring

his ale. She is a plain thing if you ask me, but I am sure she serves the purpose that most of the menfolk in these parts would put her to. 'You know Annie, I am sure.'

'Of course. How are you, Annie?'

'I am well, Parson. Thankye for askin'.'

I often find the obsequious nature of the poor – form without substance – grating. 'And your mother is well?'

'She is, sir.'

'Well, I will take some mutton stew.'

'I was just telling little Annie how she would do well on the stage,' Tyrone continued. I was sure she would. No doubt every slattern could make a living being gawped at by unwashed men if she had the inclination. 'Would you not like to see her on the stage in Colchester? The Theatre Royal. Or London!'

The girl's gaze turned quite glassy. I could see she was dreaming of a life quite apart from the Hard.

I smiled indulgently. 'As a man of the Book, such things are rather beyond my gamut,' I said. And I lowered my voice for her. 'The Church rather frowns on such places, seeing them as cauldrons for all sorts of irreligious practice.' She giggled at that.

Tyrone and I took a table and talked of minor matters – the people in the inn, my plans for a little holiday on the south coast. And then he steered the conversation around to the house we had visited on the previous occasion.

'It is like supping at G—d's own table,' he said. 'And no sin, I'm sure.'

'Are you?' I said, with some scepticism.

Yet, strange as it seems, he came back with genuine religious arguments for it being so. As he pointed out, the Bible makes a point of stating how the patriarchs of the Hebrews enjoyed relations

with their many womenfolk. Are they not held up as models for our behaviour in the absence of more direct exhortations by our Saviour?'

'But such relations are within sanctified marriage,' I disputed.

'Ah, but who is delegated by G—d to perform such sanctification? His representative.' He meant me, of course. 'The priest is the mortal man who declares marriage, doesn't he? So what is sanctified is within his gift. There is nothing to stop him bestowing such gifts on other priests — doesn't the Lord encourage it? — so there is nothing to stop him bestowing that sanctity on his own self.'

I did not like being tutored by a man who . . . in fact, as I considered it, I realized I barely even knew what he did by way of employ, something in the way of a merchant sailor, I thought. But he had theological strength behind his argument.

'True enough, yet a cleric must also pay heed to the great authorities.'

'Ah, but how did those authorities become authorities themselves? Why, by considering and testing,' he countered.

I thought this over too. Again, there was force there. We walked out to talk more.

'Lot of ruffians around tonight,' he said, checking over his shoulders and peering into the doorways.

'More than usual?'

'For sure. I saw a man beaten to within an inch of his life this evening.'

'For what offence?' I asked, shocked.

'Nothing. Looked at a man the wrong way. Criminal times we live in.'

'That is for certain.' I had myself been concerned, having read frequent reports in the newspapers of needless brutality.

'Yes. In fact, I was thinking. You should carry this,' he said. I

looked down at his palm. Lying across it was an evil-looking dagger. My mouth fell open.

'What need have I of that?' I demanded. 'I do not shed men's blood.'

'But you have to be ready to stop someone else shedding yours. And there's enough of them around these parts as have the want and the time to do it.'

I sighed unhappily. Once more, he had a point. And there is no sin in self-preservation – if anything, since suicide is the wilful and ungrateful disregard of the life that G—d has granted us, there is a compunction on us to defend ourselves when others would cut our throats. So, reluctantly, I took the knife. It was a sleek thing, long and slim but with a razor edge. I did not ask to what use he had previously put it. I placed it inside my coat, into a pocket where it fitted snugly.

14 June 1879

I met Tyrone on the Hard. It had been more than two weeks since I had seen him last and I had been looking forward to continuing our conversation; there were some points that I wanted to discuss in his argument that the Hebrew patriarchs should be our model with womenfolk when there is no more direct exhortation from Christ Jesus himself. We were walking to my house and had just come off the Strood.

'Parson!' I heard someone shout at our backs. It was not often that I would hear my honorific cried at my back as I approached my home. And it was not being yelled out in a friendly fashion. 'Parson!' it repeated.

I glanced at Tyrone. His eye met mine darkly.

'Hide yourself,' he said.

'I will do no such thing.'

'All right, you d—mned fool,' he growled. 'I'll be the one to hide.'

I continued on my course without breaking my stride, as if I had not heard the man hailing me. Tyrone slipped from the path and down the side of the creek, onto the mudflats. His mottled black garb made him quite invisible in the dusk to anyone who knew not that he was there. Even I felt his presence more than I saw it.

The thudding step of my pursuer came within earshot. I gave it no heed. He would come, whoever he was — in fact, I had a good idea whom he might be — and I would deal with him as required. There is a reason that we divines are addressed as 'Father'. It is because, like any good parent, we must often dole out remonstrance as much as guidance.

When I could no longer stand the sound of his uneven, beastly tread, I suspended my motion and awaited his appearance.

'Parson!' he barked. I looked him up and down. A heifer in a man's body: heavy and stupid. I cared little for what he was to say, so did not trouble myself to invite it. When he finally reached me, he was huffing and puffing as if he would keel over. When he had recovered a little, during which time I waited patiently for whatever nonsense was due to be spilled from his lips, he straightened up and stared me in the face. 'My sister,' he growled — I was mistaken, he was no heifer, he was a street hound. 'What you did to my sister.'

'I have done nothing to your sister,' I answered him. And it was the utter truth. Anything that had been done to this man's sister — it was now clear to whom he referred — was done by Tyrone, and without instruction from me. My conscience was clear.

'Annie . . . She was to be married.'

'Then let her marry,' I said. 'I will happily perform the ceremony myself.'

'She cannot now. She is not clean!'

I was beginning to tire of the conversation. 'That is hardly a barrier for most of you people. She is probably five times as "clean" as the average bride around these parts. Now, if you will excuse me, I have a sermon to write.'

And that was when he made his great error. He grabbed my frock-coat as I recovered my path to the house and wrenched me back. I almost toppled from his strength. In these parts, men are bred for toiling the land and drawing in a catch and it is proved in their bulk, not their brains. 'How dare you attack the Church this way!' I upbraided him. My outrage took him aback, and he paused his assault on my person. I could see his slow mind recalling years sat on pews while I or my brother priests taught him right from wrong in the sight of G–d.

But then his animal grimace returned. 'No, Parson. You have ruined her.'

And here he drew something from his jerkin. A rumpled slip of paper, greasy thumbprints upon it. It was a scrap torn from something else. I perused a brief, barely legible missive scrawled upon it.

'Sir. I am very sadd. I wonted for you to be my darlling. I am no good for no man nou. I thot you to be my husbant. Annie.'

I know I should have felt this as a poor thing, but I must confess I simply burst out laughing. 'Fancies country life, does she? Think your slattern sister will make a good parson's wife? Oh, my dear man, you have brightened up my day with your lunacy. But I fear I must leave you to it.' I tried to betake myself away, but he threw his arms around me, caging me and crushing me as if he

184

wanted to squeeze the life right out. My hands were free but next-to-useless against his brawn.

'No, Parson. No.' He was growling like a dog again. 'She has drunk of something now. Something that has sent her to sleep. She does not waken.'

I felt the air leaving my chest, and with every expiration he tightened, so that my lungs could suck in no more. I think he really did mean to suffocate me. As I cast about for aid, I looked into his eyes and saw such hate that I scarcely noticed when his torso began to sag against mine. But in an instant, we changed. Where his body had been sapping mine, suddenly mine was holding his upright. Something warm spread over my hands. I peered down and saw it was blood, gushing from a series of wounds in his side, each made by the long blade in Tyrone's hand. As I watched, White staggered away, and Tyrone, like a Fury, leaped behind him, reached around White's neck and plunged the dagger twice deep into his back. My assailant's body slumped to the ground.

I stood stock still, amazed. But in a moment, I recovered myself. Thank the good Lord for ensuring there was no one in sight.

'I told you to carry a blade,' Tyrone said. 'Now you see why you need it.' He spat on the man at his feet. To my shock, I realized White was still moving, his breathing laboured and rattling. 'Don't fright. I'll deal with him,' Tyrone muttered. I retreated a pace to let him do his work. And as I watched, the man's life became thinner. And then it left him.

'Say nothing,' Tyrone anticipated me. 'This is my work, and will continue to be my work. Stand aside.' He bent down and hefted up my assailant's lifeless body, dragging it on its haunches into the muddy creek. I noted I had a fair degree of blood on my person that I would have to wash away. I could hardly give my garb to my

housekeeper. I watched as Tyrone pulled the corpse further across the mud and into the parts that are like quicksand, where anything will sink completely out of sight. Tyrone's coat masked them both, but I fancied I saw John's hand slip down into the dirt. And that was the last anyone ever saw of him.

Tyrone came back to me and laughed. 'You'll need this later,' he said. And he slapped to my chest the letter — if you can call it that — that the girl had written. 'I'll see to this man's boat. It will look like he capsized.'

'Do be careful,' I said. He had thrust the letter to my breast just where a spot of my assailant's blood had soaked my shirt, and it was now seeping into the edge of the letter. I wiped the liquid away. I had an inkling how he meant me to use the missive and I was proved right as he outlined his plan to me. It was, I must admit, a subtle one. And at no time would I sinfully bear false witness, I made certain of that.

Yes, I thank our Lord for Tyrone, for sending him to me just when I needed him. Truly, the Great Shepherd's power and beneficence is something to behold.

When he had finished, I retraced my path and headed towards the village on Mersea and the girl's home to see what her brother had spoken of regarding her mental and physical state. I buttoned up my coat and it hid the blood stain quite effectually.

Upon reaching the attractive little cottage, I was led in by a blind old woman — they all seem to share the same mother, her class — to the bed where her daughter lay. I am no physician, but it appeared to me that Annie was heading to the same place whither her brother had already arrived. I placed my hand on her forehead. It was wet and quite cold. I saw the buds of her breasts panting up and down through a thin night slip. A terrible pity to lose such a

child from this world, a child with so much to offer, but such is the plan of the Great One.

I blessed her and left. She was in G—d's hands then. Whether she would join Him above us or suffer the torments of the netherworld would be His choice and decision alone. But I was glad I had made the visit, because it meant the rest of my friend's scheme would be all the more predictable.

There are usually one or two ne'er-do-wells sitting around the Hard hoping for a day's work. Where they drift from I have no idea, but they seem to turn up, sit about for a few days, then disappear again, and today I would have use for one of them.

I placed my clerical collar within my pocket and waved one over. He hurried to me, the prospect of a few bob no doubt lighting his fervour. 'Take this letter to the house on Ray immediately and give it to the housekeeper,' I said. I handed over Annie's crumpled note and a small sum for him to spend at the Peldon Rose. I directed him up the Strood and he left at a good pace. I then set myself down to wait for an hour on the shoreline before returning home. I felt the Holy Spirit filling me with jubilation.

As soon as I set foot in the hallway an hour later, I heard them screaming like banshees.

'Who is she, d—mn you?' It was Florence's voice. It was rare — though not unknown — for her to shout loud enough to shake the house in this fashion.

'Have you lost your mind entirely?' James was crying back.

Tyrone really knows his game, I thought.

'If I have, it was when I consented to marriage!'

I betook myself to the study while they continued in the same violent vein, and changed my shirt.

I had spent no more than five minutes reading a treatise on

missions in southern India when my brother burst in. He was clutching a handkerchief to his cheek and it was clear that the linen was soaked red. It reminded me to dispose of my shirt before Tabbers washed it. 'Dash it, Oliver, I have no idea at all what she is referring to,' he said, throwing himself down in a chair.

'Would you like to explain?'

He groaned. 'She has been questioning me about some girl I am supposed to have abused.'

'Did you abuse her?'

'I barely even know the girl. John White's sister. Flo claims to have been delivered of some G—d-awful note claiming I have used this girl, promised to marry her and tossed her aside like a worn pair of shoes. Utter madness.' He booted at a side table. 'Never liked that table. Would be better as firewood,' he said.

'What happened?'

'Flo lobbed a decanter at me. Gin sloshing all over the floor. Good stuff that I had brought over from Flanders last month. Crying shame.'

'And your cheek?'

'Well, it broke, didn't it? Right on my face. Oh, I'll live.' He pulled away the handkerchief, but some of the blood had dried, sticking it to the skin.

It is sometimes a difficult task to remain on the right side of the moral dividing line. But after examining my conscience, I know that I am in the white. I have spoken no false words.

15 June 1879

A more tranquil day. I spent the forenoon on accounts. I have asked the diocese for more funds to employ a sexton, but have received a

negative reply. It appears we shall have to delay the repairs to the church roof. James complains of a burning in the gashed flesh.

16 June 1879

I watched over James for a while. He is in pain and angry for it, but being so does him no good. He refused supper. I finished the short treatise on ecumenicism in the Colonies that I was sent by the Anglican Communion Corresponding Society. It was quite instructive.

17 June 1879

Very hot today. James grows ill. His flesh is turning yellow where Florence attacked him. Well, he is in the hands of our Lord and we must bend to His will. He is raving. I repeated my request for a sexton, setting out more reasons for his necessity.

18 June 1879

A tinker has been caught stealing from the Rose. He will be sent to the Assizes for the next quarter-session. James worsens. His condition looks grave.

19 June 1879

There is no wickedness in joy. There is no sin in advantage unsought. I am not Cain, I have slain no brother. And yet he has been slain. He is still breathing, but that will not last long, I am sure. And the perpetrator? His wife. The wound he received at

Florence's hand is green now and drips a foul liquid. The flesh around it is blackened and eaten away. You can see his teeth and bone through it. The doctor for whom we sent — a drunken local fellow little better than the village herbalist — is at a loss, other than to instruct prayer and hopes. I have, indeed, been praying. By turns James sweats and shivers and his lips are cracked dry. He yells from time to time, but thankfully his words are nonsensical.

When I went to him, I held his hand tight and he turned his vision on me. 'Oliver,' he mumbled. 'Be kind to her.'

'I will,' I said.

Tomorrow or the next day, I am certain, I will place my brother in the family crypt and consign him unto G—d's hands.

News also from the village. Annie White has recovered. As soon as she could walk, she left her mother's home, saying only that she was bound for London and would send word when she was able. G—d has stayed her voice from telling tales. Thank Him.

Chapter 16

Simeon turned the page but found nothing more. The leaves of the book were blank from there on. And yet, as he looked more closely, he saw a series of small relics of paper still attached to the spine.

'Where are the other pages, Florence?' he asked. She lifted the glass model. Beneath it was a small pile of pages. Like the journal itself, she had left them in his full sight for days. He had to hand it to her: she was playing her game well. 'Will you give them to me?'

'I might.'

Her intention was clear. 'But you want something in return.'

'How perceptive you are, Simeon! Quite the gallant psychologist.'

'And if I don't provide you with your desire, what happens? You put the lamp flame to them?'

'I think that's likely.'

'So what's the price?'

'The price is my portrait that hangs above the fireplace in the hall.'

He was surprised. 'You want a painting?' It was a curious request – but a cheap one.

'I do.'

The small portrait above the fireplace, of Florence painted some years earlier on an imaginary landscape soaked by the American sun, was easy to lift away from the wall. Cain, who was carrying a bucket of coal through the hall, stared at him, but Simeon affected not to have noticed and took the picture back to the library.

'Ah,' she sighed as she saw him return. 'You are faithful.'

He pushed it through the hatch and she gazed on her younger self. Then she reached for her side table, took a tumbler in her hand and dashed it against the table, breaking it into a dozen pieces. She picked one of the larger shards from the floor and Simeon feared she was going to use it as a weapon against herself. But instead, she stabbed it into the picture at the edge where it met the frame and cut out the canvas.

'What are you doing?' he asked.

'You'll see.'

Behind the picture he saw her real target: a clutch of letters.

'What are those?'

And as he saw them, he saw tears in her eyes. 'These? These are the billets James wrote me. When we were young. I had them put here so that . . .'

'. . . you would always know where they were,' he finished her thought.

And at that, he felt like a voyeur. He departed the room, leaving her to read her old love letters. He could not free her, but he could give her time with her past, with her thoughts and the love she had borne for her husband.

An hour later, he returned. She was standing at the side of her demi-room, leaning against a shelf of books, staring at the line of windows that she could not reach.

'Thank you,' she said. He nodded, accepting the gratitude. Without looking at him, she pushed the remaining pages of the journal through the hatch and he returned to reading Oliver Hawes's unknown history.

20 June 1879

I did indeed inter James today. We were a sad procession – I was sad, myself, that it had come to this. But we are tools of the Lord and must not question.

We stood as one black gathering in the back parlour, where he had been laid out, and I remembered the monograph that I read about the sin-eaters in our part of the country; those wretches who were paid to eat cakes laid out on the body of the deceased in order to take upon themselves all the sins of the newly dead. In the eyes of G–d and the Tempter, those black marks were then transferred from the book of the deceased to the book of that living man and he would

have to answer for them on Judgement Day, while the dead man could enter Heaven without hindrance. For sure, it is an atheist's profession. They will get a dread shock when their coffins are cracked open and their souls called up before the final judge.

I fulfilled my priestly duty well, I think, delivering words of deep comfort to all, including Florence. Had it been entirely up to me, I would have allowed her some time to mourn. But Tyrone rightly stated that the immediate aftermath of the funeral would be the most effective time for us to act.

To that end, some hours later I was reading in my library by gaslight. Florence had gone for a walk to clear her head. Tyrone was in the corner, paring his nails in an unpleasant manner.

I had rarely seen such rain even in these soaked parts. Any heavier and Noah himself would have baulked! Tyrone was not the only other man in the room. I had invited Watkins to dine, and he was asleep in the corner, snoring like an African beast. I had filled him with wine and suggested he doze it off here before returning to his house. The servants had been sent home for the night.

'Dirty night,' Tyrone muttered. 'How do you think she will fare?'

'Not well,' I replied, looking up from a volume of commentary on the Pentateuch. 'She is in a fragile state, I am sure.'

'You can be d—mn sure of that.'

'I do wish you would temper your public-bar language when in this house,' I admonished him. 'There is a time and place for it, but this is neither.'

'Sorry,' he grumbled, and he went back to working on his fingernails. 'How long has it been now?' he asked, after a while.

I checked the clock in the corner. 'Nearly an hour. She cannot last for much longer. The chill must be into her bones.' I shut the

book and removed my spectacles, so I could better concentrate. The sound of her wailing rose again. It had been angry, then plaintive and was now outwardly threatening.

'Open the doors or I'll skin you, you whoresons!' she was screaming from below. Pebbles rattled against the window pane, but she could find nothing more substantial to throw, nothing to break the glass. And against the sound of the Biblical torrent, I could barely make it out.

'No fine lady, is she?' Tyrone commented. 'Sounds like one of the three-shilling girls in London. Some of them, oh, I could tell you stories! There was one girl, Jessie, who liked it every way. Now, she once—'

I slammed my book down on the table, quite angry. 'I told you to temper these vile stories. If you will be like that, you can leave this house!'

'Oh, pipe down,' he muttered. 'You need me as you need food.'

'I do not!'

I do not like the off-hand way he has been with me of late. After seeing to Florence, I am beginning to suspect I will have to see to Tyrone. It is a dangerous state of affairs when the lackey thinks himself the master.

'Why in the Devil's name you consider that harpy, I'll never know,' Tyrone muttered.

'I want to save her from becoming worse,' I informed him. 'Holy office is anathema to you, is it not?'

'Oh, holy office. That is what you desire from her. Ha!' He cast me a filthy look. 'I'll leave. I don't care what you and she get up to. Treat her like the sailors treat Jessie, for all I care.' And he stomped out of the room. Watkins seemed to stir a little at his leaving, but did not wake.

*And then, with an almighty crash, the window bust inwards!
A rock had flown right through it, across the room and into
the fireplace. Watkins woke with a cry, an amount of the glass
showering him. I was sorry, for it quite cracked the tiles around the
grate. It was a very unpleasant event.*

*Without the window between us, her voice seemed to grab hold of
the room and shake it about. 'Open the door, you bastards. Open it
or I'll beat it down!'*

*This was followed by a fresh hail of pebbles through the broken
window. Some hit Watkins, making him leap out of his skin. 'What
is happening?' he cried.*

*I affected to look as astonished as he. 'I . . . I believe that is
your daughter's voice,' I told him.*

'Florence? Good G–d, I think it is!'

*We stepped cautiously to the broken casement. The rain was
lashing through and the curtains billowing in. Once again, I thought
of Noah, in the storm of the Flood, tossed on the sea, praying for
the survival of his race.*

*'You animals. Open the door. I'll wring your necks! The Devil
help me, I will wring your necks!'*

*'What in G–d's name is wrong with her?' he asked, frightened.
We peeped through the broken glass. She was below, soaked as if
she had fallen into the frothing sea in all her clothes. And she was
staring back at us with all the hatred of a daemon.*

*'I see you!' she screamed up. 'I'll do you both with my own
hands! Open the door!' Those hands were above her head, reaching
up as if to fulfil her promise to strangle us. Then, incredibly, they
ceased grabbing at the empty air and instead began grabbing at the
stones of the house. She was attempting to climb the very walls, to
break in through the window like a monkey. However, she made it*

no more than a few scrabbled steps up, aided by some vines that held fast to the stone, before falling down to the sodden soil.

Watkins and I shrank back. She was like one of the semi-human creatures in Tyrone's sailor's tales.

'I have never seen her like that!' was all Watkins could exclaim. His words were slurred. His fear at his daughter's state was heightened by the drink that still addled his brain.

'I wish I could say the same,' I replied quietly.

'You mean, it has happened before? She has been like this in the past?' I made no verbal reply, only sighing deeply and allowing our esteemed local magistrate to draw his own conclusion. He looked very troubled. 'I thought the incident with your brother was the only occasion.'

'Would that that were the case,' I said in an unhappy tone. Tyrone had schooled me. 'But I shall go down and let her in.'

'Is it safe?' he said fearfully. And then he recognized the absurdity of a man afraid of his own daughter. 'I mean, of course you must. I shall see to it that she calms herself.'

I took myself down to the front door. The wind was finding ways through the bricks and it sounded as if the house itself were howling in distress.

She was banging on the door hard enough to beat her way in. It was thick oak, and yet the vehemence of her attack was like to splinter it soon, I thought. I could not understand how she could beat with such force with her bare hands. But I did not have long to wait, because before my sight, it started to splinter. Long cracks appeared and I was stopped in my approach by amazement. And then the tool she was using burst right through: a huge flint she must have pulled from the garden for the task. It had become a hatchet in her grasp. I considered, for a second, whether my life

truly was in danger – if her mind had shattered like the door, then James might not be the last of our family to die by her hand.

But I saw Tyrone standing in the entrance to the kitchen and one angry look from him was enough to give me a burst of courage. I moved more quickly to unbar the house to her.

The moment I turned the key in the lock, the wind wrenched the door from me, slamming it against the wall and affording me the first glimpse of the changed Florence.

What a sight she was! Oh, that I could say it did not affect me, but the truth is that it stirred me greatly. Her clothes clung to her, the pink of her skin through the white linen as rosy as if it were open to the air and my eyes. Such waifish, sylvan beauty was never meant to be hidden.

'Lord above, you poor child!' I exclaimed. 'You did not take a latchkey?'

'Why would I take a latchkey?' she demanded. And she threw aside the flint. Droplets of red blood went with it – she had cut open her palm as she beat again and again at the door. She pushed me aside as she bundled into the hallway.

'The servants have been sent home,' I explained.

'You heard me shouting. I was out there for an hour.'

'The storm is very loud.'

'The storm? To Hell with the storm.' She cast aside her outer layer, stripping to her undergarments. 'Stare, don't stare. I don't care what you do!' she declared. And she began to pull away the straps keeping even her skimpy covering in place.

'Florence!' It was shouted from above us. At the top of the flight of stairs, her father was witnessing her apparent attempt to show all of her woman's body to me, her brother-in-law, her divine. 'Stop that! Put your clothes back on! What on earth has entered your head?'

'Oh, good G—d. Father,' she muttered with irritation. 'From a storm to a squall. It's my house, Father, I'll be naked as Eve if I want. You have seen me that way at some point in time, haven't you?' He seemed flustered and stumbled as he tried to descend the staircase. 'Though sometimes I wonder that I was conceived at all. Mother must have been as drunk as you are right now.'

'How dare you!' he cried. And he missed another step, catching at the banister for his life. 'Cover yourself. James's death has distressed us all, but—'

'It hasn't distressed you one hundredth of how it has distressed me,' she hissed. 'You — what? — knew him? Had been in a tavern with him while he bought the drinks and entertained with stories? What's that next to what he was to me? You can leave it behind and find another man to stand the beer and talk about wenches he once knew. I can't. So don't tell me how to mourn my husband's death or how I must behave between my own four walls.'

And she swept up to her chamber. A dirty night, but a pleasing end to it.

21 June 1879

A shock this morning — may the Lord send me fewer in future — as Tyrone stormed into my chamber to shake me out of slumber and inform me that Florence had gone for the morning train to London. I have become concerned with the upstart beginning to develop ideas above his station in life. I must not let him play Cassius to my Caesar.

'Where do you think she's going?' he snarled.

I thought for a second. 'To find Annie White, I presume,' I answered. 'And I agree that it is most disagreeable.'

'So what are we going to do about it?'

'We will follow her to London – not to forestall her, but to beat her to the quarry. We will find Annie and see to it that no inconvenient utterances issue from her lips,' I explained. And I feel that he was impressed by my resolution.

I made the arrangements and soon enough we were waiting for the afternoon train from Colchester to London.

'Good afternoon,' I bade the stationmaster as we stood on the platform. He was from Mersea originally and I knew him a little.

'Afternoon, Parson.'

'I am following my sister-in-law to London. She was supposed to tell me where she was putting up there.'

'Forgot, did she?' he chuckled.

'She did that.'

'Women, Parson. Forget them own names.'

'Quite. So, did she happen to mention it to you? Or anything else that could help me meet her there?'

'No, sir, no.' He shook his head and I set foot on the running plate. 'Oh, but wait! One thing. You see, when she asks me which London station we get into, I tell her it was Liverpool Street.' I presumed there was more of the story to come, but at that point he seemed to find tapping his foul pipe against his heel to loosen the spent tobacco to be of the utmost importance.

'So?' I prompted him.

'So she asks of me,' his mind was still on the pipe, 'how far that is from Covent Garden.' I was pleased by this. Would there be more, perchance? There would. '"Going to see the Punch and Judy box?" I ask her. "No," she says. "Finding someone there." So I tell her that it's twenty minutes by Hackney cab.'

Finding someone there. I thanked the Lord for His Providence.

And yet, oh my! What a journey we had. While I have usually enjoyed my sojourns in the nation's capital, the rickety journey has generally left such an imprint on my body that I have forsworn ever returning. This time was no better.

Finally, we arrived and, upon our stopping at Liverpool Street Station in the early evening, I made my way to the station mail office. I had a stratagem to execute. I found a grubby little man inside and left him instructions and a bank note for a pound.

Thence we made our way to Covent Garden market. We were wary of being seen by Florence before she saw us, so I had changed into common clothing and wore a low-brimmed hat. Tyrone wrapped a black kerchief around the lower portion of his face. It disguised him and made him hardly more noticeable in that den of thieves. Yet if there is one thing that I hate about London, it is the smog, and it was hanging over the whole city, pierced only slightly by the overhead lamps.

So Florence was searching for Annie in Covent Garden. It was clear why such as Annie would be drawn to that place — its night women were legendary from there to Vienna. And they hardly kept their strumpetry to the night. 'Over here, sir!' 'I will make you happy!' Such cheap sin. As Tyrone and I walked, we were subject to a hundred calls and invitations from painted females of all ages — as young as twelve and old as fifty, some of them, I would guess when I came close enough to make them out.

'Later, ladies!' Tyrone called back. 'Be ready, because I have a lot to send your way.' He was rewarded with a cat's choir of sharp laughter. He was quite prepared to descend to their level of pleasures, but first we made a quick sweep of the market and the surrounding alleyways. Neither Annie nor Florence was in sight. That would have been too much to ask for. And so we spent much

of the day on foot, making discreet enquiries. But nothing presented and we retired to a nearby hotel.

22 June 1879

We resumed our search, tramping again for hours before something occurred.

'Are you looking for a woman?' It was not a female voice this time. It was whispered from a doorway, and as I came close in the gloom, I saw a thin man, his face more pockmarked than any I had ever seen — it was a wonder he was still alive, with that series of pits and eruptions on his flesh, and I made certain not to step within breathing distance, lest I catch what he had.

'I am not,' I said, keeping back, waiting to see how he would respond.

His evil-painted face broke into two at that and his voice changed, became somehow knowing of me. 'I know. You are looking for two women. From distant parts.' And without another breath, he disappeared into the shadow of the doorway.

I hesitated, quite unsure about following this man into his lair. 'Go on then,' Tyrone insisted.

'We know nothing of him,' I replied.

Tyrone sneered at me. 'What, are you still a coward?'

'Be quiet!' I snapped at him.

'Don't trouble yourself. I'll go,' he said. 'You wait here.'

His hand went to the bulge beneath his jerkin that I knew to be the knife that had done for Annie's brother. I knew he was itching to use it on the sister too.

On this occasion, I thought it prudent to accede to his suggestion

and I went to the other side of the street. 'Up you come, then, sir,' I heard the pander tell my friend as I withdrew.

I remained in the narrow lane, which was just wide enough for one of the fruit or flower carts to trundle along. Its cobbles were wet with moisture, no doubt having been washed through with Thames water to cleanse as much of the daily filth as possible. I looked to the upper storey of the house. A shuttered window showed evidence of a lit candle behind. That would probably be his destination.

There was another girl at the end of the street, standing under a lamp. 'Only three bob, sir!' she called over. 'Lying down. Two upright.'

'Be quiet, whore,' I ordered her.

I waited, beginning to chill, for two minutes at most, before Tyrone came flying out. 'We must leave!' he growled, grabbing my coat and yanking me up the lane.

'What has happened?' I demanded.

'There's no time.' I stared at him. The lamplight was in his eyes as if there were fires behind them. I shook him off and hurried towards the doorway. I would let no man tell me what I could or could not do.

I went quickly up the stairs and into the sole room on the floor above. I was expecting a rough bedroom, a place of work for the pander and his stock beasts, but I found something else. I found a charnel house.

On the bed, their throats torn, were two street geese. They wore the clothes of their trade – sluttishly arranged to show as much skin as possible. They were draped across the cot without care, their blood sprayed not just on the floor, but up the walls too. And neither bore the slightest resemblance to Annie or Florence.

But someone was still alive. 'My, my . . .' I heard someone

groan. The pimp was slumped against a stool. He was stretching a hand to me, while the other seemed to hold his innards, which were spilling from his torso. 'Please . . .' The word turned into a hiss like a snake, which was no doubt appropriate, for surely the Devil himself was there in that room.

'I told you we had to leave.'

This voice I knew. Tyrone had followed me in and stood now behind me.

'What in Heaven's name has got into you?' I demanded.

'Hush your voice.' It was a most stern command. 'I'm in charge in these matters.'

'I . . . water. Surgeon.' The whoremaster was yet alive and moaning. Tyrone's gaze met mine. Then I turned my back and he went to the man on the floor. I heard no more words from that person.

'I'm in charge in these matters,' Tyrone repeated. And there was a very slight rustling, as if he was wiping metal on cloth.

I overlooked the scene again. It would be something to make the penny blood pamphlets. Carnage such as something from the Old Testament. But, of course, that made sense. G—d's hand was in that room, as it was in the Israel of old.

But still. Tyrone had angered me.

'From now on, you do nothing like this!' I declared. 'You overstep what is decent.'

'And that is exactly why you need me!' he countered with the same fury I had exhibited.

'What do you mean?'

'What do I mean?' he said in a mocking tone. 'I mean only what you know: that I have been your sin-eater.'

I stopped, amazed by this assertion. 'How do you even know that term?' I demanded.

'How? Where I grew up, everyone knows it.'

'Well, it is certain that this was sinful,' I said, waving my hand at the bloody scene, not interested in a theological discussion at that moment.

'They sin forty times a day.' He said it utterly dismissively, as if he did not care a jot for these lives. And he prodded the foot of one of the whores with his own. It swung a little, dangling over the edge of the bed. 'Sin always comes around. I am resolved to it.'

'Well, I am not.'

He grinned horribly at that. 'Then maybe you should be.' And there was something in those words that I found quite chilling. 'Now, come on,' he instructed me, grabbing my jacket and this time brooking no refusal. In the doorway, he looked out onto the street, holding the wicked knife in a shadow. 'It's clear,' he said, beckoning me with him. And as we stepped out, he slipped the knife back into a leather scabbard under his tunic. We strode quickly along the lane.

'Want me now, sir?' It was the slut who had enticed me earlier. 'You look ready for it.'

Yet it was not me who replied, but Tyrone. 'I am that,' he said, surprising me. 'Quite ready for it.' And amazing as it was, he made to go to her.

'Are you out of your wits?' I demanded in a whisper and catching hold of him.

'No, just hungry,' he replied with a chuckle. He shook me off and went over to the girl – a younger example of that profession than those lying ripped in the room above us – and without prologue seized her by the shoulders, turned her round, bent her over and went straight at her like a dog in a garden. I looked away, furious at being made a party to this, as well as at the recklessness of the timing.

'There's six bob for you,' I heard him say. 'Treat the girls

205

upstairs to a drink. Courtesy of Dr Black.' He smirked over his shoulder at me.

'Much thanks to you and the doctor, sir,' she replied, her tone quite happy.

I felt his hand on my back, telling me he was ready to leave, and I strode away, pondering how long it would be before I abandoned my erstwhile friend to whatever fate he had waiting for him: the hangman's rope, no doubt.

I took care — more care than he did — to be seen by few people as we returned to the lodging I had engaged near Liverpool Street Station. Tyrone seemed to exult in his recent act and wanted to be seen. 'Let's go to St James's Park. There are more geese there,' he informed me. 'They run about between the hedges, ripe for plucking.' Had he not had his hand on the covered hilt of his knife, I might have given him a stronger admonishment than words alone; but as it was, I called him five different words for a fool and almost dragged him with me back to our hotel. I made sure, though, to take a roundabout path to reduce the chances of our being traced to that establishment and possibly even identified by the Queen's authorities. Tyrone seemed to care nothing if a noose were to wind around his throat, but the prospect was a distinctly unpleasant one to my mind.

When we arrived at the hotel, the owner offered us supper. But when he mentioned that trussed goose was being served, Tyrone burst into laughter and I had to give him a swift kick to stop it.

24 June 1879

For a long while, Tyrone and I searched for our quarry. We tried boarding houses, bagnios and Christian missions. Nothing. All I gained was a deeper anger. He was ready to tear more whores apart

in the belief that one of them was harbouring Florence, but I held him back. We would not benefit from the increased attention. And our luck eventually changed.

On the third morning, Tyrone came to me. He had been out all night – I did not want to know where – and had gleaned some information. He told me to wait in the hotel and that night he would bring Florence and the village girl to me. I thanked G–d.

I did as he wished, waiting patiently, but far from bringing the two fugitives, he returned around midnight with a deep wound in his shoulder. I dragged it from him that, despite his assurance, his venture had been far from successful. And from then on, I knew I should not believe a word or promise he uttered. I went to bed angry that night and barely slept.

But thank the Holy One again!

I was woken at perhaps eight o'clock in the morning by the grubby little mail master from Liverpool Street Station. As I admitted him to our chamber, he held a letter in his hand.

'Sir, that matter that we spoke of,' he said, holding it up. 'This morning, this was consigned to the early Colchester train. It is the address you told me to watch for.'

It was indeed addressed to our esteemed Justice of the Peace, Watkins. And I knew his daughter's hand, of course.

'You have done very well,' I said.

'You know, sir,' he said in an innocent tone, 'it is not legal to take letters from Her Majesty's mail.'

I sighed. 'The other gentleman will pay you.'

'Other gentleman?' the idiot echoed, peering around him.

I was in no mood for such folly and drew my pocket book from under the pillow, doling out six shillings. It briefly occurred to me that that was the sum Tyrone had given the streetwalker the other night.

'You may leave us,' I said.

'Yes, Father.' He seemed somehow confused by the simple words. I dislike it when rough men I know not address me as 'Father'. It smacks of my having a spiritual or even pastoral duty towards them when I have none.

I opened the packet.

'Florence?' Tyrone enquired.

'For certain.'

I read it thoroughly. It described what had happened to her across the previous three days. It was an amusing read. And there was something far more important about it: it was composed upon hotel notepaper.

And so, I had her address without the slightest trouble: The Crown Hotel, Bishopsgate.

Chapter 17

Simeon looked up from the pages before him and took some time to think over what he had read, what he had learned about this unassuming country parson. Into his mind slipped the memory of Watkins telling him that Oliver Hawes had been cashiered from the army for cowardice and desertion. He wondered if the new psychologists could take that humiliation and connect the links to the man he had become. But there would be time anon for such supposition; now he only needed more information. 'He writes that your letter to your father told him what you had been through in London, but does not include the details. Will you tell me?' he asked.

'I don't enjoy thinking about it.'

'I can understand that. I can't know what it was, but it must have been foul.' She nodded. 'Can I offer you something else, something that would make you happy?'

'Such as?'

'Perhaps you can suggest something.'

She looked thoughtful. 'What's happened to Oliver's body?' she asked.

'It's currently in the morgue at Colchester Royal Hospital.'

'You'll have it interred in the family crypt?'

'I presumed that I would,' he replied, and as he spoke the words, he saw the direction her mind was moving. 'Do you have another idea?'

'I have. I want you to put John White in his place. He deserves a decent interment.'

It was a striking demand. At first, Simeon thought it impossible, but then, as he considered, it would not be so hard to accomplish. He would oversee the oysterman's body being placed in a coffin and would accompany that casket to the crypt. No one but he would know who was in it. White would otherwise be cast into a pauper's grave.

'And what about Oliver's body?'

The flame-light glinted on her yellow silk. It was as if she were in the fire itself. 'Bury him in the mudflats where you found John. Let him sink. And weigh him down so no one ever finds him.'

Watkins covered his ears.

There was a certain balancing justice to her plan. And what more could he offer but balance? 'I will,' he said.

There was silence for a while. 'Will you now tell me what happened to you?'

'Do you have time to listen?'

'I have all the time in the world.'

He sat on the parson's seat, in silent expectation.

'That accusing note from Annie, the one that Oliver sent to the house to make it look as if she were accusing James of abusing her, not Oliver,' she said, almost to herself, remembering. 'Well, it seemed to me afterwards a very queer coincidence that, at the same time as it arrived, her brother should have an accident, and the next day she should attempt suicide. So I went to visit her, to discover what had happened.'

'I see.'

'I found Annie quite ill, of course, and she said little, but what she said made me suspicious that I had been unfair to James by accusing him on the basis of that note of an involvement with her. But she was keeping much to herself. So when I heard that she had recovered and taken the first train that she could to London, I knew I had to go too.' She poured herself a little water from a jug. 'First off, I decided to throw any pursuers off my scent. Oh, I was a wily fox, Simeon. I asked myself, where would a girl like Annie possibly end up in London? Well, it's sadly obvious, isn't it? If you're a young woman thrown out or without a family to support you, you end up on the streets and in the only profession that doesn't ask for experience. So I put it about that I was heading for Covent Garden, where a good number of these poor women ply their trade. Anyone following me would guess that I had information about her being there.'

211

'Very subtle of you.'

'It was. But in truth, I had no idea of where she was. Yes, she might well be on the streets – but what about Whitechapel or Camden or Mayfair? The locations where that business goes on are endless. So instead, I planned a search, aided by some money I took from James's strong-box. As a first step, I called in at an emporium where I made a purchase that you men wouldn't approve of.'

'Are you sure we wouldn't?'

'Quite sure.' But then she relented a little. 'In most cases. Well, we'll soon see.' She stopped for a moment. 'The owner of that emporium also recommended the ser-vices of a man operating from an office in a backstreet of Soho. It was above a tobacconist's shop and between the fumes from that place and the general fug of London, I thought I was going to pass out at any second. The name of the man who operated from there was Mr Nathaniel Brent. "I have no idea of my true surname. I was found in Brent and they gave me that name, since it was as good as any," he told me.' She reproduced his accent as if she were the roughest guttersnipe in London.

'And who is this Mr Brent?'

'Mr Brent – or any other surname you want to give him – described himself as "an agent of enquiries". In essence, if you want someone tracked like a wounded stag, he's your man. He's of the thin sort, tall. Somehow overbearing. I told him I wished to find a former servant of mine whom I thought had got herself into trouble. The usual sort of trouble.

'He sat down in a chair of his – the only seating in the

whole room, leaving me standing, which I thought a bit off. And he spoke. "Funny thing is, miss, 'most everyone who comes through that door tells me one story, then it turns out the truth is something quite different." I flushed a bit, which made me angry at myself. "So, how 'bout you tell me the real reason you want to find this Annie White, and we both pretend it was the first tale you came in with?"' Simeon's mouth creased in amusement. 'Well, I was annoyed, but at least he had proved some wits. I told him the truth. "Devil of a story," he said, though I think it was to himself rather than me. "Poor floozy. Right. Go to your lodging. I'll come with what I can find out. I'll come by the name of Mr Cooryan. Anyone else comes a-calling for you, start screaming the place down. Remember: Mr Cooryan."

'"If someone uninvited comes calling, I shall use this, not my screaming voice," I said. And I opened my clutch bag to show him what I had bought at the emporium that afternoon. It was a rather pretty little four-shot muff pistol, you see. Snug little thing that fits entirely in my hand-warmer. You wouldn't know it was there until you got a bullet or two through the brain.' She fixed Simeon with her gaze. 'So now, what do you think of that?'

'A necessity of modern life,' he said with a shrug, presuming she was hoping for a sharper reaction.

'Ah, yes.' And she inclined her head a little to address Watkins. 'Sorry, Father, I know you brought me up to sew samplers, but times change, don't they?'

Watkins attempted a reply, but failed and sank back into himself.

'Anyway, at that I returned to my boarding house and waited. Do you know, Simeon, there's an army living on the streets of London, should any man or woman require them. For a small price, they will fan across the city asking at hospitals, inns and servants' entrances for any name or description that you give them. Most of what they hear will be bunkum, but eventually one will come back with the truth.'

'I was not so aware, no,' he said.

'But it's true. And a few days later, Nathaniel brought me what I was looking for. It was an address in St George's Fields in Southwark.'

St George's Fields. He understood immediately. Yes, he had seen that place himself and had sympathy for any who resided there. 'I can guess the address you mean.'

'I thought you might. Well, Nathaniel asked me if I knew about these places. I told him that I had read about them, but never thought I would be visiting one. "No, miss, not many do."'

'And yet, the very next day, I was in a Hansom heading for it.'

Simeon interrupted. 'The Magdalen Hospital for the Reception of Penitent Prostitutes,' he said. 'You don't forget that name.'

'You don't. So, there I was before this large brick building that looked much like a prison.' In her glass cell, she ran her hand along the front of that edifice. 'Have you ever been inside?'

'No. But my brother medics have told me strong stories.'

She nodded in understanding. 'It's all locked and

barred, with wooden blinds over the windows so that no one can see in. That's to stop the inmates from plying their trade from the hospital itself.'

'I've heard so.'

'Men get some sort of thrill from looking at fallen women, it seems. I wondered about James then, if he would have had that thrill.' She gently shook her head. 'But I'm getting away from the point. I marched up to the gate and spun them some story about wanting to contribute to the asylum, but requiring a tour of it first. I did my best to sound like you, Father, when you have a prisoner in the dock. Imperious. Puffed up.'

Here, Watkins summoned up his last vestiges of dignity. 'It is the law, Florence. It must be respected!'

And she lost her temper in full for the first time that Simeon had known. 'The law? Hah!' she shouted, striking the glass with her palm. 'It's your law that put me in here! Your law that means I'll never be allowed out. Isn't that right? Whether I'm behind this for madness or murder, it makes no odds, does it? I'm still here. And I'll be here until I die!'

Watkins rubbed his eyes. 'I am sorry, my girl,' he said. 'I was tricked.'

'You weren't the only one, sir,' Simeon informed him, trying to cool the waters. 'There's a long line before and after you.'

Watkins accepted the words with thanks and they watched Florence's chest heave with suppressed passion. She whirled away from them and it was a while before she came back, a colder anger in her eyes.

215

'I'll return to the story. But we'll speak, Father. We will speak.' Watkins met Simeon's gaze. 'A thin, grasping woman warden – I could tell she was looking to line her own pocket – obliged my request and I asked her a few questions which she was happy to answer. Did you know that one in three of the inmates is under the age of thirteen?'

'It's sickening,' Simeon agreed. 'Worst of all is that there's little we can do about it. Their families have no choice: it's that or starvation.'

'Hmm. Well. I steered the conversation to punishment of those inmates who were not wholly repentant. The woman looked at me shiftily. I wasn't supposed to ask about that. "There is Heaven and there is Hell. God has rewards and punishments, we his instruments must have too," I said. She told me about some minor mistreatments – reduced food, no permission to talk, work hours increased from fourteen to sixteen hours per day turning the mangle in the laundry. "That all sounds paltry," I said. "That won't change a wanton mind." And I said something dark about subscribing my money elsewhere. She looked panicked and told me of something they called "the hard room". And I knew she hadn't wanted to, because I had been told by Nathaniel Brent that that was where I had to look. "What is that?" I asked.

'"Where the really awful women go. Those that refuse to do their work or such. They're given cold baths and stay there in isolation. We only use it on those that can't leave the asylum."

'"Why can't they leave?"

216

'"Different reasons," she told me. "There's one there now that was caught robbing her customer. She pleaded so much that the judge said he would stay the rope if she came here and repented before God."

'"A very forward-thinking judge."

'"Yes, madam."

'"Why is she refusing to work?"

'"Can't say. She's not dying. Those that are dying, we put out on the street."

'She said that, you know, with utter callousness.' Simeon was not in the least surprised. '"I wish to see it. I wish to question her and make sure that her repentance is real," I told her. Well, she tried to brush me off, of course, but I insisted and she gave up and took me. After winding through the building, we came to an iron door at the end of a long passage. I could hear a strange sound as we came close. It was not speech or sobbing exactly. And then, when she unlocked the door, to my horror I saw what it was. There was Annie, utterly unclothed on the floor, huddling herself, and her teeth chattering so much that the whine coming from her mouth was being chopped up into short notes like some sort of mad songbird.

'"Cold baths," the warden said. God help me, she was proud of it. "Have her working soon. On the mangle." Then she spoke to Annie loudly and slowly, like you talk to a child. "We'll soon have you working. Unless you want Tyburn."

'At that, Annie looked up for the first time. It took her a few seconds to recognize me, but then she just looked amazed. She made an effort to speak, but she couldn't. I

think it wasn't just that her teeth were chattering so, it was having lived a month that had seen her attempt her own death, her brother gone, her flight to London, her arrest as a streetwalker and thief and her incarceration in this brutal place. Who could have remained strong in mind and body after all that?' Florence stared off to the side of her cell before returning to the story. '"I am taking her," I said, and I kneeled to the girl and spoke to her as gently as I could. "Home. Annie, we're going home."

'"I don't understand," the warden said. "What?"

'"I am taking her back to her mother. Unless you want me to write to everyone from the trial judge to the Archbishop of Canterbury to tell them how you are abusing the trust they put in you, you are going to collect her clothes and give them to me, and I am taking her home."' Florence grinned at the memory and the smile flitted to Simeon's mouth.

'Well, that put the wind up her. And within ten minutes, we were out the front gate.' She gazed up at the line of windows in the library, as if she could look through them all the way to London. 'We sat in St George's Fields, within sight of the asylum, but with our backs to it. She was too exhausted to go any further. "Annie," I said. "I'll take you home." But all she could do was look at me. And we stayed there for an hour or more, not speaking. I bought some small beer and pies from a hawker, and she ate so quickly I thought she would be ill, but it seemed to bring her back a little. And then, finally, she was able to stand and walk with me. God, how I wish that had been the end of our troubles.'

'Something tells me they were only just beginning,' Simeon replied.

'How perceptive you are. Well, as we went along the street, with Annie shivering even though it was a warm night, I saw a man on the other side of the road. He was dressed in black, with a big hat pulled down and his face covered with a scarf. If I had ever known him, I couldn't recognize him then. But I had no reason to pay him any attention. So Annie and I set off up the street towards the Thames, where we could cross by way of the new bridge. I couldn't help but look back at the asylum, though, horrible place that it is. And as I did that, I saw the man in black was still behind us, keeping pace. All my instincts told me to get away as soon as I could, so I took Annie's arm and hurried off.

'Over my shoulder, I saw he had stopped and was looking back the way he had come, which was strange. Then he raised his arm, and suddenly a carriage sped along the road towards us. The driver must have been desperate for his own death, though, the rate he was moving. As it passed, the man on foot leaped onto the running board and hung there as it bore down on us. I can't tell you how frightening that sight was.'

'I'm sure.'

'I shouted to Annie to run and we made a break for an alley opposite. If she had been well and healthy, I think we would have made it. But she was so weak, she was like a fetter to me. And then the coach was a yard away and the man in black threw himself upon us both, knocking us to the ground.' She broke off for a moment, breathing

219

heavily, before composing herself to resume her story. 'He kicked Annie hard, knocking her unconscious, I think. The driver, a fair-haired lump, jumped off the coach, straight onto me, knocking the wind out of me, and I felt him tying my hands behind my back and pulling a hood over my head.' Simeon felt a bolt of anger at the image, a man trussing her like game.

'I heard the one in black shout, "Get these bitches into the carriage." And I was lifted up and thrown in. "Stay down and you won't get hurt."

'I'd like to say I was brave and defiant, Simeon, but really I was scared out of my wits. I asked who they were. "Don't matter to you," was the only answer I got. And then I felt something cold on the back of my neck. It was the edge of a blade and I tried to press myself away from it, into the floor of the carriage, even though we were bumping up and down, galloping towards . . . somewhere. The man was bellowing, "Faster, for God's sake! Faster!" and I heard him thumping at the roof. I think my teeth nearly broke against the floor. "Now stop!" he said. And we came to a sudden halt. I could hear birds. Maybe the river, but that was probably my imagination. "All right, what will you bid me for this one?" I thought we were to be sold. I was as terrified as you can imagine. Would we be locked away? Sent overseas? Killed? But then I under-stood, because the one with the covered face whispered in my ear. "Well, Mrs Hawes?" he said. "What do you think you're worth?"'

'So they were after you,' Simeon said.

'Yes, they were. And it frightened me five hells more

than if they had just picked up two easy females from the street. "No, no easy life for you on your back," he said. I think he thought it very witty. I told him I could get him money. "My father is wealthy. And he is a magistrate, so the law won't forget me," I said.

'"A magistrate, you say? Oh, I know that, Mrs Hawes. A drunken JP. Who would care about him?"' Florence's gaze shifted to address her father. 'I wondered if he did know you, Father.'

'Oh, Florence,' he groaned.

She dismissed his words with a waft of her hand. '*Oh, Florence* nothing. I told him you were a man with friends. "Friends? Watkins? Ha!" was his only reply. Well, his contempt doubled my fear. He obviously didn't care about the law or retribution, so I pictured all sorts of suffering ahead of us. I had time to do it, too. We waited there for what felt like hours and I have no idea what happened in that time or what we were waiting for, but I heard distant sounds – a coach rumbling by, dogs barking. Time is like a weight upon you when it's all you have, you know. I learned that in that coach and in this cell.' She stared at her father. 'Well, eventually the man spoke again. "Mrs Hawes, I'm ready for you now."

'"Please," I said.

'"Beg all you want. I like it." Yes, it looked like it was all over.'

'It can't have been,' Simeon said.

'No. Just as I thought our fate was sealed, everything turned again.'

'How so?'

'Because as I lay there, trussed, unable to breathe with fear, there came the most ear-splitting explosion I have ever heard. It was as if the carriage itself had blown apart.' She paused, allowing them to guess. 'Screaming, someone in terrible pain. My heart was in my mouth and I couldn't see what was happening. Yelling as best I could, I tried to get my hands free, but they were tied tight.' Simeon felt his pulse beat faster. 'Then I felt the point of a dagger – the one I had felt against my neck, I presumed – stabbing into my wrists. "Please, no!" I called out and I felt blood running down my wrists. But there was a different voice to the one I was expecting. "It's all right, Mrs Hawes, it's all right. It's me. Annie." And the ropes around my wrists burst apart. Annie pulled the hood off my face and I could see the floor of the carriage. And to the side was the face of the lumpen blond man who had jumped on me.' The edge of her lips curled up in cruelty. 'I say his face was there, but half of it was gone. And I saw the four-shot pistol I had kept in my hand-warmer. It was in Annie's hand and had been fired.'

Chapter 18

Simeon met her gaze. 'Its purchase stood you well.'

Her eyes glittered. 'I've seen foxes torn apart and it doesn't bother me to see them. I didn't care a jot for this man, whose face had been ripped apart and thrown over one shoulder. Annie finally cut through the other ropes and I saw that the carriage only contained me, her and the dead man.'

'Quite the reversal of fortune,' Simeon said.

'"Where's the other one?" I asked Annie. "Did you get him too?"

'"No, he ran." She pointed out the open door. I looked outside. It was dark and we were on an empty stretch of scrub ground by the Thames. I couldn't see him anywhere.

I asked her how she was. "Better, Mrs Hawes. Who was that?" I said I didn't know. You see, I had to work it out, and I knew then, from what that man with the masked face had said, that it all hinged on what had happened here on Ray. So I had to know the truth. "Annie," I said. "People are saying it was my husband who ... brought you low." She looked at me quite blankly. "Was it James?"

'She shook her head. "No, Mrs Hawes," she said. "No, not him. It were the parson done it." And that's how I knew. That's how I realized Oliver was her abuser and John's murderer.

'"Annie," I said. "We need to ..." but even before I could finish, she grabbed my shoulder. "There!" she shouted. I spun around. The man with the black scarf was pulling open the door on the other side of the coach. It wasn't over yet. I grabbed the pistol from her, levelled it and drew the trigger. Oh, that sound.' She smiled. 'It shattered my ears and the gun kicked back, right out of my grip, you know. But through the barrel smoke, I could see I had hit his shoulder – his shirt was tattered and wet with his blood. But I knew he wasn't finished, because his eyes, which were still all I could see of him, met mine and narrowed. And he threw open the door.'

'The man felt no pain, by the sound of it,' Simeon said.

'He showed no sign. He just yelled, "Come here!" and pulled himself up, but I got hold of the pistol and fired again. This time, he dodged the bullet. Annie was scream-ing. But he came back to the door and I knew this time I had to be true with my shot. So I breathed, imagined the gun was part of my hand and stretched it towards him. It

was pointing dead at his heart. "This time I won't miss," I spat at him. And his eyes bore into mine. He knew I was telling the truth and I began squeezing back on the trigger. But at the last moment, he threw himself backwards, out of the carriage. I held my finger. It was my last bullet and I needed it.'

'What then?'

'I heard his footsteps running away. I gave it a few seconds, then checked outside. I couldn't see him, so I crept out with the pistol raised. Suddenly, he darted out from under the carriage and snatched for me, but I pulled away and scrambled up to the coach driver's seat. He was getting to his feet so I grabbed the reins, the horses leaped forward and we were gone.' Her hands lifted in the air as if in exultation.

'Florence,' was all Simeon could say, struck to the quick by the narrative.

'A triumph, yes.' But then a graver air descended on her. 'But it did not last.'

'How so?'

She paused for a moment. 'It would be better if you read the rest of Oliver's journal.'

He looked down. He had quite forgotten the loose pages in his hand, rapt as he had been in the live remembrance before him.

'Need we read every word?' Watkins burst out. 'The man was a murderer. Must you honour him by reading his thoughts?'

'I think I must, Mr Watkins,' Simeon replied. 'The truth will out.'

The magistrate moaned once more and dropped his hands in submission. 'Then do it. Though I for one would rather cast that book into the fire.'

'Maybe I'll do that afterwards.'

There were only a few pages left unread, continuing from the point where Hawes had intercepted Florence's letter to her father, so gaining the name of her hotel in London.

And so, I had her address without the slightest trouble: The Crown Hotel, Bishopsgate. 'Father. As you can see, I am currently in an hotel in London for reasons I am about to reveal to you,' her missive ran. There then followed a detailed description of her previous few days' exertions. Such a waste of effort, for I would see to it that Watkins was never troubled by the letter's contents.

And yet Tyrone had seemingly attempted and failed to take her by force the previous night. If I could not take hold of her and the village girl whom Tyrone had enjoyed, what could I do about them? The answer, I decided, was to allow the keepers of the Queen's Peace to step in.

The police magistrate for that parish was a very old fellow who should probably have retired many years earlier, but it was a thankless task with a low sinecure, so the Home Secretary would have been hard-pressed to find anyone else willing to take it on. I went to him with the necessary information: my sister-in-law, who was known to have killed my brother in a wild temper, had absconded to London, where she had, very strangely, removed a convicted prostitute from the Magdalen asylum. I, her parson as well as her brother-in-law, had been commissioned by her father, the local Justice of the Peace, to return her home, where she would

face justice and kindness in equal measure. I would also take the prostitute, since she was of our parish, thus removing one more disease-spreader from the police magistrate's books.

All of this was entirely true and bore no false witness, so I was pleased with the course of action.

It stands as a testament to the Sodomish nature of the capital that all I said hardly raised an eyebrow, and the man instead made an immediate order that a pair of constables were to accompany me to The Crown Hotel in Bishopsgate to retrieve the runaways. He would also write to Watkins, to warn him of his daughter's mental instability and explain that she was now in my care, so he need not worry.

I thanked him and made my way back to my lodging. On the way, Tyrone called in at some dreadful establishment near the docks. He came out with a bottle of strong laudanum, a funnel and a rubber tube, insisting that they would come in useful.

Thank the Lord for the English policing forces! These men knew their game, all right — which is why, barely four hours later, our two cats were being dragged towards the Colchester train, spitting and hissing enough to make me think twice whether I would be able to stand the journey.

'I'll cut your throat, you son of a whore!' You might have thought it would be the common girl screeching such things, rather than the daughter of a magistrate, but you would be mistaken. It was Florence who was shouting such oaths as to make Lucifer turn tail. But no matter, I had come armed for such a show of defiance. The loyal constables aided me by holding her still while I forced the funnel and tube down her throat and dosed her with the laudanum. Wonderful stuff! It was a minute, no more, before she was like a rag doll. The other harlot was less trouble, accepting her drink

without struggle. I think she enjoyed it. They were obedient as dozing lambs from then on.

I had reserved a small compartment. The guard seemed a little perturbed by our party, but my garb of office and the presence of the constables reassured him that all was 'ship-shape' as he said.

And so, the police left us and we set off. It was a predictably tedious few hours to Colchester, where we hired a trap which, at Tyrone's request, set us down on a lonely stretch of road close to the Peldon Rose. I asked him why he wanted to dismiss it there. He pointed at the village girl. 'I want to enjoy her one last time. What does it matter to you?'

'If you must,' I said. 'I'll give Florence another dose.'

'A good idea.'

I stood waiting by the roadside while he carried the girl into a copse of trees. Florence was at my feet. He was gone thirty minutes, and I began to worry that we would attract attention. In the end, I left our baggage where it lay and hauled Florence half-sensible after Tyrone. 'For Heaven's sake,' I cried at his back when I could make it out in the dark. 'We must go.' But as I came close, I noticed I could not see the girl. 'Where is she?' I asked.

'We don't need her any more,' he said, taking me by the arm and guiding me back towards the road. 'She's comforting her brother.' He grinned. 'Probably the only way she knows how.'

Well, it was true that we were lighter without her, and when I came to think on it, the police magistrate's letter to Watkins – which should have arrived by then – made no mention of us bringing the village girl, so no one was expecting her. Yes, Tyrone had done right again, although whether that was his intention is questionable.

When we arrived home, I sent for Watkins and related how Florence had been arrested. Taken with her assault on James, her

mental state was clearly fragile. He begged me to look after her and I agreed, saying that she had been quiet while in my company, thanks to the wonderful medicine in my possession. All this time, she was barely awake. Once or twice she attempted speech but failed to enunciate a syllable. I told Watkins I would arrange good medical supervision. And she would stay in the house.

And so, that night, Florence and I sat gazing at each other in the library. 'I shall have something constructed for you,' I told her. And I stroked her head and I am certain that, at last, she liked it. 'Somewhere for you to live.' I gave her more of the laudanum and she drank it well, and as she lay her head down to sleep she had a look of pure contentment that I swear before Our Father she had never had before.

Chapter 19

There, Simeon left off reading. He looked up at Florence.

'He read me his journal,' she said. 'Every night. When he reached the end, he would start again from the beginning. He always lingered over the passage where he described the delivery of the note from Annie that tricked me to violence. It was Oliver's lie that cut James's cheek, so that his blood was poisoned and he died in my arms. Oliver enjoyed watching me helpless, knowing what he had done to us.'

'Mental pain is the worst of all,' Simeon said, with sympathy. 'I cannot imagine.'

'They say that with time, you get used to anything.'

'They do.'

'But "they" lie, Simeon. Each night, I had to listen to

him crow over my suffering and how he had stolen James's
life from him.' Her very complexion seemed to darken.
'Each night, I felt fire – actual fire – in my blood. Some
nights, I was strong enough to cast oaths at him, but the
next day he would increase the dosage of the laudanum. If
I didn't drink it, I would drink nothing. The thirst forced
me to take it. But I could still hate. And do you know what
happened over time?'

That was obvious. 'I imagine you became immune to
the laudanum.'

'Precisely. My thoughts became clearer, my intentions
sharper. But I didn't let on. I didn't let him know that I
was returning to myself.'

'You were wise.'

'And yet you understood, didn't you, Simeon?'

He nodded. 'It took me time to realize. The first time I
saw this glass,' he touched the panel that separated them,
it was cold to his skin, 'I saw my own reflection in it, my
twin. But in time, I understood that I hadn't been the only
man in the room with a double.'

'When did that realization come?'

'When I went to the Red Lantern, at your direction. I
think you sent me there because you wanted me to understand the nature of Oliver Hawes's relationship with Mr
Tyrone. It worked.'

'He mentioned that den in his cups from time to
time.' There was a blaze in her eyes. She was savouring
the moment.

He pulled from his jacket the sheet of paper with a
man's portrait drawn in violet ink. 'A picture of Tyrone,

231

drawn by the owner of that place. She doesn't want to see him again.'

'Ah.' Florence gazed at the paper, at the ink that stained it. 'She has talent.'

He had to agree. Looking into the rendered eyes, he saw all that that woman and all the others who had met him had seen of this hard subject. 'It's strange how a picture can capture the essence of a man,' he said. 'You can see right into his soul. She said he was hollow. I think that's true.'

'Yes,' Florence said. 'It's quite true.'

He walked to the cold grate and threw the picture in, tossing a lit match after it without another thought. 'And it was at the Red Lantern that I understood how you killed Oliver.'

'Oh, don't stop now, Simeon,' she laughed. 'More, please.'

'As you wish. You killed him not by poisoning him, but by depriving him of poison.' She smiled from ear to ear. 'And he never knew a thing of it. Isn't that right?'

'What?' Watkins asked, in utter confusion.

'Tincture of laudanum,' she asked her father happily, 'do you know what exactly it contains?'

Simeon informed him. 'The normal recipe includes brandy, opium, acetic acid.' He knew where she was leading, but he allowed her the moment of joy.

'That's correct. And you know how it is administered,' she prompted.

'Drunk. Warm or cold.'

'But . . .'

'But one must stir the bottle hard. Yes, I was reminded of that fact when I went to the opium house.'

'So, you do see,' she said approvingly.

'I do.' He spoke to Watkins, explaining what the old man did not understand, without taking his gaze from Florence. 'You stir it because the opium sinks to the bottom of the bottle. Otherwise, the upper drink is pure brandy and the dregs are pure opium.' His eyes explored her face, her cheek, her chin. 'A year ago, while he was still allowing you to sit with him in this room, you poured a bottle of laudanum into his brandy.' She took in a deep breath, as if drinking in the old day. 'It would make no difference at first, but because he ladled the spirit from the top of the barrel, and the opium was at the bottom, as he drank his way through it he was receiving higher and higher doses.'

Her expression took on a faraway look. He knew she was exhilarated by the memory. 'He had dropped his spectacles,' she said, her voice drifting through the creeks. 'He was quite blind without them, so he was hunting about on the floor for, oh, ten or twenty seconds. I poured in the laudanum he used to dose me, gave it a moment to disperse, then refilled the bottle from the keg.' She chuckled to herself. 'But there would be hardly any opium in my bottle.'

'And by the end of the barrel, he was drinking pure poppy,' Simeon added, picturing the man ladling out his drink. 'He must have had a raging addiction without even knowing it.'

'He must.'

'And then, at the end of last month, he finished the barrel and overnight his supply was cut off. The burning

in his joints, the vomiting – they were his body crying out for the drug.'

'But there was none to be had.'

'But there was none to be had,' he echoed. 'It might not have killed him, it might have just wracked him with tremendous pain. But in the end his heart gave out. And there will never be the slightest proof that anything unnatural happened.'

There was silence for a while. 'A woman sits here day and night,' Florence said to him. 'She has time for thoughts. For ideas, Simeon.' The lightest of smiles drifted along her lips. 'So much time for ideas.'

THE END